"WHY DID YOU ABDUCT ME?" ALISON DEMANDED.

The Falcon's admiring dark eyes drifted over Alison's beautiful face, then dropped to sweep slowly over her body from head to foot, lingering at her full breasts until Alison felt as if he were touching her instead of just looking. A hint of a smile played at his sensuous lips. "I should think that would be obvious. I want you. I am an Apache. What I want, I take."

Alison's face paled. "Then you intend to rape me?"

He smiled. "There is no need for fear. Apaches do not rape their captives. However, if the woman is willing, that is an entirely different matter. I will wait for you to become more willing."

His audacity infuriated Alison. "Never!"

He chuckled. "Yes, you will. Someday you will beg me for it."

QUANTITY SALES

Most Dell books are available at special quantity discounts when purchased in bulk by corporations, organizations, and special-interest groups. Custom imprinting or excerpting can also be done to fit special needs. For details write: Dell Publishing, 666 Fifth Avenue, New York, NY 10103. Attn.: Special Sales Department.

INDIVIDUAL SALES

Are there any Dell books you want but cannot find in your local stores? If so, you can order them directly from us. You can get any Dell book in print. Simply include the book's title, author, and ISBN number if you have it, along with a check or money order (no cash can be accepted) for the full retail price plus $2.00 to cover shipping and handling. Mail to: Dell Readers Service, P.O. Box 5057, Des Plaines, IL 60017.

Joanne Redd

APACHE
BRIDE

A DELL BOOK

For my brother, Raymond—
for whom the Apache hero of this
book was named—
with love

Published by
Dell Publishing
a division of
Bantam Doubleday Dell Publishing Group, Inc.
666 Fifth Avenue
New York, New York 10103

ISBN: 0-440-20513-1

Printed in the United States of America

Published simultaneously in Canada

May 1990

10 9 8 7 6 5 4 3 2 1

RAD

"Where the rainbows wait for the rain, and the big river is kept in a stone box, and the water runs uphill, and the mountains float in the air—except at night, when they go away to play with the other mountains."

Words spoken by an unknown Mexican cowboy over a hundred years ago describing the Big Bend country of Texas and the Chisos Mountains.

1

"My God! Indians!"

Samuel Carr whirled around at his niece's alarmed cry and looked down from the high gravelly cliff where Presidio del Norte overlooked the Rio Grande. Riding across the alluvial river bottom just before they crossed the river, he saw a score of Mescalero Apaches, their horses' hooves kicking up sprays of golden sand behind them. Sam squinted his eyes against the bright sunlight and stared hard at the leader of the band, and then, recognizing the man, he relaxed.

Sam turned to his niece. The young woman's face had drained of all color, making her skin deathly pale against her coal-black hair and her searing-blue eyes look even more startling. "There's no need to be afraid, Alison," he said in a soothing voice. "That's just Chief Ramon and some of his warriors."

Alison glanced down and saw the Indians' horses splashing across the shallow, muddy river. With the tails of their red headbands fluttering in the breeze, their fierce countenances, and the barrels of their Winchesters glittering in the sunlight, the Apaches looked menacing. "But how do you know they're not coming to attack the town?"

"Because that's not the way Apaches attack, my dear. They don't make sweeping mounted charges, howling to the tops of their lungs, like the Comanches. Their methods of warfare are much different. They're silent, crafty guerrilla fighters who sneak up on you and attack so suddenly and swiftly that they seem to materialize right out of the ground. Believe me, if those Apaches meant to attack us, we'd be dead by now."

A shiver ran through Alison's slim body. "You make them sound much more dangerous than the Comanches."

"They are. General Crook has called them 'the tigers of the human species with an unquenchable thirst for rapine and murder,' and if anyone should know the Apaches' nature, he should. He's been fighting them for years."

Another shiver ran through Alison's body. The Indians had reached the rocky Mexican side of the river just below where she and her uncle stood. Then, as they raced up the riverbed to the place where the bluff sloped down to a gentle incline and the Chihuahua Trail entered the town, they were hidden from her view.

"Come, my dear," Sam said, taking Alison's arm. "If we hurry, we can see them riding through town."

Alison had no desire to see any more of the fierce-looking Indians, but nevertheless she allowed her uncle to hurry her along. Had she not been taller than most women—five foot eight—she wouldn't have been able to keep up with her lanky uncle's long-legged stride. They followed a narrow dusty street that wove its way around the flat-roofed adobe buildings. Most of the homes were nothing but *jacals* in which the Mexican peons lived, pitiful mud shacks that were cracked and crumbling under the searing Mexican sun, with withered cornstalk lean-tos that served as their kitchens and looked as if they would collapse any minute. Scattered among these were the large, gleaming white *casas* of the well-to-do Mexican and Anglo merchants who made their living from the Chihuahua Trail that passed through Presidio del Norte on its way to Chihuahua City, hundreds of miles farther south.

When Sam reached the main street of the sunbaked town, he stopped and peered down it. Seeing the Apaches in the distance, he said, "Yes, here they come."

The Indians had slowed their horses to a leisurely walk, the lean, brown men looking completely at ease in this Mexican border town. But Alison still thought they looked dangerous and threatening. "What are they doing here, if they don't mean to harm us?"

"They've probably come to trade with their Mexican friends here in Presidio. Or perhaps Chief Ramon and his warriors have been invited to one of the Mexicans' *fiestas.*"

"Are you saying that the Mexicans actually socialize with those savages?" Alison asked in disbelief.

"Yes."

"But I thought the Apaches preyed on the Mexicans as much as they do us."

"That's something that's peculiar to the Mexicans' and Apaches' relationship that we Americans have trouble understanding. We believe every Indian is bad and our enemy, but the Mexicans differentiate between those Apaches who are their friends and those who are their enemies. However, it's the Indians who decide which Mexicans they want for their friends. They do the choosing. Almost every Apache tribe has a select few villages that they trade and socialize with, while all other Mexicans are their deadly enemies. Those villages that are out of the sphere of their friendship they will raid and plunder regularly."

"But how can the Mexicans accept that kind of a relationship?" Alison asked in outrage. "How can they be friends with savages who are raiding and killing their own countrymen?"

"Before you criticize the Mexicans too severely, you must remember their position," Sam answered patiently. "Most of these Mexican villages are made up predominantly of poor peons. They have no weapons with which to defend themselves from either the Indians or the *bandidos* that infest all of Mexico, and until recently the Mexican government has done nothing to protect them from either, except for the northern states offering bounties for Apache scalps. It would be out-and-out suicide for a Mexican village to refuse the Apaches' offer of friendship. Besides, that friendship usually provides them with protection from other tribes that are hostile toward them. If anything, they count themselves fortunate to have such powerful Indian friends. So you see, it's a matter of both prudence and survival."

It sounded a little cold-blooded to Alison for the Mexicans to turn a blind eye to the plight of their countrymen, but she supposed if it was something beyond their control, they really had no choice. "I can understand the villages that have no protection accepting the Indians' friendship, but there's a garrison of Mexican soldiers here at Presidio. These people don't need the Apaches' protection."

"My dear, the garrison has only forty men in it, and Chief Ramon has several hundred warriors at his command. Besides, there isn't a Mexican soldier who can match one of those fierce Mescaleros man for man, and they know it. No, if truth be known, they too consider themselves lucky that Presidio has been singled out by the Apaches as a friendly town."

Alison could understand the defenseless peons bowing to the Indians' superior strength, but not soldiers whose job was to protect them from such hostiles. "Then, even though Mexico is officially at war with the Apaches, those soldiers will do nothing to confront that band of Indians?"

"No, my dear. The garrison will pretend that they never saw them. That too is a matter of prudence. To confront them, as long as the Indians come in peace, would be foolhardy."

Alison frowned. It seemed that everyone kowtowed to the powerful Indians. Why, the Apaches' offer of friendship was nothing but out-and-out blackmail, and no one had the courage to stand up to them. No wonder the savages were so bold and arrogant. They wouldn't dream of riding into an Anglo town that way. They'd be mowed down on sight.

Alison turned her attention back to the group of Apaches, expecting to see the Mexicans who had wandered out of their houses cowering in fear as the warriors passed. To her utter surprise, she saw the townspeople calling greetings to the Indians, while their dark-eyed children clung to the women's skirts, staring at the Apaches with awe. Were the Mexicans only pretending, or were these warm greetings and looks of blatant admiration sincere? Did they really consider these savages their friends?

Alison's gaze swept over the approaching Apaches, and then, as if drawn by some mysterious magnet,

locked on the man riding at the head of the column.
The Apache's black eyes stared straight ahead, and he
looked as if he were totally unaware of the commotion
he was causing. Alison knew that this had to be Chief
Ramon. It was more than the proud tilt of his dark head,
the almost arrogant expression on his face, and his erect
seat on his mount that told her so. There was an air of
command about him, and every fiber of his being be-
spoke supreme self-assurance and unleashed power.
She sensed that here was a man who was a cut above all
others, whether white or red. An aura of greatness surrounded him.

Alison was shocked that she would think such
thoughts of a lowly savage. She gave the tall, broad-
shouldered Apache a more critical scrutiny, thinking
she must have been mistaken in her impression, for no
man had ever struck her with such a strong impact. To
her surprise, she found the Apache actually handsome,
in a rugged, masculine sort of way. His lean face, with its
high forehead and prominent cheekbones, had a rather
hawkish appearance. His nose, straight and narrow, had
an almost aristocratic look about it. And he was much
younger than she would have expected a chief to be.

She glanced up, noting that his hair didn't hang in
long, straight strands almost to his elbows like that of
the other Apaches, but was cut short, just brushing the
top of his collar, and had a natural wave. And she had
never seen hair that black, so black that it shone with a
bluish luster.

Then, catching sight of something glittering in the
bright sunlight, Alison's eyes widened in disbelief as she
realized that it was a silver earring with a turquoise
stone that dangled from his ear. She glanced quickly to
the opposite side of his head and saw its mate. Alison

had never seen a man wearing earrings before and would have expected it to make him look effeminate, or ridiculous, but nothing could detract from the Apache chief's strong masculinity. If anything, the earrings gave a rakish dash to a man who radiated his power and sexuality the way sand radiates heat waves in the desert sun. Never had a man fascinated her as much as this man. She couldn't take her eyes from him.

Despite his aloof, detached appearance, Chief Ramon was aware of everything going on around him. Nothing escaped his attention; his warriors swore he had eyes in the back of his head. He was accustomed to the Mexicans staring at him with awe and admiration; even the Anglos in this town showed him respect. But who was the dark-haired young woman staring at him so boldly? He had never seen her on his previous visits to Presidio. He knew she was a *norteamericana* by her dress and her pale skin. *Dios*, she was beautiful, tall and slimly built, as graceful as a willow tree. But the feminine curves were there in all the right places. From his peripheral vision Ramon noted, in mute appreciation, the gentle flare of her hips and the proud thrust of her breasts. And those eyes! He had never seen eyes so vibrant, a blue as searing as a summer sky. Surrounded by her thick, long lashes, they looked like exotic jewels against her creamy, flawless complexion.

A heat rose in Ramon, and he felt a stirring in his loins. The unexpected arousal stunned him, for he was a man who exercised a firm control over his sexual urges. He was no callow youth to become excited by a beautiful woman staring at him. He was accustomed to pretty women throwing themselves at him, both the Apache widows and divorcées in his tribe and the Mexican *señoritas* in those villages he was friendly with. There was always a woman more than anxious to share his pallet, but he was a man of discerning tastes. Then why had the *norteamericana* attracted him? She was a *pindah-lick-oyee*— a white-eyed enemy. But there was no denying that he desired her. His body had spoken with a will of its own.

As the Apaches passed, Alison stared at the thick cloud of dust they left in their wake, then asked her uncle, "Who is this Chief Ramon?"

"One of the greatest, fiercest, most powerful Apache chiefs."

Alison had sensed a greatness about the man. That, combined with her fascination with him, irritated her no end. How could she admire a man who was nothing but a cold-blooded killer, a savage barbarian? "I've never heard of him," she replied, thinking to discredit his claim to greatness.

"It's true that he hasn't received the notoriety back east that some of the other Apache chiefs have, but he's just as powerful, just as fierce, just as cunning as Cochise and Mangus Coloradas were in their day. You might not recognize his name, but everyone in Texas and half of northern Mexico does. He's a man much admired and respected by the other Apaches and feared by his enemies. Why, just the mention of his name can strike terror in their hearts. He leads a band of Mescaleros who make their home in the Chisos Mountains to the east of here, in that section of Texas that juts into Mexico. For that reason his band has become known as the Chisos Apaches."

"He seems too young to be of any importance," Alison objected, still inexplicably hoping to discredit the Apache who had such a strong impact on her.

"Yes, he's young," Sam admitted. "I'd say around

twenty-seven or twenty-eight. But age has nothing to do with it. Apaches take on the responsibilities of manhood much earlier in life than we do, and their chiefs are chosen for their leadership qualities, not their maturity as measured in years. In El Halcon's case, no one can dispute that they made a wise choice in choosing him for their leader. Under his skillful guidance they've never been defeated, and while all the other Apache tribes are slowly being brought to heel and put on reservations, he continues to elude the cavalry. No matter how hard they try, they can't catch him."

"El Halcon? The Falcon?" Alison asked in confusion. "I thought you said his name was Chief Ramon."

"It is, but the Mexicans call him El Halcon because in their opinion the falcon is much swifter and more powerful than even the eagle."

"And the falcon is a much more skillful bird of prey," Alison pointed out.

"Yes, and that too."

Alison frowned. "You almost sound as if you admire him yourself."

"To be perfectly honest, I do."

"But he's a cold-blooded killer, a savage!" Alison said in outrage. "He's our enemy!"

"Ah, my dear, a man can admire his enemy's skills and strengths without approving of his deeds."

"I'm afraid I don't agree with you," Alison answered in a voice that brooked no argument. "A man's deeds speak for him, and I find nothing admirable in murdering, plundering, and preying on those weaker than you. Unlike these Mexicans, I can't turn a blind eye to what he really is."

Sam smiled. His niece most definitely had a mind of her own. It was one of the many things he had learned about her that had both surprised and pleased him over the past two weeks. He couldn't stand a meek woman who bowed to others' opinions, nor could he tolerate a weak-willed woman who let men dominate her. That was the reason he had never married. He had never found a woman who was as strong-willed as himself, and he didn't want a mere shadow for a mate.

When Sam's brother had asked him to meet his daughter Alison in San Antonio and accompany her to Sonora, where his brother managed a silver mine, Sam had agreed reluctantly, afraid he would find a replica of the weak, fearful woman his brother had married. But Alison was nothing like her mother. Her strength and adventuresome spirit could only come from her father's side of the family. Nor had her genteel life in her well-to-do maternal grandfather's home, where she had spent most of her life, spoiled her. He was still amazed at how well she had dealt with the hardships of the long trip across west Texas on the freight wagon train that they had attached themselves to, not once complaining about the choking dust, insufferable heat, and bone-jarring ride, to say nothing of the rough language and crude manners of the teamsters. Sam would have never subjected her to it if it had not been out of necessity. There were no stages to Presidio del Norte, nor would there be any to where they were going in Mexico.

Seeing the smile on her uncle's face, Alison bristled. "Are you laughing at me?"

"No, my dear, far from it. You're entitled to your opinions. But why don't we put our discussion of El Halcon aside for now? What I want to know is, now that you've been in Mexico for a full day, what do you think of the country?"

Alison looked about at the adobe buildings whose

roofs radiated heat waves under the blistering sun and remembered that Presidio sat on a barren, almost treeless desert that didn't look any different from the rugged, godforsaken, lonely land on the opposite side of the river. "To be perfectly honest, I thought Mexico would be prettier."

"You can't judge all of Mexico from what you've seen here. There are some really beautiful places in this country. Farther inland there are towering mountains with breathtaking waterfalls and thick pine forests. Then, around the coast, the vegetation is tropical, so thick and lush that you have to chop your way through it, and thousands of birds with the most spectacular plumage, and flowers as big as your hand in vibrant colors you never dreamed existed."

"And where I'm going in Sonora?" Alison asked curiously. "What's it like there?"

There was a slight hesitation before Sam answered. "I'm afraid it's much like here, hot and barren, except that it's in the mountains."

Alison couldn't hide her disappointment. Seeing it, Sam asked, "Do you want to change your mind? I can take you back to San Antonio."

Alison was disgusted with herself. She had been utterly bored in Baltimore and had looked forward to this trip and visit with her father for over a year, and here at the first sign of disappointment she was wavering. This was going to be the adventure of her lifetime, her opportunity to see a country and culture different from her own. Why, she had even been tutored in Spanish in preparation for this visit. No, she wasn't going to throw it away just because she might have to suffer a few discomforts. There was no telling what exciting, new experiences awaited her, and then there was her father.

She couldn't disappoint him. "No, I'm not going to change my mind. I said I was going to visit my father, and I am."

Sam smiled. "I'm glad to hear you say that. He's looked forward to this for so long. He's been a very lonely man all these years without his wife and family."

Alison felt a pang of guilt in behalf of her mother. Feeling compelled to defend her, she said, "I know that my parents' understanding in the beginning was that my mother would stay with my grandparents until my father was established someplace and then we would join him, but my mother was afraid to give up her comforts and her social life. She wouldn't join him in Colorado, when he was managing a mine there, either, for the same reasons."

"Yes, I understand her reasons," Sam answered in a carefully guarded voice, "but it hasn't made things easier for your father. Other than the few times he has gone back east to visit, he hasn't seen any of you since the end of the war. That's a hell of a life for a man— working himself to death in a lonely, isolated spot in Mexico to support a wife and family who don't even seem to care for him."

Alison's blue eyes flashed. "That's not true! I care! Why do you think I insisted on my mother allowing me to come?"

"Oh? Then it wasn't just the prospect of an adventure?"

"No, it wasn't. Oh, I admit that was a part of it. But whether you want to believe it or not, I felt sorry for my father, and I wanted to get to know him better."

"I'm glad to hear that. Your father would like to know you better too, and I'm sure he'll be just as pleased with you as I am."

Alison searched her uncle's rugged face but saw no sign of pretense there. "Why are you so pleased with me?"

"Because you're all Carr, right down to the color of your hair and your build. And you've got our determination and sense of adventure. Deep down, there's not anything you're afraid to tackle. The only things I can see that you inherited from your mother are your eyes, and as far as I'm concerned, they were her only admirable quality."

Alison was a little taken aback at his bluntness. "You really dislike my mother, don't you?"

"I've never made any pretense to care for her. She's a weak woman who thinks more of her comforts than her husband. Any woman worth her salt would stand beside her husband, no matter what."

"That's asking a lot of a woman, to leave a comfortable, secure home and brave the dangers and hardships of the western frontier, to say nothing of coming down here to this backward country."

"Other women have done it. You're doing it right now."

Alison frowned. As much as she hated to admit it, her mother was a weak woman, and an incredibly selfish one. Because of her, Alison and her sisters had never had the opportunity to know their father. Yes, her mother had put herself before the needs of her husband and her children, not that it had bothered Alison's sisters any. They were just as selfish and self-centered as their mother. "I suppose I am different from my mother and sisters. And who knows? Maybe I'll fall in love with Mexico the way you have and never want to leave."

"I hope so. I've never regretted coming to this country."

As Sam took her arm and guided her down the dusty street, Alison looked across at him curiously. She knew even less about her uncle than she did about her father. "I know my father was sent to Mexico by the company he works for, but how did you happen to come down here?"

"After the War Between the States, when we lost our plantation and means of livelihood, we both headed west to build new futures for ourselves. Your father went to Colorado in hopes of striking it rich, while I traveled to Texas. When I arrived there, I discovered the lucrative trade going on with Mexico over the Chihuahua Trail. Until then, I'd never even heard of the trail. I was amazed to learn that more gold, silver, copper, and other products were transported over that trail than over the celebrated Santa Fe Trail, and that, pound for pound, the trade was far richer. I invested in a dozen wagons and some mules, hired a crew of teamsters, and went into the freighting business. For eight years I went back and forth from Indianola and Chihuahua. Then, five years ago, I sold my freighting company and bought a home and business in Chihuahua City."

Alison's gaze swept over her uncle's tall, lean frame. With the silver wings over his ears on both sides of his dark head and his well-tailored suit, he did indeed look like a successful businessman, but the marks of his previous hard, outdoor life were still there. His face was deeply tanned and leathery from its long exposure to the sun, and there were lines fanning out on the sides of his eyes from squinting to see in the bright sunlight. Yes, there was a ruggedness about him beneath his polished exterior that made him a very appealing man. She wondered why he had never married. "But don't you find

the life of a merchant dull after all those years of freighting?"

Sam laughed. "After eight years of eating dust, riding
on a wagon that jarred my bones and rattled my teeth,
going through freezing blizzards, blinding sandstorms,
and torrential rains, and crossing over scorching deserts
that fried my brains—fighting Indians all the way—I
was more than happy to settle down to a more comfortable, peaceful life. After all, I'm not a young man. Besides, someone has to sell all that freight coming over
the trail, and I get my fill of excitement by just listening
to the wild and woolly tales that the freighters bring
back."

Alison imagined that her uncle probably had a few
wild and woolly tales to tell himself, and on the long trip
to Chihuahua she was determined to seek out every one
of them. But at the moment she was curious about
where he lived. "What is Chihuahua City like?"

"It's a beautiful place, full of magnificent cathedrals
that can rival any of those in Europe, theaters, opera
houses, fine restaurants, huge plazas and parks, thriving
businesses, and lovely homes. You and your father must
come visit me while you're here in Mexico, and I'll show
you all the sights. Surely there must be some time when
he can get away from that mine. Why, we can even go
to a bullfight and see some of Spain's greatest matadors
perform. They tour here in Mexico, you know, and bull-
fighting is the national sport."

Alison wasn't too sure she wanted to see a bullfight.
She had heard that the bull was killed.

Seeing her frown, Sam said, "It's really very exciting,
the rousing music, the spectacular colors, and the
crowds calling 'Olé' every time the matador passes the
bull with his cape."

Yes, that was one of the main reasons she had come to Mexico, to see new and exciting things, Alison thought. She'd be a fool to turn any of it down. "I'll be looking forward to our visit," she answered in all sincerity.

By this time they had reached the house of the merchant they had been staying with in Presidio del Norte. Sam pushed open the heavy wooden gate between the high adobe walls, and Alison stepped into the courtyard. She looked about her appreciatively, seeing the colorful baskets of trailing flowers that were hanging from the arches of the building, the huge pots of greenery all about, the tinkling, tiered fountain in the middle of the courtyard, and the stone bench beneath the cool shade of a spreading mimosa. "I still can't get over this courtyard," she commented. "It's like a miniature oasis in the middle of a desert, so cool and restful. And the rest of the Greys' *casa* is just beautiful."

"You father has a *casa* just as beautiful as this, with an even larger *patio,* as we call these courtyards in Mexico."

Alison was surprised at this unexpected information. When her uncle had described her destination, she had been afraid that she would be living in a squalid little hut like those of the peons. She didn't mind suffering through a few discomforts and hardships on her trip, but she hadn't been looking forward to a steady diet of it. She was glad to know she wouldn't be leaving civilization completely behind. Despite her adventuresome spirit, she appreciated the comforts of life as much as the next woman.

2

 Alison and Sam had just settled down in the *sala* with their hostess, Sarah Grey, when William Grey rushed into the room.

"My goodness, Will!" Sarah exclaimed, seeing her beefy husband's face flushed even redder than normal. "What are you so excited about?"

"El Halcon and some of his warriors rode into town—"

"Yes, I know," Sarah interjected. "I saw them from our bedroom window. But I don't know why that has upset you. He and those savages of his are frequent visitors here."

"Well, this is the last time that damn Apache is going to visit Presidio," Will answered in a hard voice, his eyes glittering with satisfaction. "This time he's staying. We're finally going to get rid of that plundering bastard!"

Sarah glanced quickly at Alison. "Watch your language, Will! There's a young lady present." Seeing the embarrassed expression on her husband's face and knowing that she had done her duty in chastising him,

Sarah asked, "Now, what in the world are you talking about, getting rid of El Halcon?"

"Did you notice anything strange about him when he rode past?" Will asked his wife.

"Not that I can recall. Besides, I only glanced out the window."

"Well, Mrs. Griffin noticed, and thank God for that. That red bastard was wearing her husband's overcoat!"

Sarah was so surprised at her husband's announcement that she didn't even bother to correct his language. "But where in the world did Chief Ramon get John's overcoat?"

"El Halcon stole it from him—after he murdered John!"

"My God!" Sarah gasped. "When did that happen?"

"Who knows! He must have attacked John's freight train somewhere on the trail and wiped it out. That's the only way that damn Apache could have gotten possession of John's coat."

"I noticed that he was wearing an overcoat," Sam commented from where he was sitting and listening to the conversation.

Will turned to face Sam and asked angrily, "Then why in the hell didn't you confront him?"

"Confront El Halcon?" Sam asked in astonishment. "Single-handed?" He laughed. "Why, even if he had been alone, I wouldn't be that big a fool. Besides, I didn't think it suspicious. Almost without exception, the Apaches have forsaken their traditional Indian dress for white man's clothing. They wear the same type of loose shirts and pants the Mexicans do, except when they're on the warpath and strip down to their moccasins and breechcloths. I just thought El Halcon had taken a fancy to the white man's duster that seems to be becoming so much of a rage out here as of late."

Sam's admission that he had noticed the coat stunned Alison. For the life of her, she couldn't remember what the Apache chief had been wearing, other than those intriguing earrings. No, she had been too engrossed with the man.

"Well, he took a fancy to it all right," Will answered. "Knowing him, he was probably flaunting that coat on purpose. He's the boldest damn—"

"Will!" Sarah quickly interjected in a hard, warning voice.

Will shot his wife a frustrated look, for he had been about to say "bastard." Then he continued, "—Apache that ever walked this earth." A gloating expression came over the merchant's face. "But he won't be walking it for long. Mrs. Griffin went to the *alcade* with her suspicions, and El Halcon and his men have been arrested and thrown into prison. He's going to be tried for murder tomorrow."

Sam couldn't believe his ears. "How the devil did the soldiers manage to take him prisoner? Didn't he put up a fight?"

"They caught him completely by surprise when he was walking out of a store. Pounced on him so fast that he didn't even have time to pull his knife."

"But what about his warriors?" Sam asked. "Didn't they put up a fight?"

"They didn't dare, not with the soldiers threatening to kill their chief on the spot if they so much as raised their rifles. Besides, they were surrounded. They would have been mowed down in a cross fire, and El Halcon knew it. He ordered them to surrender."

Sam frowned. He couldn't imagine Chief Ramon giving up that easily, knowing how fiercely that Apache felt about his freedom. He would have thought El Halcon would have fought to the death for it. "What did Chief Ramon have to say about how he had come into possession of John's coat?"

Will snorted. "He claimed John gave it to him, and the damn fool actually expected the *alcade* to believe that ridiculous story. When the *alcade* demanded the truth, El Halcon refused to say another word." Will paused, then said, "Well, we've finally got him behind bars, and by tomorrow, when that trial is finished, he'll be dead. And I say good riddance! That red devil has played hell on the Chihuahua Trail between here and the Pecos River for years. He hit three trains in just the past four months. And that damn cavalry is useless against him. He hits and runs for those mountains he and his band live in and then disappears like a wraith in the gigantic pile of jagged rocks. Hell, the only way the army would ever be able to flush him out of there would be to blast those mountains to kingdom come!"

Sarah rose from her chair and said in a calm but firm voice, "That's enough, Will. Rather than expounding on your feelings about El Halcon, we should go over to the Griffins' *casa* and give our support to Mrs. Griffin. I would imagine that she's in a terrible state."

"But she has John's family here to comfort her," Will objected, not relishing the thought of being around John's weeping relatives.

"Still, it's our Christian duty to at least pay her a visit." Sarah turned to Sam and Alison. "Do you mind if we leave you to yourselves for a while?"

"No, of course not," Sam answered, politely coming to his feet.

"I'll leave word with the servants to go ahead and

serve your dinner if we're not back by then," Sarah said, walking toward the door. "In the meantime, make yourselves at home."

As soon as the Greys had left the room, Alison said to her uncle, "I thought you said the soldiers wouldn't confront Chief Ramon."

"I don't believe the *alcade* would have demanded it of them if anyone else but Mrs. Griffin had asked him to. You see, the Griffin family is one of the oldest and most influential here in Presidio del Norte. The *alcade* didn't dare refuse Mrs. Griffin. Even though there had been no bloodshed, confronting Chief Ramon was a very risky thing to do. I still find it hard to believe that he offered no resistance."

Alison was troubled. The thought of a man as vitally alive as Chief Ramon being hanged disturbed her. No man had ever touched her as strongly as the powerful Apache chief. She couldn't understand it. He was a bloodthirsty killer. He deserved his fate. If anything, it was long overdue. Then why did she feel so . . . so depressed?

"Is something bothering you, my dear?"

Alison jumped at the sound of her uncle's voice. She didn't dare tell him her thoughts. How could she explain something she didn't understand herself? "Well, yes, there is. It seems to me that the evidence against Chief Ramon is rather flimsy. I can see him being tried for theft, since the coat was found in his possession, but there's no evidence of a murder having been committed. It seems he's being tried more for his reputation than for any crime. Even if he deserves to die, it doesn't seem just."

"This isn't the United States, my dear. And even there, I'm not too sure our American justice would prevail. You might not be able to convict a white man on such flimsy evidence, but we're talking about an Indian, or at least a half Indian."

"What do you mean, half Indian?"

"Chief Ramon is only half Apache. His father is a Mexican who was stolen in his youth by the Apaches and later adopted into the tribe. If the stories I've heard are true, he came from a rather well-to-do Creole family."

"Creole?"

"Those Mexicans with pure Spanish blood. They're the aristocrats in this country."

That explained Chief Ramon's nose and wavy hair, Alison thought. "But how did he become chief, if he's a half-breed?"

"Blood lines have no more to do with choosing a chief than his age. To the Apaches' credit, they don't go by the color of a man's skin when they pick a leader, but by the man himself. But don't get the mistaken impression that because he has white blood in him Chief Ramon isn't Apache to the bone. He was born and raised among them. Their manner of living is all he's ever known. As I said before, he was chosen because of his leadership abilities and his fighting skills."

"You didn't say anything about fighting skills," Alison objected.

"Didn't I? Well, I should have. The Apaches are a people who seem to be constantly at war. They need a man to serve as their general as well as their leader. And El Halcon is a master at guerrilla warfare. His hit-and-run tactics have left the cavalry chasing around in circles."

"Hit and run. That sounds cowardly to me."

"The Apache is in no sense a coward. He believes in

doing the greatest damage with the least possible losses
to the tribe. The way their members are decreasing, it's
the only way they can survive. Because he is so grossly
outnumbered, the Apache plays his cards to suit himself. His ambushing tactics are masterpieces of skill. He
chooses the time and the place for the battle, and he
doesn't hesitate to break the engagement if the situation begins to look bad. He sees no dishonor in running.
To him, the biggest dishonor is to lose a man unnecessarily."

Alison had no idea that the Apaches had such a high
regard for individual lives. It somehow seemed to be at
odds with their warlike ways. "Do you think that's why
Chief Ramon ordered his warriors to surrender? Because he knew it was hopeless and would be a waste of
lives?"

"It's possible, although I seriously doubt that the Mexicans will turn his warriors loose. He may be the one
being tried for murder, but they want them all. But
surely he must know that." Sam paused thoughtfully for
a moment, then said, "No, I think Chief Ramon expected his story to be believed, that if he had realized
the *alcade* wouldn't believe him, he'd have made a
break for it."

"Do you believe his story? That the coat was given to
him?"

"Yes, I do, but I'm going more by his reputation than
anything. I don't believe Chief Ramon would lie. That's
the coward's way out, and El Halcon is not a coward. I
think if he had murdered Griffin, he would have admitted so right then and there."

"Then why didn't he offer any further explanation?
Mr. Grey said he refused to say anything more."

"He's a proud man. Perhaps he thought to offer any

further explanation would make it look as if he was groveling. That Apache bows to no man." Sam gazed off thoughtfully. "Or perhaps he decided to save his breath for the trial. If so, I want to hear what he has to say." He turned to Alison. "Would you like to go along?"

At the thought of seeing the handsome, fascinating chief again, Alison's heartbeat accelerated, an unexpected reaction that irritated her. She thought to refuse, but the lure was too great. "Yes, I would."

The next morning, Alison and Sam walked through the dusty streets of Presidio on their way to El Halcon's trial. As they strolled along, Alison became aware of her uncle scrutinizing her from the corner of his eye. "Is something wrong?" she asked. "You've been starting at me as if I'd suddenly grown warts on my nose."

Sam chuckled. "Forgive me, my dear. I guess my staring was rude. But I was just thinking how changed you were from the gawky six-year-old with enormous blue eyes and freckles on her face I saw on my last visit back east."

"Oh, I haven't changed so much. The freckles are still lurking there on my face. If it weren't for this bonnet I'm wearing, they'd be popping out all over. And I'm still gawky, only taller."

"I'm afraid I'll have to disagree with you. There is absolutely nothing gawky about you, and I think your height is quite striking. A shorter woman could never look so graceful. As a matter of fact, I was just thinking that you have grown into a remarkably lovely woman."

"Why, thank you," Alison answered graciously. "I wish my mother could hear you say that. She was horrified when I grew so tall. She swore I'd never find a husband."

"Does your height bother you?"

"To be perfectly honest, no. It has it advantages."

"Such as?"

"Well, I could say it enables me to look over crowds or reach things on the highest shelf, but that would only be partially true. No, I find my height gives me an advantage over men that I wouldn't have if I was shorter like most women. Did you know men are uncomfortable around tall women? Somehow our height bothers them." Alison looked her uncle in the eye and candidly said, "This may shock you, but I get a great deal of satisfaction out of intimidating men with my height. It's an excellent way of getting rid of a pesky salesman, or an arrogant boor trying to impress you, or making a rude coachman mind his manners. And you wouldn't believe the men who try to make women feel inferior because of their sex. If I find a man's attitude or behavior annoying, I simply pull myself up to my full height and look him straight in the eye." Alison laughed. "Why, they seem to shrivel right before me."

Sam chuckled, finding Alison's honesty refreshing. He had used that trick a few times himself. "And what about that bit about not finding a husband? Does that bother you?"

"Goodness, no! Marriage is the last thing on my mind right now. I want to see some of the world before I settle down."

"Now, there I heartily agree. A beautiful girl like you can always marry. And your height will be no detriment. There are many men around who would be proud to have you as a wife."

Yes, Alison thought, but she had yet to meet one who interested her. They all seemed so dull. But then, ¬maybe when she was ready for love and marriage, she'd find someone who would appeal to her. Until then, she wasn't going to worry about it. There was much more to life than finding a man.

When they reached the *juzgado* where the trial was to be held, a crowd of spectators had gathered before the door. As Alison and Sam waited for the people in front of them to file into the adobe building, she glanced out the window over the bluff where the building sat and across to the Rio Grande. She saw a freight train on the Texas side slowly making its way across the hills, the twenty mules that pulled each heavy wagon laboring in the deep sand. No one else paid any attention to the wagon train, for it was a common sight here in Presidio, but Alison stared at it. Somehow, she sensed the wagon train had something to do with El Halcon, something important, and she found herself wishing it would hurry and arrive. It was a strange experience, a premonition of sorts that she couldn't understand or shake loose.

Not until she was seated at the end of one of the wooden benches in the courtroom was Alison able to push the strange feeling aside. She looked about her curiously, noting that the spectators were the well-to-do Mexicans and Anglos of the town. The peons in Presidio were conspicuous by their absence, and Alison wondered if it was because they had been denied entrance by the upper class, or if it was the peons' way of showing their disapproval of the treatment of a man they considered their protector.

Turning her attention to the other side of the courtroom, where the Apaches were already seated on the wooden benches, Alison quickly scanned their faces. They sat staring straight ahead with stony expressions on their dark countenances. Then, noticing that El Halcon was missing, a sudden thought occurred to her, one that upset her deeply. Had the Mexican soldiers decided not to risk the outcome of this trial and instead killed the chief during the night?

Alison whirled around to face her uncle and asked in a demanding voice, "Where is El Halcon? Why isn't he with his warriors?"

Stunned by her furious look, Sam stammered, "Why . . . why, he hasn't been brought in yet. They've kept him separated from his men for fear he would plan an escape."

"Oh, I see," Alison replied lamely, feeling a wave of relief washing over her and wondering at her peculiar behavior. Why in the world was she allowing herself to get so involved in this trial? El Halcon was just a lowly Apache, a murderer and a thief.

Feeling confused by her emotions, she sat back and found herself facing a table at the opposite end of the room. Beside it, hanging on a small pole, was the Mexican flag, and on the wall behind the table was a large picture of a muscular man with a thick head of silver hair and a bushy mustache. Taking note of his elaborate military uniform and the array of medals on his chest, she frowned in distaste, thinking him a little ostentatiously dressed, then glanced at the bottom corner of the picture and read the signature there. "So that's Porfirio Díaz, the president of Mexico," she commented to her uncle.

"Yes, that's Díaz. He overthrew the government a few years ago and now rules this country with an iron fist."

"Are you saying he's a dictator?"

"More or less. At least, he's been able to stay in power, and considering how fast presidents come and go in this country, and how torn with revolutions Mexico has been in the past, that's saying something. And he's the first ruler to make any serious attempts to bring the bandits in this country under control. He's formed a national mounted police force known as the *rurales*. In truth, most of them are ex-bandits themselves, but it seems it takes one to catch one. The *rurales* are turning out to be surprisingly efficient, if you can overlook their rather brutal tactics."

"But still, he's a dictator," Alison objected with obvious disapproval.

"Yes, I know. It goes against our Anglo beliefs of democracy. But unfortunately, right now, Mexico needs a firm hand, and Díaz is trying to rid the army of its corruption and give the country a better economic health. He's encouraging foreign investments in the country. That's how the company your father works for got its mine."

Alison frowned. Regardless of the fact that her father might indirectly owe his job to Díaz, she didn't like the idea of a dictator ruling the country. She was a woman with a strong sense of freedom, of the right of people to rule their own lives, to make their own choices. She glanced around the courtroom, then asked, "Where does the jury sit?"

"They don't have juries in Mexico. A three-man tribunal of judges tries all major cases."

"But wouldn't a jury be fairer?"

"To our way of thinking, yes, but this is how it's done down here. And considering the circumstances, El Halcon may get a fairer trail from a tribunal than a jury." Dropping his voice so that those sitting around them couldn't overhear him, Sam added, "Particularly if the jury was picked from the people in this courtroom. Almost everyone present is a merchant or freighter, either directly or indirectly connected to the Chihuahua trade that El Halcon preys on. Naturally, they harbor ill feelings toward him."

Yes, Alison thought, and they were determined to punish him for past crimes. A strange anger filled her, one that Alison could attribute only to outrage at the injustice of the Apache chief being tried for a crime no one could prove had actually occurred.

The minutes ticked by slowly. Alison wondered what the delay was. Then the double doors at the back of the courtroom were flung open, and everyone jumped and turned to look as the room was suddenly flooded with bright sunlight.

El Halcon stood in the open doorway, flanked by four soldiers with their rifles pointed at him menacingly. Despite the fact that his wrists were heavily manacled, he stood erect, his dark head held proudly, a totally inscrutable expression on his bronzed face. Dressed in a red shirt that matched his headband and was belted at his waist and a pair of tight white pants that were tucked into his knee-high moccasins, he looked magnificent. His presence filled the room to such an extent that he seemed to crowd out everyone and everything.

One of the guards prodded the Apache chief in the back with the end of his rifle, and El Halcon walked down the aisle. Or rather, his walk was so graceful that he seemed to float down it. Alison stared at him. She hadn't realized he was so tall. Then she spied the turquoise necklace that hung from his neck. Like the matching earrings, the piece of jewelry did nothing to detract from his considerable masculinity. As he passed, Alison became acutely aware of the muscles in his thighs rippling beneath his skintight pants, of the shirt straining across his broad shoulders, of the power that radiated from him. A little thrill of excitement ran through her, and a warm curl formed in her stomach.

Irritated at her reaction to his presence, Alison tried to tear her eyes away from the compelling chief, but she found she couldn't. Her fascination with the powerful Apache was too great. Even after he was seated in a chair beside the table, she stared at him, taking in every detail of his appearance as if she were trying to imprint it in her mind forever.

Everyone rose when the judges and the *alcade* entered the room. Because Alison's eyes were still glued to Chief Ramon, only she was able to see the fleeting flash of anger in his dark eyes when the four men entered, before the look on his face was replaced with the same stony expression. But however brief the show of emotion was, it was enough to make Alison's blood run cold.

The *alcade* called the court to order and produced the evidence of the lightweight overcoat. Mrs. Griffin, teary-eyed and choked with emotion, swore to the duster's identification. Alison watched Chief Ramon during this exchange, then whispered to her uncle, "Does he understand what's being said?"

"Chief Ramon? Why, of course he understands. All of these Apaches speak fluent Spanish."

The *alcade* turned to El Halcon and asked if he had anything to say. The Apache chief stared straight through the Mexican as if the man didn't even exist, his lips set in a firm line.

"I asked if you have anything to say in your defense, other than that ridiculous story you told me that the overcoat was given to you," the *alcade* persisted.

For all practical purposes, the Apache might have been made of stone instead of flesh and blood. There wasn't even a flicker of an eyelash. His stubborn refusal to speak up in his own defense angered Alison. "Why doesn't he say something?" she whispered to her uncle.

"I don't know, my dear. I assume he has no intention of giving any further information."

"Then why doesn't his lawyer say something in his behalf? Just because he has the man's coat doesn't mean he's killed him. Why, there aren't even any bloodstains on it."

"He doesn't have a lawyer," Sam explained. "He refused counsel."

"Why in the devil did he do that?" Alison asked in a much louder voice, her strange fear for the Apache overriding her good manners. "Doesn't he realize this whole trial is nothing but a sham? That they're trying to hang him for past crimes? Look at the expressions on those judges' faces. It's obvious that they've already tried and convicted him."

Alison's indignant outburst brought her several enraged looks from a few of the Anglo spectators around her. Even the judges were glaring at her from where they sat. But Alison refused to be cowed by their looks. She glared back at them.

Sam chuckled, secretly admiring Alison's courage and fiery spirit. "Perhaps you should act as his counsel."

"Maybe I should!"

A puzzled expression came over Sam's face. "Why are you getting so upset, my dear?"

Why, indeed? Alison wondered. "It's just that the injustice of this whole thing angers me," she answered, trying to convince herself as much as her uncle of the reason for her outrage. "He was tried and convicted before he even walked in here."

"He's an Apache," an American sitting down the bench from Alison said in Spanish.

Alison turned to the man and retorted hotly in the same language, "He's an innocent man until proven guilty! And possession of that coat doesn't prove him guilty of murder. Why, you don't even know if a murder has been committed. If you want to try him for theft, try him for that. But not murder!"

A Mexican merchant sitting in front of Alison turned in his seat and hissed, "Sssh!"

"Don't you tell me to be quiet!" Alison threw back angrily. "I can't stand by and watch any man, even an Indian, convicted of murder on such flimsy evidence. This isn't a trial. It's a farce!"

Before the Mexican could respond, the doors at the back of the room were suddenly flung open. The spectators in the courtroom whirled around in their seats, fearing a surprise attack by Chief Ramon's tribesmen. Then, seeing the man standing in the open doorway, Mrs. Griffin cried out in joyous relief, "John! You're alive!"

Alison's eyes widened in surprise at the sudden turn of events. She watched as the dusty American quickly strode down the aisle and embraced his happy wife as she ran to meet him. Then, when the courtroom had settled down, the freighter related how El Halcon had come into possession of his coat. It seemed Griffin had joined forces with two other freighting outfits that were coming to Presidio with a load of salt from the salt lakes east of the Pecos River. Griffin had gone ahead of the train to scout a particularly dangerous pass that the Apaches were known to favor as an excellent place for ambush. He had suddenly been attacked by a mountain lion that jumped from the rim of the pass above him and knocked him from his horse. Just when he thought he was looking certain death in the eye, El Halcon had suddenly appeared and shot the lion. Then, to Griffin's immense relief, the Apache chief had told him he was free to leave. In appreciation for saving his life, and since El Halcon scorned his offer of money, Griffin had given the Apache his coat. Later, after the train had safely traveled through the pass, they had been attacked by El Halcon and his warriors. For hours the freighters had fought off the Apaches without loss or injury to either side. Then, becoming tired of the stalemate, Griffin and another freighter had invited El Halcon to meet them for a parley. When the Apache chief met them in the open area between the circled wagons and his men, the two Americans drew the pistols they had concealed and threatened to kill him if he didn't order his warriors to withdraw to a distant place. Since he had no recourse, El Halcon had agreed.

While Griffin related the story, Alison watched El Halcon's face. No longer was his expression inscrutable, and Alison knew he was still furious with Griffin for tricking him. If the two men ever met again, she was sure there would be a much different story to tell. A shiver ran over her at the murderous look in the Apache's dark eyes. But why should the Indian be so angry? she wondered. Hadn't he been just as deceitful in attacking Griffin after saving his life? And why had the Apache saved the American's life? The red and white man were supposed to be enemies. Then a sudden thought occured to Alision, one that completely pushed the questions she had been pondering aside. She realized why El Halcon had held his silence. He had known Griffin would be arriving in Presidio shortly and would make an appearance at the courtroom as soon as he heard the news. The knowledge infuriated her. Here she had been worrying about the Apache's fate and actually defending him, while the arrogant bastard had been calmly biding his time!

When the *alcade* told El Halcon that he was free to go, Alison was so shocked that she forgot her anger at the Apache. "Why are they letting him go?" she asked her uncle in surprise.

"Because he didn't steal the coat. It was just as he had told the *alcade*. The duster was given to him."

"But when he attacked that train, it was attempted murder. Aren't they going to try him for that?" Alison asked in confusion.

"No, in view of his saving Griffin's life, they aren't. Besides, that was only attempted murder, and unless it's successfully carried out, it isn't deemed important in these parts," Sam explained. "You heard what Griffin said. No one was even injured."

"But El Halcon meant to injure when he attacked the train," Alision persisted. "He meant to kill!"

"Still, we have our own code of justice out here. A life for a life, so to speak, and no harm was done to the train. Had that been the case, it might have been a different story."

Alison pondered this information briefly, then, remembering her earlier puzzlement, asked, "Why do you suppose El Halcon saved Griffin's life in the first place?"

"In order to understand that, you would have to understand the Indian's way of thinking. He and the white man are mortal enemies, until another more traditional common enemy appears, in this case the mountain lion. The dangerous animal has been mankind's enemy since the beginning of time, and therefore, to El Halcon's way of thinking, he and Griffin were allies. A white man might not have done the same, but El Halcon was simply following his own code of honor."

"Code of honor?" Alsion asked in disbelief. She scoffed and said scornfully, "Some code of honor. He saves a man's life, then attacks him."

"That had nothing to do with what occurred earlier. El Halcon and Griffin being allies was only a brief, temporary situation. Once the common enemy was destroyed, the two reverted back to their original positions, and Griffin expected no less than that. The freighter has been out here for a long time. He knows how the Apaches think and what to expect from them. But that doesn't stop him from coming to El Halcon's defense. Just as Griffin knew El Halcon would probably attack him later, so El Halcon fully expected Griffin to come to this trial and tell the truth of how he gained possession of the white man's coat. Our reasoning may seem strange to an easterner, but as I said before, we have our own code of justice out here, particularly those of us who have been out here for a long time."

Yes, it was a strange code of justice, Alison thought. First, the townspeople tried a man for murder, using the flimsy evidence of the supposed victim's coat, then they totally ignored the fact that the Apache had attacked the wagon train with theft and murder in mind and turned a much feared and hated enemy loose because he had earlier saved the freighter's life. Why, her uncle had even implied that El Halcon would have been turned loose even if he hadn't saved Griffin's life, simply because his attack had been unsuccessful. She'd never heard of anything so ridiculous. And she'd never heard of an Indian saving a white man's life before either, particularly not one as fierce and savage as El Halcon was reputed to be. Both sides seemed a little peculiar, switching their feelings about one another back and forth, like a king in a game of checkers. But then, maybe they looked at it as a game to be played, in which only they knew the rules.

Chief Ramon rose, and the manacles on his wrists were removed. As the tall, broad-shouldered Apache walked back down the aisle, Alison again found that she couldn't keep her eyes off him. She stood before her seat at the end of the bench waiting for him and his warriors to pass before she walked out, secretly glad that they were giving the handsome, fascinating chief his freedom.

Then, when he reached where she was standing, El Halcon came to an abrupt stop and looked Alison directly in the eye. Her breath caught. She had never felt a look so profoundly. It was as if those dark, piercing eyes were pinning her to the spot and reaching into the depths of her soul. Then El Halcon was gone, leaving her feeling shaken and trembling from the strange encounter.

As she walked from the courtroom, Alison was bewildered. Why, of all men, did the tall, compelling Apache affect her so much? Why had she felt so defensive in his behalf, and why did he arouse such peculiar feelings in her? And even more disturbing, how had she known the wagon train she had seen earlier would have something important to do with El Halcon? Even the townspeople hadn't recognized it as Griffin's train. A cold shiver ran over her.

3

That night Alison stood at her bedroom window and looked out past the heavy iron grille at the town below her. Here and there she could see the flickering of candlelight through a window, but other than that, nothing. The night was pitch black, and the lights seemed to be suspended in midair.

All day she had been puzzling over the strange look that El Halcon had given her. She didn't believe the explanation her uncle had made. Sam had suggested that the Apache had overheard her saying she wouldn't stand by and watch a red man sentenced and executed for a crime he didn't commit and had only wanted a closer look at her out of curiosity. But that had been no curious look the Apache had given her. It had been much too pointed, almost as if he were trying to convey some silent message to her. No, Alison corrected herself. It wasn't a message. It was much too forceful. It was as if it were a command!

Alison shook her head in disgust. Why was she mulling over it? It was done and past, and the Apache chief was gone. Mr. Grey had said El Halcon and his warriors had ridden away shortly after they were released. They were probably halfway to their home in those mountains by now. But the knowledge that she would never again see the arrogant, totally fascinating chief did nothing to lift her strangely lagging spirits. She could only feel regret that the exciting man had left her life as unexpectedly as he had entered it.

She must be insane, wasting her time thinking about a man—a half-breed no less! She had never been one of those silly girls who entertained romantic fantasies, as her sisters had before they had married. They were always mooning over some man who had caught their eye. She wondered what they would have thought of El Halcon. Why, they would have probably swooned at the very sight of him, not out of infatuation, but out of terror. The silly things were scared of their own shadows. They would have never had the courage to do what she was doing, traveling across the dangerous Texas frontier to a backward country whose northern states were wild and uncivilized, a land plagued not only by savages but by bandits who were cruel and bloodthirsty.

Alison forced herself to think about the adventure that was awaiting her. Tomorrow she and Sam would leave Presidio del Norte with one of the freight trains going to Chihuahua City. They would follow the Rio Concho halfway to that city; then she and her uncle would leave the train and cut across the desert to the western state of Sonora, where her father lived. The long trip would take weeks, but it would be an experience that few American women had ever had. When she went back to Baltimore, she would be able to boast that she had traveled over a thousand miles, halfway on horseback, through some of the most arid, rugged country in the world. It was a challenge that left her tingling with excitement.

Her spirits buoyed by the prospect of what lay ahead of her, Alison quickly undressed and slipped on her nightgown. But sleep was elusive, not merely because of her excitement but because of the stifling heat. While the long-sleeved, button-to-the-neck gown was comfortable in the night air in Baltimore, it was oppressive here in Mexico. She'd had no idea that the country would be so warm in the late spring.

For over an hour, Alison tossed and turned, trying to get comfortable. She even considered stripping off the gown and sleeping naked, but she wasn't quite that daring. She finally rose, snipped off the sleeves at the shoulder seam, and unbuttoned the gown to her breasts. When she lay back down, her arms and chest felt cooler, but her long legs were still much too warm. She hiked the gown up around her thighs, then she finally fell asleep.

Hours later she was awakened by the feel of the mattress suddenly dipping. Her eyes flew open to see the vague outline of someone hovering over her. Terrified, she opened her mouth to scream, but the sound never left her throat. A gag was shoved in her mouth and tied in place with a swiftness that momentarily stunned her. She pushed at the person leaning over her, but the body was as immobile as a heavy rock. She knew that it had to be a man by the feel of the hard muscles on his chest. Instinctively she reached for his face, her nails bared. She had the brief satisfaction of hearing his sharp intake of breath as the nails on her hand raked one cheek. Then, to her dismay, he was straddling her, catching her flying hands and holding them firmly in one hand while he deftly looped a piece of thin leather around them over and over.

Alison struggled, bucking wildly and kicking out with her feet. With an agility and swiftness that amazed her, the man reversed his position and caught her feet, tying them in the same manner. As he did so, Alison beat on his back with her bound fists, but the blows seemed to have no effect on him.

Her abductor leaped to the side of the bed and jerked her to her feet. With her ankles firmly bound, she swayed precariously, but before she could lose her balance and fall, he tossed her over his shoulder as if she weighed no more than a sack of meal.

As he rapidly walked from the room, Alison twisted and turned, but with his arms firmly holding her thighs against his chest, it was a wasted effort. She pounded at his buttocks and the backs of his legs, to no avail. She might as well have been beating on a rock. She had never been so frightened or so frustrated in her entire life.

The man descended the stairs with a sure-footedness that astonished her. She couldn't see a thing in the inky darkness. Who was he, and why was he abducting her? Was he one of those *bandidos,* intent upon holding her for ransom? Or did he intend to carry her off for more nefarious purposes? Did he intend to take her someplace to rape her?

She struggled with renewed determination as he carried her through the dark, silent house and then the courtyard, his footsteps so light that they were soundless. Her wild exertions gained her nothing but a lightheadedness, for breathing through her nose wasn't supplying her with enough air. She whirled dizzily, fearing she was going to faint.

He bent and briefly set her on her feet before Alison felt herself again flying through the air. Her midsection landed on something hard, knocking the breath from her. Then, smelling the scent of horse, she knew it had to be a saddle. As her abductor mounted behind her, she went wild in a last, desperate effort to escape. The man's hand came down hard on her back, pressing her down as the horse lunged forward.

As they rode through the dark streets of the town, Alison couldn't believe this was actually happening to her. Who would be so bold and daring as to abduct her from her bed in the middle of the night, right under the noses of her uncle and the Greys? Surely this must be a nightmare. But as much as she hoped it was, she knew it wasn't. She could hear the horse's hooves pounding on the packed earth and feel every jolt of its gait in her midsection. And then there was that hand on her back bearing down on her and seemingly searing her skin.

The blood rushed to her head, giving her a headache that seemed to be pounding in unison with the horse's hooves, and she could feel the wind rushing past her. Then, as she heard the splash and felt the water hit her face, she knew they were crossing the river. But why would a *bandido* take her to Texas? Then she remembered something she had felt pressing against her side when the man had carried her over his shoulder, something metallic. An earring! Her abductor could be none other than El Halcon!

A little thrill ran through her, but the brief tingle of excitement was lost as other, more powerful emotions emerged: terror at what the fierce savage might have in mind for her—she had heard that Apaches tortured their captives—and outrage at the chief's audacity in stealing her from her bed. The two emotions warred for supremacy inside her. Her anger won out. It raged in her for the next hour, until the Apache brought his horse to a standstill beneath a small mesquite, dismounted, and lifted her to the ground.

Being suddenly set upright made Alison again feel light-headed, and her numb, tingling feet would not support her. She swayed, and then found herself being swept up in El Halcon's strong arms. Alison was acutely conscious of the feel of the hard muscles on his chest pressing against her side and of the heat of his body as he carried her to the trunk of the tree. She was surrounded by his slightly musky and strangely exciting scent. Suddenly his powerful masculinity seemed overwhelming. She felt as if she were smothering in it. She pushed at him with her bound hands, but it was unnecessary. He was already placing her on the ground. Then, to her surprise, he untied the rag around her head and removed her gag.

The anger Alison had been nursing rose and erupted like a volcano. "You bastard!" she threw out in Spanish, but to her utter disgust the words came out sounding like a weak croak and not the forceful curse she had meant them to be. Her mouth and throat were as dry as parchment.

Nonetheless, El Halcon had understood the curse. Instead of angering him, it amused him. He hadn't expected less from the *norteamerica,* not after the way she had fought him, like a wild lioness. *Dios,* she was a fiery one! But secretly he was pleased. Meek, fearful women disgusted him. No, his estimation of her had been correct. She would be well worth the trouble he had gone to.

Chief Ramon rose, walked to his horse, and removed his waterskin. Carrying it back to Alison, he knelt on one knee and held it to her lips. Alison jerked her head away.

"Drink!" he demanded.

Alison was determined that she would accept nothing from the Apache, even though her throat was aching from thirst. Stubbornly she held her head away. She gasped when the chief roughly grabbed the back of her head with one hand and turned it. As he poured the water down her throat, she found she had no choice but to swallow. It was either that or drown. Then she remembered her arms. She threw them up, knocking the bag from his hand.

El Halcon muttered an oath and quickly picked up the bag, from which the precious liquid was pouring out on the thirsty, parched ground. He jerked his hand from the back of her head and glared down at her. "You fool! Don't you realize that's all the water we have? I admire a woman with spirit, but not a foolish one."

"I don't give a damn what kind of woman you admire, you filthy savage!"

A long moment of silence followed, a silence that seemed ominous to Alison. She wished it wasn't so dark and she could see the expression on his face. Had her calling him a filthy savage angered him? A renewed tingle of fear ran though her. Then, when he made no move toward her, she gathered her courage and asked, "Why did you abduct me?"

Chief Ramon rose to his feet. "We will talk in the morning."

As he turned and walked to his horse, Alison shrieked, "No! We'll talk now! What do you want of me?"

"I said we would talk in the morning."

The carefully measured words were softly spoken, but they were as hard as steel. Alison had seen how utterly unyielding the Apache could be at the trial and knew she would be wasting her breath to argue. No one could force the chief to talk if he didn't want to, and she strongly suspected no one could force him to do anything if he put his mind to it. He was the most obstinate man she had ever met.

She watched as he unsaddled his horse, then lay down a few feet from her and rolled over, turning his back to her.

"Do you intend to leave me tied up for the rest of the night?" Alison asked.

There was no answer.

"I can't sleep with my hands and feet tied."

There was still no answer.

Alison realized that she could be talking to a rock for all the good it was doing her. She lifted her wrists to her mouth and tried to untie the leather string that bound them with her teeth.

"Do not try that," El Halcon said in a hard voice, his back still to her. "That is an Apache knot, and you will never be able to loosen it. All you will accomplish is to wet the rawhide with your saliva. Then when it dries, it will shrink and bite into the skin of your wrists."

Alison was startled, wondering how he had known what she was doing. She glanced down at her ankles. Undoubtedly that knot was the same. Alison had never been so frustrated. For a moment she considered saying please but quickly rejected the thought. She'd never beg for anything from the damn Apache.

She lay down and awkwardly rolled to her side, glaring at El Halcon's vague outline. For a good hour she railed at him silently. Then, exhausted from both her emotional turmoil and her long day, she slept.

Alison awoke in bright sunlight. A shadow suddenly

fell over her, and she saw El Halcon. He looked menacing. Alison bolted to a sitting position, and then, realizing that her ankles had been untied, quickly scrambled to her feet.

As Chief Ramon's black eyes slowly swept over her, Alison was acutely conscious that her nightdress was her only covering. Surely he couldn't see through the material. It wasn't that thin. But she felt stripped to the bone by his penetrating look.

When his eyes rose to meet hers, Alison summoned her courage and boldly held out her hands to him, saying in a firm voice, "Untie them."

"No, not yet."

She fought down her frustration, then said, "I demand that you take me back to Presidio."

Seeing that he found her demand amusing, her anger rose. "My uncle will come looking for me. He'll kill you!"

"Your uncle will never find you where I'm taking you."

Then he planned to take her back to his camp? But why? She wasn't a tough, country woman. She wouldn't make a good slave. "Why did you abduct me?"

El Halcon's admiring dark eyes drifted over Alison's beautiful face. Slowly—ever so slowly—they swept over her body from head to foot, lingering at her full breasts until Alison felt as if he were touching her there, instead of just looking. When he lifted his eyes, Alison saw they were smoldering with unconcealed desire. A strange little shiver ran through her before she repeated her question. "I asked why you abducted me."

A hint of a smile played at El Halcon's sensuous lips. "I should think that would be obvious." His voice dropped several octaves and seemed to pulsate in the air while his dark eyes seemingly burned her skin as they once again slowly roved over her curves. "I want you."

Alison should have been afraid, but strangely his straightforward answer infuriated her. How dare he stand there and boldly say that to her. "Because you want me?" she yelled. "Damn you, I'm not a piece of property! I'm a human being!"

"Would you have come with me if I had asked?"

"Of course not!"

"I thought not. That is why I stole you. I am an Apache. What I want, I take."

Alison's face paled. For the first time, she felt real fear. She could hardly force the words from her mouth. "Then you intend to rape me?"

"I do not think I will have to force you."

His words took her by complete surprise. "What do you mean by that remark?"

"I think you are as physically attracted to me as I am to you."

Alison remembered the strange effect he had had on her and those peculiar sensations he had aroused in her and was mortified. Then, seeing the smug smile on his lips, her anger returned. Why, he was the most arrogant, conceited man she had ever met. "That's utterly ridiculous!"

"You stared at me the day I rode into Presidio."

"I stared at you because you were the only Indian chief I'd ever seen."

"You could not take your eyes from me in the courtroom."

A guilty flush rose on Alison's face. Feeling the heat rise and knowing that she had no control over it only infuriated her more. "I did no such thing! You just imagined it."

"You came to my defense. You said you would not stand by and let them convict me of a crime I did not commit."

"I said I wouldn't stand by and watch *any* man convicted of a crime he didn't commit. It had nothing to do with you personally."

"Then you deny that you are attracted to me?"

"Deny?" Alison asked in exasperation. "Are you deaf? Didn't you hear anything I've said? I can't stand you! I'd never consort with a cold-blooded killer, a filthy, uncivilized half-breed!"

For a horrifying moment, Alison feared her reckless insult was her undoing. The look that came into El Halcon's eyes made her blood run cold. The Apache looked furious enough to kill her with his bare hands, and there was no doubt in her mind that the tall, powerful chief could break her in two if he so desired. She'd been a fool to tangle with this dangerous savage.

She watched breathlessly as his eyes narrowed. With the swiftness of a striking snake, he caught her shoulders and jerked her forward. Alison's heart pounded with fear as he glared down at her. "You lie! You lie to me, and to yourself."

"No, I—"

El Halcon's mouth came crashing down on hers in hot, fierce demand, his lips grinding against hers. He forced her lips open, and his tongue darted into her mouth. Alison stiffened in shock. No man had ever kissed her that way. As his tongue plundered the softness of her mouth, a fury rose in her. How dare he take such indecent intimacies with her! How dare he invade her with his filthy tongue!

She struggled, pushing against his chest and trying to twist her head away. El Halcon snaked one arm around her and brought her full-force against his lean body, pinning her bound arms between them. Catching the back of her head with his other hand, he held it firmly while his tongue ravished her mouth, swirling, sliding in and out in a wild, savage kiss that seemed to go on forever. With his mouth firmly sealed over hers and his powerful arm crushing her to him, Alison couldn't breathe. Her heart pounded so violently that she feared it would jump from her body. A light-headedness came over her, and she sagged limply against him.

Vaguely, as if from a far distance, she became aware of his hard male body pressing against hers, her breasts flattened against his broad, muscular chest, his taut belly against her soft one, their legs touching full length. An insidious warmth crept over her, and she began to tingle all over. And then she became aware of the long, hard length of his readiness pressing against her thigh, seemingly scorching her with its pulsating heat right through their clothing. A strange shiver of excitement ran through her.

Abruptly El Halcon lifted his head. Her senses still spinning dizzily, Alison looked up at him. His dark eyes were blazing with the heat of his desire. The part of him pressing against her suddenly seemed enormous and terrifying.

Taking note of the stark fear that flared in her eyes, El Halcon smiled. "There is no need for fear. Despite what you have heard, Apaches do not rape their captives. We are too proud to force ourselves upon a woman. That is unmanly, and one who does so is scorned by my people."

He released her and stepped back. Alison was

shocked at how weak her legs felt. "However," he continued, "if the woman is willing, that is an entirely different matter. I will wait for you to become more willing."

"I'll never be willing for you to do *that* to me!"

The dark eyes flashed dangerously. Then as quickly as it came, the anger was gone. "Yes, you will. Some day you will beg me for it."

His audacious boast infuriated Alison. "Never!"

He chuckled, a deep rumble in his chest that totally took Alison aback. She hadn't expected this fierce savage to be capable of something so human as laughter. He seemed so hard, so intense.

"You are a stubborn woman," Ramon answered with a maddening calmness. "Not only will your body welcome mine, but you will come to love me too."

It was the ultimate audacity. "Love an Indian?" Alison shrieked. "I'd die before I'd sink that low!"

Again the dark eyes flashed briefly, bringing a tingle of fear to Alison. Then he smiled smugly and said softly, "We shall see."

The softly spoken words were said with supreme confidence, and Alison knew that he was issuing her a challenge. But he wasn't just pitting his will against hers to lay claim to her body. The arrogant bastard was so damn sure of his masculine charms that he was actually predicting she'd become smitten with him. Damn his black soul! Undoubtedly he had the adoration of every female in his tribe and expected it as his due. Well, she'd show him!

Alison looked Ramon directly in the eye and said in a determined voice, "You've made a serious error in your judgment of me, El Halcon. I'm not a weak-willed woman. No man will ever bend me to his will. And I'd never be so foolish as to become infatuated with you. I'll never surrender my body to you, and the only thing I will ever feel for you is hatred!"

The Apache showed no reaction to Alison's strong, determined words. The expression on his bronzed face was totally inscrutable. "We shall see," he repeated, then turned and walked to his horse.

4

As El Halcon strode to his horse, Alison stared at his broad back, knowing her strong vow had had no effect on him. He still planned on taking her with him against her will. She realized that accepting his challenge was a serious mistake. If anything, it had only made him more determined to prove her wrong. He was an unbelievably stubborn man.

She glanced about her, wondering if she could find her way back to Presidio if she could manage to escape from him.

"Don't even contemplate something so foolish," the Apache said, his back still to her. "Even if you could escape, you would never find your way back. You would only get lost and die from thirst out here in this desert—that is, if a rattlesnake or wild animal didn't get you first."

Again Alison was started. Could the bastard read her mind? But as much as she hated to admit it, she knew he spoke the truth. Nothing looked familiar. Or rather, everything did. A lonely desert stretched out all around her, an immense, empty land that held nothing but rolling sand hills studded with clumps of cactus and mesquite brush. Because of its very sameness, there were no identifying landmarks that she might have recognized from her earlier trip through here. Besides, she wasn't even sure she had traveled over this desert. Perhaps it was another. She had no idea if they had ridden north, or east, or west once they had left the Rio Grande. She wouldn't get lost if she escaped. She was hopelessly lost already!

El Halcon turned from his horse and held out his waterbag to her. "Do not do anything as foolish as you did last night," he warned in a hard voice. "And do not refuse to drink. This time I will not force you. But it will be the last water you will get until we make camp tonight."

"Why? Are we that short?" Alison asked, feeling a tingle of fear. Without water, they could both die out here in this desert.

"No, we have enough, but drinking water in the heat of the day only makes you thirstier. Then it becomes like a living, clawing thing inside you."

Alison thought she had never heard of anything so ridiculous. She accepted the bag and drank, a few drops dribbling down the front of her gown. She lowered the bag and asked, "Can't you untie my hands now? You've made your point. I know it would be foolish to try to escape. It's awkward with them tied together."

"And have you try to scratch my eyes out again?"

Alison looked at the long, angry scratches on one lean cheek and felt immense satisfaction that she had put them there.

Seeing her look and knowing she was gloating, Chief

Ramon took the bag from her. "No, I will not untie your hands. Not until you are more submissive."

"I'll never be submissive!" Alison threw back defiantly.

"Then you'll never get your hands untied," he answered calmly.

Ignoring her angry glare, he took her arm and led her to his horse. As he hung the bag over the large horn, Alison asked in a biting voice, "Where did you get the Mexican saddle? Is it stolen too?"

Instead of angering him, as she had hoped it would, her question amused the Apache chief. "No, I traded for it. It is much sturdier than the Apache saddle. My people have no objection to adopting the use of a white man's possessions, when they are more practical."

Alison glanced at his shirt, noting that it was one like the Mexicans wore—a collarless, tuniclike garment that slipped over the head. Then, seeing the rifle hanging in his saddle holster, she asked in a scathing voice, "Like the white man's gun?"

"Most definitely the white man's gun. We'd be foolish to fight him with our bows and arrows."

"And I suppose you trade for them too?" she asked sarcastically.

"Sometimes. Sometimes not."

There was no doubt in Alison's mind as to how the Apache got the guns he didn't trade for. By murdering the white man who possessed them. "And when you trade, what do you trade with?"

"Horses and cattle."

"That you've stolen from the Texas ranchers?"

"Yes."

Seeing the look of utter contempt on her face, El Halcon's eyes flashed. "Don't look down on me with such contempt," he said angrily. "Your people are no better. This land was ours and you stole it from us. You murdered my people for it. You took what you wanted, and now you condemn us for doing the same. We plunder to live. You plundered out of greed."

"Greed?" Alison asked indignantly.

"Yes, greed! Always you want more. More land, more cattle, more horses. Who do you think we trade those stolen Texas horses and cattle to? The whites in New Mexico! Those ranchers know how we acquired them, that they are stolen property, but they do not care. They come cheap, and the whites are greedy. So they trade their guns to us, so we can steal more to bring them."

"I don't believe that!" Alison said in a shocked voice. "I don't believe Americans would do that to other Americans."

"Then you are a naive fool."

With that El Halcon caught her waist and swung her onto the saddle. Alison came down on the leather with a loud slap. Her eyes widened in horror as she realized that her bare bottom was on the saddle and that her legs were straddling it. Why, even if she hadn't been naked beneath her gown, it was a shockingly indecent position.

"I can't ride like this," she objected.

"Would you prefer to ride the way you did last night?"

"No, but—"

Alison's breath caught as the Apache chief swiftly mounted behind her and she felt him pressing against her back and buttocks. Suddenly she was acutely aware of her near nakedness and his hard muscles. His skin seemed to be burning hers right through her thin covering.

Ramon, too, was acutely aware of their bodies touching, and it was all he could do to keep from throwing Alison to the ground and taking her then and there. He wanted her so badly, he could taste it. But he was determined he wouldn't lower himself to forcing her. With supreme will, he tried to suppress his rapidly rising desire. However, he couldn't resist the temptation of taking the opportunity to touch her full breasts. As he reached for his reins, he deliberately let his forearms slide over the sides of the soft mounds, hearing Alison gasp and feeling a tingle run up his arms as she did so. It was with great reluctance that he picked up the reins and urged the horse forward with his knees.

As they galloped off, Alison quickly forgot Ramon's devastating touch and nearness with her fear that she might fall. She grabbed the horn of the saddle and then glanced down and saw that her gown had hiked up to her thighs. Feeling Ramon's bronzed muscular thigh pressing so initimately against the back of her naked thigh, a furious blush rose on her face. Completely forsaking her hold on the horn, she frantically tried to cover the nakedness of one leg, then heard El Halcon chuckle.

Alison's anger that he found her acute embarrassment amusing overrode her modesty. She abandoned her futile attempts and pulled herself up further in the saddle to get as far away from him as she possibly could, hoping to show the despicable Apache her contempt. It was a miserable position. Instead of her buttocks absorbing the shock of each gait the horse took, a most delicate part of her was taking a terrible beating. If only there was something between her and that hard leather.

"Sit back," El Halcon commanded.

"The devil I will!"

He muttered an oath, caught her around the waist with one powerful arm, and yanked her back. "Now tuck your gown beneath you."

Alison was horrified that he was aware of her naked flesh on the saddle and had guessed her dilemma.

"Do it, or I will do it for you," he threatened.

Alison didn't doubt his words for one minute, and she'd be damned if she'd suffer the indignity of having that savage shove his hands between her legs. She let go of the saddle horn and shoved the bunched-up material in her lap beneath her. The cushioning was a blessed relief. Then she looked down at her thighs and in consternation noticed that her action had made the skirt hike up even higher. It seemed that she had a choice of either protecting her bottom or exposing more of herself to the hated Apache's eyes. Deep down, Alison was a practical woman. She wouldn't sacrifice her comfort for her modesty.

"I'm glad to see that you are not as foolish as I thought," El Halcon remarked.

Damn him and his mind reading! Alison thought. "I'm sure you've seen a woman's bare legs before," she retorted recklessly.

"Yes, many." He paused, and Alison could feel his eyes on her bare legs. "But never any as long as yours."

Alison stiffened. Had he meant that as an insult? How dare he criticize her long legs! Indignant, she tried to pull away from him, but his arm was a steel band around her waist.

"Let go of me!" she demanded.

"No, you are more comfortable back here. Now be still. I am getting weary of fighting you. I'm beginning to wonder if you are worth the trouble."

His words stung Alison's female vanity. "If you don't like what you got, you can take me back!"

There was a long pause, and Alison wondered if he was actually considering it. Then he said softly, "No, I still want you."

The husky timbre of his voice sent a thrill through her, irritating Alison no end.

Alison found out that day what a harsh, unrelenting land that part of Texas was. The sun beat down on them unmercifully, and the air was so hot that every breath seemed to sear her lungs. The skin on her face and exposed arms and legs burned like fire, and she was drenched with sweat. The tender flesh on the inside of her thighs was rubbed raw, and her lips were cracked, her throat so dry it ached. Even when they stopped in the middle of the day and took refuge from the blistering sun beneath some bushes, she was miserable. The heat surrounded her like a heavy blanket, and her thirst was unbearable.

She did what she had sworn she would never do. She rolled to her side to face El Halcon. "Please," she begged, "let me have a drink of water. Just a swallow to wet my throat."

"No, it will only make you thirstier."

Furious at Chief Ramon's refusal, she jumped to her feet and ran to his horse, reaching for his waterbag. El Halcon was right behind her, his hand closing over hers like steel. "I said no!"

"You're just doing this to be cruel!"

"No, I am doing what is best for you."

He shoved her hands aside and slipped his hand into a small sack hanging on his saddle horn. Pulling out a piece of jerky, he offered it to her. "Chew on this."

"I'm not hungry, damn you! I'm thirsty!"

"It will bring saliva to your mouth."

Alison placed the jerky in her mouth, then quickly removed it. "It's salty. It will only make me thirstier."

"You need the salt to replace what you have lost. Now do what I said!"

Alison resented his demanding attitude, but she was too weak to defy him. The insufferable heat seemed to have sapped every bit of energy from her.

As she bit off a bit of jerky and began to chew, El Halcon led her back to the shade of the bushes. "You must trust me in this," he said in a firm voice. "The Apaches have learned how to survive in this harsh, arid land out of necessity. Much of what we have learned was by trial and error. We now have survival down to a fine art." He lifted the branches of the bush for her to lie under. "Eat the jerky and then rest. We leave in an hour."

As much as Alison hated to admit it, the jerky did ease her terrible thirst. She even felt the return of some of her strength and managed to doze. But as soon as she was back in the saddle and under the blistering rays of the white-hot sun again, the sweat poured from her, plastering her gown to her upper body and trickling from her forehead and into her eyes.

Seeing her wiping the stinging sweat from her eyes with her arm, El Halcon reined in and reached for the hem of her gown that lay over one blistered thigh. As he started to rip it, Alison asked in alarm, "What are you doing?"

"Making you a headband." He tied the white strip of

material around her head. "Why do you think we
Apaches wear them, if not to keep the sweat from our
eyes?" Glancing at her sunburned arms, he untied her
hands with a swiftness that stunned her, then stripped
off his shirt and handed it to her. "Put this on. It will
protect your arms."

Surprised, Alison turned in the saddle and looked at
him. The sight of that magnificent bronzed chest with
the turquoise stone resting between the bulging muscles took her breath away. Again she felt the impact of
his strong sexuality, and again that strange warmth
crept over her, a heat that she knew had nothing to do
with the sun. She quickly turned around and slipped on
the shirt, then realized, with no small horror, that the
material held his tantalizing male scent. She closed her
eyes and clenched her teeth, trying to fight off the dizzying waves that were washing over her. Damn him!
Why couldn't he just stink of sweat like other men did?

But as they continued their ride on the desert under
the searing sun, Alison had a more pressing problem to
contend with: her utter misery. Now she could understand how heat killed. It fried you alive, draining all the
moisture from your body. She was so dehydrated that
she couldn't even sweat anymore. Even her eyes felt
baked from the white-hot glare of the sand, and her
tongue felt three times its normal size.

When she saw a green band shimmering in the distance before her, she thought it was just another of the
mirages that had plagued her all afternoon. Not until
they rode closer and she saw that they were actually
trees did she dare to believe her eyes.

El Halcon reined in beneath the blessedly cool shade
of a rustling cottonwood. As he lifted her from the back
of the horse, Alison spied the nearby stream. Before her

feet even touched the ground, she was running for it, or trying to, for she was so weak she was staggering. When she reached the bank, she collapsed and buried her face in the water, taking long swallows.

El Halcon caught her shoulders and lifted her from the stream. "That's enough!"

"No! I want more. I only got a swallow or two."

"You can have more later. If you drink too much, too fast, it will make you sick."

"No, damn you! I'm thirsty!"

He shook her roughly. "Listen to me! Too much will give you terrible stomach cramps." He forced her to sit on the ground. "In a minute or two you can have another swallow."

If he had released her, Alison would have made another dive for the stream. But he held her firmly, forcing her to wait, and she didn't have the strength to fight him. Even then, he didn't release her. Holding her firmly with one hand, he cupped his other hand and dipped it into the water, then held it to her mouth. Alison didn't hesitate. She took his hand in hers and drank thirstily. Another moment ticked by with agonizing slowness before he offered her another drink.

He released her and stood. "Now, in another minute you can have another swallow. I don't care if you drink the entire stream, just as long as you space your drinks." He smiled. "Providing you leave a swallow or two for me and my horse."

Alison felt a twinge of guilt, knowing he must be as thirsty as she and had put off assuaging his own thirst to assure that she didn't make herself sick.

She watched while he led his horse to the stream and noted that he didn't let the animal drink too much either. Then he lay on his belly, taking a drink before he began splashing the water over his head and shoulders.

It looked so cool and inviting that Alison couldn't resist. But instead of being content to just splash the water on her, she waded into the stream until the water came to her thighs. Then she sat. Water had never felt so good in her life. She ducked her head in, letting it take the stinging heat from her face as well as her arms and legs.

For a long time she sat in the water, letting it soothe her burned skin and wash away the gritty salt, taking a drink now and then to ease her thirst. She was so occupied with soothing and refreshing herself that she didn't even notice when El Halcon walked away until she rose and waded from the stream.

She looked at his horse and then back at the water. The stream had to go someplace, she thought, and since water was scarce in this part of Texas there were bound to be villages along it. He couldn't catch her, not if she was mounted and he was on foot. And as long as she stayed near the stream, she'd have water.

Quickly Alison walked to where the horse was tied to a tree. But as she approached, the animal neighed and shied away. "Sssh!" she cautioned, catching the reins and jerking them loose. But to her utter frustration, the horse wouldn't let her get within mounting distance.

"You're wasting your time. I've trained him not to let anyone mount him. He wouldn't have allowed you on his back if I had not placed you there."

Alison jumped at the unexpected sound of El Halcon's voice. She dropped the rope and whirled around, seeing him standing at the edge of the clearing with a load of firewood in his arms. A guilty flush rose on her face, making her sunburn look even redder.

But Ramon was unaware of Alison's blush. His full attention was on the luscious curves of her body, fully revealed to him through Alison's wet, clinging gown. Hungrily he took in the sight of her full breasts with their rosy, pert nipples, then dropped his eyes to gaze avidly at the dark triangle between the apex of her rounded thighs.

Alison was painfully aware of Ramon's dark, smoldering gaze on her, a look that made her feel strangely weak and seemed to paralyze her. Then when he directed his gaze once more to her breasts, caressing them with his eyes, her nipples hardened and rose, seeming to beckon to him. Quickly she covered her breasts with her arms and turned her back to him.

Ramon's sharp eyes had not missed the sight of Alison's arousal, and even though he knew it was something she had no control over, he was elated to know he could excite her. He took a moment to savor this small victory, then, pretending indifference, shrugged his shoulders, turned, and walked to the center of the clearing. There he dropped the firewood and asked, "If you had managed an escape, where did you think you would go?"

Alison was greatly relieved to know Ramon hadn't noticed her body's response to his avid staring, for surely if he had, the arrogant chief would have thrown it in her face. My God! What was wrong with her? How could she be so shameless? She also knew it would be pointless to deny that she had tried to escape and was actually glad that he had changed the subject. "I thought if I followed the stream, I'd find a village," she answered without hesitation.

"There are no villages on Arroyo Tres Lenguas except Indian villages."

My God, Alison thought. She had never even considered that. Yes, that would have just been her luck, to run from one Indian into a whole village of them. At least she knew where she stood with this one. She walked to a tree and sank down beneath it, feeling more secure in knowing that her near nakedness was obscured from Ramon's prying eyes in its shadows. "Why do they call it creek of three languages?"

"Because three different Indian nations have lived on its three branches. The Apache, the Comanche, and the Shawnee."

"I didn't know there were any Shawnees in Texas. I thought they were eastern Indians."

El Halcon didn't tell her that the Shawnees were no longer in Texas, nor where the Comanches and Apaches were who had once lived on this stream. They had all been put on reservations, either in the Indian Territory or New Mexico. He didn't want her to try to escape him again. "They were pushed west by your people too."

Alison heard the bitterness in his voice and decided to drop the subject. She didn't want him getting off on a tangent as he had that morning. Strange, she had never thought of America's westward expansion as stealing the Indians' land. All she had ever heard was how wonderful it was the way her country was growing. But the land must have belonged to someone before the settlers arrived.

She watched as El Halcon dug a small hole, placed a flat sotol stick in it, then carefully placed small twigs around it. Then he picked up his fire drill and placed the tapered, blunt end on the flat stick and began to twirl it with his hands. She had heard of Indians starting a fire in this manner but was absolutely amazed when she saw the sparks flying out and the twigs catch fire.

Then he set the drill aside and carefully pulled the flat stick from the hole, adding more small twigs and kindling.

When he had the fire going to his satisfaction, he rose and said, "I will see if my snares have caught anything."

"Snares?" Alison asked in surprise. "Why don't you just shoot game?"

"It is a waste of a bullet to shoot small game."

El Halcon returned awhile later with two skinned rabbits. As they roasted over the fire, Alison's mouth watered, for other than the piece of jerky she had had nothing to eat since the night before. No wonder the Apache was so lean, she thought, if he ate only once a day. But it certainly didn't seem to affect his strength. He was all sinewy muscle.

"What is your name?" El Halcon asked from across the fire.

Stubbornly Alison refused to answer. She'd be damned if she'd give any information to the half-breed savage who'd had the audacity to kidnap her. Instead she pursed her lips together tightly and kept her eyes glued on the rabbits that Ramon was slowly turning on the spit he had fashioned.

"I asked what your name is," Ramon repeated in a hard voice.

Alison shot him a defiant look, then answered, "That's none of your damn business!"

Alison's feisty answer sent a surge of anger through Ramon. He took a moment to bring it under control, then said through clenched teeth, "And I say it is my business. Now answer me."

When Alison obstinately held her tongue, Ramon said in an ominous tone of voice, "Have you forgotten that we Apaches have ways of acquiring information we desire? Would you prefer that?"

Was he threatening to torture her? Alison wondered. But surely he wouldn't go that far. Or would he? He looked awfully determined. Deciding to humor him, Alison answered with obvious reluctance, "Alison Carr."

A smile crossed El Halcon's lips, much too smug to suit Alison. When he asked, "Where are you from?" she once again refused to answer, until he glared at her, a look so threatening that it gave her pause and made her seriously reconsider. Damn, as much as she hated to, she was going to have to back down again, but God knew how she hated to. "From Baltimore, a place far, far away from here."

"Then what are you doing here?"

"I was going to visit my father in Mexico," Alison answered in a clipped voice that clearly told Ramon her continued resentment of his cross-examination. "He manages a mine in Sonora."

The rabbits suddenly stopped turning. Alison glanced up and saw the Apache's black eyes glittering dangerously. A shiver ran through her, for she had never seen him look so angry. "What's wrong?"

"Do you know who works those mines?" Ramon asked in a hard voice.

Caught off guard by his sudden change in questioning, Alison stammered, "Why . . . why, Mexicans, I suppose."

"Some are Mexican convicts, but most are Indians who have been captured and sold by the Mexican government to the mine owners."

"Sold?" Alison asked in a shocked voice.

"Yes, the Indian prisoners are sold as slaves to work in

the mines and on the great plantations all over Mexico. Those that are strong enough, that is. The old, the women, and the children are sold as house servants."

"But how can they do that? Sell them as slaves?"

"How?" El Halcon asked in a biting voice. He laughed harshly. "They just do."

"I . . . I wasn't aware of that," Alison said, feeling very uncomfortable under El Halcon's accusing glare. "I've never been to Mexico before."

The hard expression on his face softened slightly. "No, I suppose you wouldn't. And even if you had known, it wouldn't have been your doing. It's just one of the ways Mexico has handled its 'Indian problems' over the years. At least I'll have to hand it to the Mexicans. They manage to make a profit from Indians they capture, unlike your government, which puts my people on reservations and then has to feed them, or so they claim."

Alison wished he'd change the subject. All this talk about the unjust treatment of Indians made her feel ill at ease, and the anger she had seen in his eyes had frightened her, reminding her only too well that he was a dangerous savage.

To her immense relief the Apache chief started turning the spit again. Juice from the roasting meat dropped into the fire and sputtered. Alison watched the rabbits going round and round, the tantalizing aroma in the air making her stomach rumble in anticipation. Wouldn't they ever get done? She was starving.

Chief Ramon broke the silence. "How did you learn to speak Spanish?"

After Ramon's angry flareup, Alison wasn't willing to risk his wrath by refusing to answer. "When we learned I would be coming to Mexico, my father hired a man from the Mexican embassy in Washington to tutor me. It's not all that far from Baltimore. He came to my home three times a week for a year to give me lessons. And then I insisted on speaking Spanish when my uncle picked me up in San Antonio. He helped smooth over the rough edges."

"The man who was with you in Presidio?"

"Yes, he was taking me to see my father, since my father couldn't get away from his job to meet me."

As El Halcon opened his mouth, Alison said quickly, "No! No more questions. I have a few of my own that I'd like answered. How did you find me?"

Ramon shrugged his broad shoulders and answered, "That was not difficult. Presidio is such a small town that every stranger is noticed, especially one as beautiful as you."

Alison had assumed that the Apache had stolen her because he thought she was pretty, but hearing him call her beautiful brought a strange warm curl to her belly. "That still doesn't explain how you knew which bedroom I was in."

"A Mexican friend of mine asked one of the Greys' servants."

"Are you saying that one of their servants knew you planned to abduct me?" she asked angrily.

"No, my friend said he knew a young man who was enamored of you and wished to serenade you beneath your bedroom window. The servant didn't think it unusual. It's a common practice in Mexico."

"And the gate to the courtyard? How did you manage to slip that heavy bolt from it?"

"I didn't go through the gate. I went over the walls."

"But those walls are at least fourteen feet high!"

"If you stand on your horse's back, the top is just a good jump away."

Well, Alison thought, that explained how he had accomplished it.

After they had eaten, El Halcon again disappeared into the woods. With her hunger appeased, Alison felt the effect of their long day's ride. She lay back on the ground, feeling utterly exhausted. But she couldn't sleep. The burns on her face, arms, and legs were too painful. She considered going back to the stream to sit in the water again, but she was just too tired to make the effort.

A shadow fell over her. She looked up to see the Apache towering above her. She bolted to a sitting position. With the firelight dancing over his hawkish features and the powerful muscles on his chest and arms revealed to her, he looked very dangerous.

El Halcon sank to the ground before her, resting his weight on his heels. "Why did you startle so?" he asked with a faint smile on his lips. "Did you think I meant to pounce on you?" He shook his head, making his earrings sway and glitter against his bronzed neck as they reflected the light of the fire. "I told you I was a patient man. I will wait until you are willing."

Alison might have flung back a retort, except she was just too exhausted to expend the energy. As he bent forward to touch something to her face, she pulled back.

"It is just something for your burn," he explained.

"What?" Alison asked suspiciously.

"A medicinal plant that we Apaches use. Its leaves have a thick, sticky juice that takes the sting from burns and helps them heal. Now be still, so I can rub it on your face."

Alison suspiciously looked down at the fleshy, spiny-toothed leaf that he extended toward her, seeing the end where he had cut it from the plant glistening in the firelight. Alison had heard of medicinal plants but never used one. In her sheltered world, medicines came out of bottles. "Close your eyes," El Halcon directed. "You do not want it to get in them."

Still half afraid that he might be up to some trick and dubious as to the plant's healing powers, Alison reluctantly closed her eyes. As he gently rubbed the end of the leaf over her face, she was amazed. It felt so cool, as if the plant was taking the heat of the burned skin right from her. She was so absorbed in the blessed relief from the pain that she didn't object when he began to rub it on her neck and the burned skin at the vee of his shirt and her open gown. Then, as his forearm brushed against her breast, she felt the nipple harden and a bolt of fire rush to her loins. She gasped, her eyes flying open.

"Did I hurt you?" he asked.

His face was just inches from hers, and Alison could feel his warm breath. She stared at his mouth and remembered his torrid, passionate kiss that morning, a kiss that left her feeling already violated. Her heart raced in fear. Yes, he was a dangerous man, but on a much more personal level. By just touching her, he could make her feel the most shocking, indecent things.

"No, you didn't hurt me," Alison answered in a shaky voice, "but I can do it myself."

Alison knew by the amused glitter in Ramon's dark eyes that he had again guessed his effect on her. Damn him! she thought hotly. She held out her hand and said in a hard voice, "I said I can do it myself."

"No, I will do it," Ramon insisted in a voice that

brooked no argument. "You are my captive, and I am your master. You will obey me."

"I'll do no such thing!"

Ramon's black eyes bored into her. "Do not argue with me. You have no choice but to obey me."

There was something in Ramon's eyes that warned Alison to hold her tongue and submit. She tried to steel herself against his touch while he stripped his shirt from her and gently rubbed the end of the plant over her burned arms, then pushed up her gown and smeared the juice over her legs. It was an agony for Alison, for even though the juice had a cooling effect, each brush of Ramon's fingertips—light, incredibly sensual touches that she strongly suspected were not accidental—sent her heart racing wildly and her muscles quivering in a silent plea for more. By the time Ramon had finished, she was trembling like a leaf in a windstorm. Unknown to Alison, the dark-eyed Apache felt pleased that he awakened her passion and sensitized her to his touch. He handed her the plant, saying, "You may want to apply more during the night." Then he rose and walked away with that graceful stride that was so much a part of him, leaving her with her senses spinning. It wasn't until he was seated across the fire from her that she had the presence of mind to ask what the plant was named.

"Aloe," Ramon answered. "It grows like a weed all over this area. Tomorrow I will cut more for you."

Alison frowned. Now that Ramon had stopped touching her and put distance between them, she was aware of the numbing effect of the aloe on her burned skin. She wished that he wasn't being so kind to her, making her a headband, loaning her his shirt, soothing her hurts. Why couldn't he be harsh and cruel, as she expected a fierce Apache to be? He was making it difficult for her to hate him. Then, as a sudden, suspicious thought occurred to her, she glared at him and said, "If you think your concern for my welfare is going to change my feelings about you, you're sadly mistaken!"

He chuckled, that damn husky rumble that sent shivers of pleasure running through her. "Did it ever occur to you that I might only be trying to keep you alive long enough for me to claim the reward for my patience?" he asked.

A tingle of fear ran through Alison. If she submitted to him, would he no longer want her? He had issued her a challenge. Is that all this was to him, a contest of wills? And once he had won, would he toss her aside? Then what would become of her? Would he abandon her someplace in this desolate, godforsaken country to die of thirst? Or would he sell her to one of the other Apaches as a slave? And how would they treat her? He had told her that Apaches didn't rape their captives, but they could beat her or starve her. Why, they might even torture her just out of pure meanness.

She swallowed hard and said, "Please take me back to Presidio."

"No! You are my captive."

"I'm sure my uncle would pay you a large ransom."

"I do not want his white man's gold. I am not a Comanche! Apaches do not take captives for the ransom they will bring." His voice was scornful. "Nor do we trade them to the Comancheros for guns."

"Who are the Comancheros?"

"White men and half-breeds who supply the Comanches with guns, whiskey, and supplies."

"What do they do with their captives?"

"Sell them as slaves in Mexico. Except for the women. Those they keep and use to slake their lust, until they are so used and eaten up with disease that even they don't want them any more. Then they sell them to the lowest brothels in Mexico."

Alison was horrified. Even torture looked better than that, a degradation that destroyed both body and soul. But she had to give it another try. "I will be no good to you. I'm accustomed to all the comforts of life. I will not be able to survive your harsh life."

El Halcon gave her a long, thoughtful look, then said, "No, I think you have a strength you do not realize."

Feeling utterly frustrated, Alison shrieked, "Damn you! I demand that you take me back!"

"No! And do not ask again. You are mine. I keep what I take."

El Halcon lay down and rolled to his side with his back to her, telling her in no uncertain terms that the discussion was ended. If Alison had had a knife, she would have gladly sunk it into his broad back, except she knew she'd never get a chance. The damn Apache had eyes in the back of his head.

Instead, she lay down and shot daggers at him with her eyes until her fury abated. Well, at least she had found some small measure of comfort in his words, she thought. He had said he kept what he took.

She remembered what he had told her earlier about how he had found and captured her. He must have been very determined to have her to take such a risk. She had just enough female vanity to feel a tingle of pleasure that he had gone to such lengths. Why, if this had happened back in Baltimore, she would have been the envy of every woman in the city. They would have thought it terribly exciting and romantic to have a virile, handsome, dangerous man be so enamored of you that he dared to steal you right out of your bed and carry you off. Then Alison remembered that El Halcon was an Apache. Going over walls and sneaking through a house to steal something was nothing more than a night's work for him. A thief was a thief, and El Halcon had stolen her most precious possession. Her freedom. She'd never forgive him for that. Never!

5

When Alison and El Halcon left the trees around Tres Lenguas Creek the next morning and rode back out onto the hazy Chihuahual desert, Alison saw the blue mountains in the distance. With their bases concealed in an early-morning mist, they seemed to be floating in the air. "Are those the mountains where we're going?" she asked Ramon.

"Yes, the Chisos."

Alison heard the hint of warm pride in the Apache's voice. "They look . . ." She hesitated, not knowing quite how to describe them.

"Ghostly?" El Halcon suggested. "That's what the white man calls them. The Ghost Mountains."

Alison frowned. True, they seemed to be floating, but there was nothing frightening about them. They seemed to have more of an ethereal quality about them and were really quite beautiful.

As they rode farther into the desert and closer to the mountains, she noticed things she had never seen before: huge piles of volcanic ash as white as snow and fascinating rock formations that jutted from the ground. One formation looked as if its flat rocks had been stacked like dishes, a few leaning this way, a few that, then this way again, and she marveled that they didn't tumble over. Another spire towered into the air several hundred feet, and at its tapered peak a huge rock teetered, seemingly defying all the laws of gravity. They rode through huge boulders in which the wind and rain had carved windows and tunnels, and all around her in this hot, forbidding desert there were signs of the struggle between the land and elements of nature. It was a dry, harsh, lonely country that had a wild beauty about it, whose silence was oppressive and whose sheer vastness made Alison feel very small and insignificant.

She gazed in awe at a forest of giant yuccas whose tops were crowned with clusters of white, bell-like flowers, and wondered where they got the water to survive. She smelled the strong scent of a creosote bush that they were passing. Then, spying something ahead of them, she asked, "Why are those long, curved sticks placed in the ground that way? Are they some kind of Indian sign?"

"No, it's a plant, a lechuguilla, and its limbs are not dead, although they appear to be. After a rain, it looks like a green fountain spurting from the ground. This entire desert comes alive after a rain. All the cactus breaks into bloom, and there are wildflowers everywhere."

"You mean in the spring?"

"No, at any time of the year. It is a beautiful sight."

Alison looked about her. "It's a strange land. I've never seen anything quite like it."

"Despoblado."

"Uninhabited land?" Alison repeated to herself in English, then asked in Spanish, "Is that what you Apaches call it?"

"No, that is what the first Spaniards who explored it called it. They found it so forbidding that they never came back. Nor did the Mexicans."

Alison could see why civilization had passed it by, and the Spaniards' name was certainly appropriate. Its only inhabitant seemed to be a hawk that was lazily circling in the sky high above her.

Looking down from watching the hawk's gliding flight, she saw that the mountains were much nearer and that they no longer looked blue. They had taken on a copperish color and did not look like she had always imagined mountains to look. Instead of a gentle, undulating rising from hills that gradually got taller and taller, they rose from the open plain with a startling suddenness and appeared to be made of solid rock, looking like huge castle turrets towering in the air, their summits cathedral-domed, flat-topped, and razor-backed.

Shocked at what she saw, she said, "I can't believe you actually live in those mountains. Why, they're nothing but a mass of huge rocks."

"We Apaches have a legend about the Chisos. When the Creator finished shaping the heavens and the earth, he had a huge pile of rubble left. He tossed them down to the earth, and they became the Chisos."

Alison knew why El Halcon was sure her uncle would never find her where he was taking her. No one would ever find her in that gigantic pile of rocks. "But how do you live? They're completely barren."

"No, they only appear to be so from here. Wait and see."

As they rode into the mountains, twisting around huge boulders and piles of rubble that lay at their bases, Alison could see the scattered, twisted mesquite and cactus on the mountains above her, seemingly growing out of solid rock. And the mountains no longer looked copperish. Now they were streaked with red, yellow, gray, black, white, and all possible shades of brown.

Alison and El Halcon followed a deeply shaded trail where the rocks rose up on both sides of them like towering walls, in some places so narrow that they could barely pass through. Despite the shade, the mountains held the heat of the sun. She felt as if she were in an oven, the heat and closeness so oppressive it was smothering.

Then, hearing a tingling sound, she asked in disbelief, "Is that water I hear?"

"Yes, there is a *tinaja* nearby. We will stop there for water and rest for a while."

"*Tinaja*? Is that an Apache word?"

"Yes. It means a temporary water hole."

Alison was amazed when she saw the *tinaja*. It sat under a rocky ledge in a depression no bigger than a washbasin. Water trickled into it from a fissure in the wall. It seemed unbelievable that water could flow from solid rock, but even more amazing was its taste. It was the sweetest water she had ever put in her mouth, and actually cool. After she had quenched her thirst, she asked, "Are there many of these water holes in these mountains?"

"They are scattered all over, some even smaller than this and some as large as twenty feet in diameter. But only we Chisos know where they are."

"I've heard that if you dig in a dry stream bed you can find water."

"That is not true. Only if it is at the bottom of a dry waterfall. It must be forced very deep in the sand to keep from evaporating."

They continued their ride, and as they twisted and turned down a maze of trails, the scrubby mesquite gave way to piñon pines, oaks, and maples. Twice they dipped into valleys where a lush green grass grew and wildflowers bloomed in a riot of color, amazing Alison at their unexpected appearance, and once they traveled through a deep canyon where cattails towered a dozen feet into the air and scattered golden pollen over their heads and shoulders. As they rode through yet another deep pass where the walls went straight up and the horse's hooves clattered on the rocky ground, Alison finally asked wearily, "Just where is this place?"

"In the very center of the mountains."

Alison looked up. Beyond the rims of the deep ravine she could see a huge mountain, its summit so high that it was obscured with wisps of clouds. "Up there?" she asked, feeling even wearier, for the mountaintop looked very far away.

"No, that is the highest mountain in the Chisos. It overlooks our village. My camp is not much farther from Panther Pass."

"Panther Pass? Where is that?"

"We are traveling through it right now."

Alison shot a fearful look up at the rim of the pass, fully expecting to see a panther come flying down at them with its teeth and long nails bared. "Do not be frightened," El Halcon told her with an amused smile. "If there was a big cat up there, my horse would know. He can smell them a mile off." Despite his assurance, Alison didn't relax until they left the pass.

Suddenly, as they came around a jagged mountain

peak, El Halcon reined in, and Alison looked down on
the large, beautiful valley. She glanced up at the magnificent peaks all around her, at one in the distance that
looked like a giant castle with its towering turrets, then
down at the shadowy emerald valley, then up again at
the mountains, their summits a play of gold and copper
in the bright sunlight, and finally at the azure sky with
its band of gold at the horizon. "This is the most beautiful place I've ever seen," she said in an awed voice.

"This is my home, where the rainbows wait for the
rain, and the big river is kept in a stone box, and the
water runs uphill, and the mountains float in the air,
except at night when they go away to play with the
other mountains."

Alison turned her head and stared over her shoulder
at El Halcon. She would have never expected such a
poetic description from the fierce Apache chief. "That's
beautiful," she whispered. "Why, it sounds almost like a
poem."

"Yes, it is, but I am afraid I cannot take credit for it. I
overheard a Mexican cowboy in Santa Rosa saying it.
But it is an apt description of my homeland. Except for
one comment, I would not change a word."

"And what would you change?"

"The part about the mountains going away at night to
play with the other mountains. That is not true. They
are always here to protect us. If they play with anything, it is the clouds."

Alison glanced up at the sky. She saw fluffy white
clouds drifting past several of the higher peaks, obscur-
ing them from view momentarily, then revealing their
majestic, jugged summits, making it look as if the mountains were indeed playing hide and seek among the

clouds. "What river was that Mexican talking about, being kept in a stone box?" she asked curiously.

"The Rio Grande. It passes through three deep stone canyons as it makes its wide bend into Mexico. The river marks the southern boundary of the Chisos. If we were on the opposite side of this basin, we could see it."

"And the rainbows? Why did he say they wait for the rain?"

"Because when it rains in the distance, out on the deserts surrounding these mountains, you often see the rainbows long before the rain."

Alison looked back down at the deep, shadowy valley. "I would have never dreamed these mountains had such a beautiful hidden place."

"That is what has protected us all these years, the forbidding desert and rugged mountains all around us. From the open plain, they look like solid rock where nothing could possibly live. Even after you have entered them, they look like solid rock. Only we Chisos know how to find this place and the other isolated valleys in these mountains."

Alison could understand why. They had twisted and turned down so many deep canyons and narrow passes that she had no earthly idea how they had managed to arrive here. "But how do you get down to the valley?" she asked.

"Over there."

He nodded his head to the mountains across from them, and Alison saw a break in the rim of towering peaks. "That is where the valley drains," he informed her. "If not for it, this would be a huge lake. We call it the window."

They picked their way across the rim of mountains, following a narrow, rocky trail that hugged the sides of the jagged peaks. Alison was terrified at the deep drop she saw below her, a spine-tingling expanse of nothing but air for thousands of feet. "Isn't there any other way to get to the valley but this?" she asked nervously.

"Of course. Through the window."

"Then why didn't we come in that way?"

"Because I wanted you to see the valley from the heights of the mountains. To just ride into it is not nearly as impressive."

It had been impressive, the most beautiful, breathtaking sight Alison had ever seen, but at that moment she would have gladly given it up to have her feet planted firmly on level ground.

An hour later they rode through the window and into the wide valley. Alison was amazed at how cool and green it was. They rode beneath stands of tall ponderosa and shorter piñon pines, their fragrance scenting the air, and crossed several fast-flowing, shallow streams. As they passed a small cornfield, its plants only a foot tall, she looked at it in surprise. "I didn't know Apache raised crops."

"Only corn."

"But why not other vegetables? You certainly have enough land here, particularly if you cleared out some of these trees."

"We are not farmers."

Alison heard the scorn in his voice, and it angered her. "No, you prefer to plunder, to steal, to kill!"

Alison didn't have to turn her head to know that she had finally aroused his anger. She could feel it coming from him in powerful waves. She held her breath, knowing that she should never have baited the dangerous Apache. He could easily kill her with his bare hands.

When he finally spoke his voice was terse. "We have

never become tied to the land so that we are dependent upon it to feed us. Then when you lose it, you starve. That is what happened to the Navaho. Instead we have learned to use what nature gives us. What nature does not provide us with, we attain by raiding. It is to us what hunting is to the other Indians. We have never had large herds of buffalo to sustain us, not since the Comanches, with their superior numbers and the guns they got from the French, chased us from the Plains hundreds of years ago. The Spanish were not so foolish. They did not let Indians have guns. And so now we must raid to obtain the necessities of life. We do not do it out of blood thirst. We do not take fiendish pleasure killing. We do not seek encounters. We take only what we need to survive. We are not greedy."

He gave Alison time to absorb this, then said, "So we were pushed north by the Mexicans, south by the Comanches, and west by the Americans, until all we have left is this miserable, arid land around the Rio Grande, land not fit for anything but rattlesnakes and scorpions."

Alison had never realized any of what he had told her, but she still thought his refusal to farm was nothing but pure stubbornness. "But if you raised crops, utilized this land—"

"Will the land give us blankets?" he interjected in a harsh voice. "Will it give us clothes for our backs? Will it give us guns and ammunition to protect ourselves? Will it give us meat? How much game do you think there is in these mountains? Not enough to feed us indefinitely. We are not like the white man, who kills game thoughtlessly, until it is all gone. We do so judiciously. And so we steal cattle when necessary, or we trade what we have stolen for those things the land has not given us."

Alison frowned. The Apaches did need more than vegetables, and there certainly wasn't enough land here to feed them and trade too. Besides, fresh vegetables were perishable. They would never survive the trip across that desert, even if the Apaches could find a market for them. She realized that she owed Chief Ramon an apology, but she couldn't bring herself to apologize to a man who had denied her her freedom. She admitted she could understand his stealing necessities to live, but she, Alison Carr, *wasn't* a necessity. That had been nothing but arrogance on his part. She held her silence.

As they entered the *rancheria,* Alison looked about her, seeing the igloo-shaped *wickiups* scattered all around, their entrances all facing east. Most had an attached windbreak made from brush, and from her elevated viewpoint on the horse she could see the women tending their cooking fires in their outdoor kitchens. Without exception, they all wore high-necked, long-sleeved blouses similar to the men's shirts over long, full skirts that were belted at the waist. Every one of the two-piece dresses was made of printed calico. There wasn't a solid-colored dress or shirt in the entire camp other than El Halcon's that she was wearing. She was left to assume that the Apaches had a fondness for prints.

As they rode into the center of the village, all of the Apaches came from their crude huts to welcome El Halcon back, crowding all around him and Alison, their high esteem for their chief obvious on their bronze faces. Alison was surprised to see that the entire camp held no more than several hundred Indians, and a good three quarters of them were women, children, and older men. She had expected to see many more braves than were visible. "Where are the rest of your war-riors?" she asked El Halcon.

"Some are tending our horses and a few are posted as sentries."

"I thought you had a much larger band. My uncle said you had several hundred warriors at your command."

"The white man always exaggerates our fighting strength. If makes them look less cowardly when they have to admit that we defeated them if they can claim that we had superior forces."

Alison bristled at his calling her people cowards. She might have flung back a retort if her attention hadn't been caught by a young girl running through the camp, pushing her way through the crowd and crying out in an excited voice, "Ramon! You are back!"

El Halcon reined in sharply and swung down from his horse. As the girl threw herself into his arms, he lifted her from her feet, and the two embraced warmly. When the chief sat her back down, Alison realized that the girl wasn't a child, but a dainty young woman. The top of her dark head barely came to the middle of the chief's broad chest. Alison wondered who the pretty girl was. She obviously adored the man at whom her black, sparkling eyes were gazing. And El Halcon seemed very pleased to see her. Was she his wife?

The thought sent a wave of raw jealousy through Alison, then was quickly replaced with fresh anger at El Halcon. How dare he steal her when he already had a wife to warm his bed. The greedy bastard! And how demeaning for both of the women. But as the girl turned and looked up at Alison, she saw only curiosity, and no signs of hostility in the Apache's eyes, as she would have expected a wife to feel. The young woman's lack of jealousy baffled Alison.

As the girl and El Halcon carried on a brief conversation in Apache, Alison seethed in anger, both at El Halcon's gall in stealing her to satisfy his animal cravings when he already had a wife, and at the couple's rudeness in conversing in front of her in a language that she didn't understand. It was obvious they were discussing her. Damn him! He humiliated her at every turn.

El Halcon turned and saw the furious glitter in Alison's blue eyes. Having no idea what she was thinking, her anger took him aback. Now what had he done to raise her ire? *Dios*, she was an exasperating woman. He wondered briefly if she was worth the trouble. Ignoring the daggers she was shooting at him, he reached up and lifted her from his saddle.

As soon as Alison's feet touched the ground, she shoved his hands away. "Don't touch me!"

El Halcon gave her a hard, warning look that would have made his bravest warrior cringe in fear. To his frustration, Alison just glared back at him. "This is my sister, Jacita," he said in a terse voice. Turning to the dainty girl, he said, "The captive's name is Alison. She speaks Spanish."

His sister? Alison felt very foolish and then, as the girl stared up at her, very self-conscious, knowing she must look a sight with her sunburned skin, her face smudged with dirt, her torn gown, and her long hair hanging about her in wild tangles. But why should she care what the girl thought of her? Alison wondered with renewed anger, this time at herself. Jacita was just a lowly Apache like her brother.

"She is so tall," Jacita said in an awed voice, gazing up at Alison with a dumbfounded expression on her face. "Almost as tall as you. I have never seen such a tall woman."

Despite her burned face and tattered appearance, El Halcon thought Alison looked magnificent. There was something about her bearing that was almost regal. Yes, she was worth the trouble, he admitted, but while he had come to admire her spirit, she was much too proud and much too defiant. Perhaps teaching her humility would make her more manageable. After all, she was a woman, a captive woman at that. She needed to be taught the proper order of things.

El Halcon's dark eyes slid over the length of Alison's body. "Yes, she's much too tall for a woman. And a little too skinny. But then, hopefully, she will make a strong, good worker."

Alison stiffened. If he didn't find her height and shape to his liking, why had he stolen her? she thought, her female vanity piqued. And if he had any notions of making a slave out of her, she'd quickly set him to rights. She opened her mouth to fling back a retort, but El Halcon took her arm in a tight grasp and firmly led her away. "No!" he warned in a lowered voice so that the others could not hear. "Do not insult me or defy me. I will not tolerate it when my people are watching. I am their leader. You will obey me just as they do."

"But you can insult me any time you want?" Alison asked in an icy voice.

"You are my captive. I can do anything I like with you." His dark eyes bored into hers. "I can even kill you."

The words were said calmly and, because there was no heat in them, seemed much more threatening than anything he had said to her thus far. But Alison was determined that she wouldn't show any fear. As soon as they stepped into the brush arbor beside the large *wickiup* he had led her to, she jerked her arm away and turned to him. "I don't care what you do me! If you think I'm going to slave for you, you've got another thought coming. I'll die before I'll be anyone's slave!"

"I did not capture you for my slave, but you will earn your keep while you are here, just as everyone in this camp does. The one thing an Apache cannot abide is indolence."

"I didn't ask to come here!" Alison threw back. "You forced me, remember?"

"That has nothing to do with it. You are here, and you shall work just as the other women do. Since I have no wife, you shall cook for me, wash my clothes, tend to my *wickiup.* Now that I have a woman, there is no need for my sister to continue to do these things for me."

"If you wanted a cook, as well as a woman to slake your lust on, you should have captured an Indian woman. I know nothing about cooking over an open fire, or even how to build one."

"Jacita will teach you. She will teach you everything you need to know."

"And if I don't do these things for you?"

"You will not eat."

Alison drew herself up to her full height and glared at him. But any hopes that she might have had of intimidating him with her size were futile. He still had a good six inches on her. Besides, even if he had been three feet tall, she knew she wouldn't have been able to intimidate him. He was the most unyielding man she had ever known.

"Now sit," El Halcon said in a hard voice. "Jacita will bring us food."

"I won't eat," Alison announced defiantly.

"That is up to you. But you will sit and keep me company while I do."

El Halcon sank to a mat on the ground with his legs
crossed before him. Seeing Alison still standing, he mo-
tioned to a mat across from him and said, "Sit."

Alison glared at him, her lips tightly set.

Ramon's dark eyes flashed. "Your defiance is becoming tiresome."

Before Alison could guess his intent, Ramon was on
his feet and taking her in his arms, his lips covering hers
in a fierce demanding kiss that was clearly meant to
bring her to heel. She tried to struggle, but it was useless
against his superior strength. He was holding her so
tightly against him that she feared he would crack her
ribs, and she had difficulty breathing with his hard, insistent lips ravishing hers. Domineering brute, she
thought angrily, and then she was beyond coherent
thought as he kissed her deeply, his artful, devastating
tongue shooting into her mount and playing wild havoc
on her senses. The world seemed to tilt on its axis, spinning crazily, and her bones seemed to melt.

Just as abruptly as he had taken her in his arms, Ramon broke the kiss and stepped away from her. "Now
sit," he said in a firm voice.

Alison really had no choice. Her legs were so weak
they refused to support her. She sank to the ground,
sitting on her heels, still feeling light-headed, her lips
swollen and throbbing from Ramon's masterful kiss.

Jacita entered the brush enclosure carrying a woven
willow tray with two pottery bowls on it. El Halcon took
it from her, sat down, and set the tray on the mat between him and Alison. As the Indian girl turned and
left, Alison looked down at the bowls, the tantalizing
aroma of the steaming food making her mouth water.

"Do you still refuse to eat?" El Halcon asked.

Having had nothing to eat but a few strips of jerky

that day, Alison was starving, but she was determined
she wouldn't back down, particularly after Ramon had
just forced her to sit against her will. No, she'd prove he
hadn't broken her defiance, despite his brutish treatment of her. She lifted her head and answered coldly,
"Yes, I do."

El Halcon shrugged his broad shoulders and answered, "Suit yourself. But you are only hurting yourself with your stubbornness. It is your stomach that will
cramp, not mine."

He picked up one of the bowls and one of the crude
wooden spoons sitting on the tray. As he ate, Alison
could see it was a meat stew with something resembling
dumplings in it. Watching him eat while she was fam-
ished was an agony. Her stomach rumbled in protest.
She was forced to admit that her refusal to eat was only
punishing herself and that starving to death, when food
was available, would be very difficult if not impossible to
do. She wondered if she could sneak food, then rejected
the idea. That would make her a thief, no better than
him. No, she was going to have to back down, but God,
how it galled her.

She reached for the bowl of food sitting on the tray,
acutely aware of his dark eyes on her. "All right!" she
spat. "I'll eat! But I'll only do enough work to earn my
keep. No more!"

Wisely Ramon held his silence, knowing that any remark on his part might only goad her into keeping her
threat. When they had both finished eating, he rose to
his feet. "I will show you my *wickiup* now."

Her gnawing hunger appeased, Alison was feeling a
little less hostile. She followed him into the oval-shaped
structure that was made from bent willow limbs and
covered with brush and loose animal hides. Like him,

she had to bend to keep her head from touching the ceiling except in the middle of the low *wickiup*. Looking up, she saw the smoke hole in the center of the ceiling, then glanced around her curiously. Several pallets made from trade blankets lay about on the dirt floor, and a large hide bag lay to one side. Besides that, the only furnishings were a few mats. The dwelling seemed awfully austere, especially for a chief. Then, spying a basket shaped like a jar, she bent and picked it up.

"That is a *tus*, what we call our water jugs," Ramon informed her. "They are made from twining willow or sumac twigs together and are caulked with pine gum to keep them from leaking."

Alison was amazed at the open wicker jar. She was still marveling over it when El Halcon nodded to a pallet and said, "You will sleep there."

Alison's head shot up. "Surely you don't expect me to sleep in here with you?" she asked in a shocked voice.

"You are my captive. It is my duty to house you. Where else would you sleep?"

"Outside, in that enclosure."

"It is cool at night in these mountains, even in the summer. You will sleep in here."

Alison had slept in the open with El Halcon the past two nights, but what he was suggesting seemed much too intimate, especially in view of the fact that his strong sexuality was almost smothering in the small confines of the *wickiup*. A panic rose in her. "No, I'll sleep outside. I don't mind the cold."

"You will sleep inside."

"No! What you're suggesting is . . . indecent!"

"I told you I will not force you to submit to me, if that is what you are afraid of. You will sleep in here."

"Why are you being so stubborn about this? If I don't object to sleeping outside, why should you?"

"I am chief here. I have an image to uphold. I will not have it said that I mistreat my captive by not offering her the protection of my *wickiup*. Now, do not argue any further. It is settled. You will sleep in here, with me, regardless of how you feel about it."

Alison knew it was futile to challenge his authority. His fierce male pride would never allow it. And now she knew why he had seemed even more unyielding since they had ridden into the Apache camp, even more determined to force his will upon her. As chief, he was accustomed to being obeyed without question, and he had an image to uphold before the others. He wouldn't tolerate a captive openly disobeying him and causing him to lose their respect.

"All right!" she flung out. "I'll sleep in here, and I'll work to earn my keep. But I won't grovel to you like the others. You may be their chosen leader, someone they obey out of respect, but you aren't mine. If I obey, it will be out of prudence, and not because I admire you in any way."

"Are you saying you will not defy me in public?"

"Yes, if that's what your stupid pride demands of me!"

"But in private?" There was a husky timbre in his voice that gave his words a strong sexual innuendo.

"In private, I'll fight you tooth and toenail!"

Ramon wasn't surprised by Alison's fierce vow. She was wise enough to see the futility of defying him in public, but she was equally determined that she wouldn't surrender to him on a personal basis. The strong-willed Apache chief was just as determined that she would. If anything, her defiance only made her all the more desirable. A hard-earned victory was always much sweeter that one easily won. Yes, Ramon vowed, he'd have her respect as well as her body and her love. In the end, she would deny him nothing.

His dark eyes met hers as he said in a calm, self-assured voice, "We shall see."

His supreme self-confidence was more than Alison could bear. She raised her hand and threw the water jug at him with all her might.

Ramon ducked just in time to avoid being hit by the flying object. He rose and warned in a hard voice, "Do not do that again. I will not tolerate anyone throwing things at me."

Staring at those flashing, black eyes, Alison had no doubt that Ramon meant what he said. He could be pushed just so far by her shows of anger. Any further, and she would be risking retaliation, and she wasn't sure just what he might do to her. He had said he could kill her, if he liked. She was seething with frustration as he turned, pushed back the skin flap hanging over the doorway, and ducked beneath it.

6

In the two hours that passed after El Halcon's departure, Alison had time for her anger to cool and to seriously consider her position. She was an unusually practical woman, despite her privileged upbringing. She was forced to admit that, like it or not, she was his prisoner and there was no hope of escaping him, nor was there much likelihood that she would be rescued. She was in a strange place, among people who were inured to hardships. It would take all her energy just to survive under such harsh and primitive living conditions. She would be foolish to waste it on fighting him, unless he tried to force himself on her, and he had given her his word that he wouldn't do that. She would be wise to make the best of a bad situation, not to waste energy struggling against him until it really mattered.

By the time Ramon returned to the small *wickiup*, dusk had fallen, and there was a decidedly cool nip in the evening air, enough so that Alison felt chilled even with a blanket wrapped around her where she sat on one of the pallets. She was relieved to see that he carried a load of firewood in his arms, and she watched silently as he placed it in the middle of the structure and built a fire.

Sitting back on his heels, El Halcon gazed at Alison thoughtfully. He had sensed a change in her the minute he walked in. "Am I mistaken, or are you in a more amicable mood than when I left you?"

"I've decided to make the best of a very bad situation, since I have no other choice," Alison answered coldly.

"Then there will be no more fighting me?"

Alison looked him straight in the eye. "Only when it matters."

Alison didn't have to tell him what mattered to her. He knew. She wouldn't surrender to him, and El Halcon would have been disappointed in her if her answer had been anything else. "A wise decision. A continuous struggle of wills can be very tedious. It will be much easier for both of us if we can be more civil to one another."

He sat down on the pallet opposite hers, and Alison felt very uncomfortable under that steady gaze. She wished he would say something, instead of just staring at her. Hoping to distract him, she asked, "Is Ramon really your given name?"

"No, I have an Apache name, but it is our custom not to address one another by our given names except in times of mortal danger or utmost gravity. For that reason, most of us have nicknames or have taken on Spanish names. It's much easier than referring to someone in the third person."

It sounded like a strange custom to Alison. Why have names if you couldn't use them? "What is your Apache name?"

"It does not matter. I would prefer you to call me Ramon."

Alison sensed his answer was evasive. Were all Apaches secretive about their given names? she briefly wondered. "I'm afraid not," she answered in a firm voice. "Ramon sounds much too personal. I will call you El Halcon."

Ramon frowned deeply and replied. "That is a silly name the Mexicans have given me, one I am not particularly fond of."

"Then I will call you Chief Ramon."

"Why not just Ramon?"

"I told you. It's too personal. After all, I'm your captive," Alison answered bitterly.

"I would still prefer you to call me Ramon."

"Are you ordering me to do that?" Alison asked, her resentment on the rise despite her vow not to fight him unless it mattered.

Chief Ramon's dark eyes met hers. "Yes, if I have to."

Alison fought a silent struggle with herself, a part of her wanting to defy him and another reasoning it would be foolish to do so. Her pride finally gave way to her practical self. "All right," she relented with obvious reluctance, "if you insist. I will call you Ramon."

Her concession seemed to satisfy the Apache chief. He smiled, then removed his knee-high moccasins, placing the knife he had concealed in them carefully to the side. As he rose to his feet with that fluidness that was so much a part of him, Alison was so distracted by the graceful movement that it took her a moment to realize he had removed his belt and was untying the string that held up his pants. "What are you doing?" she asked in alarm.

"I'm removing my clothes for bed."

"You mean you're going to strip naked?"

"That is how I sleep in my *wickiup.*"

"But I'm here!"

"I see no reason why I should change my sleeping habits for a captive."

As the string gave way and Ramon started to slip the pants down his hips, Alison gasped in shock, then quickly turned her back to him, horrified that he would actually strip off all his clothes in her presence. Besides, it was downright indecent for someone to sleep in the nude. Yes, he was nothing but an uncivilized savage.

"You can turn back around now if you like. I have my blanket over me."

Alison heard the amusement in Ramon's deep voice. It angered her that he found her modesty humorous. "No, thank you," she replied icily, then reclined on her pallet, careful to keep her back to him.

"You can take off your own clothes if you like. I have no objection to your getting comfortable."

Alison would have given her right arm to take off her gown, which was now both filthy and smelly. But she knew she didn't dare do anything of the sort. Ramon might misinterpert it as an invitation to take more intimacies with her, and God only knew the arrogant Apache didn't need any encouragement along those lines. He seemed to have a one-track mind, with his prime objective in life being to get her to submit to him. "I don't sleep in the nude."

"Why not?"

"Because it's disgusting!"

"No, it's comfortable with nothing binding around you. You should try it sometime."

Alison wouldn't give the brazen Apache the satisfaction of answering. She lay on her side and stared at the willow branches beside her. The only sound was that of the fire crackling and popping, but despite her proximity to its warmth, her exposed feet were cold, for the blanket she had tossed over her shoulders did not protect them. Only when she heard Ramon's steady breathing and knew he was asleep did she sit up and rearrange her blanket over her, studiously averting her eyes from him. But when she lay back down, she found she couldn't resist stealing a glance.

Ramon lay on his side facing her, his body covered with a blanket from the waist down. She stared at the broad expanse of his bare chest, then the muscles on his shoulders and upper arms. Even asleep, he exuded power and masculinity. She turned her attention to his face, her eyes slowly roving his rugged, chiseled features, noting that he had indecently long, thick eyelashes for a man and that his mouth seemed softer in his sleep. Gazing at those lips, she remembered what they had felt like on hers, and how his tongue had ravished her mouth. She felt a warm curl deep in her belly, and a tingle ran through her. Horrified at her body's reaction, she rolled to her side with her back to him. But even then, she couldn't get comfortable. His masculinity seemed to be overpowering her, smothering her, and she was acutely conscious of his nakedness beneath the blanket. It was a long time before she slept.

Ramon was gone from the *wickiup* the next morning when Alison awoke, much to her relief. Shortly thereafter she heard a noise in the brush enclosure and then a feminine voice calling softly in Spanish, "Alison? Are you awake?"

Knowing that it could only be Jacita, Alison walked to the skin flap hanging over the door and lifted it.

"Good morning," Jacita said brightly, remembering

her brother had firmly cautioned her that Alison was not to be treated like an ordinary captive, but with some measure of respect, in view of the fact that she was the chief's woman.

Alison didn't want to be friendly with this girl. After all, she was the sister of the man who had taken her captive. But to refuse to greet her would appear churlish. "Good morning," she replied stiffly.

"While I am cooking your breakfast, I thought you might like to change clothes."

"I don't have any other clothes but these," Alison answered bitterly.

"Yes, you do. I brought them with me. See?"

Jacita nodded her head to a pile of clothing on the ground. "Where did you get those?" Alison asked in surprise.

"Ramon asked me to see if I could find something for you to wear. I knew my clothes wouldn't fit you, so I asked some of the larger women if they could spare a blouse or skirt. Take them inside and see what fits."

She had really sunk low, Alison thought, to have to accept hand-me-downs from savages. But it was either that or run around in her nightgown and Ramon's shirt. Even then, she wouldn't have a change of clothing. Knowing that she really had no choice, she accepted the pile of clothing Jacita was holding out to her. "Is there anywhere I could take a bath?"

"This evening I will show you the women's bathing area."

"But it seems pointless to put on fresh clothing when I'm so grimy myself."

"By evening you will be grimy again. That is why we bathe at that time of the day."

Knowing it was pointless to argue against Jacita's

logic, Alison turned and walked back into *wickiup*. Of
the four printed blouses and skirts Jacita had brought
her, only two fit, and then the skirts only came to her
midcalf. There had been no underwear in the pile, leaving Alison to assume the Apache women didn't wear
any. That alone was disconcerting, but when she discovered that none of the moccasins fit, Alison was even
more flustered.

When Alison stepped from the *wickiup*, she knew by
the expression on Jacita's face that she looked a sight.
Not only was the skirt much too short, but the blouse
was decidedly too snug over her bust, to say nothing of
her bare, dirty feet and tangled hair. "None of the moccasins fit, and this was the best-fitting blouse and skirt,"
she said defensively.

Embarrassed by her own rudeness at staring at Alison, Jacita dropped her eyes and muttered, "I'm sorry,
but you are much . . ."

Jacita's voice trailed off, and Alison realized she was
too polite to say "larger," which surprised her, since she
hadn't expected Apaches to have any manners. "I
know. I'm bigger than you Apache women are. But I
can't go around barefoot."

"No, you cannot, not with all the sharp rocks lying
about. I will have to see if I can find a man's moccasins
for you."

Alison had never been ashamed of her size, but she
had never had to wear a man's shoe before. Towering
over the dainty girl in her too-short skirt and her long
bare feet, she felt like an awkward giantess. "Can't we
make me a pair?" she asked, thinking how humiliating
it would be if everyone in the camp knew how big her
feet were. Besides, she didn't particularly like the idea

of wearing someone else's shoes, something that couldn't be washed.

"I suppose so, but it will have to wait until tonight. Ramon wanted me to teach you how we gather food and build a fire today."

"I'll wait until then."

"Your feet may get bruised by the rocks," Jacita warned.

"I'll still wait," Alison replied stubbornly.

After they had eaten, the two women set out, each carrying a large basket that Jacita had called a *tuts-ah*. As they walked through the camp, Alison was aware of the Apaches staring at her height and came to realize for the first time that not only were the women small statured, but the men were also. She was as tall as, or taller than, most of the warriors. She knew her height was unusual for a woman, even in the white man's world, but their stares made her feel like a freak of some sort. Ramon was unusually tall, but they didn't stare at his height. No, he was a man, she reminded herself. Height was always admired in the male. Besides, they expected their chief to be larger than life.

When a group of women fell in behind her and Jacita, each carrying her burden basket, Alison heard them snickering and knew they were laughing at her big feet. The sudden urge to bend her knees in an effort to shorten herself and hide her feet beneath her skirt came over her. Then, realizing what she was considering, she was furious with herself. She had never been ashamed of her height before, and she'd be damned if she'd let a bunch of savages make her feel that way. Nor would she let them intimidate her. If there was any intimidating to be done because of size, she'd do it, not they.

Alison whirled around to face the women who had
been laughing at her, catching them totally off guard.
Drawing herself up to her full, imposing height, she
glared down at them. Her trick worked even better
than it had with any man. The smirks on their faces
disappeared like magic, and their eyes widened in fear,
for Alison looked very dangerous towering over them
with her searing-blue eyes glittering with anger.

Seeing them cower brought Alison an immense satisfaction. She smiled, stunning the women even more,
then turned and walked away, managing to look very
regal despite her ill-fitting garments and dirty, bare
feet.

Jacita ran a few steps to catch up with Alison's long
strides, thinking not many captives would dare to face
up to a crowd of Apache women, for fear they would
beat her. And Alison didn't know Ramon had left strict
orders that there would be none of that with this captive. A secret admiration of the white woman's courage
was born.

The women walked from the valley, through the window, and out onto an area covered with steep rocky
hills. Alison looked about her, wondering what food
they could possibly gather, for the only thing she could
see growing here were cactus, yuccas, and the century
plants with their huge, low-lying leaves. She soon found
out what the women had walked all that distance for.
They came to cut out the hearts of the century plants, or
agave, which looked like giant artichokes. It was tricky
business, cutting out the cabbage-sized heads without
being scratched by the sharp edges of the plants, thick
leaves. And Alison soon learned not to approach one of
the plants before shaking the bottom leaves with a long
stick to scare out any snakes. All morning long they

worked under the hot sun collecting the hearts and placing them in their baskets. Then, when they were full, they carried the heavy baskets to a huge pit filled with flat rocks that had been heated in a fire until they were glowing red hot. If Alison thought the hard work was behind her, she had much to learn. She was kept busy pulling up grass, which was dampened and thrown on the rocks, followed by the agave hearts, then another layer of wet grass. By this time her back and arms were aching, and she was perspiring from both the heat of the sun and the steam rising from the huge baking pit. She sank to the ground wearily.

"No, Alison, we are not finished yet," Jacita said patiently. "We must pile dirt on the pit."

"But you'll smother the fire," Alison objected.

"No, it will hold the heat from the hot rocks, and we build another fire on top of the mound of dirt, so that the mescal will cook evenly."

Alison frowned. "I thought mescal was a drink."

"If you squeeze the juice from the baked mescal and ferment it, it is."

"Ferment it? Are you telling me we've gone to all this work to make liquor?" she asked angrily.

"Some of the Mescaleros, as the white man calls us, use a part of their harvest for that purpose, but mostly the baked hearts are eaten. Mescal is our most important source of food. It is to us what the buffalo is to the Plains Indians. Some of the hearts we bake, but they must be eaten right away. Some we dry in the sun to preserve. Some we pound into thin sheets and then preserve with a glaze made from the juice we extracted, so that we will have food during the Ghost Face." Seeing Alison's puzzled frown, she explained, "That is what we Apaches call winter."

"Are you saying you do this all year long, except in the winter? Collect those damn hearts and bake and preserve them?"

Jacita frowned at Alison's use of the word "damn," then answered, "No, we can only collect them during the Many Leaves—early summer to you. Soon they will be gone until next year. That is why we work so hard while they are here."

Jacita turned and walked away, then began shoveling dirt with her hands into her basket. Alison marveled at the tiny girl's endurance, since she herself was exhausted. Feeling a twinge of guilt, she wearily pushed herself from the ground and began shoveling dirt into her basket.

Later that afternoon they left the baking pit with the fire still burning on top. The fire would be kept going for several days by a few of the women. According to Jacita, it took that long for the tough mescal to bake. Much to Alison's disappointment, the remaining women did not go right back to the camp. Instead, they collected more hearts to be pounded the next day and the creamy bell-like blossoms from the yucca plants to be used for making soup, braving the plants' sharp, swordlike leaves to pick them. Alison was amazed. She would have never thought flowers could be edible.

By the time they trudged back to the valley carrying their loaded burden baskets, Alison was so exhausted that she could hardly force herself to put one foot before the other, much less think about Ramon and her anger toward him. And now she knew why Jacita had said it would have been pointless to bathe that morning. She had never been so filthy in her life, her hands, forearms, and feet caked with dirt from where the earth had clung to her sweaty skin, and her body gritty from the salt left on it where her perspiration had evaporated. As soon as they lowered their heavy baskets to the ground inside the enclosure beside Ramon's *wickiup,* Alison turned to go inside, wanting only to lie down and sleep.

Jacita stopped Alison by placing her hand on her arm. "No, we will go and bathe now."

"I'm too tired to bathe. All I want to do is lie down. Besides, I don't think I can walk another step. My feet are bruised and cut from those rocks."

"The cool water will soothe them and your scratches."

Alison was acutely aware of the scratches on her body, for they burned like fire. The yuccas' sharp daggers were particularly treacherous, and she wasn't as adept as the Apache women in avoiding them. They had even ripped her dress in several places.

"Get your fresh clothing and bring your soiled along with you," Jacita said. "We will wash them while we are there."

Alison was too tired to argue any further. She obeyed the tiny girl.

They stopped at the *wickiup* where Jacita said she lived with her father, for the girl had to pick up her fresh clothing and laundry. Alison was curious to see Ramon's Mexican father, but to her disappointment, he was nowhere around. Then she and Jacita walked to the side of the camp, and there, in a thick copse of trees that served as a screen from the rest of the camp, they found the women's bathing area.

When the stream came into sight, Alison came to a dead halt, shocked by what she saw. The women were bathing together stark naked. As Jacita started to strip off her clothing, a mortified flush rose on Alison's face. Surely she didn't expect her to do the same.

Seeing her embarrassment, Jacita asked, "Is something wrong?"

Alison directed her gaze over the naked girl's shoulder. "I've never bathed with anyone else before."

"But there are only women here and a few children."

"My people don't strip naked before others, not even other women."

"But we are all made the same. What difference does it make?"

Alison might have pointed out that she felt it was indecent, except she had come to admire Jacita too much to insult her. "Isn't there another stream we could go to, one that's more private?"

"No, this is the stream that has been set aside for bathing and washing. We women use this end, and the men use the stream at the other end of the valley. Ramon does not want soap in the streams where we get our drinking water."

It made sense. And Alison could understand why the Apaches practiced communal bathing. They had no private bathrooms, as her family had. She supposed she should be glad that they even bathed at all, considering they were savages, but she just couldn't force herself to strip before them. "I'll just wash off my arms and legs."

Jacita shrugged her shoulders. "If that is what you prefer."

Jacita walked off, taking her long hair down from its neat bun at the back of her neck as she did so. Then, after dropping something on the ground, she waded into the stream. Alison wandered down to the water's edge and began to wash off her lower legs and feet, then her forearms and face. The cool water felt wonderful, and she longed to immerse herself in it. She glanced up and saw several women shampooing their hair, including Jacita. Alison ran her hand through her tangled locks, acutely aware of how dirty it was, and then became aware of the women casting curious glances in her direction. She supposed to them she looked ridiculous trying to take a bath with her clothes on. Her modesty was only making her conspicuous. She hesitated for a moment, her white upbringing struggling with her practical self, then threw her modesty to the wind. She stripped off her clothes and waded into the water, but to her dismay the Apaches' curious glances turned into gaping stares.

Stopping beside Jacita, she asked in an angry voice, "What are they staring at? As you said, I'm not built any differently from them."

Jacita pushed a wet strand of hair from her face before answering. "It is not your body they are staring at. It is your pale skin."

"Of course my skin is pale. I'm white! What did they expect?"

"Do not be angry. I don't think they mean to be rude this time, as they did when they laughed at your size. Your skin is quite lovely, as creamy as the yucca blossoms."

Alison glanced around her and saw that the stares were more admiring than anything. But she still felt very self-conscious.

"Just ignore them," Jacita suggested. "Once the novelty has worn off, they will take no more notice of you than anyone else." She handed Alison a soft ball of soap. "I am through with my bath. You may use my soap."

Alison decided to take the girl's advice and ignore the others' stares. She'd be damned if she'd let them ruin her bath now that she had gotten the courage to strip before them. She accepted the soap and, as she rubbed it over her skin, marveled at its rich lather. The fact that it had a pleasant scent was even more surprising. Then she shampooed her hair, thinking it was the most wonderful feeling in the world. As she and Jacita waded from the pool, Alison did feel much refreshed. The water had not only soothed her bruised feet and the scratches all over her body, but seemed to have taken some of the soreness out of her aching muscles.

"I'm glad you persuaded me to come," she admitted to the Apache girl. "I do feel much better. Where do you get the soap? I've never seen soap that lathers the way it does."

"We make it from an aloe we call soapweed." Jacita handed her a length of heavy flannel. "We will use this to dry off with."

When they had dried off and put on their fresh clothing, Jacita sat on the bank and brushed her hair with a crude instrument whose bristles were made of the tips of a sturdy grass, while Alison tried to comb her tangles out with her fingers. Handing the brush to Alison, Jacita said, "You will never get the tangles out that way."

"Thank you," Alison replied. As she brushed her hair, she watched while Jacita picked up the object she had dropped earlier—a piece of leather shaped like a bow. She wound her long hair around it, then fastened it at the nape of her neck with a piece of colored cloth that hung down her back. "That's very clever," Alison remarked. "What is it called?"

"A *nah-leen*."

"Do you suppose I could get one? This long hair of mine gets so tangled and makes my neck so hot with nothing to even tie it back with."

"Only maidens are allowed to wear them."

"Well, I'm a maiden." Seeing the startled expression on the girl's face, Alison said, "Why do you look so surprised?"

"I thought Ramon had . . ." Jacita's voice trailed off, and a flush rose on her pretty face.

There was no doubt in Alison's mind what Jacita thought Ramon had done to her. "That may have been his reason for abducting me, but I quickly set him straight," Alison said in renewed anger.

"You refused him?" Jacita asked in amazement.

"Of course I did!"

"You do not find him attractive?"

For the life of her, Alison couldn't deny it, not in view of Jacita's candid honesty. "Even if I did, that wouldn't make any difference. I've been brought up to believe that . . . having relations with a man you aren't married to is wrong."

"That is what we believe too. My people are very strict with their maidens. Those women who do that with a man before they are married are looked down upon and their families shamed. Even the divorcées and widows who give their bodies too freely are not respected. Apaches do not approve of loose women."

Jacita's information surprised Alison, and infuriated her all the more. She had assumed that Apaches had low moral standards, since Ramon had stolen her simply because he desired her. How dare he treat her with less respect than he would have shown one of the maidens of his tribe! Then a sudden thought occurred to her. "Why did you act so surprised when I said I had refused him?" she asked. "I told you I was a maiden."

"It is just that Ramon is so . . . so—"

"So forceful?" Alison supplied.

"Yes, and so very attractive. There are many maidens that would risk their families' wrath if he desired them, and he is our *nantan,* our chief. There are many women that would consider it an honor to lie with him, even without marriage."

Yes, it was just as she suspected, Alison thought. The arrogant bastard was used to getting anything he wanted, to having everyone bow to his wishes. "Well, I'm not one of them!"

"I am sorry if I insulted you. Ramon said you are his woman."

"Not in that sense, I'm not. Nor will I ever be!"

Jacita thought Alison objected just a little too strongly. She wondered how long the white woman would be able to resist her brother's considerable masculine charms. Every maiden in the tribe, and half the married ones if truth be known, were enraptured with him. He was one of those rare men whose presence alone sent a woman's pulses racing, regardless of her age. There was something about him that brought out a woman's primitive nature, some mysterious call of the wild that one felt compelled to answer. But Jacita was wise enough not to voice her doubts to Alison. Instead she said, "I will bring you a *nah-leen* for your hair tomorrow."

Alison could hardly wait to wear it. It would serve as a reminder to Ramon that she was off limits. And she couldn't wait to get back to the *wickiup* to tell Ramon just what she thought of him. How dare he think her a loose woman just because she was white!

But to Alison's frustration, they didn't go back to the camp immediately. First they had to wash their soiled clothing. As they left it hanging over bushes to dry overnight, Alison asked, "Won't someone steal it?"

"No, an Apache never steals from another Apache."

Alison couldn't resist saying, "No, you just steal from other people."

"It is not the same. If an Apache needs something that another has, he has only to ask. He will not be refused."

"I find that hard to believe. He's expected to just give up his possession because someone asks for it?"

"A man who makes too many requests soon gains the contempt of the tribe. He becomes known as someone who is no man at all. Apache men are very proud."

Yes, she knew just how proud they were, Alison thought, thinking of one particular Apache.

As they walked through the camp, the sun was setting, a white ball against a golden sky that turned the mountains all around them a blood red. When they reached Ramon's *wickiup*, Jacita taught Alison how to start a fire with a firestick—something that she discovered was much more difficult than it had looked when the Apache chief had done it. No matter how fast she twirled the stick, she couldn't seem to make it spark.

Frustrated, she asked, "Can't I just get a light from someone else's fire?"

"No, you must learn how to do this yourself. Try again."

To Alison's relief, the firestick sparked and the small twigs beside it caught fire. Then Jacita taught her how to build it slowly so as not to smother it. When it was going to her satisfaction, Jacita rose and said, "I will bring you something to eat. Tomorrow we will set up your kitchen and I will teach you the rudiments of Apache cooking."

"Then we won't be gathering agave hearts tomorrow?"

"No."

Alison was vastly relieved. She didn't think she could take another day of such hard labor. She needed time to recuperate.

Jacita brought her a bowl of stew similar to what Alison had eaten the night before. "Would you like me to stay with you tonight?" Jacita asked as Alison accepted the bowl.

"What do you mean, stay with me?"

"Ramon will not be here. If you are afraid to stay by yourself, I will sleep here. But there is nothing to be afraid of. No one will harm you."

"Where did Ramon go?" Alison asked, a little taken aback at this surprising news.

"He and some of the warriors have gone on a raid."

He had gone off and left her without even so much as a word? Why, he had no sooner brought her to this camp than he had cast her aside, leaving her to his sister's care. Alison felt a twinge of hurt at his lack of concern.

"Would you like me to stay?"

"No, that's not necessary. I'm not afraid, and as exhausted as I am, I'm sure I'll have no trouble sleeping."

Jacita was pleased with her answer. Apaches scorned fearful women. "Then I will see you in the morning."

But despite her exhaustion, Alison lay awake long after Jacita left, again seething with frustration. She had hoped to tell the Apache chief just what she thought of him, and his leaving with no explanation still piqued her. She jumped at the sound of a pack of wolves baying in the distant mountains, then wondered if the wild animals ever wandered into the camp. She glanced apprehensively toward the skin flap hanging over the door, knowing it would be no determent to them. Then, remembering their fear of fire, she relaxed. Ramon probably couldn't care less if they tore her to pieces, she thought morosely. He didn't need her to cook and wash for him. No, he probably didn't even want her anymore, since she had refused him her body. And he was too proud to return her. The wolves would be doing him a favor. She fell asleep with this depressing thought on her mind.

7

The next day Alison and Jacita set up her kitchen in the brush enclosure next to Ramon's *wickiup*. Her utensils consisted of a pot or two, a large tin that had once contained coal oil for boiling, a metal skillet, and a huge grindstone, which Jacita called a *metate*. There were also a few pottery bowls, a few wooden spoons, a wicked-looking knife, an herb basket, several other baskets for storing food, a second wicker water jar, and two *tsahs*, one to be used as a serving tray and another to carry seeds that could be placed over the hot coals and roasted. With her burden basket, her own firestick, and a stack of wood for her fires, Alison's kitchen was complete.

"I brought you this *parfleche* to store your clothes in," Jacita said, nodding to a cowhide bag sitting on the ground that was similar to the one Alison had seen in the *wickiup*.

"So that's what was in that bag," Alison commented. "Ramon's clothes."

Jacita was pleased to learn that the white woman had not snooped through her brother's belongings, although she was obviously curious as to what the bag contained. "I put some soap in it and a hairbrush, to use until I can teach you how to make your own."

"Thank you, but you didn't forget the *nah-leen,* did you?" Alison asked, anxious to get her hot hair off her neck.

"No, I didn't forget." Jacita walked to the *parfleche* and pulled out a leather bow. "See? I thought you might like one that was decorated with beads, but if you prefer I have another with brass knobs that you can have."

Alison wasn't the least interested in decorations. She just wanted something to keep the hair off her neck and out of her face, and also something to remind Ramon that she was a maiden, forbidden fruit by his own people's dictates. She could hardly wait to throw *that* in his face!

"I also brought you these," Jacita said, pulling out a string of trading beads and another necklace from which a small mirror dangled.

Alison had noticed the Apache women's jewelry and thought them gaudy, but she didn't dare refuse for fear she would hurt Jacita's feelings. The girl had been so kind to her. "Thank you, Jacita. I think I'll wear the blue beads."

As Alison slipped the beads over her head, Jacita said, "I thought they would look pretty with your eyes, but they don't really match their color. I have never seen eyes so blue." She laughed. "But then, I have never seen anyone with blue eyes. Are they all as beautiful as yours?"

Alison flushed at Jacita's compliment, then admitted, "I've been told that they're a rather striking color."

"Yes, they certainly are." Seeing that she was embarrassing Alison, Jacita picked up the leather bow and said, "Here, put this on."

"How do I do it?"

"Just roll your hair around it."

Alison tried to roll her hair around the hard leather bow, but the strands were elusive, and no matter how hard she tried, she could not get all her long hair in the bow. "I guess I'm not used to it."

"No, I think you are having so much trouble because your hair is so wavy, while ours is perfectly straight. You will have to practice with it. In the meantime, let me do it for you."

After Jacita had rolled Alison's long hair into the bow and tied it with a bright-colored strip of cloth, she stepped back and said, "That looks very pretty."

"I don't know what to say, Jacita. You've been so very kind to me. I'm sure your brother didn't tell you to do all these personal little things for me. After all, I'm nothing but a captive. But I do appreciate it. 'Thank you' just doesn't seem enough."

"I understand. We Apaches have a special thank you for a very serious expression of gratitude. *Asoog'd.*"

Alison tried to say the Apache word, but it didn't come out sounding anything like Jacita's. It sounded more as if she were choking. Both women laughed at her effort. Then Alison said, "I'm sorry, but I just can't seem to twist my tongue around that one."

"It does not matter. You do not need to thank me. It's true my brother did not tell me to do these things, but I wanted to."

"Why?"

Jacita had come to admire Alison's determination and willingness to work as well as her courage. "Because I like you. I had hoped we could be friends, despite the fact that you are my brother's prisoner."

Alison sorely needed a friend, someone she could talk to in this camp of people who were so different from her own. And the tiny Apache girl certainly couldn't help it if her brother was an arrogant bastard. No, it wasn't Jacita who had stolen her freedom, but Ramon. The thought occurred to her that Jacita might help her escape, then Alison quickly tossed it aside. Jacita might like her well enough to offer her friendship, but she would never do anything that would displease Ramon. She stood in awe of her brother, and Alison sensed it wasn't fear that motivated her, but worship of the man she thought absolutely perfect.

Alison smiled and said, "I'd like us to be friends too."

Jacita smiled back, then asked, "How much do you know about cooking?"

"Very little, I'm afraid."

"There's really not that much to it. We fry, bake, roast, or boil our meat. Other than that, we serve mostly soups or stews."

"I'm afraid you're oversimplifying it. I have no idea what goes into a stew or soup, especially an Apache stew or soup. You don't have vegetables like we do, and I have no earthly idea what's edible and what may be poisonous."

"Then we will have to start from scratch. Today we will make soup from rabbit, yucca blossoms, and wild onions. And I will teach you how to make the Mexican's flat bread."

"*Tortillas*?" Alison asked in surprise. "How did you learn to make them?"

"There are many things we have learned from our Mexican captives and adopted, particularly when they are practical. And we are as fond of their red peppers as they are."

Jacita put Alison to work grinding dried corn on her *metate*. It was a backbreaking job and hot under the blazing sun, particularly with her long sleeves and high-necked blouse. Alison wondered why the Apaches hadn't adopted the Mexican women's short-sleeved, low-necked blouses if they were so fond of Mexican things. They would certainly be much cooler. But then, the heat didn't seem to bother Jacita as much as it did her. There were no circles of perspiration beneath her arms or sweat trickling down her forehead. She seemed to be immune to the sun's hot rays.

After the tortillas had been baked in a small mud oven that Jacita taught Alison to build, the two went out into the woods to dig up wild onions. It was while they were on their hands and knees that Jacita looked at Alison and then sat back on her heels, a horrified expression coming over her face.

"What's wrong?" Alison asked.

"There are spots on your face."

Those damn freckles, Alison thought. "I know, they're what we whites call freckles."

"Are you sure you are not getting the red-spotted disease?" Jacita asked fearfully.

Alison frowned. "Do you mean measles?"

"I do not know what the white man calls it, only that he brought it to my people."

"But measles aren't serious."

"They are to my people. Several years ago, a Mexican captive brought the red-spotted disease to our village. She whose name I cannot speak and thirty others died from it."

Alison's frown deepened. "Who is she whose name you cannot speak?"

"I cannot tell you. Apaches never speak the names of the dead."

"Why not?"

"Because it might bring their spirits back."

Alison couldn't believe the girl actually believed in ghosts, but Jacita's expression was deadly serious. Wisely she didn't laugh at her, but she was consumed with curiosity to know who she whose name she couldn't speak was. Seeing the girl still staring fearfully at the spots on her face, she said, "There's nothing to be afraid of, Jacita. I don't have the measles. My spots aren't red. They're brown. Freckles are quite common among my people. They're just a discoloration of the skin that comes out when I've been exposed to too much sun."

Jacita laughed. "I'm sorry. I guess I seemed foolish to you."

"No, if you didn't know what they were, I can't blame you. If I saw something odd on someone's face and thought they might have a disease, I'd be just as frightened."

As the two walked back through the camp, Alison noticed that the only Apaches about were the women, and they were all performing backbreaking tasks: hauling water, carrying wood strapped to their backs by a sling tied around their heads, on their knees grinding corn, pounding mescal, or scraping hides. There wasn't a man in sight, and Alison couldn't believe that they had all gone with Ramon. "Just what do the men do around here?" she asked Jacita. "It seems to me that the women do all the work."

"They hunt and tend the horses. And of course, they provide us protection."

"That doesn't sound very hard to me. In my society, the men do the hardest work, because they're stronger."

"That is not the Apache way, and Apache women are not weak. We have the women's work to do, and they have the men's."

Alison could tell by the tone of Jacita's voice that she resented Alison's criticism of the Apaches' ways, and she was forced the admit that the women were unusually strong, undoubtedly because they had been doing the hard physical labor for so long. Alison had muscles aching that she had never used, never even dreamed existed. She decided to change the subject. "Where are the horses? I haven't seen any around."

"We keep them in a valley far away from here, so our enemies cannot find us."

"But isn't that a little difficult, having to walk far to get a mount?"

"Apaches do not mind walking. We have strong muscles in our legs. We are not like the Comanches, who have become so dependent on their mounts that they are helpless if their horse is killed and they are left stranded. See those children, running up the side of the mountain? They are not playing. It is our way of strengthening their leg muscles and their lungs."

Alison was amazed, but she supposed the white man had become overly dependent on horses too. They rode them, used them to pull their carriages and wagons, and even their plows. The white man never walked unless he absolutely had to.

By the time they reached the *wickiup,* Alison was feeling a little winded, and she was limping on her bruised feet. Glancing down, Jacita said, "I'm sorry. I completely forgot about your moccasins. If you'll get the fire going for our stew, I'll go over to my wickiup and bring back the items we'll need to make you some."

Alison nodded, saying a silent prayer that the firestick would cooperate with her.

It took a lot of furious twirling and some unladylike curses, but Alison finally got a spark. She was feeling rather proud of herself when Jacita returned and she actually had a fire going.

Jacita was proud too, and said so. Then she placed a piece of hard cowhide on the ground and asked Alison to place her foot on it so she could trace its outline with a bit of charcoal.

"I thought Indians made moccasins from buckskins," Alison said as she watched Jacita.

"Not the soles. Deerskin is much too soft in this rocky country. Apaches use cowhide for the soles and buckskins for the upper moccasins." She looked up from what she was doing. "I will take this home and sew your moccasins for you tonight."

"Can't you teach me how to do it? I hate to have you laboring over my moccasins. You've already done so much for me. Besides I might as well learn that too."

Jacita was pleased with her answer. "As soon as we have our stew simmering, I will teach you."

It was a painstaking task, forcing the awl through the tough leather to sew the buckskin to the sole with a thin string of rawhide, but Jacita didn't leave her side for one moment, and offered many helpful suggestions. In the end the moccasins didn't look nearly as neat as the Apache girl's, for in many places the buckskin was puckered where it wasn't supposed to be, but even so Alison was very proud of her work. She held up the finished product and said, "I know they don't look like much, but do you realize that I've never sewed a thing in my life?"

"Then who sewed your clothes?" Jacita asked in surprise.

"A dressmaker."

"Then you should be proud of yourself. And don't worry, the next pair will be much better. It takes practice."

That night Alison went to bed feeling a glow of satisfaction. She could start a fire with nothing more than a stick, make tortillas from dried corn kernels, cook a stew from the most unlikely ingredients, and sew moccasins. They were accomplishments that she had never aspired to, had never dreamed of acquiring, but because they were so unusual for a white woman, she felt all the more proud of them. She couldn't wait for Ramon to return to see all she had learned.

The thought shocked Alison. She wasn't learning these things to please him. She was learning them to survive in this new, harsh environment. She didn't give a damn about him, or what he thought of her. No, she was only doing them for herself, so that he couldn't accuse her of not earning her keep. Only for herself, she vowed fiercely.

But despite this vow, Alison hadn't been able to get the handsome, exciting Apache out of her mind. It seemed much more than two days since Ramon had ridden off, and she wondered how much longer he would be away. She told herself that she wasn't anxious to see Ramon, the man. No, his absence only frustrated her because the savage had aroused her anger and then put himself out of her reach where she couldn't vent her fury at him. That was the only reason she was anxious for his return, to put the bastard firmly in his place.

Two days later, when Alison and Jacita were returning from the stream after their bath, Alison spied a gray-haired man sitting on the ground in front of Jacita's *wickiup* with his long legs crossed before him. No one had to tell her who the man was, for despite his deeply tanned, leathery face, he was obviously a white man. This was Jacita and Ramon's Mexican father.

"Good," Jacita said, "my father is home. I have been wanting you to meet him."

As the two young women stepped up to the older man, Alison could see the strong resemblance between him and Ramon. The Apache chief had his father's build, his nose, his mouth, and his wavy hair, but it was obvious that Ramon had inherited his mother's black Apache eyes, for the Mexican's eyes were a light brown.

"Who is this stranger you have with you, my daughter?" the Mexican asked.

"She is Ramon's captive. Alison, this is my father."

"How do you do," Alison responded, for there was a certain dignity about the old man that seemed to command respect.

"I am pleased to meet you," the old man answered politely. "I nderstand you are an American?"

"Yes, I am,"

As he gazed up at her, Alison became aware that his eyes were focused on a point over her shoulder and not on her face. She realized, with something of a start, that he was blind.

"You will have to tell me what Alison looks like, Jacita. I would like an image to go with the voice."

Alison spoke up before Jacita could answer. "I'm tall and skinny," she informed the old man, still smarting at Ramon's uncomplimentary description of her, "and have spots on my face."

Jacita shot her a quick, startled look, then said, "That is not true! She is not skinny, just slender. But she is tall, almost as tall as you and Ramon. And the spots on her face are called freckles. She is really very pretty, particularly her eyes. They are blue, Father. But you have never seen such a deep, lovely blue."

The old man smiled. "I did not believe her description of herself. I knew my son would not bring back an ugly woman."

Alison wondered if the Mexican knew why his son had taken her captive, and if so, if he approved of Ramon's audacity.

"I will walk back with you to your *wickiup*," Jacita said to Alison. "I left my burden basket there."

Alison looked down at the man and said, "Good day." She paused, wondering how to address him. "Señor . . . ?"

"Apaches do not have last names," the Mexican informed her.

"But you're a Mexican."

"Not anymore. I am an Apache. Call me Miguel, or he who is the father of Ramon."

That peculiar third person Ramon had told her about, Alison thought. She laughed softly. "I will call you Miguel. The other is much too long-winded for me."

As soon as the two women were out of Miguel's hearing, Alison asked, "How did your father lose his sight?"

"He was hit in the head by a bullet on a raid several

years ago. He did not die, but when he regained consciousness, he could no longer see. The *di-yins* tried to restore his sight, but nothing helped."

"Who are *di-yins*?"

"That is what we call our medicine men."

"What did they do?"

"They sprinkled him with *ha-dintin,* the pollen of cattails, because it is very powerful, shook their gourds and chanted over him, and tried to purify him with smoke. They even asked the *Ganhs* for their help. They sang and chanted and danced over him all night. They even laid their tridents on him, trying to transfer the blindness to the air, but that did not work either."

"Who are the *Ganhs*?"

"I'm sorry. Of course, you do not know who they are. They are the Mountain Spirits who serve as the Apaches' link to the Highest Spirit. We only call on them when we are in great need or joy."

"Are you trying to tell me that ghosts actually came and tried to cure your father?" Alison asked in utter disbelief.

"No, they are not ghosts. They are members of our tribe whom the Mountain Spirits have entered. But no one knows who they are."

Alison wasn't surprised that the medicine men and *Ganhs* hadn't been able to cure Miguel's blindness. Why, it all sounded like something out of the Dark Ages.

"How did your father know I was a stranger when we walked up?"

"He probably did not recognize your step. He says his other senses are much sharper since he lost his sight. Would you believe, he claims he can even tell someone by their scent? I can't imagine that."

Alison could. Ramon had a scent about him that she had never smelled on another man, a mixture of leather, wood smoke, pine needles, and some faint musky scent that did strange things to her.

After Jacita had picked up her burden basket and left, Alison walked through the brush enclosure, ducked her head, and pushed back the skin flap on the door of the *wickiup*. Stepping inside, she came to a dead halt. Ramon sat on one of the pallets across from her, his legs crossed before him, eating a bowl of the stew that she had left simmering. As his dark eyes rose to meet hers, Alison was again stunned by his rugged handsomeness and his powerful presence. A spontaneous thrill of happiness that he had returned ran through her, before she realized what she was doing and quickly suppressed the unwanted emotion.

"This is good stew," Ramon remarked. "I must remember to compliment Jacita on it."

"I cooked it," Alison said, taking immense satisfaction from the surprised expression that came over his face.

He set the bowl aside, then asked, "Did you miss me?"

"If you mean did I notice you were gone, of course I did," Alison replied tartly.

"That is not what I meant, and you know it. Did you miss my company?"

"Of course not!"

Ramon's lips twitched with amusement. "I thought I saw a brief glimmer of happiness in your eyes when you first saw me, but I must have been mistaken."

The arrogant bastard! Alison thought hotly. "You most certainly were," she replied in a frosty voice.

"How have you fared in my absence?"

As if he cared, Alison thought bitterly. "Fine."

"And Jacita has been teaching you our women's work?"

"She has. I think you will find that I am quite capable of earning my keep."

Alison sat down on the pallet across from him. He glanced at the bow at the back of her neck and said, "I assume Jacita gave you that."

"Yes, she did. She's been very kind to me." Alison's blue eyes flashed angrily. "She also told me its significance, that Apaches have a high regard for their maidens."

Ramon shrugged. "That is true."

"May I remind you that I too am a maiden? You wouldn't abduct an Apache maiden simply because you wanted her. I deserve the same respect!"

Ramon had never wanted an Apache woman, or any woman, the way he wanted Alison, but his pride wouldn't let him admit that to her. "You are not an Apache. You are my captive. That rule does not apply to you."

"Damn you! How dare you treat me like a loose woman just because I'm white!"

"I did not say you were a loose woman."

"You implied that I would surrender to you."

As his dark eyes feasted hungrily on her beautiful features, Ramon reached out and touched Alison's cheek softly with the tips of two fingers, then ever so slowly moved them across her jawline. "You will . . . eventually."

A spontaneous shiver of sheer pleasure ran through Alison at Ramon's senusal caress, infuriating her all the more. She jerked her head away angrily and spat, "No, I won't! My morals are just as high as any Apache woman's. I will never submit to you willingly!"

"We have already been through all of this. I told you, I am a patient man."

Alison knew she was beating her head against a brick wall. Ramon was a man who did what he damn well pleased, running roughshod over her feelings and even the code of decency of his own people. She glared at him with impotent fury.

It was a wasted effort. Ramon ignored her, turning his attention to cleaning his rifle.

But Ramon wasn't as cool, calm, and unaffected as he appeared. He hadn't been able to get his beautiful, spirited captive out of his mind the entire time he had been gone, and thinking about Alison only made him want her more. His desire for her was like a tight coil ready to spring, and he was finding it more and more difficult to keep his promise to wait until she was willing. Knife and awl! Why did she have to be so obstinate?

The next thirty minutes passed with excruciating slowness with Alison seething in frustration and Ramon pretending indifference to her while he struggled to keep his passion in check. The silence wore on both their nerves. Finally Alison, realizing that nothing had changed between them and nothing would be gained by maintaining this uncomfortable silence, broke it by saying, "There is something I would like to ask you. Jacita told me that someone whose name she could not speak had died from the measles. I was curious to know who she was talking about."

There was just the slightest pause. "Our mother."

Alison frowned. She hadn't realized that it was someone so close to Jacita. No wonder the girl had gotten so upset. "She said Apaches do not speak the name of the dead for fear it will bring back their spirits."

"That is true."

"You did."

"I personally do not believe in spirits."

"And the *Ganhs*? Do you believe in them?"

"Who told you about the Mountain Spirits?"

"Jacita. She said they couldn't cure your father's blindness either."

"No, I don't believe in them either, but that is between just you and me."

"Then why did you allow them to perform all of that . . . that black magic?"

"For Jacita. She believes. And she wanted our father's sight to be restored very badly. Now, because she knows that everything that could possibly be done was, she has come to accept it."

"How can you say that?" Alison asked with a hint of anger in her voice. "That everything that could possibly be done for him was done? You should have taken him to a doctor!"

"A white man's doctor?"

"Yes!"

"Could he remove the bullet from my father's head?"

"Are you saying it's still in there?" Alison asked in a shocked voice.

"Yes, lodged somewhere behind his eyes."

"Why, it's a miracle that he's even alive!"

"Yes, it is," Ramon agreed, setting his rifle aside and coming to his feet. "So what harm did my allowing the medicine men and *Ganhs* to practice their magic on him do? None at all. It comforted Jacita and it comforted the other members in the tribe."

He gazed down at her thoughtfully, then asked, "What prompted Jacita to tell you about our mother dying of the measles?"

A flush rose on Alison's face. She hated to mention her

ugly freckles to him, particularly after he had made that sarcastic remark about how tall and skinny she was. It would only give him more ammunition with which to humiliate her.

When she held her silence, Ramon crouched before her and looked her directly in the eye. "I asked you a question."

Alison knew he wouldn't leave her alone until she answered. He was the most persistent man she had ever known. "She saw the spots on my face and thought I was coming down with the red-spotted disease. I had to explain to her that they were only freckles."

Ramon's eyes drifted over the bridge of her nose where her freckles lay. "Yes, there are exactly eleven of them."

"How do you know that?" Alison asked in surprise.

"I counted them while you were asleep."

He had hovered over her, close enough to count her freckles while she was sleeping, while she was totally defenseless? "How dare you stare at me while I was asleep!"

He chuckled. "You do not like me staring at you while you are awake either." His hand rose, and he trailed his fingertips over her nose. "Besides, I think they are intriguing. I wanted a closer look."

Alison was stunned by his words. She had always considered her freckles a mar on her face. And then as his fingers drifted down along her jaw, his masculinity suddenly seemed overpowering, so much so that she found it difficult to breathe. "Don't," she muttered, trying to shove his hand away.

He pushed her back on the pallet and lay half over her. Alison was acutely aware of his hard body pressing against hers, of his corded thigh lying over her legs. She looked up and saw his dark eyes smoldering with desire. Frantically she tried to push him away. "Don't! You promised you wouldn't force me."

As his head descended, Alison knew he meant to kiss her. She turned her head away. Ramon ran his mouth down her neck, saying, "I promised I wouldn't force you to submit totally to me. I did not promise I would not kiss you."

"You're still forcing yourself on me!"

He nibbled at her earlobe, causing a jolt of pleasure to run through her. "No."

As he dropped soft kisses over her jawline, moving closer and closer to her mouth, Alison felt sheer panic. "Then what do you call this?"

"Gentle persuasion."

He cupped her chin and firmly turned her head. Alison steeled herself for his wild, passionate kiss. But instead his warm lips brushed back and forth across hers with a feather lightness, coaxing and wooing until her lips were aching. His gentleness stunned her, for she had never credited the fierce Apache with being capable of tenderness. When his tongue flicked out at the ultrasensitive corner of her mouth, an incredibly sensuous act that was rich with promise, a tingle of excitement ran through her; then as his tongue slid back and forth over her lips, teasing and tantalizing, she thought she would scream if he didn't stop tormenting her and kiss her, really kiss her.

He did. But there was none of the wild forays his tongue had made in the past. It slipped into her mouth, sliding down the length of her tongue, the tip tracing the insides of her teeth and touching the roof of her mouth before it returned to softly caress her tongue, then withdrew, bringing a little moan of protest from

Alison. Again his lips played with hers, before his tongue dipped inside once again, not plundering her sweetness but tasting it, savoring it, stealing her nectar little by little. As he dropped kisses over the bridge of her nose, then her eyelids, Alison was floating on a warm rosy cloud. The feel of his lips brushing across her eyelashes was more than she could bear. The world seemed to turn on its axis, spinning dizzily. She wrapped her arms around his shoulders, needing something to cling to.

She could feel the warmth of his hand cup her breast through the material of her blouse. She fought her reeling senses, but the feel of his teeth nipping on her neck left her weak with longing. Then as his fingers brushed across the nipple and she felt it come alive, straining eagerly for his touch, the full impact of what she was letting him do struck her.

"No! Stop!"

Ramon raised his head and looked down at her. "You don't mean that," he said in a voice thick with passion.

"Yes, I do!" Alison answered, feeling incredibly breathless. "I told you I can't stand for you to touch me."

"Is that why you're trembling and why your heart is racing so fast?"

"Yes!"

"You still lie! You are not adverse to my touch."

To prove his point, Ramon brushed his fingers once more over her throbbing nipple, and Alison felt it like a bolt of fire. She gasped.

He smiled smugly. "You see?"

It was the smile that did it. A fury filled her. "If you think I gasped from pleasure, you're mistaken. No one has ever touched that part of me with such impunity! It's indecent! Disgusting!"

Ramon's dark eyes flashed. Then to Alison's utter dismay, he smiled. "No, Alison, it will not work. You will not make me angry by insulting me. I will kiss you and touch you whenever I like. But I will not force the ultimate act upon you. I will not have to. Your body will hunger for mine, and ache for my disgusting touch."

"No! You can't seduce me either!"

He rolled away from her and came to his feet with one smooth movement, then turned and walked to the door. Lifting the flap, he looked back over his shoulder and said with that calm self-assurance that was so maddening, "We shall see."

As he ducked beneath the flap, Alison shrieked, "Never, you damn arrogant bastard!"

The only response was a chuckle, infuriating Alison all the more.

8

The next morning, when Alison walked to Jacita's *wickiup*, there was an air of excited anticipation about the entire camp, and she had never seen so much activity. The women and children were rushing about everywhere, chopping wood in the forests all around the *rancheria* and carrying it back to build huge fires in the center of the camp, rather than the small ones usually built beside their *wickiups*.

Alison walked up to Jacita, who was busy sharpening her butcher knife in her brush kitchen, and asked, "What's going on? Why are they building such big fires?"

"The men's recent raid went so well that we are going to celebrate with a feast and dance tonight," Jacita answered. "The men are off hunting, and as soon as they return, we women will start cooking for the event."

"So early in the day?"

"Yes, it will take us all day long to roast the large game they will bring back."

Soon the men started returning to the camp, carrying

deer and antelope hung by their hooves on long poles
slung between the braves' shoulders. Jacita had set up
her grinding stone in front of her *wickiup,* and she and
Alison were busy grinding corn with their cucumber-
shaped *manos* to make tortillas. Looking up, Alison saw
Ramon coming from the woods with a buck draped
around his broad shoulders. She had seen nothing of the
virile chief since their confrontation the evening before. If he had returned to the *wickiup,* he had come
and gone while she slept. She briefly admired his graceful walk and the ease with which he carried his heavy
burden, then remembered she was angry with him. She
shot him a look that could kill before she turned her full
attention back to her grinding, determined that she
would ignore him if he made any effort to speak to her.

He strode up to the two women, then dropped the
deer to the ground beside Alison. It was an act so delib-
erate that Alison couldn't have missed it, but she pretended that she hadn't even noticed.

"This is for you," Ramon said, motioning to the deer.

Alison glanced at the dead animal, then up at the tall
chief. "What am I supposed to do with it?" she asked in
an icy voice.

"Skin it and cook it."

"Skin it?" Alison asked in surprise.

"Yes."

"But I have no idea how to skin a deer," Alison objected. "Why don't you do it?"

"Skinning deer is woman's work. The man only kills
the game."

"You skinned those rabbits we ate on our trip here,"
Alison pointed out.

"That was different. We were not in camp then and
you knew nothing of our ways."

"I still don't know how to skin a deer!"

"No? I thought you said you were quite capable of earning your keep."

Alison knew he was taunting her. She glared at up at him.

"A woman who cannot skin game is no woman at all," Ramon informed her, ignoring her heated look. "You still have much to learn. Jacita will teach you."

He turned and walked away, and Alison was sorely tempted to hurl her *mano* at him, despite his previous warning that he wouldn't tolerate anyone throwing things at him.

Jacita showed Alison how to skin the deer, then gut it, a chore that left the white girl's stomach churning. Then, after rubbing the raw meat with herbs, the two women spitted it and placed it over one of the big fires with the rest of the roasting meat. All day long the women worked in preparation for the feast, turning the meat over the fires, chopping more wood to keep them going, grinding corn and baking tortillas, then trudging to the mescal pits to bring back heavy loads of the baked agave hearts for that night's celebration. While the women labored, the men, their work of supplying the meat done, entertained themselves with wrestling, horse racing, and gambling games, a situation that irritated Alison to no end but which the Apache women took in stride.

Finally, when all the preparations for the feast had been completed, the women hurried to the bathing area to prepare themselves for the night's festivities, dressing in their best as they chatted gaily in excited anticipation. As they walked back to the camp, Jacita, looking very pretty in a turquoise printed blouse and skirt and a pair of beaded moccasins that she used only for special occasions, asked Alison, "You are coming tonight, aren't you?"

Alison was very conscious of her ill-fitting clothing and pitiful-looking moccasins. Compared to the Apache women dressed in their finery, she felt like a ragged street urchin. "I don't think so. I'm rather tired."

"But you have to come," Jacita objected. "There will be dancing afterward. You wouldn't want to miss that."

Alison assumed the dancing would be done by the warriors and didn't particularly care to watch a bunch of frenzied, half-naked men howling and jumping around a fire to the beat of wild tom-toms. She'd already seen that at a wild-West show.

Seeing Alison's hesitation, Jacita said, "You are coming, and that's that. You worked as hard as any of us and deserve a little relaxation."

When they entered the center of the camp, everyone was there. Many were already seated around the campfires and eating, while their children ran helter-skelter through the crowd, too excited to be bothered with something as mundane as food. There was such an air of festivity about the camp that Alison found she couldn't remain aloof and disinterested. A tingle of excitement ran through her, despite her earlier reluctance.

As she and Jacita ate, she glanced around her, secretly hoping to see Ramon. She saw nothing of the powerful chief, but did spy Miguel sitting with a group of older men off to one side. Then, noticing that the men were making frequent trips to the big wicker jars that were sitting about, she asked, "What's in those jars?

"*Tulapah*. It's a beer made from corn mash. Ramon will not allow the men to drink mescal at these tribal celebrations. It's too potent and its effects too unpre-

dictable. Some men go wild on it." Jacita glanced
around, then said in an excited voice, "Look! The dancing is about to start!"

Alison saw a crowd of Indian men standing to the side
of the fire, a few holding drums in their hands, but there
were no half-naked, painted warriors anywhere
around. The men were dressed in their usual shirts,
pants, and knee-high moccasins. Then women, mostly
young maidens, began forming pairs around the fire,
leaving Alison to assume, with surprise, that *they* were
going to dance. But instead of the music starting right
away, as Alison expected, the girls walked away from
the fire and into the crowd of warriors, many of them no
more than teenagers, tapping them on the shoulder.

"They are about to perform the wheel dance," Jacita
informed Alison as the couples walked back to the fire,
the maidens hanging their heads shyly. "Only the single
men and women can participate, and as you saw, the
woman chooses her partner from among the men who
wish to dance. Most often it is a young man the maiden
is attracted to."

"Is that why you're not dancing, because there's no
one you're particularly attracted to?"

A flush rose on Jacita's pretty face. "There is someone," she admitted, "but he is not here tonight. He is
standing night watch."

As the drums started, the couples faced each other
about a yard apart and danced a simple two-step, a few
paces forward and then a few back, slowly revolving
around the fire. Alison noted that several couples had a
blanket thrown over their shoulders and asked Jacita
about it.

"They are couples who are openly courting."

"Why are the teenage boys wearing those funny caps with feathers sticking out of the top of them?"

"They are braves who are still serving their apprenticeship. They must go on four raids and serve beneath an older, experienced warrior before they can become full warriors themselves."

Alison enjoyed watching the young people dance, for although it was rather sedate, they seemed to be enjoying themselves immensely. As the dance ended and the couples drifted back into the crowd, Jacita said, "Now they will dance the property dance. The steps are similar, but only the young widows and divorcées can participate, and they can pick any man in the camp to partner them. For the privilege of dancing with her, the warrior must give her a substantial present from his share of the spoils from the raid, and he cannot refuse."

"Do you mean married men too?"

"Yes. It is the only way those women who have no man to support them can gain any material goods."

Alison glanced around her, then spied Ramon standing in the crowd. How long had he been there? she wondered. She caught sight of something from the corner of her eye. It was a young woman weaving her way through the crush of people toward the tall chief. She stopped before him and tapped him on the shoulder. As she walked back toward the fire, Ramon followed.

Then something happened that shocked Alison. As the drums began to beat, the women began stripping off their clothing, baring themselves completely except for a thin piece of material over their pubis. As they began to dance lewdly, their breasts bobbing and their hips swiveling suggestively, moving within inches of their partners and then backing away, Alison said in a shocked voice, "Why, they're not just dancing. They're trying to seduce those men!"

"Yes, they are inviting them to their pallets after the dance is over," Jacita answered, so embarrassed at the women's nudity and gyrations herself that she could not look at the dancers.

"In full view of the entire tribe? Why, I've never heard of anything so indecent!"

"This is the only time the tribe allows promiscuity."

"The tribe? What about those men's wives? Don't they object?"

"They don't usually complain. They know the warriors have faced much danger and gone through many tribulations on the raid and are ready for a good time. And this is the only" —Jacita hesitated; she was still a maiden and reluctant to discuss such intimacies— "outlet of that nature available for those women, except for those who allow braves to slip at night into their *wicki-ups,* and that is not openly condoned."

"I should think not!" Alison said in outrage. "But what I don't understand is how your people can condone it at any time, particularly after you told me how strict your people are with the maidens."

Jacita shrugged, then answered, "It is our way. Those women are lonely and miss the physical pleasures they once shared with their husbands. And as for the wives being jealous, they know it does not mean their husbands especially care for those women. They are just being men."

How true, Alison thought angrily. All the act meant to men was gratification of their lust. Sex for the sake of sex and nothing more. Men! They were such disgusting creatures. And the women who sold their bodies for a gift were nothing but out-and-out prostitutes. She couldn't understand how the men's wives could calmly accept their husbands having a lusty romp with other women, even if it was accepted by the tribe in this case. She'd be furious!

A sudden thought occurred to her. "And the married women? Are there occasions when they too are allowed to take other lovers?"

"No, but that does not mean that some do not do it. But Apache men are very jealous. If he catches his wife, he can kill her. But usually, he just cuts off her nose, so she will not be attractive to other men any more. And then, too, she must suffer the humiliation of the entire tribe's knowledge of her infidelity. That is usually enough of a punishment."

Alison was horrified, and then angered. A man could slip around with no punishment if his wife caught him, but he could disfigure her, even kill her for her own adultery. She wasn't so naive not to know that the white man had a double standard too, but they certainly didn't carry it to such extremes.

Noticing that the drumbeat had gotten wilder, she looked back at the dancers, seeing that the men were matching the women gyration for gyration, many of the couples' bodies actually rubbing together. With the women's naked, sweaty skin glistening in the firelight from their exertions and the men's eyes glittering with unconcealed lust, Alison was sickened by the obscene display. She rose to her feet, saying, "I'm leaving."

"I will go with you," Jacita said, feeling a little uncomfortable herself.

As they wove their way through the crowd, Alison noted that the spectators' eyes were glued on the dancers, and from the expressions on their faces, there was no doubt in her mind that they found the lewd dance

exciting. She also noticed that the crowd was mostly
older people, as the young maidens and teenage boys
who had danced earlier made themselves scarce for the
most part, and those who remained stared at the
ground in embarrassment. Their discomfiture made
Alison feel somewhat better. At least the younger
Apaches had some sense of decency about them.

Then, as the music suddenly stopped, Alison looked
back. Standing as she was, she had no trouble seeing
over the seated crowd and over the fire, and for the first
time since the dance had begun spied Ramon. The
Apache chief stood just inches from the young, almost
naked woman who had asked him to dance, the firelight
playing over his bronzed, chiseled features. Even from
the distance that separated them, Alison could see the
smile on his face and his eyes locked on the woman's
nude body. Quickly Alison's eyes swept over the
Apache woman, secretly hoping that her body would be
ugly, with sagging breasts and fat, squatty legs. But she
found nothing of the sort. The young woman's full
breasts seemed to be standing at attention, the dark
nipples jutting from the mounds, leaving no doubt in
anyone's mind as to her aroused state, and her legs,
while a little fleshy around the thighs, were far from fat.
Alison quickly glanced up at the woman's dusky face
and, much to her dismay, found that she was quite
pretty. To make matters even worse, the woman's dark
eyes were half closed, glittering with desire for the man
standing before her. Then, smiling seductively, the
young widow stepped closer to Ramon and boldly
reached between his legs. Alison knew by the intense
expression that came over Ramon's handsome face that
he wasn't in the least bit averse to the woman's indecent caresses. A wave of intense raw jealousy ran over

Alison. She longed to scratch the little bitch's eyes out. As Ramon and the pretty widow turned and walked toward the woods, Alison knew where they were going and what they would do. She was filled with fury.

Having watched the whole scene and observed Alison's reaction to it, Jacita said, "Do not be so upset. Ramon does not really care for her. No man would turn down such an obvious invitation, particularly when he has no woman to share his pallet."

Alison started, having not realized that her feelings were written on her face. "I couldn't care less who he beds, much less if he has any feelings for her," she answered in a cold voice, furious with herself for becoming jealous. She turned and walked toward the *wickiup*, but her quick, agitated strides gave lie to her words, and Jacita practically had to run to keep up with her.

Long after Jacita left her, Alison was still seething. She told herself that it wasn't jealousy that angered her, that she didn't give a damn about the chief and couldn't really care less whom he made love to. No, what angered her was that he had stolen her unnecessarily. It was quite obvious he could get a woman to satisfy his animal needs any time he wanted one. He didn't need her, and he certainly didn't care anything for her. But despite her efforts to soothe her injured feelings, Alison was both hurt and angry that the handsome, virile chief had so quickly forgotten about her. And the possibility that he might care for the young Apache woman, despite what Jacita had said, gnawed at her, making her feel absolutely miserable.

She was still tossing and turning when Ramon walked in. Without even realizing that she might be giving herself away, Alison shot daggers at him.

"Were you at the dance?" he asked.

Alison sat up, saying, "I certainly was."

"Then that is why you are so angry with me. You saw me dancing with Margarita."

"I'm not angry," Alison denied adamantly. "I couldn't care less whom you dance with." Her blue eyes flashed dangerously. "Or rut with!"

So she had seen him walking away with Margarita and assumed they had made love, Ramon thought. Well, he wouldn't bother to correct her, to tell her that his ardor had quickly cooled once he and the bold widow were alone, something that surprised him. He had shared Margarita's pallet in the past and found her an exciting and accommodating lover. She had also been faithful to him, but he had discovered that he no longer desired her. The only woman he wanted, at least for now, was Alison. And the captive must care a little, enough to feel jealous. A smug smile spread across his rugged face. "I think you are jealous."

"That's ridiculous! I told you I couldn't care less. If anything, I'm glad! If you have her to slake your lust on, you won't be bothering me with your indecent advances."

Alison wondered at the twinge of disappointment her words brought her, but before she could ponder them, Ramon said, "You are wrong. I still want you."

A tingle of excitement quickly replaced the twinge of disappointment. "But why? When you have her?"

It was a question that Ramon didn't know the answer to himself, and he had refused to delve too deeply into why he desired the white woman so much. Perhaps it was because she was so different from Apache women, he thought. There was nothing meek and submissive about her. Alison was all fight and fire. Yes, that was it.

She presented a challenge to him, and once she had surrendered her body to him, he was sure the powerful fascination he felt for her would disappear.

Aware that Alison was awaiting an answer, he shrugged and said, "Perhaps I am too much man to be satisfied with only one woman."

Alison had heard that Indians took more than one wife. Was that why? Because one woman couldn't satisfy their lusty appetites? Well, she'd be damned if she'd share a man with another woman, be she his wife, or mistress, or a common whore. He'd give her his all or nothing. "Well, I'm afraid you're going to have to settle for Margarita to keep you happy. Or find another. You can have a whole damn harem for all I care. I'm not in the running for your attentions, remember? And besides, even if I were, I would never accept sharing you with another woman. I have too much pride for that."

Alison's strong words gave Ramon pause. Then he said, "You are in no position to demand anything, much less total commitment. You are my captive, not an honored member of this tribe. When you become my woman, do not expect fidelity from me."

Alison's eyes took on a hard glitter. "You're forgetting something, Ramon. I'm not going to become your woman. Now less than ever."

With that, Alison lay down with her back to him, leaving Ramon standing with a deep frown on his face, for there had been a fierce determination in her voice that he had not believed a woman capable of possessing. For the first time, his supreme assurance that he would bring her to heel wavered. She seemed to have laid down new yet subtle battle lines, proclaiming that if she gave her all, she would expect the same in return. But that was impossible. He was not prepared to give his all to any woman, much less a white-eyes, no matter how desirable she was. No, he would allow no woman to dictate such stipulations to him. She would surrender, and on his terms.

9

Over the next week, Alison fervently wished Ramon would go on another raid. He seemed even more determined to force her to surrender to him, using every seductive trick he could think of. Just as he had threatened, he would turn to her in their *wickiup* and touch her at will, brushing his fingers across the sides of her breasts, her throat, the nape of her neck, the bridge of her nose—hot, feather-like caresses that sent tingles running through her despite her determination to remain cold and aloof. Or he would walk into her brush-enclosed kitchen with that damn silent walk of his and slip his arms around her waist while she had her back to him, kissing and nuzzling her neck and throat until she could finally twist away from him. Twice he boldly took her in his arms, kissing her once with such passionate ardor that she was left breathless and weak-kneed, then once with such agonizing sweetness and tenderness that she secretly longed for it to go on forever. Sometimes she would look up from whatever she was doing to find him staring at her, but Alison found those scorching looks just as disconcerting as his touch. His eyes seemed to strip her of her clothing, making her feel as if it were his hands that were caressing her and bringing a warm flush to her body that she knew had nothing to do with embarrassment. He seemed to be waging a war on her nerves as much as her senses, for she never knew when he might suddenly appear or what he might do, leaving her feeling jumpy all the time. Even when he seemed to ignore her, giving his full attention to the arrows he was making which he would use to kill game, Alison couldn't find relief. His virile presence filled the *wickiup*, and she could feel his heat and smell his scent, a masculine essence that played havoc with her senses.

Since he never made any advances to her in public, Alison spent as much time as she could outdoors, but she found that even then she couldn't get away from his disturbing presence. She was acutely aware of his lithe walk as he strolled across the camp, of his dangling earrings swaying against his bronzed neck, of his black hair shining beneath the sunlight. His deep voice drifted across to her, and his power filled the entire valley, seeming to crowd everyone else out. She had never dreamed a man could be so compelling. It was almost as if the rest of the world had ceased to exist and there was only Ramon.

She was grinding corn one morning when she suddenly knew he was standing beside her, not because she heard him walk up, but because she smelled him. She glanced across and saw his moccasins with the beaded stripe that ran down to his toes. Then, looking up, she gasped.

"What's wrong?" Ramon asked.

"You're naked!"

"I am not naked. I am wearing a breechcloth."

Alison glanced at the cloth, which hid only the bare essentials and hung to his knees. It left a great deal of bronzed skin exposed. She could even see his hipbones, for the only thing covering the entire length of his side was a thin piece of rawhide around his lean hips. With his broad, muscular chest, his taut, ridged belly, and his long, corded thighs revealed to her, Alison felt assaulted by his blatant masculinity. She suddenly found it difficult to breathe, and a peculiar weakness invaded her. She jerked her eyes away and said, "You might as well be naked for all the good that flimsy piece of material does you. It's indecent to walk around that way."

"This is the Apache's traditional dress. A few of the tribes still do not wear pants, just shirts over their breechcloths."

"Then put on your shirt! At least you wouldn't look quite so bare."

"But that would defeat my purpose. Apache men strip to their breechcloths in the heat of summer to be cooler, particularly in the privacy of their camps."

Alison glanced around her; all the men were wearing nothing but breechcloths. But somehow their near-nakedness didn't disturb her. She wondered if it was just because the tall chief was so powerfully muscled, so blatantly male that his lack of clothing was so disconcerting. Regardless, it was doing peculiar things to her, arousing feelings that she had been trying her damnedest to fight down.

She breathed a sigh of relief when he turned and walked away, hoping that if he removed himself from her close proximity she wouldn't feel so light-headed. She looked up, only to find that his tight buttocks were almost totally revealed to her eyes—powerful muscles that contracted with every step he took. A sudden heat

suffused her. She tore her eyes away. Damn him! He
hadn't stripped down just to be cooler. Maybe the others had, but not him. No, he planned on parading his
magnificent physique in front of her just to taunt her. It
was just another one of his seductive tricks. Well, it
wouldn't work. He could walk around half naked until
doomsday, and she wouldn't look at him. Besides, she
didn't find his body at all appealing. Well, maybe his
chest was a little exciting, she admitted with reluctance.
But the lower part of his body was too male. There was
nothing attractive about a man's belly and buttocks and
bare thighs. But much to her disgust, Alison couldn't
resist stealing glances at the tall, virile chief.

The Apache season of Many Leaves gave way to the
season of Great Leaves. The valley in the mountains
was pleasantly cool at night and in the early morning,
but at midday, when the sun bore down on them, Alison
found it terribly hot. During those times the *wickiup*
was stifling, and even the brush enclosure was swelter-
ing, for not a breath of air stirred and there was no
nearby tree to shade her. She felt as withered as the
wild grapes she was drying for raisins, and her grindstone reflected the heat, making grinding the wild
seeds and grains all the more exhausting, for the heat
seemed to drain every bit of energy from her.

She was on her knees before the grindstone one hot
summer day when Ramon entered the brush enclosure.
She glanced up at him, acutely aware of the sweat trickling down her armpits, her back, her thighs. How dare
he stand there looking so unaffected by the heat, while
she was burning up.

Seeing her scowl, he asked, "Now what have I done to
displease you?"

"Nothing!"

"Then why are you in such a foul humor?"

Alison shot to her feet. "Because I'm hot, that's why! I'm not used to this heat like you Apaches are. You men may strip down to something more comfortable, but your women don't. I can't understand why they don't wear something cooler, like those blouses the Mexican women wear. I'm burning up in these long sleeves and this high neck."

Ramon glanced over Alison's clothing. The two-piece dress was so faded from washing that it hardly had any color to it, and it was ripped in many places. He hadn't realized that he had been negligent in providing better clothing for his captive, since Alison's ill-fitting clothes had not made her any less desirable in his eyes. And he supposed that a Mexican blouse would be cooler. "Can you sew?"

"Why do you ask?"

"I have some bolts of material from my last raid."

"Well, I can certainly learn. Jacita can teach me, just like she taught me to sew my moccasins."

Ramon glanced down at Alison's pitiful moccasins. "On second thought, I think we will get you some clothes that are already made. If you can make that big a mess out of moccasins, I hate to think what you might do a dress."

Damn him! Now he was criticizing her sewing. Nothing she did pleased him. She worked herself to the bone, gathering food and cooking for him and washing his clothes, not that it had consisted of much since he had taken to wearing only that obscene breechcloth. But still it was the principle of the thing. Just once she wished he would show some appreciation, or at least acknowledge that she was earning her keep. Her keep.

That was a laugh. All he contributed to that keep was a shelter and meat. "Thank you all the same, but I'll just keep what I've got," she said in a haughty voice.

"You are just being stubborn again. Besides, Jacita doesn't know any more about making that kind of a blouse than you do."

"Then I'll just hack off my sleeves, as I did those on my gown."

"I said I will get you new clothing," Ramon said in a firm voice. "Now stop arguing with me. You are the most exasperating woman I have ever met. First you complain about your clothes, then you tell me you don't want new ones. Since you can't make up your mind, I will. Tomorrow we will go to San Carlos to get you new clothing."

"We?" Alison asked in surprise. "I'm going with you?"

"Yes. If you don't, they will fit no better than what you are wearing."

"I'm supposed to stand there in the dark and try on some woman's clothing that you're stealing?" Alsion asked in an incredulous voice.

"I did not say I would steal the clothing," Ramon answered in total disgust. "I will trade for it, at the marketplace." Considering the matter closed, he turned and walked from the enclosure.

As Ramon strolled across the camp, his thoughts were still on Alison. He had sensed that she had a strength about her, but he was amazed at how well she had adapted to the Apaches' harsh life. The others had noticed, too, and made remarks about it. Her quickness to learn and dogged determination to keep up with the other women despite the fact that she was not accustomed to the hard labor was slowly earning their respect. He had even heard the story of how she had stood up to the women who had tried to humiliate her the first day, something that the Apaches viewed as an act of courage. And he had never heard her complain, except today when the heat got the better of her. In truth, he was proud of her, but he was determined not to tell her so until she surrendered to him. There was no point in encouraging her stubborn pride. She was obstinate enough.

Yes, she was the most stubborn woman he had ever met. After all this time, she still resisted his advances. He knew she found him attractive. He could feel her eyes on him when his back was turned. And he knew she wasn't averse to his touch. Just the brush of his fingers could make her tremble and her heart race. He had seen the telltale proof of his effect on her by the pulse beating in her throat. He knew the others assumed she shared his pallet, despite that stupid maiden's bow she insisted upon wearing. He was chief. His word was law in this camp. No one dared defy him. Besides, he had a reputation for being an extraordinarily skillful lover, thanks to the gossip of the widows and divorcées who had chosen him as their partner for the property dance. It would be humiliating if the others ever learned that Alison had refused him, that she was still holding him at bay after weeks of sleeping in his *wickiup*.

Perhaps he should change his tactics, Ramon thought. Maybe if he treated her a little kinder, she would be more receptive. Buying her new clothes would be a beginning. Every woman liked pretty things with which to adorn themselves. But he would have to be careful not to be too kind. It would be just as humiliating for the others to find out he was actually wooing her with presents, a woman who was nothing but a lowly captive, his slave, as for them to discover she had refused to share his pallet. *Dios,* she was a stubborn woman!

Again Ramon wondered if Alison was worth the trouble. A woman was a woman, and he could have his pick. But he wanted only the white-eyes. Each night was an agony for him. Her sweet, womanly scent intoxicated him, and her nearness tormented him. He was plagued by the memory of her softness when he had held her in his arms and the incredibly sweet taste of her mouth and skin. Invariably he became aroused, and his manhood throbbed painfully, demanding release. It took all his willpower to keep from reaching for her and forcing her surrender. And the days weren't much better. Even when she wasn't within sight, visions of her beautiful face and eyes drifted across his mind. She had become a fire in his blood, a fire that only she could quench. He *had* to possess her soon. Both his pride and his sanity demanded it.

Alison couldn't hide her excitement the next morning. Not only was she thrilled at the thought of having some new clothing that would be cooler and better fitting, but it gave her the opportunity to get away from the women's drudgery for a day or two. Why, the trip would be like a holiday for her.

When she discovered that Ramon was giving her her own mount to ride, she was even more pleased. The only thing she had been dreading about the trip was having to steel herself against the feel of his powerful body pressed behind hers. She found to her vast relief that she would not have to fight a constant battle with herself to keep her eyes off him, for he was dressed in a shirt and pants, and not that obscene piece of white cloth dangling between his thighs, drawing her attention like a red flag to the very root of his masculinity.

As Ramon handed her the reins, Alison didn't hesitate. She knew she was expected to ride astride, for she had seen several Apache women riding and admired their skill. She put her foot in the stirrup and swung her leg over the saddle, noting as she flew through the air that it was covered with a small blanket. When her bottom hit the saddle, she was surprised at its softness. She pushed her fingers against the blanket, then said, "Why, it's padded beneath this blanket."

"Yes. I remembered what a tender bottom you have and padded it with moss."

Alison was pleased with his thoughtfulness and was on the verge of actually thanking him when Ramon added with a grin, "I would not want you to be disabled, just in case you change your mind."

There was no doubt in Alison's mind as to what he was referring to. "Oh?" she asked in a frosty voice. "Well, I'm afraid you went to all that trouble for nothing. I won't change my mind."

Ramon wasn't surprised by her pert answer. He turned to his mount and flew into the saddle with a smooth, fluid movement that took Alison's breath away. Damn, she thought, why did he have to be so graceful in everything he did? And why did he have to wear that bright turquoise shirt? It only drew attention to his fascinating earrings and accented his bronzed skin tone. He was such a magnificent specimen of manhood with his superb physique and dark coloring. His devastating good looks, combined with his aura of power and command, decisiveness, and supreme self-confidence, all strong masculine attributes, made it very difficult, if not impossible, for a woman to remain indifferent to his powerful sexuality.

They rode from the camp and through the window, passing by the huge mescal pits with their mounds of ashes and sooty rocks. It took them the entire morning to weave their way down through the jagged mountains, again following narrow trails that twisted and turned and wove through a maze of deep canyons. Alison spied a mountain that she had never seen before, whose twin peaks looked like mule's ears, and knew that they were taking yet a different route from the one they traveled when Ramon had brought her to his camp.

When they left the mountains and rode onto the desert floor, Alison was stunned by the heat. In comparison, the valley in the Chisos was cool, even in midday. The blazing sun beat down on her with a vengeance, and she seriously doubted that new clothing was worth the torture she was going through. Had it not been that Ramon might think it a sign of white female weakness, she might have asked him to forget the entire trip and turn back, but she'd be damned if she'd risk leaving herself open to his ridicule. If he could take this intense heat, she could, even if it killed her!

"Just where is this San Carlos?" she asked.

"In Mexico, across the border.?"

"How far into Mexico?"

"Once we reach the border, it will not be far."

"How many miles?" Alison persisted.

"Miles?" Ramon snorted in disgust. "Apaches do not use miles to determine distances. We use time."

"Then how long from the border?"

"A few hours' ride."

"And to the border?"

"We should reach there by sundown."

Alison didn't know if she could endure the heat until sundown. It sounded like an eternity.

It was an hour later when she noticed the bleached bones laying all around her on the desert, a testimonial to the harsh, arid country they were riding through. There were piles of skeletons everywhere. "How did all these bones get here?"

"We have swung onto one of the Comanche Traces that the Texas tribes use on their raids into Mexico. Those skeletons are those of the horses and cattle that didn't make it back, and a few of the captives too," he added in an ominous voice, eyeing a bleached human skull.

"Comanches?" Alison asked in alarm, looking about her fearfully. "Aren't they your enemies?"

"Yes, but there is no need to be afraid. They only raid into Mexico during September, the month they call the Comanche Moon, and return in December. Besides, almost all of the northern tribes have been put on reservations by your people. Even the renegades rarely bother to make raids into Mexico anymore. The only Comanches that bother us are the Mexican tribes."

The trail was clearly marked by hundreds of hoof-prints that seemed permanently etched into the ground. Alison watched the sun as it slowly moved across the sky. She was dying for a drink of water, but knew better than to ask for one. Finally she did ask, "How much farther is it to the river? And dammit, don't give me that foolishness about you don't measure in miles!"

"In which direction?"

"What do you mean, in which direction?"

"If we traveled west, it would only be a half hour's

ride. If we continue the way we are going, it will be another hour."

"Then why don't we travel west?"

"Because there are only a few places where the river can be forded. At Presidio del Norte, at a place we call the little rocks, at the pass of the Chisos, and at Santa Rita, farther down river."

"Which will we be using?"

"Paso de Chisos."

About an hour later, Alison spied the river, sitting in a broad flood plain. "There it is!" she cried out excitedly. "The Rio Grande!"

"No. Rio Bravo del Norte."

"Brave River of the North?" Alison asked in surprise. "Why did you call it that?"

"Because that is what the Mexicans who live around here call it. The Rio Grande is just one of its names, one more frequently used by your people."

"But the brave river? Where in the world did they get such a ridiculous name?"

"They use the term to mean bold, not brave. You have only seen the river at Presidio del Norte, where it is wide and shallow and slow-flowing. But there are places where it is wild and dangerous. Do you remember me telling you that the river was kept in a stone box around the Chisos? It runs through deep canyons that have been cut through the mountains and are filled with dangerous rapids and sharp rocks. If you could see it there, you would not think it the same river."

When they reached the water, it was placid, shining under the bright sunlight like a tin roof. She quickly dismounted and quenched her terrible thirst, but she was careful not to drink too much too fast. Then she heard a strange noise, a low continuous roar. She looked about her.

"What you hear are the rapids in the canyons on both sides of us," Ramon explained. "The Santa Elena Canyon lies to our right, and the Little San Vincente Canyon is to the left."

Alison looked upriver and saw the canyon, but could spy no rapids. Beneath the tall, brooding cliffs, the olive-green water was calm and serene. Then, seeing some tall cane growing beneath one of the cliffs, its plumelike flowers silvery in the sunlight, she smiled. "Can I dig up some cane roots before we leave? They would taste good with our evening meal."

"You can dig up as many as you like. We will cross the river and camp here tonight."

After they had set up camp, Ramon searched out game while Alison busied herself with digging up cane roots and wild potatoes, and gathering raspberries that she found growing on a bush beneath one of the cliffs. She had the roots roasting over the fire and was munching on one of the potatoes, which the Apaches ate raw, when Ramon returned. As he tossed down a furry animal, Alison looked at it and asked, "What in the world is that?"

"A beaver."

"You eat beaver?"

"Why not? It is meat. Roasted it tastes similar to possum."

Alison hadn't eaten possum either, but undoubtedly Ramon would bring one of the ugly creatures home for her to cook someday. She was sick and tired of game. She longed for beef, or even turkey. She had seen some around the camp, or rather heard them gobbling in the woods, but the only birds Ramon ever brought her were doves and quail, small birds that were hardly worth the trouble of dressing. She gazed at the river longingly. "I was hoping we might have something different to eat tonight. Like fish."

"No! Apaches do not eat fish."

Alison was stunned by his answer and the force with which he said the words. "Why not?"

"Because they have spots."

"What does that have to do with it?"

"Long ago, when my people first contracted your white man's spotted disease, they went into the rivers to cool their fevers and died there. Since then, Apaches will not eat fish."

"But that's ridiculous! Do you think the disease invaded the fish?"

"That is our belief."

Alison couldn't believe her ears. Ramon was too intelligent to place credence in such foolishness. "If I should go in that river to bathe, and you bathed after me, do you think my freckles would appear on you?"

Ramon's dark eyes drifted over Alison's beautiful face in mute admiration, then her curvaceous body. A slow smile spread across his face. "I am willing to risk it, providing we bathe together."

Alison glared at him.

Once again Ramon was forced to suppress his desire for Alison and pretend indifference to her spurning him. He shrugged, then said, "It does not matter if I personally believe or not. My mother died of the disease. I prefer not to eat something that reminds me of that."

Well, at least that was an explanation she could accept, Alison thought. She turned and picked up the beaver and her knife. As she walked away from the camp, Ramon called, "Be careful not the ruin the pelt. Beaver fur is good for lining moccasins in the winter."

Alison bristled and fought back the urge to throw the beaver in his arrogant face.

10

Ramon awakened Alison the next morning long before sunrise. She sat up and looked groggily around her, then asked, "Why do you want to leave so early? It's still dark."

"I want to be out on the desert when the sun comes up."

"But why?" Alison persisted, wanting only to lie back down and get a few more moments of sleep.

"You shall see."

As Ramon turned and walked away into the darkness, Alsion glared at his outline. His answer irritated her, for it seemed to be his favorite method of ending the conversation, vague words that seemed to be veiled with a half promise and a half threat that he never kept and which, for that reason frustrated her no end.

As they rode out on the desert a few moments later, the morning star was burning like a bright lamp in the eastern sky. Then, as the other stars faded from view, a pearl flush spread from crest to crest of the Sierra del Carmen in the distance, becoming peach-colored as the sun rose higher. The low-hanging clouds on the horizon took on a violet tinge, then turned salmon pink as the giant white orb topped the jagged peaks, spilling golden shards of light over the desert and making the night dew on the cactus and yuccas glitter like diamonds. The night that had been so quiet came alive with sounds as the desert larks joyously sang and a pack of coyotes howled, greeting the new day.

"That was the most beautiful sunrise I've ever seen," Alison said in an awed voice, still gazing out at the desert in wonder.

"It's always that way on the desert. Each sunrise seems more beautiful than the last."

That's what he had brought her out here to see, Alison realized, and this time he had kept the promise of his words. She *had* seen, and it had been well worth the wait. In truth, he couldn't have told her what she would see. It was a sight that was truly beyond description. She frowned, thinking that he was such a strange man. Who would have ever thought an uncivilized Apache would have such appreciation of the beauty of nature, particularly one as strong and manly as he? And yet he did. Once more, he had made a point of sharing something beautiful with her, presenting the spectacular sunrise to her as if it were a gift. Despite her animosity toward him, she was touched and said softly, "Thank you."

"Don't thank me. Thank the Great Spirit. He was the one who created it, not me."

His answer did nothing to dispel Alison's feelings. It was true God had created the sunrise, but it was Ramon, the man, who had shared the gift with her.

Several hours later they rode into San Carlos. The Mexican town was built on the site of an old, abandoned Spanish fort, and its crumbling walls were still in evidence. From the number of adobe homes scattered at random on the arid plain, Alison judged the town to be larger than Presidio. Over the flat, tiled roofs of the houses she could see the twin bell towers of the church. Alison and Ramon wove their way through the narrow streets, passing Mexicans on foot carrying their merchandise to be sold at the marketplace on their backs or transporting their fresh produce in little carts pulled by shaggy burros.

When they entered the edge of the square in the middle of the town, Ramon reined in, and Alison looked about her in amazement. She had never seen an open marketplace. Before her, in the bright sunlight beneath the towering walls of the church, were hastily constructed stalls where the Mexicans were displaying their products. In many cases the merchandise had simply been laid out on the ground on straw mats. Even more amazing was the wide variety of goods that were for sale: delicate silver jewelry, colorful pottery, leather goods, clothing, fresh vegetables, live chickens, pigs and goats, firewood, spices and red and yellow peppers, rounds of cheese, and cooked foods such as tamales and tortillas. In one stall only straw goods were sold: wide-brimmed sombreros, *huraches*, mats, dolls, and miniature animals. Staring at a straw toy that depicted a Mexican wearing a sombrero and serape riding a burro, Alison marveled at the maker's craftsmanship in being able to create something so lifelike out of something as simple as straw.

On the crowded plaza she spied a large fountain in the middle of the square. Was it her imagination, or could she actually hear the tinkling water beneath the hum of the crowd? Then, looking up at the elaborately carved facade on the church, she wondered who among these simple peons was such a talented sculptor and marveled at the time and toil that must have gone into etching those intricate carvings into that hard adobe. Here, in this little obscure town, was the Mexico she had come to see, a land where extraordinary beauty blended with stark simplicity. A tingle of excitement ran through her.

A sudden realization came to Alison. She was no longer in an Indian camp. These were Mexicans all around her, white people, like her. If they knew she was Ramon's captive, would they help her escape him? Briefly she wondered why this hadn't occurred to her before, why she hadn't realized from the very beginning that this trip would offer her the opportunity to escape. As precious as her freedom had become, she would have expected that possibility to be her first thought.

Spying a stall that sold women's clothing, Ramon nudged his horse with his heels. As the animal walked out into the square, Alison followed on her mount, looking about her excitedly and wondering who of all the people in the crowded plaza to appeal to for help. Then, as a sudden cheer came from the crowd, she jumped at the loud sound.

"*Viva* El Halcon! *Viva* El Halcon!"

She watched with amazement as the people of San Carlos greeted the Apache chief, waving to him and cheering, some even throwing flowers at him. While the Mexicans in Presidio had held the chief in respect and awe, it soon became apparent that the populace of San Carlos had a genuine affection for him, treating him as if he were a much-loved king, not just a blackmailing savage who offered them protection in exchange for their friendship. If Alison had entertained any secret hopes that she might enlist their aid in escaping him, they were quickly dashed to the ground.

Ramon accepted the people's adoration calmly, smiling benevolently and nodding now and then as he threaded his way through the excited crowd, acting as if their tribute was his right, something that irritated Alison no end. Even the *padre*, dressed in a brown robe and wearing long wooden rosary beads, rushed from the church to welcome him. No wonder the chief was so arrogant, Alison thought bitterly; everyone bowed and scraped to him, Apaches and Mexicans alike. Well, he'd never have her groveling to him, nor would he ever earn her respect, she vowed. He was nothing but a savage who wielded the fighting strength of his band over these poor people like a weapon. Surely if the Mexicans realized how he was using them, they would feel differently. Yet, deep down, Alison felt bewildered at the Mexicans' sincerity.

By the time they had reached the other side of the plaza, the people had settled down and returned their attention to the business at hand. Ramon reined in beside a stall where colorful skirts and embroidered blouses were thrown across strings strung from one side of the flimsy wooden structure to the other. As he dismounted, Alison followed suit, still feeling resentful at the Mexicans' tribute to him.

The old woman who tended the stall beamed at Ramon as he approached her, her dusky, leathery face creased as she smiled broadly up at him. To Alison's surprise, he smiled back—a genuine, friendly smile— then announced that he wished to look at some clothing for his captive.

He turned to Alison and said, "Pick out what you like."

In view of her renewed resentment toward him, Alison was tempted to tell him she had changed her mind. She didn't want anything from the arrogant bastard. But she was wise enough to know she would be spiting herself, to say nothing of raising Ramon's ire, if she refused his offer at this late date. Very aware of the old woman staring at her curiously, she stepped forward and picked up a skirt from one of the lines, then held it up against her. While the waistband looked as if it would fit, it was much too short, hitting her, like the faded Apache skirt, at her calves instead of her ankles. To her utter dismay, the same was true of every skirt she picked up.

Seeing Alison's frown, the old Mexican woman offered to sew a ruffle of the same material on the end of the skirts that she choose. Alison expected Ramon to say that wasn't necessary, that she was nothing but a lowly captive, but to her surprise, he agreed. Feeling relieved, Alison picked out a red and a dark blue skirt and handed it to the woman.

She turned her attention to the blouses. It was hard to make a choice, not because of fit, however, but because they were all so beautifully embroidered. She finally selected two and handed them to the woman.

"Is that all you want, just two of each?" Ramon asked.

Alison would have loved to have a bigger wardrobe, but her pride prevented her from saying so. It was bad enough that she was forced to accept this much from him. "That's all I need," she replied in a tight voice. "One to wear, and one to be drying for the next day."

Ramon stared at her for a moment, noting the proud tilt of her head and the obstinate set of her chin, and replied bluntly, "I think you are being stubborn again."

"I'm not being any such thing!" Alison denied hotly,

then added bitterly, "I wouldn't think a lowly captive could expect much more."

It was a good point. She *was* just a captive, and Ramon had vowed not to go to extremes in being kind to her. But Ramon found he wanted her to have more, and not because it might soften her toward him. Strangely, his feelings of generosity had nothing to do with his hopes of seducing her, a fact that puzzled him. Exasperated with both himself and her, he snorted in disgust, turned to the lines, and quickly chose four more blouses and skirts, tossing them to the old woman.

Aware of the astonished looks on both the women's faces and hoping to cover up his perplexing generosity, he said to Alison in a terse tone of voice, "I did not ride all this way to buy two outfits that you will quickly have in tatters from wearing so often. If we are to make the trip, we will make it worth our while, for I will not repeat this foolishness." Turning to face the old woman, he asked, "How long will it take to lengthen the skirts?"

"I'm afraid I will not be able to finish them all today," the woman answered apologetically. "Sewing on so many ruffles will take time, and my fingers are not as nimble as they used to be. But I can have them ready by tomorrow morning."

Alison fully expected Ramon to decide against purchasing so many, thinking that he would not want to be delayed that long on her behalf, but to her surprise, he was agreeable. After the old woman explained where the altered clothing could be picked up the next day, he walked to his horse and untied the Winchester that was lashed to the back of his saddle. Alison had wondered at the extra rifle and, as he carried it to the woman and offered it to her, realized that he had brought it along to trade for her new clothing.

A disagreement between the two followed. The old woman refused to take any payment, saying she wished to give the clothing to him in appreciation for all he had done for the town, but Ramon insisted upon paying. Seeing that she was getting nowhere, the woman then pointed out that the rifle was too costly to exchange for the clothing, but the Apache still persisted. To Alison's dismay, the old woman's entire male family joined in, a good dozen sons and grandsons drifting in from all over the plaza, all arguing that it was too much, and Ramon adamantly insisting that they accept it. Alison wasn't surprised when the Apache chief won the long, drawn-out argument. She had learned for herself how strong-willed he could be. But what did surprise her was his insistence upon paying. It didn't fit in with her image of him as a thief, nor as an arrogant man who accepted the Mexicans' tribute as his due.

As she and Ramon walked away, the Mexican family calling out "*Gracias*! *Gracias*!" Alison was still struggling to come to terms with this new side of himself Ramon had revealed to her. When he took his mount's reins and started walking back through the plaza, Alison did the same with her horse and followed, hardly paying any attention to where they were going as they wove their way through the maze of stalls. Finally, when they reached the other side of the plaza, she asked, "Where are we going?"

"To where my warriors and I always stay when we are in San Carlos, the old abandoned church."

The ancient church sat off to one side at the far corner of the plaza, one adobe wall collapsed and lying in rubble. After turning their horses over to a small Mexican boy to stable at the back of the church, they walked into what was left of the musty building. Half of the roof was gone, the sun shining in picking up dust motes that drifted in the air, and Alison discovered that there were others in the abandoned church. Mexican women cooked over the small fires they had built, while their small children played all around them.

"Do they live here all the time?" she asked, noting the piles of straw that were covered with blankets.

"No, they have come from outlying areas for market day and take shelter out of the hot sun here. While their husbands are tending to business, they cook and take care of the children. Many will spend the night here, so they can take part in the dance that always concludes market day, and go back to their homes tomorrow."

"Then every day isn't market day?" Alison asked in surprise.

"No, it's just one day out of seven. However, some of these people only come once a moon, or once every several moons. That's why it's such an adventure for them, and the whole family tags along if possible."

Ramon led her to a corner of the building and spread one of their two blankets down on the straw, then placed his rifle and second blanket on it. "That will reserve our place for tonight."

"What will we do until then?" Alison asked.

A slow smile spread over Ramon's face. "I could make a suggestion of what to do to occupy our time if all of these people were not here."

Alison's eyes flashed. "Can't you think of anything else?"

"No, not when you are around."

"Dammit, be serious!"

"I am serious."

When Alison just glared at him, Ramon sighed deeply and forced himself to consider her question of how they would pass the time. When he had come to San Carlos before it had been in the company of his warriors, for trading purposes. Sometimes they stayed overnight for the dancing and festivities, and sometimes not. If they had spare time during the day, they passed it by gambling with the Mexicans, or watching the cockfights that were held in dingy, smoky *cantinas*, or racing their horses against the Mexicans on the outskirts of the town, or just talking among themselves. He shrugged his broad shoulders, then found himself asking, "What would you like to do?"

The question surprised Alison as much as it did Ramon. Since when did the arrogant Apache care what she liked or didn't like? She stared at him for a moment, then, recovering, said, "I'd like to browse through the marketplace."

"Why? You have no money to buy anything."

"That doesn't stop me from wanting to look."

Ramon was reluctant to grant Alison her request. That was one of the reasons Apaches didn't bring their women with them when they came to trade. When they looked, they wanted, and often what they wanted were frivolous things to adorn themselves with. It seemed to be a woman's weakness, wanting things that had no practical value, things the Apaches could ill afford. Yet he had seen many a warrior trade his hard-earned plunder for some silly little trinket that would please his wife or sweetheart. Ramon scorned such men, thinking they were as weak as their women. Kindness was one thing, foolishness was another, and he had vowed that he would never become so smitten with a woman as to let her make a fool out of him. Then he remembered how he had just traded a valuable rifle for clothes for his captive. Hadn't he been doing the same thing? No, he told himself firmly. Clothing was a necessity. "I will not buy you anything else," he warned in a hard voice, as much for Alison's benefit as for himself.

"I didn't say I wanted anything else!" Alison retorted. "All I want to do is look. Is that too much ask? Or would you rather just sit around here being bored to tears until we can leave in the morning? At least it's something to do!"

It was a point Ramon couldn't argue. The thought of wiling away their time in this smoky building didn't particularly appeal to him either. "All right, we will browse, but nothing more."

As they walked through the marketplace, Alison surprised Ramon. He had expected her to ogle the feminine things, but she seemed to be interested in everything, stopping at all the stalls to admire their wares whether it be sombreros, or silver-studded saddles, or pottery, or gilded statues of the Madonna, or wheels of cheese, and asking delving questions on how they had been made. Even when they stopped at the jewelry stalls, she seemed to be interested only in how the Mexicans had been able to create such delicate silver filigree and where they had gotten the semiprecious stones, not showing any desire for obtaining the beautiful creations. Ramon found himself fascinated with her fascination and actually enjoying himself.

Throughout the day, as they wandered through the plaza, people in the food stands offered them things to eat: a handful of hot tamales, fresh-baked tortillas in which a spicy meat mixture had been wrapped, warm, sweet Mexican bread that contained a pumpkin filling, cookies sprinkled with anise seeds, slices of juicy melons, a brown sugar candy that had been rolled in chopped pecans and was so sweet that it made Alison's teeth ache. She noted that the Mexicans didn't seem to expect any payment, nor did Ramon offer any. Apparently, offering their food was yet another tribute they afforded him.

Toward dusk, when the church towers were casting long shadows over the square, the Mexicans started dismantling their stalls and loading up their wares. Ramon and Alison returned to the ruins of the old church and sat on their blanket in the corner of the building, watching the Mexicans eat their evening meal. Again they were offered food, which Ramon declined, saying they had already been fed. Alison didn't object to his refusing. She felt stuffed from all she had eaten.

A Mexican man wandered over to them and offered Ramon a thin, black cigar. Alison was surprised when he accepted it and the light, for she had never seen him smoke any of the wild tobacco that the Apaches used. She watched as he leaned back against the wall and smoked, his long legs crossed before him. At that moment he looked more Mexican than Apache, despite his earrings and headband. Yes, he really was a very attractive man.

Alison wasn't the only female in the church who was very aware of the Apache's strong masculine appeal. Several *señoritas* walked past them, casting inviting looks in his direction and swinging their hips provocatively, totally unconcerned that he was in the company of another woman. Apparently they didn't consider a lowly captive of any consequence. Their attitude infuriated Alison. How dare they brazenly flirt with him in front of her, and how dare he smile back at them! A raw jealousy consumed her, and she glared at the bold women.

Ramon was very aware of the daggers that Alison was

shooting at the young women. She cared enough to be jealous, he noted, but still persisted in keeping him at bay. Why did she have to be so obstinate? Why couldn't she accept him as a lover, and nothing more? That was all the *señoritas* wanted or expected. *Dios,* she was an exasperating—if irresistible—woman! He hoped when he finally seduced her that it would prove to be worth all this trouble.

After the Mexicans had eaten, there was a mass exodus as they left the church ruins for the dancing in the square, leaving the younger children in the care of grandmothers. Through the high window above them, Alison could hear the musicians warming up. She rose and stood on her tiptoes, peering out at the plaza, which was crowded with excited Mexicans. Lamps had been strung across the open area, their lights blinking as they swayed in the evening breeze.

"Would you like to go outside and watch?"

Alison jumped at Ramon's voice. She hadn't even heard him rise and step up behind her, and he was standing so close that she could feel his warm breath fanning her neck. She turned, fighting off those peculiar feelings that always besieged her at his nearness. "Yes, I would."

He placed his hand on the wall to one side of her head and leaned into her. Alison sucked in her breath sharply at the feel of his hard male body pressing against hers. His black eyes bored into hers, and his mouth hovered over hers. "Perhaps, if you gave me a kiss, I would consent."

His words infuriated Alison. Her blue eyes flashed dangerously. "Your blackmail may work on these Mexicans, but it won't on me!"

Ramon scowled. "What blackmail?"

"The way you offer these people protection in return for their friendship. If that's not blackmail, I don't know what is!"

An angry look came across his rugged face. He stepped back and said in a tight voice, "No, it is the other way around. Because the people in this town are my friends, I protect them."

"The devil it is!"

His hand shot out like a striking snake and caught her arm. "Have you seen fear in their eyes? Do they cower to me?"

"No, but . . ."

"But what?"

"But they bow and scrape to you all the same. You'd think you were their chief, their king, the way they treat you."

"That is the peons' way of showing respect. It has been drilled into them for centuries by the Creoles, the aristocrats in this land. The peon is the lowest of the low, except for the Indian. He is at the very bottom of the social scale, next to animals."

"But you're part Indian."

"I am *all* Indian!"

Ramon glared at her. Then his expression softened. "I am not ashamed of my Indian blood, as they are. Every peon has some Indian in him. He will not admit it, except when he is drunk, but he and we know, and because of our shared blood, he trusts us more than the Creoles, but he still has trouble accepting our protection as a part of our friendship. He associates it with the upper classes, those with Spanish blood, and feudalism still exists here in Mexico. There are the serfs and the nobles."

"And you consider yourself a noble?" Alison asked in

a scornful voice. "You accept their adoration as your due?"

"It is true that I am not their chosen leader, as I am with my band, but they have still set me above them. To refuse this position would insult them. The Mexican peon is proud, despite the lowly position he has been put in."

"Then why did you insist upon paying for my clothes? You took the food they offered you."

"I will accept food from these people. I will accept lodging. These are things friends offer other friends. But I will not accept clothing for my captive. That is too much to ask of friendship from these poor people." He released her arm and stepped back, glaring. "Now, do you wish to watch the dancing or not?"

Alison walked to the door of the church, perplexed by Ramon's words. He was an admitted thief, yet he didn't take more than he considered within the dictates of friendship from these Mexicans. And, to keep from insulting them, he wouldn't refuse their adoration. Apparently he had principles, principles that perhaps only he understood. This new insight into Ramon's character didn't set easily with Alison. It was much easier to fight off her strong attraction to him if she could convince herself that he had traits she disliked. But there appeared to be more to the Apache chief than met the eye.

When they entered the plaza, the dancing was already going on as the Mexicans performed their traditional hat dance. The couples danced with the man's sombrero laying on the ground between them, and Alison got the impression that it was a courtship dance of sorts, one partner turning his or her back and showing indifference while the other partner wooed, then reversing their positions, until at the end when they faced each other, furiously stamping their feet to the throbbing beat of the guitars and the women swishing their colorful shirts provocatively.

Long into the night, beneath the glittering stars and swaying lamps, the Mexicans performed their spirited folk dances, and Alison marveled at their endurance. Their dancing seemed to be more than just enjoyment for enjoyment's sake. It seemed to be a means of releasing their hot-blooded emotions, for there was a wild, uninhibited quality about every dance. Even more amazing were the glorious sounds that the musicians coaxed from their guitars and trumpets. She had never heard such stirring, exciting music, music that seemed to send her blood racing through her veins and made her all the more aware of the electrifying man standing next to her.

When the dancing stopped, Alison felt a keen disappointment. As the Mexicans started walking back to their homes and those that were staying overnight strolling arm and arm back to the church, she turned to Ramon and asked, "Do you ever dance those dances?"

"No."

"Why not? You're half Mexican."

"I am Apache! I have told you that over and over."

"Why do you deny your Mexican blood?"

"Because it is my white blood, and the whites are my enemies. They are treacherous and not to be trusted. My Indian blood is my strength. In spirit, I am a full-blooded Apache."

He turned and walked into the church. Alison stared at his broad back in confusion. How could he accept these peons as his friends if he hated his white blood so badly? Like him, they had mixed blood. He was the most baffling, contradictory man she had ever met.

She walked back into the church. When she reached their pallet, Ramon had already reclined. The blanket looked awfully small and their sharing it seemed much more intimate than their sharing his *wickiup*. She glanced around her, wondering if she could sleep somewhere else, but every available inch of space was taken up by the Mexicans.

Then she became aware of Ramon's dark eyes on her and of the amused curve of his lips. "What are you afraid of?" he taunted. "That I will seduce you in the night?"

When Alison didn't answer, he laughed and said, "Stop worrying. Your precious virtue is perfectly safe with all these people about."

As he had proven in the Apache camp, Alison knew Ramon would never make a spectacle of himself by making amorous overtures to her in public. She stepped over him and lay down. He tossed the blanket over them, and she jerked away, bringing a snort of disgust from him. She rolled as far from him as she could get, facing the adobe wall. But the distance she put between them didn't seem to help. She was acutely aware of the heat of his body and his heady scent. The combination of the titillating dancing and the stirring music and his exciting company had aroused her, leaving her with a yearning that was a physical ache.

Secretly, so secretly that she would never have verbalized it to herself, she wished they were alone.

11

Alison was rudely awakened at sunrise by the sound of the bells ringing in the church across the plaza from them. She sensed something drastically wrong, for the pealing was not a joyous sound—it had a frantic quality to it. Ramon had the same realization; he grabbed his rifle and sprang to his feet, and the women in the church began screaming hysterically, the shrill sound bouncing off the walls.

Alarmed, Alison jumped up and asked, "What's wrong?"

Before Ramon could answer, she was on her tiptoes and looking out the window he was peering through. "Get down!" he said sharply, pushing on her shoulder.

Horses' hooves were pounding on the cobblestones in the plaza, and gunshots were heard. "What's going on?" Alison asked. "Who's doing that shooting?"

"We are being attacked by bandits."

A bullet hit the edge of the window, sending broken pieces of adobe flying everywhere. Ramon grabbed Alison's hand and, keeping his head low, pulled her away from the window. She looked around her. Pandemonium reigned in the small church. Women were screaming and children were crying in terror, while the men rushed about in confusion, their faces ashen.

"Stop that screaming!" Ramon yelled out over the loud noises.

To Alison's surprise the women stopped, so suddenly it was almost as if someone had turned off a spigot. "Tend to your children," Ramon said in a stern voice. "All that hysteria is just frightening them more."

As the women turned to their terrified children, taking them in their arms and trying to soothe them, Ramon said to the men, "Those of you who have guns protect that crumbled wall, the rest man the doors and windows."

A few of the men ran off to do as he had commanded, but most remained where they were, and Alison realized that they had no weapons. "What are you standing there for?" Ramon demanded. "You can throw rocks, can't you?"

"But we can't fight them off with rocks," one man objected.

"I do not expect you to fight them off. Just keep them out of this church and in the plaza. I will do the rest."

He rushed to a stairwell filled with rubble. Alison followed, calling out to him as she ran after him, "Where are you going?"

Ramon turned at the bottom of the stairs and answered, "To the old bell tower. You stay here, and keep your head down!" He leaped over the pile of rubble and sprinted up the crumbling stairs, leaving pieces of broken adobe bouncing down the stairs in his wake.

Alison peered up the shadowy stairwell, but could see nothing of Ramon. The only sign of his recent presence was a thick cloud of adobe dust that floated in the narrow passageway. Despite his orders, she was tempted to follow him. She would feel much safer up there with him than down here with these virtual strangers.

Deciding against it, she turned and walked to one wall where the women were cowering with their children and hunched down beside them. Soon the church was filled with the sounds of gunshots, both from the bandits outside and the men firing their ancient muskets inside. Gun smoke floated in the air, stinging their eyes and making them cough. Babies cried and children whimpered, while women mumbled fervent prayers on their rosary beads. Alison glanced up at a small, chipped statue of the Madonna that was sitting on a pedestal beside her, thinking that the Lady's serene expression seemed out of place among all this violence. The Mexicans' fear was so strong it was almost palpable, and Alison could swear that she actually smelled it.

A man at one of the windows was hit. He flew back from the impact of the bullet and collapsed on the straw, blood pouring from the gaping wound on his chest. A woman screamed, the piercing sound reverberating in the church, then pushed a toddler from her lap and ran to him, hovering over her husband and begging him to speak to her. Then as she began to sob pitifully, Alison felt tears of compassion coming to her eyes.

"Madre de Dios," someone muttered.

"We will all die," another mumbled, clutching her child to her bosom.

Another man at the wall was killed, for there the bullets seemed to be coming in a steady stream. "What do they want in here?" Alison asked. "There's nothing to steal here."

"But there is," a young woman answered. "The pesos we made yesterday."

"Pesos? They'd kill for pesos?" Alison asked in shocked disbelief.

"They kill for fun, for the power it makes them feel," an old woman answered bitterly.

"And we are here," another young woman pointed out in an ominous voice.

They'd rape them? Alison thought, a horror filling her. What kind of men were these that they would violate the sanctuary of a church in such a manner? Even if it was abandoned, it had once been a holy place.

She came to her feet, crept over a window, and carefully peered out. Through the drifting smoke she could see that the plaza was littered with dead: dead peons, dead bandits, dead horses. Other bandits, with bandoliers strapped across their chests and wearing huge sombreros with coins sewed to their brims, raced their horses around the plaza, shooting at the Mexicans in their houses. Across the square, Alison saw a mean-eyed bandit with a fierce, curved mustache shoving a young girl from her home. When her half-crippled grandmother tried to stop him, he pushed the old woman to the ground, shot her dead, then laughed at the horrified expression on the young girl's face. Bile rose in Alison's throat, and she clamped her hand over her mouth while she fought it down. She had never seen killing, much less the senseless carnage she was witnessing. Why, they were nothing but animals!

A shot rang out above her. To Alison's immense satisfaction, the bandit who had cold-bloodedly killed the old woman fell beneath the bullet. Then, hearing another shot coming from the same direction and seeing another bandit fall, she realized that it was was Ramon shooting from the bell tower. She watched as he systematically picked them off, one bandit, two, three, four, then gasped in fear when she saw the bandits riding toward him en masse, their guns all aimed at the tower. The roar of their guns made her ears ring as they blasted the tower, and without even thinking, she screamed, "No!"

Her scream drew the attention of one bandit, and Alison barely had time to duck the bullet he fired at her. She sank limply to the ground and leaned weakly against the wall. Ramon was dead, she thought. He had to be! No one could have survived that hail of bullets. She stared into space, so stunned that she was beyond any emotion.

The bandits were attacking the crumbled wall in force now, riding their horses down on it like a wave. Terrified at what they saw coming toward them, the Mexicans deserted their posts and ran. Then suddenly, so fast it seemed a blur to her eyes, Alison saw a man darting from the stairwell and running to the crumbled wall. But despite his speed, she knew it had to be Ramon, for she had seen the bright red headband as it flashed by. A profound relief filled her.

The Apache chief threw himself down behind the rubble and let go with a scathing fire, furiously pumping the lever on his Winchester. Not one shot missed its mark. He mowed down the first wave of bandits, and the second wavered. Encouraged, the Mexicans who had run hurried back, firing their old muskets and cheering at the tops of their lungs. Their action drew the bandits' fire from Ramon, and gave him time to reload. As he emptied his rifle the second time with deadly expertise, the bandits turned their horses and fled.

The Mexicans went wild, cheering and slapping one another on the back, and almost beating Ramon to death in their elation. Women sobbed in relief, or laughed hysterically, or did both. Soon the sounds of the bells victoriously pealed in the church across the square, adding to the spontaneous celebration.

Alison could hardly believe it was all over. The end had come so fast, so unexpectedly. Then she saw Ramon looking over the heads of the Mexicans crowded around him, scanning the church. When he spied her, their eyes locked and held for a long moment. Alison knew she might regret it later, but she smiled at him and her eyes sparkled. She had never been so happy to see anyone in her entire life, and she was so proud of him. Then, as if her legs had a will of their own, she was running toward him.

Ramon shoved his way through the crowd to meet her and took her in his arms. They came together with an impact that knocked the breath from both of them. Ramon kissed her long and hard, each sensuous stroke and swirl of his skillful tongue an affirmation that they had both survived the attack and were vitally alive. Alison leaned into him, glorying in the feel of his hard body against hers. When he broke the kiss, Alison was breathless and weak-kneed, and it took a moment for her to realize what she was doing. She pushed away and stepped back from him, staring at him as if she were horrified by what she had done.

A look of disappointment passed over Ramon's face, before he quickly hid it. "For a moment there, I thought you were happy to see me."

She had been more than happy, Alsion realized. She had been ecstatic. But she couldn't admit that. Nor could she totally deny it. "I was relieved to see you were alive," she admitted.

"Why?"

"Because . . . because I would not want to see you dead."

"I thought you hated me."

"Not that much."

To Alison's surprise, her answer seemed to please him. He smiled, a smile that warmed her to the tips of her toes. Then he turned to the man who was tugging on his shirtsleeve in an effort to catch his attention. He waited patiently while the gray-haired man praised and thanked him at length. Alison wondered who the man was, for he was dressed in a crumpled suit, not the white tunics and pants that the peons wore.

When the man had finished, Ramon asked him, "Where did those bandits come from?"

"It is rumored that their camp is in the Sierra del Carmen."

"Have they attacked you before?"

"No, but they have attacked several nearby villages."

"They will not bother you again."

The man didn't seem to doubt Ramon's promise for one second. He thanked the Apache again profusely and then turned and walked away.

"Who is he?" Alison asked.

"The mayor."

Even the mayor came out to thank him, Alison thought in surprise. But then, Ramon deserved it. He had turned back the attack practically single-handedly. No wonder these people held him in such high regard. And Alison had to admit to a grudging admiration for the way he had handled things. She had never seen anyone so cool and decisive, or so brave. If he was always that way under fire, she could understand why the Apaches had chosen him for their leader.

But these were thoughts that Alison kept very much to herself.

Ramon helped the Mexicans clear the plaza of the dead. When the gruesome job was finished, he and Alison saddled their horses and rode to the old woman's house to pick up her new clothing. Alison noted that there was none of the cheer and elation that the Mexicans had shown when the bandits fled. The entire town was now in mourning, and more than one door had a black wreath hanging on it.

Thankfully the old woman's didn't. She greeted them warmly and insisted that they eat with her and her family before they departed. Ramon accepted graciously, and throughout the meal Alison was acutely aware of the open adoration in the Mexicans' eyes, from the youngest wide-eyed child to the oldest, bent grandfather. There was something else there too. Pride that their idol had honored them by accepting their invitation, and this time Alison couldn't summon up any resentment. Ramon had earned their respect and gratitude that day.

When they had finished eating, the old woman insisted that Alison wear one of her new outfits. Again, Alison expected Ramon to object to the delay, and again he surprised her by agreeing. The old woman rushed her to a small bedroom where she could change, and Alison quickly slipped on the new clothes. It was amazing what they did for her spirits. For the first time in two months, she felt womanly and pretty, instead of awkward and gangly. Then to her surprise, the old woman gave her a pair of *huraches.* Alison felt a little embarrassed, for she knew the woman must have noticed her pitifully sewed moccasins, then feared the straw sandals wouldn't fit, which would be even more embarrassing. To her amazement they did, and Alison realized that the woman had deliberately picked out a pair of men's sandals to fit her long feet.

"*Gracias,*" she said, knowing that the woman would know what she meant and thankful that the Mexican hadn't given them to her in Ramon's presence. It was bad enough that he thought her too tall and skinny without having him criticizing the length of her feet too.

"*De nada,*" the old woman answered.

When Alison stepped back into the outer room, she was startled at the look Ramon gave her right in front of the old woman and her family. His dark eyes slid over her body with pleasure and naked desire, and Alison would have crawled in a hole if she could have.

The old woman handed Ramon a package wrapped in a straw mat, and Alison assumed that it contained the rest of her new clothes. After thanking the family for their hospitality, something that stunned Alison, for she hadn't expected the fierce chief to be capable of such good manners, Ramon tied the package to the back of his saddle, and they mounted their horses.

As they rode off, Alison said in an angry voice, "You are the rudest, crudest man I've ever met."

He sliced her a surprised look. "What brought that on?"

"I'm talking about the way you looked at me back there. It was humiliating in front of all those people."

"I was just admiring your new clothes."

"The devil you were! There's a big difference between admiration and lust!"

"Sometimes it is hard for a man to separate one from the other." His voice dropped to a husky timbre. "You are a very beautiful woman."

Alison allowed herself a moment to bask in the warm glow his compliment gave her.

"And a very desirable one."

The mention of desire was his undoing. Alison bristled. "You can save your breath. Compliments won't get you anywhere. I'm not so stupid that I don't know that's just another trick of yours to try to seduce me."

At the moment, Alison did indeed look very beautiful with her extraordinary eyes flashing like blue fire. Ramon knew there was a deep passion in her, one that matched her fiery temper, a knowledge that only made him want her more. *Dios,* she was an exasperating woman! He offered her compliments, something that he had never done with any other woman, and she threw them back in his face. She couldn't be forced and she couldn't be wooed. What did she want from him?

Three hours later, when they were nearing their crossing at the border, Ramon suddenly spied a line of riders coming down on them from that direction. He glanced around quickly, then turned his horse sharply to the right, dug his heels into the animal's flanks, and called out to Alison, "This way! Quickly!"

Alison didn't have any choice but to follow as he galloped off at a furious pace. She glanced over her shoulder, but could hardly see the riders following them for the thick cloud of dust their own horses were kicking up. But she did know one thing. There were an awful lot of them, fifty or more.

"Who are they?" she called across to Ramon when her horse finally came abreast with his. "The bandits that attacked us this morning?"

Before Ramon could answer, Alison heard a blood-curdling howl, a terrifying scream that made the hair stand up on the back of her neck.

"Comanches! *Mexican* Comanches!" Ramon yelled back.

The knowledge that they were being chased by a band of howling, bloodthirsty savages who were the Apaches' ancient enemies galvanized Alison, for she was in the company of an Apache chief and she knew that boded her no good. Whatever horrible fate they had in mind for him, she would share. She urged her horse to a greater speed.

It was the wildest ride Alison had ever taken. They raced their horses over the arid plain, flying across deep arroyos and careening around piles of rocks and clumps of cactus, her long skirt whipping about her legs. The heat generated from her mount combined with that of the searing sun, and sweat streamed from her. Then, over the sounds of their horses' pounding hooves and the Comanches' nerve-wracking howls, she heard the sharp cracks of rifles being shot. She clenched her teeth, expecting to feel a bullet slamming into her back at any moment.

Ramon glanced over his shoulder and saw that the Comanches were gaining on them. He knew then that they couldn't possibly make it to the next crossing farther downstream. Again he veered his horse sharply, this time to the left, knowing that was the only avenue of escape left for him and Alison.

At the edge of a deep canyon he brought his horse to an abrupt halt and flew from the saddle. Seeing Alison's horse rearing at her sudden stop, he dodged its flying hooves and grabbed the animal's cheek strap, forcing it down. As he lifted Alison from the animal's back, she asked, "Why are we stopping?"

"We won't make it to the next crossing."

He took her hand and raced to the edge of the canyon. As they ran, Alison could hear a distinct roar. When they reached the rim, she looked down. What she saw terrified her: a deep, hundred-foot drop between solid walls of rock, and at the bottom, the river frothy white with wild, treacherous rapids.

"Jump!" Ramon commanded.

Alison decided that she would rather take her chances with the Comanches than jump into that. Why, it would be sheer suicide. If she didn't get killed by dashing herself against the jagged rocks jutting up from the river, she would drown in that violent, churning water.

"No! You're insane! We'll be killed for sure!"

Ramon heard the bullets whizzing past them and felt them kicking up dirt all around them. "Jump! It's our only chance!"

"No, I—"

Alison never got to finish her sentence. Ramon leaped into the chasm, jerking her with him, and Alison felt herself flying through the air, her long shirt ballooning up around her and the wind rushing past her. The drop seemed an eternity to her, even though she could see the churning water coming up at her. She was looking death in the eye, she thought frantically, and she was helpless before it.

She hit the water with a loud splash, the impact tearing away Ramon's grasp on her hand. Down and down she went, tumbling over and over in a world of frothy white. Desperately she tried to right herself, to fight her way to the surface, but her strength was a weak, pitiful thing against the power of the churning water. Her lungs felt as if they would burst, and a red haze fell before her eyes. Then, from somewhere, she felt a hand grasp her wrist, pulling on her.

Suddenly she surfaced and found herself surrounded by thrashing white water, the walls of the narrow canyon looming up on each side of her so that all she could see was a narrow band of blue sky. With the water slapping her in the face, she could see no sign of Ramon. The only way she knew he was nearby was by the steel band of his hand around her wrist.

The current swept her downstream, the walls of the canyon flying past her, the water tugging on her legs and twisting and turning her as if she were limp rag doll. Terrified that it would suck her beneath its surface again, she jerked on her arm, but Ramon's grip on her wrist held firm. "Let go, so I can swim!" she called out frantically, furiously paddling her free arm.

"No!" His voice came back to her, sounding far away over the roar of the rapids. "Do not fight it! Let the current carry you!"

Alison found that she really didn't have any choice. She was at the mercy of the angry water. She was helpless against its tremendous power. It tossed and turned her, flung her against sharp rocks, pounded at her, dunked her, then brought her once again to the surface, spitting out water and gasping for breath. Her heart raced; she had never been so terrified in her life.

Only once during that wild descent down the river did she spy anything of Ramon, and that was just a brief glimpse of his dark head bobbing in the agitated water before her. Then she heard a howling over the roar of the rapids. My God, she thought, had the Comanches

followed them down river? Had all this been for nothing?

Then she realized that it was a wind, a tremendous
wind that was trying to push them back upriver. The
water whipped this way and that as the two forces of
nature fought one another, and she was caught in the
struggle between the river and the wind.

She felt Ramon release her wrist, then heard him yell
over the deafening noises, "Now swim! Swim down-
river!"

Alison paddled her arms and kicked her feet furiously. If she was making any headway, she couldn't tell
it. Waves as big as those in a surf hit her, washed over
her, trying their damnedest to push her back. Still, she
tried valiantly, putting every ounce of strength she had
into it. Exhaustion overcame her, and a hopelessness
invaded her. She couldn't fight it any longer. It was
futile. She was going to drown in this damn river.

She was so exhausted and dispirited that she didn't
notice she had passed the bend in the canyon, or that it
widened, or that the current was again sweeping her
downstream. She didn't even notice the absence of
rapids, nor did she see the hands reaching for her.

As Ramon pulled her to him and she felt something
graze her knees, she realized he was standing in the
river with the water swirling around his hips. She
looked around her in a daze, seeing that the river had
pushed them to one side and that the canyon was much
wider and the walls not nearly as high. He brought her
to her feet, but Alison's legs were too weak to support
her. Her knees buckled. He swept her up in his arms
and carried her to a narrow, sandy bank, laying her on
it, then collapsing in exhaustion beside her.

For a long while there were only the sounds of their

rapid breaths over the roar in the distance. Alison was too tired to move, and every muscle in her body ached from where the water had pounded her. She was too exhausted even to close her eyes against the bright sunlight, and she was only vaguely aware of the stinging of the scratches all over her body where she'd been cut by the sharp rocks.

The first thing that recovered from her traumatic experience was her mind. She had come to Mexico for adventure, she thought, and in the last twenty-four hours, she had survived a bandit attack, had been chased by Comanches with bullets whizzing all around her, had taken a death-defying leap into a deep chasm that was more rocks than water, and had ridden for miles down dangerous, treacherous rapids that should have, by all rights, drowned her. She'd had enough adventure in one day to last her a lifetime, and she had the savage next to her thank for it. Remembering how he had given her no choice but to jump in the river, a sudden anger seized her.

She rolled to her side and propped herself up on her elbow, glaring down at him. "That was an insane thing to do!"

"What?"

"Jump into those dangerous rapids! We could have been killed!"

"We would have been killed if we had stayed where we were," Ramon answered calmly.

"At least it would have been a quick death," Alison retorted. "Instead I died a thousand deaths out there in that crazy river."

"You are still alive, and you still have your scalp. If I had it to do over, I would still take the risk. I would prefer death in the river to having my body mutilated and my scalp paraded through some town for the Mexicans to ogle."

"What are you talking about?"

Ramon sat up before he answered. "Those Comanches were scalp hunters, Indians that do nothing but hunt down other Indians for the bounties the Mexican government pays for their gruesome trophies," Ramon answered in a voice dripping with scorn. "After a successful raid, the entire tribe marches through town showing off the scalps they have taken. The Mexicans even provide them with a band."

Alison remembered her uncle saying something about the northern Mexican states paying bounties for Indians' scalps. It seemed a barbaric practice. "But those scalp hunters are Indians too. What's to keep the Mexicans from taking their scalps?"

"They have an arrangement with the government. They will seek out other Indian tribes and kill them for amnesty, and of course for the money the government pays for their scalps," he added bitterly. He laughed harshly. "The Mexican officials are fools. They do not know that the bounty hunters bring them more Mexican scalps than Indian. The peons are much easier prey, and the scalps all look alike."

Alison was horrified to think that innocents were killed along with the guilty. But then just what were the Indians guilty of? Protecting their right to the land they had inhabited for centuries before the white man came? Was that a crime that justified genocide, for surely that was the Mexican government's intention, to wipe out the red race totally. And why did members of that race cooperate with them? "Do some Apache tribes do this too collect scalps for bounties?"

"No, very rarely do Apaches take any scalps, and then

only of their most hated enemies for ceremonial purposes. As soon as the ceremony is over, the scalps are destroyed and the warriors who took them cleansed in smoke. We have an aversion to mutilating the dead."

Well, at least the Apaches had some redeeming qualities, Alison thought. And now she was glad they had taken the risk of jumping in the river. If she had to die, she preferred to stay in one piece.

She looked down at herself and saw that her new clothes were in tatters and that her sandals had been ripped from her. She was in even worse shape than she had been, for she was back to being barefoot. And now her other new clothes were in the hands of some barbaric scalp hunter. The entire trip and everything they had gone through had been for nothing. She felt like crying, but instead laughed hysterically.

Ramon shot her a startled look. "What are you laughing at?"

"Me. Look at me! I look even worse than before."

"They are just clothes. Mine are in tatters too."

But you have others, and I don't, Alison wanted to scream at him. Then she felt a twinge of self-disgust. She should be glad she survived, instead of bemoaning her lost clothing. "Yes, I suppose you're right."

Ramon's eyes swept over her again, this time more leisurely, then locked on her breasts. The wet, clinging material hid nothing from his view.

Seeing him staring at her chest, Alison glanced down and was horrified by her near nudity. She raised her arms to cover herself.

Ramon's eyes rose and met hers. Alison sucked in her breath. They were blazing with desire.

As he caught her shoulders and pushed her back on the sand, Alison cried out frantically, "No!"

Her objection was smothered by his mouth. His kiss
was hard and demanding, then coaxing and wooing,
then demanding again, switching back and forth from
furious ardor to tender seduction so quickly that Alison
was left reeling in confusion. He settled his body down
on hers, half covering her, and Alison gasped at the feel
of her breasts pressing against his bare skin where his
shirt had been torn open. She could feel his necklace
dangling between the valley of her breasts, the turquoise stone as cold as ice against her suddenly flushed
skin.

His tongue shot into her mouth, as sure as a bullet. As
it slid in and out and around in a sensuous dance, Alison
tried to steel herself against the sensations that were
flooding over her, but she was as helpless as a grain of
sand in a windstorm under the artful expertise of his lips
and tongue.

She was gasping for breath when he bathed her face
with soft kisses, then shivered in delight when he ran
his tongue down her neck. He stopped to sup at the
crook where her throat met her shoulder, his teeth nibbling ever so gently and sending waves of tingles rushing over her. As he pushed down the sleeve of her
blouse, the brush of his warm hand made her feel weak
with sudden yearning.

The world was spinning when he dropped soft kisses
on the rise of her breasts. Then as his head slowly descended, licking and nipping, Alison suddenly became
aware that her breasts had been bared. Alarmed, she
tried to push him away, but her arms felt heavy and
weak. Instead, she grasped his broad shoulders.

She felt his warm lips nibbling at one nipple and the
treacherous rosy peak rise to his attentions, and opened
her mouth to object. But all that came out was a low

moan from the back of her throat as his tongue swirled around the throbbing peak and she felt a rush of warmth to her loins. As his mouth closed over the peak and tugged on it, Alison was lost in a sea of confusion. His action shocked her, for she had never dreamed a grown man would do that to a woman, but excited her unbearably. When his hand cupped the other breast and began massaging it, she was awash in pleasure, and the aching between her legs grew until it was almost painful.

As his mouth left her breast, Alison muttered incoherently in protest, not wanting the wondrous sensations he had been invoking to end. She gasped at the feel of his earring trailing across her chest, then sighed when he took the other nipple in his mouth, each swirl of his tongue, each powerful tug of his lips sending thrills racing through her. She clasped the back of his head, threading her fingers through his thick hair, arching her back to give him even better access.

He shifted his weight, and Alison felt his hot arousal pressing against her thigh, the hard, searing flesh making a mockery of their clothing. Or rather his clothing. Somehow or another her skirt had gotten pushed up to her hips. She gasped as his hand slipped between her thighs and cupped her there. His touching her so intimately was like a bucket of ice water thrown on her heated senses.

"No!" she cried out, pushing him away with a strength born of desperation.

She sat up and quickly pushed her skirt down, then pulled up her blouse to cover her breasts, hating herself for letting him take such intimacies with her. Ramon watched her, seething with sexual frustration.

She looked over her shoulder and glared at him. "When are you going to learn when I say no, I mean it!"

He glared back at her. "You are still lying to yourself. Your mouth says one thing, your body another. You loved what I was doing to you."

"That's not true!" Alison denied hotly.

"You were moaning, pressing my head to your breasts, begging for more."

A flush of mortification rose on Alison's face. "No . . . no, I wasn't."

"You were twisting your hips, pushing yourself into my thigh. But it was not my thigh that you wanted."

Had she done that too? Alison thought in horror. She remembered the terrible aching between her legs, an aching she was trying to assuage by pressing herself against something. Oh, God! She had!

Her expression gave her away. "You see," Ramon said with just a hint of smugness, "you are not averse to my touch."

Alison knew to further deny it would only make her look foolish. "All right!" she admitted hotly. "So I momentarily succumbed to your seductive expertise. But it won't happen again!"

Ramon flew to his feet and asked angrily. "Why do you persist in denying us the pleasure we both want?"

"We don't both want it. Just you do!"

Ramon knew she was lying. He was torn between two conflicting emotions, his desire and his anger. One urged him to take her back in his arms and kiss her into submission, the other to throttle her. Neither would give way to the other. Finally he threw his hands up in utter frustration and thundered, "You are the most stubborn woman!"

With that, he spun on his heels and started rapidly walking away down the bank of the river.

Was he going to leave her here in this desolate country, completely abandon her? Alison wondered in panic. Had she tried his patience too far?

Then he whirled in his tracks and called, "Are you going to sit there all day?"

A wave of relief washed over Alison, to be quickly replaced with anger. "The arrogant bastard!" she muttered, coming to her feet.

As he turned and continued to walk down the bank, Alison followed, hating herself every step of the way, but knowing she really had no choice. In this harsh environment, he was her only means of survival.

12

As Alison followed Ramon down the sandy bank of the Rio Grande, she noticed that the canyon was getting wider and wider. Gradually the rocky walls gave way, and they were surrounded by a broad plain. Ramon veered from the river to a pile of rubble, ruins where a few cracked adobe walls were still standing.

When they reached the ruins, she sat down on a pile of crumbled rocks to catch her breath, rubbing one of her bare feet where the hot sand along the river had burned it. "What used to be here?" she asked. "A town?"

"It's what is left of San Vicente, another old Spanish fort. The Santa Rita crossing is just a little farther down the river, the crossing I was heading for when I saw the Comanches had cut us off from the Pass of the Chisos."

Alison looked around her. The Sierra del Carmen were red and blue and purple in the distance to her right, and across the river the mountains were copper-colored. She knew they had to be the Chisos, for she recognized several of their lofty peaks. She could have

sworn on their wild ride down the river that they had
traveled at least a hundred miles, for it seemed to take
an eternity, but they were still in Ramon's home territory.

"You wait here, while I go back to San Carlos to get us
horses," Ramon said.

"San Carlos is near here?" Alison asked in surprise.

"No, it is a good distance away."

"How far away? And don't tell me in time," she
added tartly.

He shrugged his shoulders. "About eighty miles. I
should be back by the early hours of the morning."

"Are you insane? You're going to walk eighty miles
and make the return trip in less than twelve hours?
That's impossible!"

"I did not say I would walk. I will run."

"That's still impossible!"

"For a white man, yes. But I'm an Apache. No Indian
can run as far or as long as we can."

He stripped off his torn shirt and tossed it down. "Do
not light any fires. In this desert, they can be seen from
far distances."

Alison didn't like the idea of staying out here alone,
particularly not with the Comanches and bandits somewhere in the area. "Wouldn't it just be simpler to walk
back to our camp? It can't be much farther from here
than San Carlos."

"Simpler for me, yes, but not for you. You would
never make it on your tender, white woman's feet."

With that he ran off, using a lazy, effortless lope that
was deceptive, and Alison was amazed at his speed.
Within minutes, she could barely see him. She remembered what Jacita had told her about the Apaches running up and down the mountains to strengthen their

legs and lungs. But to run eighty miles, across a desert, in the hot sun? It seemed an impossible feat for anyone. Then she remembered that this was Ramon, a man in superb physical condition, a man with amazing stamina who was inured to heat. If anyone could do it, he could.

Alison settled down in the ruins behind a wall that was still standing, in hopes that anyone crossing the desert would not be able to spy her there. The sun went down several hours later, turning the river rose-colored, then lavender. It seemed unbelievable that this serene stream was the same river that had been a raging monster back in that canyon. It was nothing short of a miracle that they had survived.

Despite her intense thirst, she waited until it was dark to venture from her hiding place and walk to the river for a drink. As she walked back, she wished she had something to eat. She was starving, but there was nothing growing around her but cactus, and the fruit on them, which Jacita had told her Apaches ate, was not yet ripe.

An hour later the moon came up, a huge golden ball that turned silver as it climbed higher and higher into the sky. Over the desert it was beautiful, bathing everything in a soft moonlight and making the yuccas stand out in bold purple relief. On the Chisos the moonlight turned the vegetation gray, giving the looming mountains a spooky appearance. Alison wondered if that wasn't why the white man called them the Ghost Mountains, rather than the way they seemed to float in the air.

She lay down and tried to sleep, but exhausted as she was, sleep wouldn't come. The ghostly mountains hovering over her and the coyotes howling mournfully played on her nerves. Every little desert noise seemed magnified: the rustle in the cactus made by a kangaroo rat, the scurrying in the sand made by a nocturnal lizard, the slight slide of rubble as a rabbit hopped through the ruins. Alison had never felt so terribly alone or so edgy in her life. Not even the soft murmur of the river could soothe her jagged nerves.

She finally dozed off, then awoke with a start when she head the crunch of pebbles. She looked up and saw a dark silhouette standing over her. She opened her mouth to scream, but no sound came from her throat. She was too terrified. Then, seeing the glitter of one earring in the moonlight, she sat up and said in a furious voice, "Damn you, Ramon! How dare you sneak up on me and scare me like that!"

"I didn't sneak up on you. If I had meant to do that, you would not have heard me. I walked up on you. What are you so jumpy about?"

Alison glanced around her. Her heart was still racing wildly from the scare he had given her. "I don't like being out here all alone," she admitted. "It frightens me. There could be anybody lurking around out there."

"There is no one in the immediate vicinity. I would not have left you if there had been."

"It was still frightening."

He knelt on one knee beside her and handed her a blanket. "Perhaps you have come to appreciate me, then, if only for the protection I offer you."

Alison refused to answer. She'd bite her tongue off before she'd admit how relieved she was to see him. She took the blanket and spread it out, then rolled up in it, for the night air in the desert was cool.

Ramon placed his blanket nearby and did the same. Almost as soon as his head hit the ground he was asleep, for his long run and hard ride back had taken its toll.

Beside him, Alison closed her eyes. Ramon was lying so close that she could feel his heat and smell his distinctive scent. But there was nothing threatening in his nearness that night. She felt safe and cared for with the powerful Apache at her side. Feeling that all had once more been set right in her world, she fell into a deep sleep.

They were up with the sun the next morning. The Chisos Mountains towered over them, hanging like a blue mirage in the early morning air, their bases shrouded in mist. Then she said in an excited voice, "Look, Ramon! Look at that mountain peak in the Chisos, the way the sunlight is hitting it. Why, it's almost as if the sun is pointing to it. It's all golden."

"It is the sunlight shining through the window that makes it look that way. There is a legend about that particular mountain, which we call Lost Mine Mountain. It is said there is a lost Spanish gold mine somewhere in it, and that if one stands in the ruins of the church here at San Vincente on Palm Sunday, the first shards of sunlight that hit that mountain mark the entrance to that mine. Of course, it is a ridiculous claim. How could it be true? Palm Sunday doesn't fall on the same day each year. But still, that does not keep the greedy gold prospectors away. Every year they come, looking for that lost mine."

There was an ominous tone in Ramon's voice that made Alison ask, "What happens to them? Do you kill them?"

"No, we don't have to. The Chisos kill them. Those white men can't survive up there without water, and only we know where the hidden water holes are. They can search until doomsday and they will not find that mine."

"Then it isn't just a legend? It really exists?"

"It's there. As are the bleached bones of the Spaniards that were left behind to guard it. But the gold seekers will never find it. We have sealed its entrance with rocks and boulders. We will not allow the white man to violate the Chisos the way they did the Sioux's Black Hills."

He turned and walked to where he had left the horses. Alison gave Lost Mine Mountain a last look and followed him, thinking it was best that the Apaches had done what they had. The gold the prospectors had brought out of the Black Hills had been the beginning of the end for the Sioux nation.

When she rounded the half-crumbled wall where Ramon and the horses were standing, she came to an abrupt halt, then said in surprise, "Why, those are our horses!"

"Yes, the Comanches' bullets frightened them so badly that they ran all the way back to San Carlos, still carrying my rifle and your clothes." He picked up a package lying in the rubble and handed it to her.

Alison couldn't have been happier to see the folded straw mat. She took it and hurried behind another wall to change, quickly untying the string that held it together. As she unrolled the blouses and skirts, she found her old Apache clothes in the middle. With a cry of gladness, she picked up her moccasins. As pitiful as they were, they did protect her feet.

She quickly changed into a new blouse and skirt, then slipped on her moccasins and laced them up, thinking if she had had them on the day before, the river wouldn't have been able to rip them from her. Perhaps the

Apaches knew what they were doing when they rejected the white man's shoes. Those straw sandals could never take the wear and tear that moccasins could.

She debated on what to do with her ripped Mexican clothes, then decided to keep them. Ramon had said he would not repeat the trip to buy her clothing, but had mentioned something about having some bolts of cloth. She could used the ripped clothing as a pattern to cut out new clothes when the others wore out, and perhaps by then her sewing would have improved.

She walked from behind the wall, carrying the folded straw mat with her clothes under her arm. Ramon shot her an admiring glance, but he was very careful to keep it brief. He didn't want his desire on the rise again, only to have it frustrated by her stubborn refusal to submit.

"I have cheese and tortillas," he said, motioning to the center of his blanket where he was sitting cross-legged. "As soon as we have eaten, we will leave."

Alison sank down on her heels across from him, her mouth watering as he cut a thick slice of cheese and wrapped it in a tortilla for her. The goat cheese was strong, but Alison thought it absolutely delicious. "It's a shame you don't keep a few goats," she remarked, "so you could make cheese like this."

"The Chisos are full of wild goats."

"Then why don't you do that, milk them and make cheese?"

"As I said, they are wild. You can hardly get close enough to shoot one, much less milk it. Besides, cheese is not Apache food."

"Neither are tortillas," Alison pointed out sharply.

"Tortillas are made from corn. Corn is Indian food."

"If you're starving, I shouldn't think it would matter!"

Alison answered in exasperation. "You eat roots and cactus, why not capture a few goats?"

"Those goats have wicked horns."

"For your information, those yuccas have wicked daggers too. If I can dodge them, I can dodge a goat's horns."

"Are you telling me you want me to bring you a goat?"

Alison quickly thought it over, then said, "No, several goats. You've got to have a billy and a nanny, to get milk."

Ramon cocked his head. "What is this billy and nanny you are talking about?"

Alison realized that she had been using American terms, but she didn't know what they were called in Spanish. A flush rose on her face. "A male and a female goat."

"Bring you a live male mountain goat?" he asked in disbelief. "That's impossible!"

"No, it isn't. You're just being stubborn!"

Alison rose and walked to her horse, muttering beneath her breath as she saddled her horse and tied her clothing to the back of the saddle. She couldn't understand his reasoning. The Apaches were forced to eat wild things to survive, and yet if they'd plant a few more vegetables than just corn and take advantage of available resources like goats, it would make things much easier on them, particularly the women, who had to work so hard to gather the things that nature grudgingly gave up to them. But then what did he care about how hard the women worked? He wasn't the one doing all that backbreaking labor.

They forded the river at the shallow Santa Rita crossing, then followed it downstream for a few miles. As

they turned their horses toward the mountains, Alison
spied a huge cornfield planted at the side of the river in
the distance, the golden tassels waving in the slight
breeze. "Does someone have a farm down there?"

"There's a small Mexican village down there where
people make their livelihood on those cornfields. Sometimes we trade with them for their corn and cache it in
caves in the mountains until we need it."

That must be where the bolts of cloth were, Alison
thought, for she had seen nothing of them, or any of the
other plunder Ramon brought back. "If there's a village
this close to your camp, why did we go all the way to San
Carlos to get my clothes?"

"It's just a village. They do not have a marketplace.
All they raise and sell is corn."

Alison looked about her. The flood plain was obviously very fertile. Why, probably almost anything could
be grown here. She shook her head in disgust, thinking
the Mexicans in that village were just as set in their ways
as the Apaches.

They passed a herd of golden pronghorns grazing on
the plain, and Alison admired the graceful, large-eyed
animals with their black horns and white rump patches,
thinking it was a shame to kill something that beautiful
only for their meat.

As they rode their horses into the mountains, Alison
glanced up, and on a ledge above her saw a huge,
shaggy animal with wickedly curved horns. My God,
she thought, if that was one of the goats Ramon had
been talking about, no wonder he said it would be impossible to bring one back alive. It was at least four feet
tall at the shoulder and had to weigh at least five hundred pounds. "Is that one of the goats you were talking
about?"

"That is a sheep," Ramon answered in disgust.

"Oh," Alison muttered, feeling very foolish.

"That is a goat," Ramon said, nodding to another ledge.

She looked up. The goat was larger than those she had seen in the marketplace and its horns were much longer, but . . . "It doesn't look all that dangerous to me."

"It is wild. A cougar does not look dangerous either, until you tangle with one. A wild animal will fight to the death for its freedom."

"Well, maybe if you captured some when they were young, they could be tamed."

"I am beginning to regret bringing back that cheese." His dark eyes bored into her from where he sat across from her. "I will not get you a goat, and that is final."

He kneed his horse and trotted it a few feet before hers. The lord and master has spoken, Alison thought bitterly, glaring at his back.

When they rode into the valley in the center of the mountains late that afternoon, Ramon got his usual reception, the Apaches all crowding around and welcoming him back. To Alison's surprise, she was greeted too, by Jacita and some of the other women who, unknown to Alison, had come to admire the white captive's determination and industry. As soon as she had dismounted, they circled her, admiring her new clothing, but when Alison offered to let them have her ripped blouse to use as a pattern to make them a cooler garment, they declined. Again, they were set in their ways.

The next day Ramon and two score of his warriors left the camp, and Alison didn't have to ask where he was going. She knew he was riding out to fulfill his promise to the mayor of San Carlos. She really wasn't worried about Ramon and his warriors being successful in their mission. If the bandits had run away before one Apache, they would certainly be no match against forty. But she found, to her utter disgust, that she missed the arrogant Apache's company.

One day, when she and Jacita were gathering wild grains, she asked the young girl, "What do Apache men admire most in a woman?"

"Do you mean their bodies?" Jacita asked bluntly.

A red flush crept up Alison's face. "Yes."

"Small feet. They judge a woman's beauty by how little her feet are."

Not their breasts, or their hips, or their legs? Alison thought in surprise. Then she remembered her long, narrow feet and was acutely conscious of how big they looked in comparison to Jacita's dainty ones. By the Apaches' standards of beauty, she was a total failure. That bastard! He *was* just feeding her meaningless compliments to seduce her.

When Ramon returned from his successful punitive raid on the bandits, he noticed a change in Alison, and it was not the change he had hoped for. Somehow or another, their relationship had seemed to slip backward. Alison was even more aloof, shooting him icy daggers if he got anywhere near her.

He stewed over her change for a time, then made a firm decision.

For several days Ramon was out of the camp, and Alison wondered at the peculiar glances the other Apaches were casting in her direction. Even Jacita acted strangely, giving her secretive little looks and smiling smugly. The Apaches' behavior set her nerves on edge.

Late in the afternoon of the fourth day, Ramon

walked into the camp wearing that damn indecent breechcloth again and leading his horse behind him. But as he came closer, Alison noticed something different. The breechcloth was elaborately beaded, as were dazzling white knee-high moccasins he wore, and he had replaced the usual red rag around his head with a beaded headband in which a large turquoise stone sat in the center of his forehead. Alison had to admit that he looked incredibly handsome, and all that white just made his sleek, bronzed body stand out all the more. She was acutely conscious of every rippling muscle.

Since he was dressed so impressively and every eye in the camp was on him, she assumed that a tribal ceremony was about to take place. But instead of stopping in front of the large *wickiup* that was used for tribal business, as she had expected, he walked straight up to her, and Alison was so stunned that she could only stare at him.

He held out his hand to her and asked, "Will you come with me? I have something to show you."

Alison couldn't believe her ears. It sounded more like a request than a demand. And she could hardly refuse, not with every eye in the camp on her.

Bewildered, she placed her hand in his, and as the warm fingers curled around her palm, she felt a little thrill. He led her to his horse, lifted her to his saddle, and mounted behind her. As they rode through the camp, she wondered at the grave expressions on everyone's face, then spied Jacita. The girl gave her a dazzling smile, which only confused her more.

As they rode through the window, Alison asked, "Why are you so dressed up?"

"This is a special day for me."

"Why? Is some ceremony going to take place?"

"Yes."

"When?"

"Later."

Alison thought perhaps he would tell her what ceremony, but he held his silence. Damn, he was acting as strange as the others.

As they weaved their way through a maze of paths, she asked, "What is it you wanted to show me?"

"A little secluded valley. Just be patient. You'll see."

When they emerged from a heavily wooded area and Ramon reined in, Alison's breath caught at the sight of the valley. Surrounded by towering ponderosa pines, it was covered with a lush grass in which wildflowers were sprinkled: orange caltrop, lavender-pink sweet william, bracketed paintbrush, looking like red flags among the grass, delicate, violet-blue day flowers, and pale yellow evening primroses. It looked as if nature had dipped her brush in every color on her palette and then sprinkled it over the meadow. Off to one side there was a small stream in which sparkling-clear water flowed around rounded stones and gurgled over flat ones in shallower places, and all around her were the majestic mountains, acting as powerful, silent guardians to the lovely valley.

"It's beautiful," Alison said in an awed voice.

"I'm glad you think so."

Ramon dismounted and lifted Alison from the horse. She walked out into the meadow, still admiring everything about her. Then, seeing a *wickiup* sitting beneath the thick boughs of two ponderosas at the edge of the grassy field, she stared at it in disbelief, for among the pine limbs that had been cut to cover it were flowers.

"Why is it decorated that way?" she asked.

"It is the *wickiup* a warrior builds for his bride."

"Who's getting married?"

"We are."

The calmly spoken words had a shocking effect on Alison. Speechless, she stared at him.

When she held her silence for so long, Ramon said, "I am a patient man, but I have grown weary of waiting for you to submit to me. I have taken you for my wife. You cannot refuse me now."

A sudden fury rose in Alison and erupted. "I didn't agree to marry you!"

"I am chief. I am affording you a great honor."

"I won't marry you!"

"We are already married. When you agreed to come with me to this place, you sealed our contract. In the eyes of my people, we are man and wife."

"You tricked me! I didn't know what I was doing!"

"Still, you are my wife."

"The devil I am!"

"Is that not what you wanted?" Ramon retorted, feeling his exasperation with her on the rise again. "A commitment? I have given to you what I have never even considered giving to another woman."

"But not out of love. Out of lust!"

"I told you in the very beginning that I desired you. Do not ask for love. That is something I can give no woman. To love someone means to give them your total allegiance. I have already made that commitment to my tribe, my people. In everything, they will always be first and foremost. I will protect you, care for you, do all the things a husband is expected to do for his wife. I am a good provider, and I can be kind. In return—"

"You don't have to tell me what you want in return! What you've always wanted. My body!"

When he remained grimly silent, Alison said, "You

promised me you wouldn't force me, and I won't submit."

"I will not have to force you."

He swept her up into his powerful arms, and Alison fought like a wildcat, kicking wildly and raking her nails down his face. Somehow, he managed to pin her arms between them, holding her so tightly to his chest that she feared he would crush her. She opened her mouth to sink her teeth into his shoulder. "Do not do that," he warned in a hard voice.

Alison thought better of it, and renewed her struggle, trying her damnedest to twist away from him. But to her dismay, her futile efforts only seemed to amuse him. He chuckled, and held her so tightly against him Alison felt the rumbling in his chest like a sensuous caress against her breasts.

He ducked beneath the blanket at the door of the *wickiup,* then stood. As he bent his head to kiss her, Alison jerked hers away. Not in the least perturbed, Ramon kissed the closest part of her—her neck—then ran his tongue slowly up to nibble on her ear. Alison felt that insidious warmth stealing over her and knew her body was betraying her again.

She turned her head back around, and Ramon's mouth swooped down on hers like the falcon he had been named for. Pinning her head between his shoulder and his neck, he kissed her long and hard, then teased and tantalized, his tongue running back and forth, back and forth over her lips, then supping at the ultrasensitive corners of her mouth until Alison was whimpering in frustration.

He dropped her legs, and Alison was shocked at how weak they were. But he didn't relinquish his tight hold on her, nor her lips. He took his time, his lips playing at

hers, his tongue darting out to lick one corner, then the
other, an incredible sensuous promise that left Alison
trembling like a leaf in a windstorm. Finally his tongue
slipped into her mouth, tasting her honeyed sweetness,
exploring all her recesses, before plunging in and out in
a passionate kiss that brought Alison to her toes and
practically begging for more.

His mouth still locked over hers, Ramon dropped to
the pallet on his knees, taking her with him. Deftly he
untied the drawstring at her neckline, then pushed the
blouse down, his hand cupping one soft mound.
Through a daze, Alison felt his fingers brush over the
crest, sending fresh tingles rushing over her. She tried
to object, to push his hand away, but her arms felt so
weak.

He lay her back on the pallet and gazed down at her,
his dark eyes blazing with the heat of his desire. "You
are my wife. Let me give you pleasure."

Alison was acutely aware of the bare skin on his chest.
Every time she took a breath and her nipples brushed
against those hard muscles, shivers of pleasure raced
through her. And his fingers softly stroking her neck
made her stomach flutter. When he tenderly kissed her
brow and then her temple, she knew she was lost. She
squeezed her eyes shut, and a tear trickled down her
temple.

"Why are you crying?" he asked in an astonished
voice. "I have not hurt you."

"Because I'm so weak. I can't fight you anymore."

A smile spread over Ramon's lips. "You will not be
sorry you submitted to me. I promise you. I will give as
much pleasure as I take. When it is over, we will both be
the victors."

It was a promise Ramon kept. He caressed her, stroking her arms, her sides, her breasts, his mouth dropping butterfly kisses over her face and shoulders. Slowly, ever slowly, his head descended, laving her breasts with his tongue, nipping the soft mounds until Alison thought she would scream if he didn't reach his ultimate objective soon. Her nipples were throbbing for want of his mouth. Then when he gave her what she wanted, his warm mouth closing over one turgid peak, she sighed in ecstasy and gave herself up to sensation.

When he unbuttoned her skirt and slipped it down, Alison didn't object. His hands caressing her stomach, her hips, brushing back and forth across her thighs, were as exciting as the magic of his mouth at her breasts. A delicious languidness invaded her. She felt only a brief tingle of alarm as his hand smoothed across the curls at the juncture of her thighs. Even when his fingers slid across her dewiness, gently exploring her most secret place, she couldn't rouse herself to object. She felt as if she were drowning in warm, thick syrup.

When Ramon found the throbbing bud he was searching for, stroking it with his fingers, Alison felt a whole new barrage of sensations attacking her. It seemed as if every nerve ending in her body had suddenly shifted to that part of her. A warm wetness slipped from her, and she felt as if her body had turned into a flaming torch, searing her clear down to the soles of her feet. Then the sweet ripples began, growing to powerful undulations that left her limp and her breath coming in ragged gasps.

When she recovered, Ramon was smiling down at her. "Did I give you pleasure?" he asked in a husky voice.

She wanted to deny it, but couldn't. "Yes."

"There will be more."

He kissed her softly, and Alison realized that they were both naked. When had he slipped off her clothes and his breechcloth and moccasins? she wondered. But her mind didn't dally over the question. All thought fled at the feel of his hard body pressing against her soft one, so male, so different from her own.

While he nuzzled her neck, her hands drifted over the powerful muscles on his shoulders and back, then slipped lower to tentatively brush across the rise of his buttocks. She heard his sharp intake of breath, and knew she was giving him pleasure. Then she became acutely aware of his manhood pressing against her hip. Bare of all covering, it seemed to sear her skin with its heat, and she could feel it throbbing. Instead of frightening her, this excited her. An answering throb began between her legs. She pressed her hip against his erection in a silent but eloquent plea.

He kissed her then, a deep, demanding kiss that gave free rein to his passion and sent both of their senses spiraling. Between the wild kiss, and the feel of his hands caressing and exciting her everywhere and his hot, male scent, Alison felt as if every nerve in her body were strung taut and on fire. As he left a string of searing kisses across her shoulders and breasts, the aching between her legs became unbearable. The feel of his scalding loins pressed against hers was driving her wild. She had to find relief. She had to!

"Please, oh, please," she whispered.

Ramon had been waiting for just that invitation. He had held his passion at bay with an iron will, determined that she would be willing when he took her. He positioned himself between her legs and slipped his hands beneath her buttocks, lifting her hips to meet his. As he entered her, he forced himself to go slow, steeling himself against the feel of her soft heat surrounding his rigid maleness. Then, feeling the barrier, he hesitated briefly before he plunged in.

Alison stiffened and gasped when she felt the sharp, stabbing pain as Ramon buried himself deeply in her. The soft cry affected Ramon more strongly than any distressed sound he had ever heard. He felt a strange, twisting pain in his chest. With a tenderness that he hadn't known himself capable of, he soothed her with caresses and whispered endearments in Spanish and Apache.

The brief pain that Alison had felt was replaced with a dull ache, and then something else: an awareness of him inside her, hot and throbbing, filling her completely. She hardly took notice of his caresses and soft, soothing words. Her full concentration was on their joining. The aching returned, seemingly throbbing in unison with his, almost as if their hearts were beating as one. She moved her hips tentatively in an effort to ease it, then moaned in pleasure at the electrifying sensation that small movement brought her.

Ramon smiled at her reaction and gave a slow thrust. Sparks danced up Alison's spine. As he began his movements in earnest, she clutched his shoulders, arching her hips and wrapping her long legs around him, pulling him deeper. She needed no tutoring as to the ways to move. It came to her instinctively, her passion driving her.

Ramon's mouth caught hers in a deep, fiery kiss. As he moved more rapidly, more urgently, his masterful strokes deeper, bolder, stronger, Alison felt herself spiraling higher and higher, her senses expanding, her heart pounding. She seemed to be racing upward to some lofty, unknown peak. A terrible urgency filled her, and an unbearable pressure began to build in her. She writhed beneath Ramon, her fingernails digging into his shoulders, as the strange tension grew, and grew, and grew to a frenzied pitch, and then burst in her brain in a blinding white flash, her body convulsing as wave after wave of ecstasy rushed over her. A split second later Ramon followed her to his own shattering release, exploding inside her and collapsing over her.

Alison drifted down from those rapturous heights slowly, as if she were floating on a cloud. Her first awareness was of Ramon's head lying on her breasts. She fingered the damp locks on his head dreamily, thinking she had never known anything could be as wonderful as what she had just experienced. And she didn't feel in the least defeated. She had received far more pleasure than she could have possibly given him.

Ramon rose to rest his upper weight on his forearms and smiled down at her, a warm smile that tugged at her heartstrings. "How do you feel?"

"Wonderful," Alison admitted.

"Did I not tell you I would give you pleasure?"

"Yes, but I never dreamed it would be like that."

"It will get better as we get accustomed to one another."

"It couldn't possibly get any better," Alison blurted.

"I have been told differently by others. They claim their lovemaking improves with time. You have a deep passion in you, but it has just been awakened. You have much to learn about lovemaking and I will teach you all I know. Then we teach each other. We will have many years together to nurture our mutual passion, a lifetime. We will work to perfect it."

He rolled to her side, then took her in his arms and placed her head on his shoulder. Lying in the protective circle of his strong arms, with his heartbeat drumming in her ear, Alison pondered over his words. He had made her his wife, a lifetime commitment that he apparently took very seriously. She knew now that he would never let her go. His fierce pride would never allow that. The world of the white man was closed to her for good. Her future lay in this world, with this powerful Apache chief, and she would be wise to make the best of it.

But Alison couldn't accept her marriage to Ramon quite that easily. It hadn't been an Anglo wedding, and she had not willingly given up her white heritage. On the other hand, she couldn't deny her growing feelings for him, feelings that had nothing to do with her strong physical attraction to him. But there were two very important things that marred the happiness she might have felt at Ramon making her his wife: He didn't love her, and he hadn't given her any choice. Again the Apache chief had trampled on her freedom, and she would never forgive him for that.

13

When Alison awoke the next morning, Ramon was gone from the *wickiup*. She stretched lazily, feeling absolutely glorious. Ramon had made love to her twice more during the night, and to her utter surprise, each time had been even more wonderful. Just thinking about all the exciting things he had done made her tingle all over. Despite a slight soreness between her legs, she wished he was there with her.

The thought shocked her. She would have thought her passion to be sated. My God, she was like a glutton who had been sat before a feast of sensual delights. She couldn't get enough. But she had to admit that his making her his wife and forcing the issue had taken a tremendous pressure from her. She had given him her body, and it would be pointless to fend off his advances any longer, particularly after the way she had wantonly behaved that last time. Her passion for him was as great as his for her, and she wouldn't sink to hypocrisy. Now she could relax and enjoy his lovemaking. As his wife, it was her due, and while she wouldn't allow herself to fall in love with him, she was going to love being married to

him—if last night was a sample of what their life together was going to be like.

She rose from the pallet and quickly dressed. Picking
up the leather bow that Ramon had removed from her
hair the night before, she stepped from the *wickiup* and
looked around her, thinking the valley, with the dew on
the grass glistening in the sunlight and the meadow-
larks singing their hearts out, even lovelier this morning
that it had looked the evening before.

Spying a movement in the woods across from her, she
saw Ramon walking from them, leading his horse behind him. She couldn't believe that this graceful, powerfully muscled, handsome man, this magnificent,
bronzed savage was her husband. A feeling of pride
swelled in her.

He stopped before her and smiled. "Good morning. I
trust you slept well."

He knew perfectly well she had slept very little, Alison thought. But she didn't feel in the least bit tired
from the lack. "Yes, after you left," she answered pertly.

Her answer brought a chuckle from him. "Is that a
complaint?"

A flush rose on Alison's face. "No," she admitted, "not
really."

Ramon was vastly relieved that she had accepted
their relationship. She was unpredictable. He had almost dreaded their first meeting this morning, for fear
he would find her cool and aloof again, and after their
passionate night together, he didn't think he could bear
going back to that. Storming her defenses was weary-
ing, even for an Apache chief.

He turned to his horse, and as he started removing
the *parfleches* that contained their clothing, Alison
asked, "Why did you bring those here?"

"Because this is where we will be living for the next two weeks."

"Here, alone in this valley?" Alison asked in disbelief.

"Yes. Apaches believe that a new husband and wife need a time of complete privacy to adjust to one another."

Alison found it hard to believe that the fierce Apaches believed in honeymoons, but the prospect of spending that much time in the exclusive company of this exciting man thrilled her. "So they can perfect their lovemaking?" she asked, then blushed at her own audacity.

"That is part of it," Ramon answered with amusement. "But there are other adjustments to be made too. Apaches generally marry when they are very young, hardly more than adolescents. Because of our strict courtship rules, they are still very shy in each other's company. This time gives them the opportunity to get to know one another better and feel more at ease."

A sudden, horrifying thought occurred to Alison. Had Ramon been married before, and had his wife died? He seemed to know an awful lot about lovemaking. A raw jealousy consumed her. She hated herself, but she had to know. "Have you been married before?"

"No," Ramon answered, her unexpected question momentarily taking him aback. "What made you ask that?"

"Well, you are older and . . ."

"And what?" Ramon prompted when her voice trailed off.

"Well, you do seem to know an awful lot about . . . lovemaking."

"Because I am older, I am more experienced than the ordinary Apache groom. I told you last night that I have been *told* it got better over the years. If I had been married before, I would have known."

Alison realized her question had been foolish to begin with. He was a man. Unlike a woman, he wasn't expected to remain pure until he married. She wasn't so naive that she didn't know the same was true with the white man. In a way, she resented his experience, hating the women he had given pleasure to, but in another way, she realized that his being a skillful lover had been to her advantage. At least she had one consolation. He hadn't loved those women either. And he hadn't wanted any other woman badly enough to make her his wife. She supposed she should be grateful for that. At least, he had set her above the others. But still, she wanted more. She wanted what every wife wanted, her husband's undying love, although she wasn't prepared to willingly give the same in return.

When Ramon stepped from the *wickiup* after placing their *parfleches* it it, he said, "We will eat beneath that tree over there by the stream."

Alison turned her mind to more practical purposes. "Is there enough firewood over there?"

"We won't need a fire. I brought back enough food to last us for a few days." Seeing her surprised expression, he said, "I told you. This is a time for the newly married couple to adjust to one another. You will not have to bother with cooking for a few days."

He removed a blanket and a sack of food from his horse and handed them to her. While she was spreading the blanket and laying out the food, he led his horse to the woods and turned it loose. As he sank down on the blanket beside her, she remarked, "These tortillas are still warm."

"Yes, Jacita cooked them and the rest of the food for us."

Alison remembered the girl's dazzling smile the day before. Jacita had known what was going to happen. Alison felt a twinge of betrayal, then realized that Jacita probably thought she knew what she was doing, that Ramon had asked her to become his wife and she had accepted. She felt a renewed twinge of bitterness at Ramon's high-handedness, then remembered the expressions on the other Apaches' faces. Jacita had been happy for her, but they hadn't all looked pleased.

"The tribe doesn't approve of you taking me for your wife, do they?" she asked in a tight voice.

Ramon shot her a sharp glance, then answered, "I would say my taking you for my wife came more as a surprise to them, and that they are withholding their judgment. I am their chief. Naturally, they expected me to choose an Apache woman."

"And certainly not a white-eyes," Alison said bitterly.

"The color of your skin had nothing to do with it. My father was a white, but he had been adopted into the tribe. He was a full-fledged member when he married my mother. You were still a captive, and a fairly new one at that. Your worthiness to become a member had yet to be proven."

"Then women can be adopted into the tribe too?" Alison asked in surprise.

"Yes, but it is not usual for a grown woman to be adopted. My father was still a youth when he was taken into the tribe. To be adopted you must accept Apache ways in all things, and that is difficult for an adult to do. But that is neither here nor there now. As my wife, you have become a full-fledged member."

He *had* honored her by making his wife, so far as to go

against the tribes' expectations of him, Alison realized. She knew now what she had seen in the Apaches' faces: doubt that she would prove herself worthy of her exalted position as wife of their chief. A fierce determination filled her. She would prove them wrong. It was something she would do both for herself and for Ramon, for surely he must have realized he would be gambling his esteemed position on her. If she failed, he failed, and she was determined she wouldn't let him down. Whatever happened, she wouldn't let him regret his decision. If she couldn't have his love, she would at least have his respect.

After they had eaten, Ramon suggested they bathe in the stream.

"You mean together?" Alison asked in a shocked voice.

"We were both naked last night," Ramon reminded her.

But that was in the subdued light of the *wickiup*, and then in the dark, Alison thought. This was broad daylight!

Seeing her reluctance, Ramon said, "We are man and wife. The whole purpose of this time together is to overcome any embarrassment between us, to make us feel at ease with one another under ordinary, everyday circumstances."

He stripped off his moccasins. Then as he stood to divest himself of his breechcloth, Alison averted her eyes. She heard the faint splash of water and risked a peek, seeing him wading into the stream. In essence, he wasn't exposing much more of himself to her eyes than he already had. The only difference was that instead of only half, she could see all of his taut buttocks, the powerful muscles flexing with each step he took. Remembering what they had felt like beneath her hands, rock hard and flexing in the same manner in the throes of their lovemaking, her mouth turned dry and a heat filled her.

When he was hip deep in the water, he turned to face her and asked, "Are you coming?"

Alison started, feeling much like the child who had just been caught with her hand in the cookie jar. She jerked her eyes away guiltily. She was acutely aware that he was waiting for her answer. "We don't have any soap," she replied as a delaying action. "I'll go back to the *wickiup* to get some."

"We don't need soap. We can scour ourselves with sand."

He was determined, wasn't he? Alison thought, feeling a twinge of annoyance. He was used to running around half naked, but she wasn't. Overcoming her inherent modesty wasn't going to be easy. "Would you turn your back, just this once?"

He gave his head a little exasperated shake, then turned away from her. As he began to scoop up sand from the bottom of the stream and wash his chest with it, Alison summoned her courage and stripped off her clothes, keeping her eyes glued on him suspiciously while she waded in. To her utter disgust, she discovered that he was standing in the deepest part of the stream. She had hoped that she could wade deeper and hide herself in the water. Then, glancing over at him and seeing his legs and buttocks clearly through the water, she knew she couldn't hide her nakedness. She had no choice but to endure this embarrassing situation.

It was the quickest bath Alison had even taken. She waded back out and quickly donned her clothes, her back to him the entire time. She looked down and saw that her blouse was sodden from her dripping wet locks of hair. Shaking her head in disgust, she bent over and started ringing the water from it, then knelt on the blanket to pick up her leather hair bow.

"No. Don't put that back in your hair," Ramon said in a firm voice.

Alison glanced up to see him standing over her. The water drops in his black hair glittered, and the bronzed skin on his shoulders and chest glistened in the sunlight. Although she strove to keep her eyes on his upper body, it was impossible for her not to see all of him from her peripheral vision, the long muscular legs, the taut belly and—God help her—that part of him hanging between his thighs that she was trying so desperately not to look at.

She forced herself to concentrate on his words, and not his magnificent body. "Why don't you want me to wear it?"

He dropped to his knees before her, a blessed relief to Alison, for it removed that rather frightening yet fascinating part of him from her view. Taking the leather bow from her hand, he answered, "Because you are no longer a maiden. A married woman wears her hair down."

"But it keeps the hair off my neck. It's much cooler."

"Still, it is not done. You will not wear it."

Alison resented his dictatorial attitude. It seemed their marriage had changed nothing. He still thought he was her lord and master. A defiant expression came over her face. She made a grab for the bow, but Ramon jerked it away.

"A married woman who wears the maiden's hair bow

is announcing to all that she is willing to take other lovers."

His explanation did nothing to ease Alison's resentment. "Maybe I will, since you didn't give me a choice in the first place," she threw out recklessly.

The look that came over Ramon's face terrified Alison. She had never seen him so furious. He tossed the bow away angrily and pushed her back on the blanket, his dark eyes glaring down at her. "You will do no such thing! You are mine! Your body belongs only to your husband."

His fierce possessiveness brought on renewed anger. "Dammit, I'm not a thing to be owned! I told you that before!"

"You are my wife!"

"And you're my husband! You have no right to demand fidelity from me, if you don't intend to give me the same."

"Who said I did not intend to remain faithful to you?"

His question took Alison aback. "What . . . what about those indecent property dances? Are you saying you won't take part in them?"

Ramon remembered the last property dance and his turning down the pretty widow who had eagerly offered to share her pallet with him. Even before he had taken this exasperating woman for his wife, she had laid claim to his fidelity. He didn't want any other woman then, nor did he now. After his tasting of Alison's passion, he seriously doubted that he ever would. But to admit such to her would give her too powerful a hold on him. "I will dance," he answered, then seeing the angry flash in Alison's eyes, added, "because I cannot refuse. But I will not make love to the women."

He waited for Alison to absorb this, then said, "By the

same token, you will not wear the maiden's hair bow. For a married woman to do so is an open insult to her husband's skills as a lover. Even though it may be cooler, I will not allow you to wear it and humiliate me by having the others think you are dissatisfied with my lovemaking."

Then it wasn't just a matter of possession, but a matter of pride, Alison thought. And she had vowed she would never do anything to make him lose his esteem with the tribe.

"Are you dissatisfied with my lovemaking?" he asked.

Dissatisfied, Alison thought, in utter disbelief that he should ask. My God, no! It was wonderful! Absolutely marvelous! But she was hesitant to admit that to him. She didn't want him thinking her a total wanton. "No, I'm not dissatisfied," she admitted, deliberately directing her gaze over his shoulders. "I didn't realize how serious wearing the hair bow would be. Now that I know, I will no longer wear it."

From the corner of her eye she saw his smile, a smile that made her bones melt. Damn him! She was really helpless against him. His smile left her weak, and his touch set her body on fire.

He nuzzled her neck, whispering against her ear, "I'm glad to hear you say that."

Shivers of pleasure ran over Alison at the feel of him nibbling her throat. "That I won't wear the hair bow?" she asked in a distracted voice.

"No, that you are not dissatisfied." He lazily circled her ear with his tongue, making her shiver, then jump as it darted inside. "But I suppose it does need more perfecting."

As he began to slip her blouse down, Alison objected. "Not here in the broad daylight."

"There's no one here but us."

He smothered any further objections, his mouth coming down over hers with teasing, nibbling kisses that fired Alison's passion and completely made her forget where she was. Her clothes disappeared like magic, and she gloried in the feel of his artful tongue dancing down her body, dallying at her breasts, her navel, the insides of her thighs. Not until he picked up her foot did reason come rushing back. Horrified, she looked down to see him sitting back on his heels and holding it in his hand.

"Don't!" she cried out frantically, trying to jerk it away.

He held fast. "Why not?" he asked in surprise.

Alison felt so ashamed she couldn't look him in the eye.

"Why don't you want me to kiss your feet?" he probed.

"Because they're so big and ugly," Alison finally admitted, a humiliated flush creeping up her face.

"A woman of your height would look foolish with little feet," Ramon pointed out calmly.

Damn him! Why did he have to mention her height? And why did he have to pick now to point out all her faults, when she was so totally exposed to his eyes? "If I recall correctly, you said I was much too tall and skinny for a woman," she answered bitterly.

"I was just teasing you."

Alison wondered, then said, "Jacita said Apache men admire dainty women with small feet."

He kissed the insole of her foot, then ran his tongue over it. Alison steeled herself to the exquisite feel, then sucked in her breath sharply as he slid his naked body up hers.

"Some Apache men prefer small women, but I don't.

I much prefer a woman's body that matches my own. See how perfectly we fit? Chest to chest, thigh to thigh, mouth to mouth? I do not like breaking my back just to kiss a woman."

Alison was acutely conscious of the lengths of their bodies pressed together and particularly of his long, hot erection trapped between their lower bellies, seemingly searing her entire pelvic area. Her heart raced.

"And you are not skinny, just slender. You have all the womanly curves where it matters." He cupped the weight of her breast in one hand, saying, "Here," then smoothed his other hand over the flare of her hip, adding, "and here." Both hands slipped beneath her and fondled her soft buttocks. "And here."

His words, combined with the feelings of his hands smoothing over her and now massaging her buttocks, brought a warm glow to Alison. His dark eyes locked on hers. "Do you think I would choose a wife who I did not find desirable in all ways? No! Even these are a delight," he said in a husky voice, his hands sweeping down the sides of her legs. "I have never seen a woman with such lovely, long legs."

If Ramon had meant to help Alison overcome her self-consciousness over her body, he had certainly succeeded. With his ardent gaze on her face, she felt as if she were the most beautiful woman in the world. It was a heady feeling, one that intoxicated her as much as his exciting scent and his thrilling caresses.

She wrapped her arms around his broad shoulders and lifted her mouth. He met it with a kiss of such excruciating sweetness that it brought tears to Alison's eyes. It was inevitable, however, that their passion would override the tenderness of the moment. They were two healthy young animals whose hunger for one another seethed just below the surface. Soon Ramon was kissing her wildly, and Alison was kissing him back, her tongue dancing around his in an erotic dance that excited him to an unbearable pitch.

Feverishly he feasted on the silky softness of her skin, kissing and placing little love bites at random all over her, sucking her breasts greedily and glorying in her moans of pleasure. She writhed beneath him while he licked away the drops of water in the soft curls at the juncture between her legs, then quaked like a leaf in the wind when he ran his tongue up and down the insides of one thigh and then the other.

Opening her eyes and seeing him kneeling between her legs, Alison glanced down and saw his manhood. This time she couldn't take her eyes off it. Standing boldly and proudly before her, it looked nothing like the organ she had gotten a glimpse of earlier. Why, it was immense! She stared at it in mute fascination, and Ramon allowed her to look her fill, her wondrous appraisal making him lengthen another inch.

Alison couldn't believe it. Why, he was actually growing beneath her eyes. Then a compulsion seized her. She sat up and reached for him, hearing his sharp intake of breath as she wrapped her hand around it. She was amazed, both at the feel of him growing even larger, and at how soft and velvety the skin felt over the rock-hard flesh. She stroked him, feeling an incredible excitement fill her at his moans of delight and the shudders wracking his body.

His hand stilled hers. She looked up to see an intense, almost painful expression on his face. Her heart beat like a wild tom-tom. When he pushed her back to the blanket she didn't object. Her need for release was as great as his. When he bent and slipped his hands under her buttocks, she arched her hips to meet his thrust, then stiffened when she felt his mouth between her legs, his tongue ravishing her.

It was shocking, for he had never made love to her in this manner before. Shocking—and absolutely wonderful! As nimble and skillful as his fingers were, they were nothing compared to what he was making her feel with this instrument of exquisite torture that was his tongue. She felt as if there were flames stroking her, circling, lashing out, dipping inside of her. Powerful waves of intense pleasure swept over her, and she feared she would die if he didn't stop. Her heart beat so hard she thought it would jump from her chest.

"Stop! Please, stop!" she begged.

But Ramon couldn't stop. The taste of her sweetness and the scent of her womanliness were exciting him unbearably. He wrapped her long legs around his shoulders, wanting to crawl inside her, feasting on her even more hungrily than he had.

It was heaven; it was hell. Alison was besieged with sensation from every side. She was hot and cold. Every muscle in her body was trembling uncontrollably. Her breath was coming in hot, ragged gasps. Her entire body was an inferno. Every nerve in her body was screaming. He seemed to be holding her on the very brink, driving her mad with intense, overwhelming need.

Then he plunged into her, and Alison felt that hot pulsating shaft of desire like a bolt of lightning. Sparks flew up her spine and exploded in her brain as she climaxed. Ramon clenched his teeth, steeling himself against the feel of her hot spasms of joy, using every ounce of his willpower to keep himself from following her. A sheen of sweat covered him, and his muscles trembled with effort, until finally he brought his passion under control.

Dazed, Alison opened her eyes to see him bending over her. Then, feeling his length inside her, throbbing and hot and still as hard as steel, she wondered what had happened. "What's wrong?"

"Nothing."

"But you didn't . . ." Her voice trailed off. What was it called? she wondered.

"No, I didn't. Not yet."

"Why?"

"Because I am not through giving you pleasure."

Alison seriously doubted if her passion could be further aroused. She felt as limp and lifeless as a rag doll, totally drained. But Ramon's first long, slow thrust proved her wrong. Her eyes widened in disbelief as she felt her passion ignite again. She gave a little cry of gladness and wrapped her long legs around his hips, giving herself up to sensation and glorying in her powerful, magnificent lover as he carried her up those lofty, spiraling peaks to give her another taste of heaven.

For a long while after it was over, they lay in each other's arms, still trembling with aftershocks, the sweat on their bodies glistening in the sunlight. Then Ramon lifted himself from her and rolled to his back, wrapping one arm around her and bringing her to his side possessively.

Alison didn't feel in the least embarrassed by her nakedness in the open meadow, in the broad daylight. It seemed so natural to be lying that way in her husband's strong arms, with the sun warming her body, the bees droning in her ears, and the smell of grass in her nostrils. When Ramon suggested another bath to wash the sweat from their bodies, she didn't hesitate for a second. They walked hand and hand to the stream, as comfortable with each other's nakedness as if they had been doing it all their lives.

And why not? Alison thought as she stepped into the water. There should be no secrets, no shame between a man and his wife.

14

The two weeks that followed were a time of utter bliss for Alison, one that she would treasure her entire lifetime. There was a magic about the little, secluded valley that made the real world seem far away, a peacefulness that stripped man of his anger, his frustrations, his cares, making them seem insignificant and meaningless, and both she and Ramon fell under the valley's tranquilizing, almost hypnotic power.

They spent a good deal of their time perfecting their lovemaking, as Ramon called it. As he had promised, he taught her all he knew, and Alison was amazed at its many moods—sometimes wild and passionate, sometimes exquisitely tender, sometimes carefree, with teasing and laughter. Then they taught each other, experimenting with new ways to bring one another even more pleasure, and Alison learned that what Ramon had predicted was true. It did get better with practice. It seemed that there were planes of ecstasy, each a little higher as their young, eager bodies became more attuned to one another.

But their time together was more than just a prolonged feast of sensual pleasure. During this period
they shared confidences, and Alison came to understand what events and cultural differences had shaped
the fascinating, compelling man who was her new husband. He told her how Apaches prized and treasured
their children and how they marked the events of their
lives by special ceremonies: first placing the infants'
umbilical cords in the branches of a fruit tree so that
their lives would be renewed each year when the tree
produced new fruit, then placing them in cradleboards
that had been constructed and blessed by the *di-yins*
amid songs and celebration, then the moccasin ceremony in which they took their first steps and were
guided to walk toward the east, the holiest of all direc-
tions, and the symbolic haircutting ceremony at five
years of age. He related how Apache infants were
bathed in cold mountain streams to strengthen their
hearts and how they were taught from the very beginning the value of silence, for a crying baby could give
away the entire tribe's hiding place. He told her about
his warrior's apprenticeship when he was fourteen, how
he had to use a stick to scratch himself, how he could
only drink from a reed, how he had to do all the drudgery chores while following a set of strict rules in which
he could use only the warpath language—eighty mysti-
cal euphemisms for common terms that protected him
from harm.

Alison was amazed at all the things he revealed. She
had thought of the Apaches as savages, an uncivilized
people with no more restraints on their behavior than
wild animals, and yet from the very beginning they had
been taught self-discipline and had to learn to live under a set of restrictive social rules that, in many cases,

made the white man's look lenient in comparison. Yet their social rules were not so oppressive as to be smothering. They believed in having a good time with feasting and dancing, and Alison was absolutely dumbfounded to learn that they held womanhood in such high regard that a girl's menarche was celebrated by the entire tribe in a four-day puberty ceremony in which she, and she alone, was honored. It just didn't seem to fit in a society that was as strongly male-oriented as the Apaches'.

Curious to know just where this custom of revering the female had come from, Alison asked Ramon. He explained that the Apaches believed their race had begun with a powerful woman whom they called White-Painted Woman, and that the girl being honored at the puberty ceremony was believed to possess her power. Alison was left to wonder how many so-called civilized peoples made a point of dignifying and glorying the female. The closest she had come to being so honored had been her "coming out" ball, and that seemed frivolous and meaningless in comparison. No one had said a thing about power. Just the idea of feminine power itself was a little mind-boggling and greatly appealed to the strong-willed Alison.

Besides learning the customs that were different from her own and had shaped Ramon, Alison had been shocked to learn he had become chief at the tender age of seventeen and that it had been he who had found this hidden spot in the Chisos and had led the band to safety from their old home near Fort Davis, where their survival had been seriously threatened by the white encroachment. It seemed impossible that anyone so young could take on such an awesome responsibility, yet he had risen to the demands made on him and proven himself over and over. Therein, she came to realize, lay the dignity that she had admired from the very beginning. From his years of leadership he had gained the maturity and wisdom of a much older man.

By the time the honeymoon was over, Alison had come to see Ramon with new eyes. She still found his overbearing attitude often infuriating, but she realized that it was an integral part of him, for he couldn't separate the chief from the man. The two were irrevocably one, and despite her vow she had come to respect him. As much as she hated to leave the magical valley and their special time together, she had to admit it was probably for the best. She had already broken two of her promises to herself. She had openly given him her body and secretly granted him her esteem, and her third vow was being dangerously threatened. She feared she was beginning to fall in love with the forceful Apache chief.

The day the two rode back to the village, there was a rainbow in the sky, a huge multicolored arch that stretched across the entire width of the valley from mountaintop to mountaintop. Alison stared at it in awe, for she had never seen such a large, vibrantly colored rainbow, then asked Ramon, "Do you think we'll make it back to camp before the rain comes?"

"That's hard to say. Sometimes it hovers over us for a day or so before the rain finally comes."

As they entered the valley and passed the cornfield, Alison was shocked to see how dry and wilted it looked. "But the rain will come?" she asked a little apprehensively. "The corn needs it desperately to survive."

"So far it has never disappointed us. Besides, listen to the katydids singing."

"What does that have to do with it?"

"Their singing predicts a bountiful corn crop."

But the rain didn't come that day when they returned to camp, and the rainbow was still there the next morning. As the day passed, and the sun beat down on them with no clouds in sight, Alison began to fear that the rainbow was just making empty promises, and the katydids' incessant, shrill singing began to wear on her nerves. Then, late that afternoon, the dark thunderheads rolled over the mountaintops, blotting out the sun and throwing a deep shadow over the valley.

Jacita was with Alison in her brush kitchen when the storm finally made its appearance. When Ramon strolled in, the wind that preceded the storm whipping his dark hair around his face, Jacita glanced up and said in an alarmed voice, "Take off your headband and hide it!"

Ramon smiled indulgently and removed the flapping piece of material, then slipped it inside his shirt. As Jacita rushed away so she could get home before the storm hit, Alison asked in puzzlement, "Why did you do that? Hide your headband?"

"Because it's red. Apaches believe that anything red attracts lightning."

"You can't be serious," Alison said in disbelief.

"I'm afraid Apaches have quite a few superstitions about lightning. They consider it the most frightening power on earth. They think it's the arrows of the Thunder People, and that the thunder is their shouting, that near-misses are dire warnings. They hide red objects, turn loose any captive wild animals, refuse to ride pinto ponies, eat no food until the storm passes."

"Surely you don't believe in that silly rubbish?"

"No, I don't, but Jacita does. Rather than have her worrying about me, I just go along with it."

They slipped into their *wickiup,* and as the storm came down on them in its full fury, they heard a terrible din over that made by the storm. "What in God's name is that?" Alison asked.

"The others are imitating the call of the night hawk. They think it helps dodge the fiery arrows."

Alison thought the Apaches' superstitions ridiculous —until the storm got worse. Never in her life had she heard such loud, ear-piercing crashes of thunder or seen such tremendous bolts of chain lightning. It seemed to pulsate in a blinding, white light like a living thing in the small *wickiup,* some bolts striking so close that she could hear the sizzling noises they made on the wet grass outside the crude structure, and the smell of ozone in the air was so strong that it was almost suffocating. Alison had never experienced such a terrifying storm, and as she cuddled close to Ramon, she wondered if it was because they were in the mountains and closer to the source of the disturbance. The heavens seemed to be torn asunder and the ground shook, and she could well imagine the Thunder People venting their rage on her. She felt very mortal and terribly defenseless and vulnerable against their wrath. When the storm finally passed, leaving in its wake a pounding downpour of rain, she was weak with relief. She vowed she would never again scorn the Apaches' fear of electrical storms.

Summer slipped into early fall, the season that the Apaches called Thick with Fruit. As nature gave up her bountiful harvest, Alison soon found out that it was well named. Not only was there the corn crop to be picked,

but the women were kept busy collecting the pods of
the narrow-leafed yuccas, preparing the seeds of sun-
flowers and the nuts of the piñon pines to be roasted,
then gathering walnuts and currants and picking beans
from screwbean mesquite to grind into flour. And still
the work was not done. The fruits called datiles from
the broad-leafed yuccas and the sweet tunas from the
prickly pear cactus were yet picked to be dried and
glazed.

The women weren't the only ones kept busy in preparation for the coming winter. Ramon increased his
raids on the wagon trains and ranches, and he and his
warriors were gone for long stretches of time.

Alison discovered she missed his company, much
more than she would like to admit. The only way she
could keep her mind from him was to keep herself busy.
But that only helped in the daytime. No matter how
exhausted she was at night, sleep was elusive. She found
she missed not only his sensuous lovemaking but the
feeling of security his sleeping beside her gave her. The
time passed incredibly slowly, and Alison measured it
not by the rising and setting of the sun but by the
forceful chief's coming and going.

One day, when the harvesting was finished, Jacita
taught her how to weave a *tus* from willow twigs, then
caulk it with piñon pine gum. When the water jug was
finished, Alison held up the finished product and admired it, thinking that her first effort had come out
much better than her first attempt at making moccasins.

"What are you going to decorate it with?" Jacita
asked.

"Decorate it? You mean paint something on it?"

"Yes. Most Apache women paint their baskets with

their symbol, something in nature that they identify with, like the moon, or the morning star, or a particular flower. My symbol is the blossom of the prickly pear cactus."

Alison remembered seeing the yellow blossom that was painted on Jacita's burden basket. Yes, she thought, the fragile flower suited the small, delicate girl, but flowers certainly didn't suit her. She was more like that tall pine over there. But she didn't want to use a tree as her symbol. She wanted something more colorful, more eye-catching. She glanced around her, then looked up. Her breath caught as she saw the magnificent rainbow in the sky. Yes, she thought, she was like that rainbow up there, always waiting, except it waited for the promise of rain, while she waited for the promise of . . . what? The promise of Ramon's undying love? How silly she was, Alison thought glumly. She'd never have that. He'd told her he would never love her. No, she just waited for his return.

"Do you have any ideas about what you might use as your symbol?" Jacita asked, breaking into Alison's gloomy thoughts.

"Yes, I think I'll use the rainbow for my symbol."

The next day, Ramon and his warriors returned from their raid. As usual, he suddenly appeared beside her, materializing, as her uncle had said, seemingly right out the ground. His abrupt, silent appearance always startled Alison, and once she had recovered from it, it was all she could do to keep her happiness from showing.

That night Ramon made wild, turbulent love to her. He couldn't seem to get enough of her; his hands and lips were everywhere. Even when he entered her, there was a certain urgency, a certain rough demand, as if nothing short of total possession could satisfy him. Alison held back nothing. She was a wanton in his arms, glorying in the ecstasy he could bring her, giving back kiss for kiss, caress for caress, stroke for stroke, urging him on and on and on. She surrendered her body completely and totally, but she held her heart grudgingly close.

Later, much later, just when Alison was about to drift into an exhausted sleep in Ramon's arms, he said, "I have something to tell you that I think you should know. Your uncle and another man, whom I assume is your father, have been searching these mountains for you for months now. My sentries have been constantly watching them and keeping me informed of their movements. They have finally given up their search and gone back to Presidio."

Alison had known her uncle and father would look for her. She wondered why she wasn't more disappointed at hearing they had given up their search. Was it because she had known from the day Ramon had brought her into these forbidding mountains that there was little hope of being rescued? Or was there another reason —one which she refused to probe too deeply?

"There was never any danger of their finding our camp," Ramon continued. "At no time did they get anywhere close. Even when I took you to San Carlos, they posed no threat to me. They were on the other side of the mountains. But I am glad they have given up their search, before the Chisos killed them. As it was, they were nothing but skin and bone when they left. Now I think I know where you got your strength and determination, your courage. Even though they failed in their quest, I admire them."

Alison was glad her uncle and father had given up

their search before it was too late. Ramon's compliments brought a warm feeling of pride to her, for both them and herself—for in an oblique way, Ramon had complimented her too. She remembered what her uncle had said about admiring one's enemy and smiled. She thought he would be pleased with Ramon's testimony to his attributes.

Again Alison wondered why she didn't feel more disappointment, then realized that, deep down, she didn't want to be rescued. Nor did she want to escape. What she wanted was for Ramon to give her freedom.

Two days later, when Alison entered the *wickiup* and saw Ramon cleaning his guns, she knew he was planning on leaving on another raid. By tacit agreement, his raiding was something that they never openly discussed, for fear it would lead to an angry confrontation. Despite the fact that Alison realized his raiding was the Apache way of life, that she had even come to understand it was necessary for his band's survival, she couldn't help but resent his plundering the wagon trains and ranches. Those were white people he was attacking and stealing from, her people, and Ramon was all too aware of her feelings. Thus, the issue was never brought into the open, for it would serve no purpose. As chief, Ramon did what he had to do, even if it displeased the woman he had taken as his wife, a woman who was beginning to unearth powerful emotions buried deep within him. His first obligation was to the people who had placed their lives in his hands.

As Alison stared at the Winchester Ramon held in his hands, a sudden premonition came to her. Like the day she had spied the wagons making their way to Presidio and sensed they had something to do with Ramon, the feeling was something she couldn't explain, but she knew with an uncanny certainty that the raid he was planning was doomed to failure, that it posed a dangerous threat to him personally. A fear rose in her, and her face paled beneath her tan.

She fell to her knees beside him and said, "Don't go on this raid."

"We do not discuss my business," Ramon answered in a terse, forbidding tone of voice. "An Apache wife does not involve herself in tribal affairs, and certainly not in the affairs of a chief."

"Dammit, I'm not an Apache!" Alison flared out. "Besides, my being white has nothing to do with this. It's too dangerous. Something terrible is going to happen. I can feel it."

Ramon shot her a sharp look. "Are you predicting failure?"

"I'm not just predicting. I *know* it!"

"You claim to be able to see into the future?"

"I haven't actually had visions. I just have this terrible, ominous feeling. Don't ask me to explain it. I can't understand it myself. I just know."

"You are just being a fearful wife. It is normal for a woman to be anxious when her husband goes off to raid."

"No! This is not normal! I don't just fear something is going to happen. I know it!"

As Ramon continued to stare at her, Alison said, "This has only happened to me once before, when I saw the wagon train coming toward Presidio the day of your trial. Somehow, some way, I knew it had something important to do with you. But this premonition is even stronger and much more foreboding. Please, don't go."

A brief flicker passed over Ramon's eyes. Then his

hand shot out and clasped Alison's wrist in an iron vise, jerking her forward. "Do not talk that way!" he said in a hard voice, his dark eyes boring into hers. "Such talk is dangerous. Only a witch can predict the future."

"A witch?" Alison asked in utter shock at his accusation. "You can't be serious."

"Apaches are very serious about witchcraft."

Alison knew that the *di-yin,* the Apache medicine men, practiced a witchcraft of sorts. Not only did they claim to be healers through their magical power, but they made protective amulets for almost everything. She also knew that there were women among the tribe who secretly sold "love magic," amulets that supposedly influenced the sexual desire of others. "But that's just more of your Apache superstitions. If you personally don't believe in the power of the medicine men, how can you believe in witches?"

"It does not matter what I believe. The tribe believes." He released her wrist and stood. Staring down at her, he said in an adamant voice, "You will never speak of predicting the future again, not even to me."

"But—"

"No! Your power is dangerous, if what you tell me is true. Never reveal it to anyone, and never mention it to me again."

Ramon quickly strode from the *wickiup* and headed for the woods. There he paced, trying to calm the terror that had filled him at Alison's words. He didn't know whether to believe her claim or not, but he did know that if she possessed such an unnatural power, it was dangerous to her. The Apaches would interpret that power as evil, and as terrified of witches as they were, not even he, their chief, could protect her. He was well aware of *di-yins* in other tribes blaming their failure to cure someone on some poor old woman, claiming she was a witch whose evil curse had negated their healing power. The *di-yin* then set about turning the family of the victim against the old woman, convincing them that she had committed incest, the proof of a witch. While it would be difficult for the medicine men to prove such a charge against Alison, since she had no family in the camp, just the Apaches' suspiciousness because she was white would set the scene. If his tribesmen ever learned that she could foretell the future, it would be much too easy for the medicine men to blame any misfortune that befell the band on her. If such happened, and they accused her, he would fight to the death to keep her from the punishment for being a witch—being burned alive. But he would be only one warrior against the entire village, and the chances of him protecting her from that fate would be very slim. Yes, Alison was vulnerable, and that terrified him. It was an emotion Ramon had difficulty understanding and accepting, for he had never known a moment of fear before in his entire life.

15

In the days that passed after Ramon and his warriors had left the camp, Alison was filled with two conflicting emotions: anger at Ramon for not taking heed of her warning, and the terrible feeling of foreboding. Eventually the stronger of the two won out, that oppressive premonition of impending doom. She performed her duties listlessly, her face pale and drawn, her apprehension a living, crawling thing inside her.

One day when the two were grinding corn in Alison's brush kitchen, Jacita looked at the white woman with concern and asked, "Are you ill?"

"No, I'm not ill. I'm just worried about . . ." Alison stopped in midsentence. She hated to admit even to herself that she was actually worried about Ramon, the arrogant man who had taken her freedom and forced her to become his wife. It didn't matter that she found the marriage to her liking. His overriding her freedom of choice still rankled, a bitterness that she clung to deep down with the tenacity of a bulldog. No, she wouldn't admit she cared about that big bully. She wouldn't!

Alison didn't have to tell Jacita whom she was worried about. The Apache girl knew. "Do not worry about Ramon. He can take care of himself. He is the most able warrior in our band. He will return safely."

Jacita's assurance did nothing to allay Alison's fear for Ramon. The feeling of impeding doom pressed down on her even stronger. "I asked him not to go," she muttered half to herself. "Oh, damn him and his stubbornness!"

Jacita's face paled. "No, you must not curse him, no matter how angry you are at him. Apaches never curse someone, for fear it will come true."

Alison had already found that out. The Apaches never used curse words. The strongest words she had ever heard Ramon say, besides an occasional *"Dios,"* was the Apache curse "knife and awl," which, compared to the white man's angry oaths, seemed ridiculously mild for such a strongly macho man. More of the Apaches' silly superstitions, Alison thought in exasperation. They actually believed they could bring someone's doom down on them by just saying the words. But realizing how seriously Jacita took her cursing and how she idolized her brother, Alison felt contrite.

"I'm sorry," she apologized. "I didn't mean it literally. The white man doesn't take cursing seriously."

"But still, you must not do it," Jacita replied solemnly.

"I know. Even the white man doesn't approve of women cursing."

"Then why do you do it?"

Alison shook her head in frustration, then admitted, "Because your brother makes me so angry it seems to be the only way I can vent my feelings. I never cursed before I met him. Women where I come from just don't do it. He seems to bring out the worst in me."

"But why does he make you so angry?"

"Because he's so damn overbearing!"

"And your men are not overbearing?" Jacita asked in surprise.

"Oh, I guess all men are," Alison admitted in disgust, "regardless of their race. It's just the male in them. They're all a little domineering, or at least try to be. But I don't like it. Just because I'm a woman, I don't know why I should be expected to obey their every wish and command. I have a mind of my own."

And a will of her own too, Jacita thought. She had never met such a strong-willed person as Alison, except for Ramon. She had sensed that the couple were at odds in some way, although they never revealed it in public. To Alison's credit, she appeared to be the perfect docile wife. Until now, Jacita had never realized what a sacrifice to her own pride Alison was making, and she was grateful to the white girl for the appearance she made before the others. The Apaches would never tolerate a chief who wasn't supreme master in his own household. But one or the other of the two was going to have to relent, or else their marriage would be nothing but a perpetual struggle of wills. It was a shame they used their strength against one another. Combined, it would be formidable.

"Why did you ask Ramon not to go on the raid?" Jacita asked, curious to know if Alison had merely been trying to inflict her will on Ramon. If so, she had made a serious mistake. Ramon would never brook interference in tribal business from anyone. His decisions were law, and the Apaches had never had occasion to question his judgment. He had always stood them in good stead.

Alison wondered if she should tell Jacita of her premonition, then, remembering Ramon's caution to tell no one, decided against it. The Apache girl was terribly superstitious. She even wondered if Ramon didn't believe in witches himself. He hadn't actually denied it, and she had seen the flicker of alarm in his eyes when she had told him about her strange foreboding. Did he secretly believe and was afraid to admit it to her, for fear it would make him look foolish in her eyes? That was the only plausible explanation but somehow, it didn't fit. To give the devil his due, Ramon was much too intelligent to believe in something as silly as witchcraft. "I was just afraid something might happen to him," Alison answered, avoiding direct eye contact with Jacita. "He's led so many raids lately, I thought he was tempting fate to go out again so soon."

Jacita accepted Alison's answer without question. The white girl and her brother might be at odds with one another, but there was no doubt in her mind that Alison loved Ramon. It was natural for a woman to worry over her loved one when he was away raiding, for even though the Apaches avoided direct confrontation with the white man, it was dangerous. "Then, if you are unusually worried about this raid, you must be on particular good behavior. We believe that a man's safety is influenced by the conduct of his family in his absence."

More silly superstition? Alison thought. How could her behavior affect what was going on miles away?

Jacita lowered her voice so no one could overhear and cautioned in a ominous voice, "And do not curse him any more. If something should happen on this raid and the others remember hearing you doing that, they will accuse you of being a witch. They will say you brought an evil curse down upon him. I know you do not have an evil bone in your body, but they do not know you as well as I do. You must be very careful of what you say."

As Jacita walked away, Alison stared at her back. How could such a fierce, warlike people like the Apaches be so superstitious? she wondered. She wouldn't have thought they would be afraid of anything. And they were such a practical people, levelheaded and efficient, making use of everything nature gave them. How could they be so reasonable on one hand and yet believe in such totally illogical things? They seemed to be a people of contradiction. They were a complete puzzle to her.

Two days later, Alison was watching the women playing *stove,* a complicated game that somewhat resembled hopscotch, when she heard the sentry's cry from the mountaintop high above them. She jumped to her feet, knowing that the call could mean only one thing. Ramon and his raiding party were back.

She rushed to the window with the others in the village, and Jacita almost had to run to keep up with her quick, long-legged strides.

"See," the Apache girl said with a twinkle in her eyes, "I told you there was nothing to worry about."

Alison frowned. The strange feeling had still not left her. She would have expected it to disappear like a puff of smoke when the sentry had announced Ramon's return. Then, as the party began riding through the break in the mountains, Alison knew why the feeling of foreboding had not gone away. The horses were pulling litters and two had bodies wrapped in blankets. A cry of alarm rang out over the camp, and Alison felt an icy tingle run up her spine. Her prophesy had come true.

Rooted to the spot, she watched as the weary warriors rode into the valley, their clothing tattered and blood-stained and their faces haggard. The women in the village converged on them, looking for their husbands and sons and sweethearts anxiously, crying out in relief or anguish, depending upon what they found. But Alison didn't hear their wails. Her full concentration was the line of warriors as she searched for Ramon. Then she spied him, riding at the back of the column where he had acted as rear guard during their escape. An immense wave of relief rushed over her, leaving her feeling weak. Then abruptly an anger rose in her. Damn him! she thought. Why hadn't he listened to her?

As he rode closer, Alison's anger fled as quickly as it had come. Even though he sat erect in his saddle, there was something about his face that alarmed her. She had never seen him looking so pale and drawn, almost as if he were in pain. Her eyes quickly swept over him, but she could see no wound. Was it grief for his dead warriors that made him look so terrible? Was he regretting what had happened and blaming himself?

As he reined in before their *wickiup*, Alison hurried to him. It wasn't until several of his warriors jumped down from their horses and rushed to help their chief dismount that she realized something was wrong with him. Waving them away with one hand, Ramon swung from his horse, then almost collapsed. It was then that Alison saw that his pants leg was covered with blood, for the wound had been concealed by his horse.

When Alison pushed her way through the circle of warriors around Ramon and stepped up to help him, he waved her aside also. But rather than step back in deference to his silent command as his warriors had, she grabbed him around the waist and shot him a furious look.

"No! Stand back!" Ramon ordered her. "I will walk into my *wickiup* on my own power."

"No, you will not!" Alison retorted in an equally determined voice.

"Do not argue with me!" he rasped beneath his breath, his black eyes boring into hers.

Alison glanced around her and saw that every eye in the camp was on her. His stupid pride again, she thought. If he didn't prove himself stronger and better than any of the others, he didn't think he had the right to lead them. She longed to throttle him, but instead, she swallowed a lump in her throat and stepped away. As he slowly limped into the brush enclosure she stuck close to his side, giving him her support emotionally, if not physically. Each flinch of pain on his face felt like a stab to her heart. It seemed an eternity until they reached the skin flap over the door. She pushed it aside, and as he bent to enter, he collapsed. She caught him, staggering under his weight. It wasn't until Jacita rushed to help her that she realized that the Apache girl had been following them.

The two women laid Ramon on a pallet. Or rather they broke his fall. His heavy weight brought them both down. Almost pinned beneath him, Alison pulled herself free and sat up, looking down at him. His face was covered with beads of perspiration from his exertion, and his eyes were glazed with pain.

"And you have the audacity to call me stubborn?" Alison asked angrily, furiously blinking back the tears that were threatening to spill over. "You damn, obstinate fool! What did you prove out there? How brave you are? How strong you are?"

"I proved that I am still chief," Ramon answered thickly.

As his eyelids closed, Alison thought he had passed out. Then, in a voice that was so weak Alison could barely hear him, he said, "We must do something about your vile language. An Apache wife would never call her husband a damn, obstinate fool."

"I'm not an Apache! And don't you dare take me to task about my language! Dammit, if you wanted a meek little wife, you should have married an Apache."

A brief smile crossed Ramon's lips. "But I did not want an Apache woman," he muttered. "I wanted you." Then he did pass out.

Alison and Jacita lost no time in tending to Ramon's wound. Alison ripped his pants leg open, then gasped at what she saw. The gaping hole in his thigh was red and angry and bleeding much too freely.

Alison had never seen a gunshot wound before, and for a moment she feared she would faint. The brassy odor of blood seemed overpowering. Only her fear for Ramon's life kept her from succumbing to such a female weakness. She had to be strong. She *had* to!

She fought back the dizzying waves, then asked Jacita, "Do you think the bullet is still in there?"

"Turn him and look on the other side," a voice said from the doorway. "If there is a hole there, you will know the bullet went through."

Alison looked over her shoulder and saw Miguel standing there. She had completely forgotten about Ramon's father. Naturally, he would be concerned for his son and had come to discover how badly he had been injured.

"Help me roll him," Alison said to Jacita.

Both women shoved and pushed, but Ramon was like a dead weight.

"If you will place my hands at the right place, I can add my strength to yours," Miguel said, sensing their dilemma.

Jacita took the old man's hands as he knelt beside them and placed them at Ramon's hips. As Miguel rolled Ramon, Alison quickly looked at the back of his leg. The material there was soaked with blood too, but she could clearly see the neat hole. "The bullet went clean through."

"That is good," Miguel said with obvious relief. "At least you will not have to dig it out."

"*Me* dig it out?" Alison asked in a shocked voice. "I thought the medicine men treated injuries."

"Not unless they are so severe that the family cannot deal with them," Jacita informed her. "They are called in only under the most dire circumstances."

And then all that they did was for show, Alison thought bitterly. Why, they were nothing but a bunch of charlatans.

Alison and Jacita bandaged the leg, but almost as soon as it was done, the bandage was soaked with blood. Three times they repeated the procedure. "We are not getting it tight enough," Jacita said.

"If we make it any tighter, it will cut off the circulation to his leg," Alison pointed out.

"But we have to do something," Jacita said in a voice that bordered on hysteria. "If we don't, he will bleed to death. Already his face is as pale as a white-eyes."

Alison glanced up at Ramon's face. His ghastly color terrified her. "Don't Apaches have something that will stay the bleeding? A poultice or something?"

"No."

"But I thought Indians were supposed to be so skilled with healing herbs," Alison said in a sharp, accusing voice.

"We do use herbs to heal. We chew osha roots for colds, make a tonic from *zagosti* for the old to thin their blood, cure earaches with salt and screwbeans, and make tea from dried Apache plume for diarrhea, but we have nothing to stop bleeding. When it gets that serious, the medicine men must be called in."

"And what will they do?" Alison asked sarcastically. "Rattle their gourds, beat their tom-toms, chant, and burn feathers? How is that going to stop his bleeding?"

"Perhaps they can give us an amulet," Jacita suggested hopefully.

Alison felt like screaming in frustration, or shaking the silly girl for her blind faith in the medicine men. But the fear she saw in Jacita's eyes tempered her anger.

"There is something that the Mexicans do to stop bleeding when all else fails," Miguel said from where he was sitting to the side. "They cauterize the wound."

"You mean burn it?" Alison asked, a shiver of revulsion running through her at the thought.

"Yes."

She glanced down and saw the pool of blood beneath Ramon's leg. She knew if they didn't do something drastic soon, he'd die. "How?"

"By placing a red-hot knife against the wound."

Alison rose and said to Jacita, "Light the fire while I get my butcher knife."

The Apache girl stared at her in utter horror, shaking her head mutely.

"Dammit, Jacita, do what I said!"

Shocked by the fury she saw in Alison's eyes, Jacita scurried to obey, and since she was much more adept at

starting fires than Alison, she had one going by the time
Alison returned, the blade of the knife the white
woman carried gleaming ominously in the firelight.

"Wrap a piece of cloth around the handle," Miguel
advised. "Even though it is wooden, the hot blade may
generate enough heat to burn your hand."

Alison looked around her, then spied Ramon's headband. Slipping it from his head, she wrapped it around
the handle, then held the blade over the flames.

"Jacita," Miguel said, "lead me around the fire to
Ramon's shoulders, so I can hold him down. He might
regain consciousness when he feels that hot blade burning him and jerk away."

Her face as pale as her brother's, Jacita led the old
man around the fire. When he was positioned, he said to
the girl, "Now you hold his other leg."

Seeing the Apache girl's face turn even whiter, Alison
said sharply, "Don't you dare faint on us; we need your
help!"

Suddenly Jacita felt ashamed of herself. She was
Apache, a people known for their strength and forti-
tude. Certainly she could be as strong as the white girl.

When everyone was positioned, Alison watched as
the tip of the knife turned red and the glowing color
spread up the length of the blade. A feeling of dread
filled her. When the knife was ready, she carefully removed it from the flames and turned to Ramon. Looking down at the gaping wound, her courage wavered. She
couldn't plunge the knife against it, not knowing
that she would be inflicting even more pain. She
glanced at Miguel, sitting on his heels at Ramon's head
with his hands placed firmly on his broad shoulders. She
wished desperately that he had his sight and could do it.
She looked over at Jacita and saw that the girl had

turned her head away and knew that there was no hope from that quarter. She felt suddenly very alone and helpless.

"Do it, before the knife cools."

Alison jerked her head around and saw that Ramon had regained consciousness. His dark eyes looked like two pieces of coal sitting in his deathly pale face.

When Alison only stared at him, he asked, "Do you want me to die, white-eyes? Is that why you hesitate? Then kill me honorably, and not by default. Sink the knife in my chest."

Tears shimmered in Alison's eyes. "I don't want you to die."

"Then do it!"

Alison summoned her courage, then, biting her lower lip, plunged the red-hot blade against the gaping hole. Ramon's entire body jerked as he felt the raw flesh being burned, and his breath left him in rush. Then he went limp, mercifully losing consciousness again.

The smell of the burning flesh made the gorge rise in Alison's throat. She fought it down, knowing that to do the job halfway would accomplish nothing. Despite the fact that she felt incredibly weak and the *wickiup* was spinning dizzily around her, she forced herself to rotate the blade, searing every exposed edge. The sizzling sounds added to her nausea. Then she pulled the knife away and sat back weakly on her heels, her forehead beaded with cold perspiration and her entire body trembling. Tears streamed down her face.

There was a moment of silence in the *wickiup* before Miguel asked, "Is it over?"

"Yes," Alison muttered.

"Did it stop the bleeding?"

Alison forced herself to look at the wound. The sight

of the blackened flesh made the gorge rise in her throat again. She clapped her hand over her mouth.

"Did it stop the bleeding?" Miguel repeated.

Alison took a few deep breaths before she could answer. "Yes, it's just oozing."

"My son made a wise choice when he chose you for his wife. You are a brave woman."

"You wouldn't say that if you could have seen me. I was terrified and shaking like a leaf."

"You cannot have courage without fear. You did what you had to do."

"You *are* brave," Jacita said, her eyes filled with admiration. "I could not have done it. I'm ashamed to admit it, but it's true."

"It wasn't your place to do it, Jacita," Alison said, hoping to ease her shame. "As his wife, it was mine. And thank God, it's over."

She looked around her. "We need to get him out of these bloody clothes and placed on a clean pallet."

The three stripped Ramon of his clothing and moved him to a dry pallet, Jacita modestly keeping her eyes averted from his nakedness. The two women could have never accomplished the task without Miguel's help, for it was he who did most of the lifting, and Alison was amazed at the old man's strength. While Alison rebandaged the wound, Jacita slipped out into the brush enclosure to prepare their evening meal.

As Alison covered Ramon with a blanket and sat down wearily beside Miguel, he said, "Jacita and I will stay with you tonight. Most bullet wounds become infected. If he gets delirious from fever, you will need our help."

"Then the danger is not over?" Alison asked in a shocked voice.

"No, the worst is still ahead of us."

"Does Jacita know that?"

"No, she has never cared for a wounded man before. When I was shot, she was just a child and my dead wife's sister cared for me. We do not consider it proper for a maiden to tend to a man's injuries."

The same was true in her society, Alison thought, remembering the public censure of the unmarried nurses who had cared for the wounded during the Civil War. How foolish both races were. Just because a woman was married didn't mean she had any knowledge or skills in healing. She was a perfect example of that. At that minute, she would have given her eyeteeth to know what those nurses had learned.

Darkness fell, and shortly thereafter a terrible din was heard from outside. The noise was horrendous, with the beating of the tom-toms and the Apaches howling and shrieking. As the noises got even louder, Alison rose and walked to the break in the brush enclosure, curious to know what was going on. She saw the Apaches dancing wildly around a huge bonfire and several men dressed in something similar to the kilts that Scots wore and huge headdresses shaped like antlers. As they hovered over something on the ground and sprinkled ashes over it, chanting the entire time, Alison realized they were practicing their magic on two wounded men who had been brought near the campfire on litters.

"The medicine men have called in the *Ganhs* for their help."

Alison jumped at the sound of Miguel's voice. She hadn't realized he had followed her from the *wickiup*. "Is that those men dressed in those strange costumes? The *Ganhs*?"

"Yes, the Mountain Spirits."

"They don't look like spirits to me," Alison remarked bluntly.

Miguel chuckled. "No, everyone knows that they are men from the camp chosen by the medicine men, but still, they believe in their power."

"Faith healing?"

Miguel heard the cynicism in her voice. "Do not be too critical. It sometimes has its place."

"Not if it blinds the people to the truth, or prevents progress," Alison countered.

"Progress is a white man's word. These are Apaches. They cling to their old beliefs."

A sudden thought occurred to Alison. "How did you know about the *Ganhs* if you can't see?"

"I can hear. That is the devil dance they are performing. At no other time do the Apache drums beat so frantically."

Alison looked back out at the scene and thought the dance well named. The Apaches had worked themselves into a frenzy, stomping, wildly twisting, leaping into the air. The flickering light of the fire only made them look more eerie, and the sound of their howling and the whirling of their bullroarers was setting her teeth on edge. Then, seeing two fires across the camp, she asked in alarm, "Why did they set those two *wicki-ups* on fire? It that part of their black magic too?"

Jacita stepped up beside them and answered, "Those are the homes of the two dead men brought back by the raiding party. It is our custom to burn all of their possessions, so that their ghosts will not return for them."

Alison shook her head in disgust. As poor as the Apaches were, they burned the deceased's possessions instead of letting the living make use of them. Again it seemed to contradict their practical nature. She hadn't just left civilization behind, she thought. She felt as if she had been transported back in time to medieval days.

She turned and walked back into the *wickiup*.

It was impossible to sleep with all the noise going on outside, but the three did lie down to rest. Since the *wickiup* was so small, Alison was forced to lie beside Ramon, but that was exactly where she wanted to be. He lay so still it frightened her, and she found herself staring at his chest to be sure he was still breathing. Then she became aware of his heat. When she placed her hand on his forehead, she found it was burning with fever.

"Water," Ramon muttered.

Feeling vastly relieve that he had regained consciousness, Alison reached for the wicker jar and supported his shoulders with one arm while she held the jar to his lips with the other. After taking a few swallows, he refused to drink any more, no matter how much Alison pleaded with him.

"Too tired," he muttered, then lost consciousness again.

Around daybreak, Ramon's fever had gotten so high that he was delirious, and it took all three of them to keep him from rising. Alison couldn't believe his strength. She thought he would have been too weak to fight from all the blood he had lost, but fight he did. He swung at them and kicked out, muttering oaths in Apache all the while. He even said "Damn you" a few times, causing a look of absolute horror to come over Jacita's face and making Alison feel ashamed of herself for teaching him the white man's cursing.

Finally he passed out again, and that frightened Alison even more. His entire body was red and so hot she could barely touch it. "We've got to get the fever down," she said to Jacita and Miguel. "If we don't, it will burn up his brain."

"If we asked the *di-yins* to bring in the *Ganhs,* they could take the fever from him with their tridents," Jacita said in a small voice, hesitating to even mention the Mountain Spirits to Alison.

Alison shot her a furious look. "No! They're nothing but charlatans, and I won't have them in here. We'll do it the white man's way by sponging him with cool water. Jacita, hurry down to the stream and fill our water jugs."

"Maybe we could put Ramon in the stream," Jacita answered, her eyes lighting up with hope.

"No!" Miguel said sternly. "That is what killed your mother. The cold water was too much of a shock."

After Jacita had left, Miguel said, "I do not blame you for not seeking out the *di-yins,* help. They *are* charlatans for the most part. But they are powerful men. They will resent your not asking for their help, particularly since Ramon is their chief. If he dies, they will blame you. They will incite the entire band. There is more at stake here than Ramon's life. You could lose your life too."

A tingle of fear ran through Alison. She knew if she called in the *Ganhs,* even at this late date, she could save herself. But to do so would mean she would be losing valuable time. Ramon's life depended upon how speedily they acted to reduce his fever. She squared her shoulders and answered in a determined voice, "He won't die. I won't let him die!"

For the better part of the morning, the three sponged Ramon with cool water. Alison could hardly bear to see him shivering, and she had to harden herself against Jacita's tears and the girl pleading for her to stop. Finally the fever abated enough for Alison to call a halt.

"He does feel cooler," Jacita remarked in amazement.

Alison pulled the blanket that had been lying across Ramon's hips up around his shoulders and answered, "Yes, it's come down considerably. At least enough that he's out of danger, but his dressing is soaked. I'll have to change it again."

As Alison removed the soggy bandage, she saw that the skin around the wound had turned a reddish purple and was so taut with swelling that it looked as if it would burst. "The wound needs to drain. That's the only way we can get the infection out. Do you know of a poultice that draws out infection?" she asked Jacita.

"No."

"Do you?" she asked Miguel.

"No."

"Do you know someone who might?"

"No."

Alison fought down her frustration. Apparently the Apaches were so dependent upon their medicine men's powers that they weren't as adept at native healing as other Indian tribes. "Then we'll just have to do it the white man's way."

"And how is that?" Miguel asked.

"When my sister had a boil, the doctor ordered warm salt compresses on it. He said it would help draw out the poison."

When Alison placed the warm salt compress over the wound, Jacita objected to the treatment by saying, "The white man's medicine does not make sense. First we worked for hours to cool him off. Now you are placing warm, almost hot, compresses on him."

"Only over the wound," Alison replied patiently. "It's the poison in it that is making him so ill."

"But how will warm wet rags get the poison out?"

"I don't really know. The heat draws it out some way or another."

"Why did you add salt to the water?"

"I don't know the answer to that either."

"I hope the white medicine man knows what he is doing," Jacita said, her voice still tinged with doubt. "You poured all of our salt into the pot. It is very precious."

Alison knew salt was a precious commodity. She had always taken it for granted, but according to Ramon, Indian tribes fought one another for possession of a salt flat in this hot, arid county. She had never realized how important it was to survival or that people could actually die from lack of it. "If it will save your brother's life, it will be worth it."

Fresh tears shimmered in Jacita's dark eyes. "I'm sorry. I should not be worrying about such trivial things. But I am so frightened."

"I know. My ways seem strange to you. But you must trust me."

Only after she had said the words did Alison realize what she was asking of Jacita, to put her trust in a white-eyes, one of the people who had betrayed the Apaches over and over. When Jacita smiled at her and said, "I do trust you," Alison felt she had been given a great compliment. She also felt a great burden. Not only was Ramon's life in her hands, but Jacita's confidence in her also. She was even more determined that she wouldn't fail.

Much to everyone's relief, Ramon's fever didn't soar out of control again. None of them relished the thought of fighting him or having to sponge him down again. All day long, the two women took turns applying the compresses. Then, at sunset, Ramon regained consciousness.

Alison's relief was short-lived. She discovered she had a new battle on her hands. Despite the fact that he was in obvious pain, he refused to take any of the jimsonweed tea the two women had brewed for him, arguing that he had to remain lucid if the tribe needed him for something. Alison pleaded and begged, but it did her no good. His obstinacy infuriated her.

"You stubborn bastard!" she flung out. "You were unconscious for almost an entire day, and the tribe got along without you!"

"That could not be helped," Ramon replied through clenched teeth.

"Just sip a little bit," Alison pleaded. "Just enough to ease the pain."

"No."

"All right! But I'll be damned if I'll sit around and watch you suffering needlessly."

Alison flew from the *wickiup* and paced the brush enclosure. But she found she couldn't stay away from Ramon, even though she knew Jacita and Miguel were with him. An age-old need to be by the loved one when he was suffering drove her back to his side.

When she knelt beside his pallet, Ramon took her hand in his and said, "I'm glad you returned, even if you are still angry with me. It doesn't seem so bad with you near."

Alison's love for him welled up in her, and she felt suddenly very vulnerable. "I only came back to make sure they changed the compresses on your leg as soon as they had cooled," she answered, her denial of her real reason for returning to his side as much for herself as for him.

A flicker of a smile passed over Ramon's lips. He knew she was lying. She came back because she cared. The knowledge gave him the strength to endure the terrible pain, and he closed his eyes.

16

By the next morning, Ramon's wound was draining. Knowing he would recover, Miguel announced that he and Jacita would return to their own *wickiup.* He told Alison to be sure to come for them if there was any sign of a relapse.

When the old man walked outside, he was approached by a group of Ramon's subcaptains anxiously inquiring about their chief. Miguel assured them that Ramon would recover, then praised Alison's virtues until Alison, hearing everything being said, blushed with embarrassment. She glanced at Ramon and was thankful to find he was asleep. If he had heard his father calling her brave and wise and strong, undoubtedly he would have laughed.

Ramon slept much of that day, but every time he did wake up, Alison was right there to pour a thick, rich soup she had made down his throat. Finally he objected, saying, "If you keep this up, I will be as fat as a pig."

"You could stand a few more pounds on you," Alison replied tartly.

"Oh? I wasn't aware that you found my physique lacking."

Alison thought he had a magnificent physique, all hard muscle sheathed in a smooth bronze skin, but she wasn't about to admit it to him. She shrugged her shoulders and answered, "You never asked. It just so happens that I prefer men with a little more meat on them."

"And where would you prefer I have more meat? In the middle?" He scoffed. "Apaches do not have potbellies like the *pindah.* We stay lean and hard, even in our old age."

"Well, if you don't drink this soup, you'll never regain your strength and live to become an old man," Alison snapped irritably.

Ramon looked at her closer and saw that she was exhausted. "How long has it been since you slept?"

"You're the patient here, not me."

"Lie down and sleep."

"No, not yet. I need to change your dressing."

"It can wait until tomorrow."

"No, it can't wait until tomorrow! And don't start trying to boss me around. I won't put up with it! I'm the boss here until you're well." She placed the bowl of broth against his lips and said, "Now drink, or so help me God, I'll drown you with it."

Ramon tried to push the bowl away, but found, to his utter dismay, that he was so weak he could hardly raise his hand. He glanced sharply at Alison's face and saw the determined gleam in her eyes. "You are a stubborn woman."

"You're damn right I am! I can be ten times more stubborn than you. Now do you drink, or do I drown you?"

Flashing black and startlingly blue eyes met and

glared at one another. It was Ramon who finally broke down with a grin, saying, "I'll drink."

Later, when Alison was changing his dressing, being very careful not to hurt him, Ramon said softly, "I think you must love me a little."

Alison's heart suddenly hammered against her ribcage. She could no longer deny the truth. She did love him. She had surrendered her heart to him just as irrevocably as she had her body. But she'd never admit it to him. Her pride wouldn't let her, not when he still denied her his love. "Where did you get a ridiculous idea like that?"

"There were tears in your eyes when I told you to cauterize the wound."

"I just didn't want to hurt you any further. Showing compassion for someone doesn't mean you love them."

"It was more than compassion."

"It was not! I would have done the same for anyone."

"You enjoy my lovemaking," Ramon said, taking a different approach.

"Yes, I'll admit to that. But that doesn't mean you love someone either. It's physical. It has nothing to do with the other."

Alison's flippant answer cut Ramon to the bone. More than anything, he wanted to hear her say she loved him. It was no longer just a matter of his ego, but a deep need. He pondered over her admission that she enjoyed their lovemaking. It was something she did not have to admit to. He knew as well as she that she enjoyed it to the fullest. But he couldn't believe her claim that it was just physical. She gave of herself too freely, too completely, and she went to great lengths to bring him just as much pleasure. He had learned long ago from his own experiences that physical love was selfish.

A deep scowl came to Ramon's face. He realized that what he had experienced with other women couldn't begin to compare with the joys he had felt with Alison. There had been no heart and soul in those encounters. Nor had those women brought him the contentment Alison had, that strange peacefulness he experienced with her just lying at his side, just being there. *Dios!* What was the white-eyes doing to him? *Was* she a witch? Had she cast a spell on him? He couldn't allow himself to fall in love with her. His total commitment was to the tribe. As their leader, he couldn't split his loyalties between them and one of the enemy. He should never have tied himself to her. He should have married an Apache woman, one of his own kind, one who knew her place. But the thought of a docile wife who obeyed every wish and command disgusted Ramon. He found Alison's high spirit exciting—infuriating sometimes, but always exciting. She was fire, while other women were lukewarm water. But could he afford the price he might have to pay for her? An Apache woman would have never threatened his heart.

The next day, Alison asked Ramon, "What happened on the raid?"

"I told you, women do not concern themselves with tribal affairs."

"Apache women. I'm not an Apache. I'm white! And white women do concern themselves with what's going on around then. I have a right to know, particularly when my husband comes home half dead."

When Ramon remained stubbornly silent, Alison erupted. "Damn you! Answer me! I'm tired of being treated as if I don't have a mind, as if I'm stupid! Apache women may be content to live in a vacuum, but I'm not. I want to know what happened out there."

Ramon stared straight ahead with his lips tight set. Alison knew that implacable look all too well. "You're the most infuriating man I've ever met! First you bring me to this prison—"

"You are not in a prison."

"Yes, I am! This valley is a prison, with those mountains out there its walls."

"You can walk out the window at any time."

"Yes, and get lost and die," Alison answered bitterly. "You don't even need walls to hold me here. No, you've imprisoned me, and now you lock me out of your thoughts. The only thing we share is our pallet. What kind of a marriage is that? I'm not a wife."

"You perform all of the duties of a wife."

"Duties? I'm not talking about duties. I'm talking about sharing! A husband and wife should confide in one another. They should share everything. Dammit, I'm not trying to stick my nose into tribal business. I just want to know what's going on. But you refuse. You give me just so much of yourself, and no more. Well, I don't want the little crumbs you throw me. I want to be a *real* wife, not just a servant and a—concubine!"

She whirled around and stormed from the *wickiup*.

Since she didn't return for several hours, Ramon had a long time to think over what she'd said. The sharing of thoughts and confidences between a husband and wife was not the Apache way. Did white men really bare their souls to their wives? An Apache would consider that unmanly. The male was supposed to bear the burden of decisions and their consequences, and as chief, he was supposed to do so even more. But deep down, he longed for someone to confide in. He couldn't do it to his warriors. He was expected to know all of the answers. If they ever realized how mortal he was, how many times he had doubts about his own judgment, they would lose confidence in him. A chief who had lost his medicine was no chief at all, but the burden of his office lay heavily on him. These were bad times for the Apaches, the worst they had ever faced. One by one, the Americans were beating the great Apache chiefs and placing their tribes on reservations, horrible pieces of desert land that no one wanted, not even the greediest of the *pindah*. How much longer could he hold out? But could he reveal his doubts, his fears to Alison? That would take a great deal of trust.

He admitted he'd come to admire her, even before his father had told him how brave and strong she had been in assuming full responsibility for his survival. Even the threat that the medicine men might kill her if he had died hadn't frightened her away. He was proud of her. She had a strength of character such as he had never known in a woman. But could he trust her? If he relented and confided in her, would she be content to just listen? Or would she try to tell him how to run his affairs? She did have a tendency to be bossy. Just look at the way she had forced her will on him with the broth. But she'd said she wasn't trying to stick her nose in tribal business. That was something he would never tolerate. There could only be one chief!

That night, when the fire had burned low and Alison had almost fallen asleep, Ramon suddenly announced, "I will tell you what happened."

She wondered what had changed his mind, but was wise enough not to ask.

"We ran into a trap at a water hole. The yellowlegs— what we call your calvary—were waiting there for us."

"But how did they know you were coming?"

"They didn't. The trap had been set for Chief Beduiat and his warriors, but to the yellowlegs, one Apache is as good as the other."

"Who is Chief Beduiat?"

"You probably know him by his Mexican name, Victorio."

Alison had heard of Victorio. Everyone had. For years, the papers all over the United States had carried the stories of the bloody trail of destruction the renegade Apache chief had left all over New Mexico and Arizona. "But I thought he had been put on a reservation."

"He broke out last spring."

"He's done that twice before," Alison commented. "Why does he keep surrendering, if he doesn't intend to keep his word?"

"It is not Victorio who is not keeping his word. It is the white-eyes. He surrendered with the promise that his tribe would be put on the Ojo Caliente reservation, in their beloved Black Mountains. For two years, they lived there in peace. Then the white man broke his word. Two companies of soldiers showed up suddenly to move them to San Carlos, the Mescalero reservation in Arizona. Victorio had already been to the San Carlos hellhole and seen his people burning under the hot desert sun, where the daytime temperatures went to 110 degrees or higher, had seen them choking to death in dust storms, had seen them dying of starvation and disease. He was enraged at the white man's treachery and bolted with a hundred of his warriors, leaving their women and children behind. Their families were marched to San Carlos in the dead of the winter, through terrible blizzards. Many died on that terrible march."

Alison frowned. She had heard nothing about the Apache women and children being marched hundreds of miles in the middle of winter. All the newspapers spoke of was Victorio's raids on the white settlers.

"Victorio was not happy living without the families of his band," Ramon continued. "He pleaded with the white man to let them return to the Ojo Caliente reservation, but they would not relent. The best they would offer him was the Mescalero reservation at Tularosa, another hellhole in New Mexico, and if they behaved, the army would move their families to join them. Victorio surrendered, but again the white man proved his treachery. Victorio saw the white men coming from Silver City and recognized the judge and district attorney. He knew they were coming to try and hang him. He gathered his warriors and fled. He has sworn he will never make peace again with the *pindahs*."

"But why did he think the white men were coming to try and hang him? Maybe that hadn't been their intention at all," Alison objected.

"He suspected a trick because of what happened over a decade ago at Camp Grant, an Apache reservation outside of Tucson. A large, armed group of citizens from that town attacked the Apaches without warning and massacred them. A hundred and twenty-five, mostly women and children, were killed, and all of the dead were mutilated. You see, most of the men were away hunting at the time. That is why the whites found the courage to attack. They knew there would be no warriors at the reservation. Since then, when Apaches see a large group of white men approaching them, whether they are civilian or soldiers, they are very suspicious of their intent."

Alison was horrified. She had never heard that story either, but she knew Ramon wouldn't lie to her.

"Over and over, the white man has tricked us, both the *pindahs* and the Mexicans. Juan José, one of our great chiefs, was tricked by a group of *pindah* mule traders near Santa Rita. They invited him to feast and drink with them, then offered him and his people a big pile of trading goods to prove their goodwill. There was a bomb hidden in the pile, and Juan José and many women and children were killed.

"Mangus Coloradas, another of our great chiefs, was peacefully on his way to a reservation when he was tricked and killed by soldiers. At Ramos, in Mexico, the Apaches were tricked by the Mexicans. They, too, invited them to feast and drink with them. Then when the Apaches were dead drunk, the soldiers and villagers massacred them. Even Cochise, as wise as he was, was fooled by the white man. He was invited to a conference by the *pindah* army, which was conducting an inquiry into the whereabouts of a half-breed who had been captured by another band of Apaches. The officer in charge told the chiefs to go into the tent where a feast had been set up for them. When they went inside, they were attacked by the soldiers waiting there. Cochise escaped only by cutting through the back of the tent. Considering the past treacheries of the white man, do you wonder at Victorio's suspicions that he was being tricked?"

"No, I can't blame him," Alison admitted, shocked by the things Ramon was telling her. "It's a wonder you trust anyone."

"We pick our friends very carefully, then still we watch our backs, so much so that we are reluctant to join with other bands. That is why the Apaches have never united. But if we ever had, the white man could not have pushed us from our country, could have never beaten us."

Alison didn't doubt his claim. Considering the hell Victorio and just his small band of Apaches were giving the army, if the entire Apache nation had united, they would have been invincible. Their division, caused by mistrust, had been their downfall.

But Alison was curious about something. The question had been teasing at the corners of her mind since Ramon had told her what happened. "Did you ride all the way back from New Mexico with that wound?"

"No. The way it was bleeding, I would have never made it. We were attacked at a water hole between here and the Davis Mountains."

"But what were they setting up a trap for Victorio in Texas for? He doesn't come this far east."

"He was forced to flee to Mexico. On his way south, he swung through west Texas. The army hopes to trap him when he tries to return to Ojo Caliente."

"But why are they so sure he'll try to go back there?"

"Because it is his home. All along, that is all he has asked for. To be left in peace there."

"It's that important to him? That he'd risk his life to get to it?"

"He is a Chiricahua Apache. They believe that Ojo Caliente, where four prairies come together, is where White-Painted Woman instructed the Apaches in the first puberty ceremony, and then went up to heaven. They believe it is a holy place, full of power. And his tribe are mountain Apaches, like my band, not desert Apaches. We cannot bear to live anywhere but in the mountains. That is where Victorio wants to go, back to his beloved Black Mountains that overlook Ojo Caliente."

"And the damn fools wouldn't let him go back," Alison muttered.

"What did you say?"

"I said the white men who decided he couldn't go back were fools. Look at all the blood that has been shed because of their stupidity."

"You are calling white men fools?" Ramon asked in disbelief.

"Yes! All this turmoil between the whites and the Indians could have been avoided if the white man had used a little common sense. You don't take a fish out of water and expect it to live. You don't take a desert plant, transport it to a cold climate, and expect it to thrive."

"You are forgetting something," Ramon said bitterly. "The white man does not want us to thrive. He does not want us to live."

Alison could think of nothing to say. She feared that what Ramon said was true. The old adage that the only good Indian was a dead one seemed to be her people's creed. Was it greed that drove them, or just blind stupidity? Regardless, she felt a deep regret that it couldn't be different between the two races.

For a long time the two lay in silence, occupied with their own thoughts. Then Ramon said, "I should have listened to you. I should not have gone on that last raid."

Was he feeling guilty? Alison wondered. But she didn't want him to feel that. And she felt no satisfaction in knowing she had been right. Just regret that it had happened. "You can't blame yourself. My prediction must have sounded strange. I couldn't expect you to accept something that I couldn't even explain myself."

"I did not want it to be true. I did not want you to be able to foretell the future. It frightened me."

Did he think she was a witch? Alison wondered. *Was* she? How had she known something terrible was going to happen? A shiver ran through her. "It frightened me too. I don't like things happening to me that I can't explain and I don't understand."

"Did you tell anyone else?"

"No."

"You must promise me that you will never tell anyone. It will be our secret."

Alison had no idea that Ramon was trying to protect her. She thought he didn't want the others to know because they would be angry at him for not heeding her warning, and she didn't want that. "I won't. I promise."

Ramon breathed a sigh of relief. Her silence about her strange power was the only way he could protect her. And he did feel better for admitting to her that he had made a mistake in not listening to her. That had not been an easy thing to do. He had feared she would criticize him. Perhaps he could confide in her. He had not expected her to be so understanding or so honest with him. And their little talk had seemed to bring them closer. It was a good feeling, this new intimacy.

Ramon pulled Alison into a tighter embrace, kissed her tenderly on the forehead, and cradled her head on his chest, keeping her close to his heart as they slept.

17

The next night, after Alison had changed his dressing, Ramon caught her before she could lie down, pulled her halfway over him, and started nibbling on her neck.

"Don't, Ramon."

"I want to make love to you."

"You're still too weak. It will drain your strength."

"I feel much stronger today."

"And you'll feel even stronger tomorrow. Perhaps then."

"No," he answered adamantly, deftly untying the string at her low bodice. "Now!"

As his hand cupped one breast and his fingers worked their magic, Alison felt those familiar shivers of pleasure washing over her. She tried to push his hand away. "I really don't think we should. What if your wound were to start bleeding again?"

"It won't," he answered, firmly pushing her hand away.

"But you don't know that. You haven't put your weight on it yet."

"When it gets to that stage, you can do all of the strenuous work. You've ridden me before."

Alison wavered.

"Does that not suit you, being on top?"

It suited her. Alison loved the position. She had full control of her movements, and she could set the pace. "No, I don't object to doing the work, but I'm still not sure you're up to it yet."

Ramon chuckled. "If you don't think I'm up to it, look down."

Alison glanced down at the blanket that was thrown across his lap. It was sticking up as if someone had stuck a pole beneath it.

But Ramon gave her no further opportunity to object. Swiftly he stripped her blouse from her and took possession of one rosy nipple with his mouth. With the feel of him suckling her, and his hands caressing the length of her bared back, Alison knew she didn't have the willpower to resist. Her passion for him, which always seethed just below the surface, rose like a monumental wave. She swung her leg over him and braced her forearms on both sides of his dark head, giving him better access to her breasts.

His hands slipped beneath her skirt and stroked her thighs. He nuzzled the deep valley between her breasts, then worked his way to the other nipple, licking and gently nipping the soft mound. When his tongue whipped out like a hot wet lash around the turgid peak, Alison cried out, feeling as if a bolt of lightning had rushed to that place between her thighs. "This is madness," she exclaimed gasping.

"Delicious madness," Ramon muttered, then captured the nipple he had been seeking, raking it ever so gently with his teeth before taking it in his mouth.

Alison felt a wetness slipping from her as that terrible aching began between her legs. She rubbed herself against his hard belly, then trembled at the exquisite sensation it brought her.

Ramon laughed, a husky rumble that made Alison tingle. "That is not where I want you to ride me."

A flush rose on Alison's face. She hadn't even realized what she was doing. "Well, how can I in this position? I might be long, but I'm not that long!"

"Ah, I do have a dilemma," he answered, licking one breast avidly. "It seems I'm going to have to give up one pleasure for the other."

He tugged on her skirt. "Take this off."

"Why? It won't get in the way."

"I want to be able to see all of you."

Alison sat up, unbuttoned the skirt, and slipped it off.

He tossed off the blanket covering his lap, but when Alison started to move down his body, he caught her and kissed her deeply. It was maddening with his hot tongue making wild forays into her mouth and his erection pressed against her buttocks, so close to where she wanted him, yet so far away. Finally she managed to pull away from that torrid kiss and ask in a breathless voice, "I thought I was going to do all the work?"

He grinned, a slow smile that made her heart melt. Then he dropped his arms and said, "Be my guest."

Alison came to her knees and slowly backed up, then carefully lowered herself over him, fighting back the shivers of pleasure as she encased his rigid length in her warm depths. She was acutely conscious of his wounded thigh against her calf and reluctant to move for fear she would hurt him.

He reached between where they were joined and

began to stroke the hard bud there. "No!" Alison objected, catching his wrist.

"Why not?"

"You'll make it happen too soon."

"It will happen again. It always does."

As he resumed, Alison was helpless against his skillful fingers. Damn him, she thought. He took delight in bringing her to that shattering peak over and over, always giving her much more pleasure than she did him. But she was determined she wouldn't let him do it more than once. Otherwise, she'd be too drained to reciprocate. But Alison was unprepared for the climax his ministrations brought her, for he had never before taken her to fulfillment with his fingers while his hot, throbbing manhood was deep inside her. The rapturous waves became powerful undulations that overwhelmed her, and she exploded in a starburst of blinding colors, then collapsed over him.

Ramon steeled himself against the feel of Alison's spasms of joy, the hot muscles surrounding him squeezing him like greedy hands. He clenched his teeth and only by sheer willpower kept from following her to ecstasy. But he had wanted that to be for her. His pleasure could wait.

Lying limply over him, with her head buried in the warm crook of his neck, Alison said, "Damn you! Now look what you've done. Now I'm too weak to do anything."

Ramon smoothed back the hair at her temple and kissed her there. "You'll recover your strength. We'll wait until you do."

It didn't take long for Alison's passion to flare anew, not with Ramon caressing her and nibbling at her earlobe. And with the return of her passion came her strength. She sat up and began to ride him, her movements slow and sensuous at first, then faster and faster as her own pressing need took command. Her breath came in ragged sharp gasps and her body was covered with a fine sheen of perspiration. It was wonderful! It was glorious! Never had she felt so powerful; never had she felt so alive!

Ramon watched while Alison rode him superbly, thinking she looked absolutely magnificent with her head thrown back and her proud beautiful breasts jutting out. He stroked her thighs and fondled the milky globes, but never did his gaze leave her face, not even when the demands of his own body made themselves known and he was writhing beneath her in his own rapturous ecstasy. Then, seeing her eyes glaze over and knowing she was on the brink, he pulled her head down and captured her lips in a fiercely possessive kiss, his tongue ravaging the sweetness of her mouth. With one deep thrust he brought them over that peak to a powerful sweeping eruption that plunged them into a dark void.

Slowly Alison floated back down to earth. When reason returned, she was trembling and again lying weakly over Ramon. Then as she suddenly remembered, she lifted her head and said, "My God! I completely forgot about your leg. Did I hurt it?"

"No."

As Alison started to lift herself from him, Ramon said sharply, "No, don't move!"

"Why not?"

Ramon just smiled and Alison became aware of him still inside her, hardening and growing larger and larger. She had always been amazed at his recuperative powers, but he had never recovered *that* fast.

Seeing the look of astonishment on her face, Ramon laughed. "I think it must be that soup you've been pouring down me. I told you I felt strong."

Alison couldn't help but laugh too. Then all thought fled as she gave herself up to the pleasure her strong, virile Apache lover brought her.

The next day Ramon insisted on getting up. Alison argued with him, still fearful that they might have injured him further with their bout of lovemaking the night before, but he was adamant. Well, he must be well, Alison thought angrily. He's back to being the same old arrogant bastard.

She was determined she wouldn't help him dress, but when she saw how much trouble he was having putting on his pants, she relented. Much to her surprise, he allowed her to assist him, then let her help him limp around the *wickiup* to get the stiffness out of his leg.

Alison knew he was in pain by the beads of perspiration that popped out on his forehead. She also knew he was much weaker than he was letting on. She could feel him trembling from the effort. She cursed his stubbornness silently, but wisely held her tongue. When he finally deemed it enough exercise for the time being, she was vastly relieved.

Almost as soon as he had sat back down on the pallet, he asked, "Where are my saddlebags?"

"I wasn't aware you had any saddlebags."

"Yes, I traded for some on this last raid. I decided the white man's bags would be easier to carry small things than that sack I've been using."

Alison remembered him telling her that he wasn't averse to adopting the white man's equipment if it had a practical value. "Now that you mention it, I do remember seeing Miguel bring something in." She glanced around, then spied the tip of one leather pouch beneath his *parfleche.* "There it is."

"Would you hand it to me?"

Alison picked up the bag and handed it to Ramon. As he unbuckled the strap, he said, "Kneel down here by me. I have something for you."

Alison fell to her knees, wondering what it could be. Then as he drew out a necklace and held it up, her breath caught in surprise. "Why, it's lovely—a turquoise necklace just like yours."

"Yes, I instructed the craftsman to make it identical to mine." He reached into the saddlebags and drew out a pair of earrings. "And these too."

"But I don't have pierced ears."

"Jacita can do it for you."

Alison wasn't too sure she wanted her ears pierced. "Does it hurt?"

"I don't know. Mine were pierced when I was baby. But I shouldn't imagine it would be that painful. Just a needle jab." He handed her the necklace. "Put it on."

Alison took the necklace and placed it around her neck. As she fastened the clasp at her neck, Ramon stared at her jutting breasts in mute appreciation. Then as she lowered her arms and the stone slipped into the cleavage between them, he smiled, thinking it was an appropriate place for his gift, close to her heart and yet visible to all.

Alison looked down and fingered the large stone. "Where did you get it?"

"The same place I got mine. In New Mexico. But I'm afraid we lost everything else we had traded for in the heat of the battle and our escape."

"You and your warriors are much more important to this tribe than those trading goods," Alison pointed out.

"That is true, but we needed those goods, particularly the blankets. They serve as our coats during the winter, as well as our covering at night."

"Does it get very cold here in the mountains?"

"Not in this valley. The mountains all around us protect us from the cold north wind that plagues the rest of Texas. Occasionally we have a little snow flurry, but generally our winters are rather mild. Remember, the Chisos sit in the middle of a desert. However, that is not true in the mountains north and west of us. They have terrible blizzards that sometimes come very suddenly. That is why we cannot risk making another trip to New Mexico."

"Couldn't you trade in old Mexico?"

"Yes, but the prices the Mexicans offer for our horses and cattle are not as good as those the *pindahs* give us. But we do trade our furs to the Mexicans."

"Furs?" Alison asked in surprise. "You trap also?"

"A little, in late winter when the pelts are the thickest."

Alison recalled the beaver they had eaten. "Is that where you trap, by the Rio Grande?"

"Yes, it's full of beaver and muskrat. We take a few fox and wolf pelts too."

Remembering that she had things to do, Alison rose. "I need to get my stew simmering or the meat will be tough." She stopped at the door and turned. "Thank you for the necklace and earrings. They're beautiful."

"You're welcome."

She laughed softly and said, "We'll have to remember to take them off when we make love, though. The silver chains might get tangled and break."

"The chains are much stronger than they look. We'd be more likely to choke each other." He grinned and added, "Particularly as carried away as we get."

A flush rose on Alison's face, half in embarrassment at how wanton she could be, and half in remembrance of how wonderful it felt.

After she had left, Ramon wondered again why he had bought the jewelry for her. He had sworn he would never buy useless trinkets for a woman. But he had rationalized, as wife of a chief, Alison needed something to denote her position in the tribe, and jewelry that matched her husband's seemed appropriate. He experienced a warm feeling inside that had nothing to do with desire and was forced to admit that he had been lying to himself. He had given her the jewelry simply because he wanted to. The earrings and necklace were a token of a much deeper emotion than pride.

Later that afternoon the *di-yins* of the tribe paid a visit to their chief. As soon as the four old men crowded into the *wickiup,* Alison excused herself. But before she left, she noticed them glaring at her turquoise necklace, a symbol of her position as Ramon's wife.

The medicine men stayed much longer than Alison had expected. Not until she saw them walking across the camp did she return to the *wickiup,* and after making a quick stop by her kettle to add more water to her simmering stew, she entered the low structure. The first thing she saw was Ramon's deep scowl.

"Is something wrong?" she asked. Then, remembering that she had promised not to stick her nose in tribal affairs, she said, "I'm sorry. I didn't mean to pry into your business."

Strangely, Ramon found he didn't resent her asking.

It was the *di-yins* glaring at Alison that had upset and angered him. He feared she had made enemies of the old men because she had not sought their aid. They were terribly protective of their positions in the tribe. If Alison, the chief's wife, shunned them, they feared the others might also. But he didn't want to reveal his worries on that score to Alison. "They came to assure themselves that I was recovering satisfactorily."

Alison was tempted to throw out some sarcastic remark, but bit it back. "It seemed to take them an awfully long time to decide that you were."

"They also questioned me about what had happened."

"Do they have that right?"

"Actually, no, but I humor them. Particularly Benito, since he claims he has powerful war medicine."

"How dare those old buzzards question you," Alison said angrily. "Were they critical?"

Ramon chuckled. The four old men did look like buzzards. "No, I think Benito was embarrassed and trying to find some way to clear himself. You see, he foretold a successful and prosperous raid."

"Oh, and how did he come to that conclusion?" Alison asked, no longer able to hide her contempt for the charlatans. "By looking at some poor chicken's innards?"

"Where did you hear that, looking at a chicken's innards?"

"I read it in a book about voodoo some slaves practiced."

"That's interesting. I have no idea how Benito comes to his conclusions. He's very secretive about his methods of deduction."

"Naturally. If anyone knew the silly things he did, he'd be found out for what he is—a big fake!"

"Watch what you say about him, or any of them. They can be vindictive men."

"Oh, I'm not going to say anything around anyone else. Miguel already warned me. I'll keep my opinions to myself. But it infuriates me how they take advantage of these poor people, giving them false hope. And look what they did to you, giving you poor advice."

"I pretend to listen to the medicine men, but I don't act on what they say. I'm not that foolish. I still follow my own judgment."

"I'm just curious, but how did Benito manage to save face?"

"He didn't. But he talked round and round the issue so long and so elaborately that I think he confused the others. By the time they left, he had somehow managed to make them believe that he hadn't made a prediction on the outcome of the raid."

Alison laughed. "We have politicians that use the same tactic."

A week later, Ramon announced that he and several of the warriors were going to the big cave where the tribe cached their trading goods, explaining that since they had lost the blankets they were bringing back, they would have to take some from their emergency stock.

"In that case, may I ask you a favor?" Alison responded. "Could you bring me back some of that material you offered me last summer? With winter coming on, I'd like to sew some long-sleeved blouses."

"I have a better idea. You can come with us and pick what you want."

"Then this isn't an all-male excursion?"

"The warriors learned long ago to take their wives along. Invariably the men brought back a calico print or color of blanket that their wives didn't like. Bringing them along saves them a second or third trip."

"What about the women that aren't going along?"

"They just have to settle for what is brought them. It's their husbands who will have to listen to their complaining, not the men who made the selection."

Alison felt a little glimmer of hope for the Apache women. Maybe they weren't so meek, after all.

The next morning the party rode out of the window and high to a mountaintop on the southern edge of the ridge that surrounded the valley. When they stopped their horses on a wide ledge, Alison looked about her. "I don't see any cave," she said to Ramon, who was dismounting beside her.

"It's concealed behind those boulders."

It took three men to roll each of the huge boulders back, and Alison found herself looking into a huge black chasm in the side of the mountain. With torches to serve as light, the party walked into the cave. Alison was amazed at what she saw: piles of blankets and bolts of cloth, stacks of boxes of ammunition and guns, sacks of dried corn, baskets of preserved agave hearts and jerky, boxes of thread, needles, and assorted knives, piles of kettles, saddles, and bridles.

Alison quickly made her selections from the bolts of cloth that Ramon informed her were his, choosing two prints and one solid color, but when it came to picking out the blankets, he did the choosing. As he sorted through the pile, Alison wondered why he was being so particular. Then he pulled out a blanket and said, "This is the one I was looking for," and tossed it over her shoulders.

Alison looked down at the blanket and knew why he had chosen it for her, for the design had a great deal of blue in it. "I was hoping the blue would match your eyes, but I see it doesn't," he said softly. "I don't think there is anything in this world as blue as your eyes, or anything as beautiful."

Alison glanced quickly around her, feeling embarrassed at his attentions before the others. Seeing that they were all occupied, she muttered, "Thank you."

She ran her hands over the soft blanket. "It's beautiful and so thick."

"Yes, to give the Navaho devils their due, they do excel in making beautiful blankets."

"Why do you call them devils?"

"They are our ancient enemies."

"But they trade you their blankets?"

"They trade them to the white man, and we in turn trade for them."

While the men were loading the supplies on the horses, Alison stood on the ledge and looked around her. The view was absolutely magnificent. She could see the entire countryside: the little village below them that specialized in raising corn, the winding Rio Grande as it made its big loop into Mexico, the rolling desert with its towering spikes and buttes, the Sierra del Carmen that stretched deep into Mexico, looking like huge breakers in the far distance.

As Ramon stepped up beside her, the wind whipping the tail of his headband around his face, she said, "I feel like I can see clear to the ends of the earth up here."

"You can see for a good hundred miles from this point."

"A hundred miles?" Alison gasped. "But that's impossible! No one can see that far."

"In a desert you can. Even a smoke signal can be seen clearly from fifty miles away."

As they rode away, Alison looked back over her shoulder, hating to leave the breathtaking view. But when they rode through the window and the *rancheria* came into view, her disappointment fled. The maples and aspens had taken on their fall colors, and the entire valley was a riot of brilliant golds and reds and burnt oranges against the lush, dark green of the towering pines. At that moment Alison thought the valley had to be the most beautiful place in the world. But deep down, she still thought of it as her prison.

Alison decided that winter was her favorite season in the Chisos, for as Ramon had predicted, the weather was mild. It was more like an extension of fall, the air crisp but not cold, and Alison wondered why the Apaches called it the season of Ghost Face, until Ramon reminded her that they had once been Plains Indians.

It wasn't just the relatively mild weather that Alison liked. The pace of living was much more relaxed. The men kept in shape by hunting, tending their horses, and playing games involving a great deal of physical activity. The women tanned hides, wove mats from dried sotol leaves, sewed, and cooked. But since there was nothing to be gathered, they too had time for games, and to Alison's surprise, they were allowed to participate in the many footraces that the men held.

But what Alison liked most were the winter nights. Then everyone would gather around a huge bonfire and listen to the storyteller. Alison had picked up enough Apache to know that the stories were always about the escapades of Coyote, a character that the Apaches held in contempt for his foolishness, and always had a moral to them. Sometimes they were rather racy, and the storyteller would always warn his audience if something naughty was coming up, so that the adolescents could leave and not be embarrassed. But it wasn't the stories that Alison enjoyed so much. It was sitting by a crackling fire beneath a sky filled with glittering stars, with the smell of pine in her nostrils, passing bowls of roasted nuts and listening to the Apaches laugh and encourage the storyteller with *"Ao, Ao,"* that delighted her. There was a warm feeling of family that she had never experienced in her home back in Baltimore.

One night, when they were sitting around the fire, a toddler plopped himself in her lap. Alison wrapped her blanket around him and pulled him closer. That was another thing she liked about the Apaches, their love for children. Each and every child belonged to the entire tribe, and everyone, male and female alike, looked after them. A child would approach anyone, for he knew there were no strangers here, that he was loved and accepted equally by all.

When the storytelling ended, the mother of the toddler came to claim her son, who was curled up on Alison's lap and sleeping with his head on her knee. Alison hated to give up the cuddly little boy. As the mother carried the toddler away, Ramon helped Alison to her feet.

"Did you notice Jacita leaving with her sweetheart during the storytelling?" she asked as they walked back to their *wickiup.*

"Yes, I expect Santo will make a marriage offer after the next raid."

"But why wait till then? Why don't they get married now? While things are so relaxed."

"I'm sure Santo would have done so after the last raid in the fall, but since it turned out so disastrous he couldn't. It is by his raiding that a young warrior attains the marriage price."

Alison hated to see spring come, but she couldn't hold back the hands of time. When Ramon and his warriors rode off, she felt fear, but it was only the normal kind any woman would feel when she knows the man she loves is going into danger and not that terrible oppressive feeling of doom that she had come to dread.

The raiding party returned two weeks later, and Alison knew as soon as they rode through the window that the raid had been successful. Every warrior was beaming, including Ramon.

Later, when they were alone, he confided, "I was almost afraid to go on another raid. I feared my medicine had been broken."

"Your luck? But you're bound to have some defeats. Things can't always go smoothly."

"I know. But losing his medicine is something every chief dreads."

Jacita stuck her head in the *wickiup*, her pretty face flushed and her dark eyes dancing. "Father says you must come!" she said to Ramon in an excited voice.

Jacita disappeared as suddenly as she had appeared. "What's that all about?" Alison asked.

"I suspect Santo is on his way to offer his marriage price. Come," he said, bringing her to her feet. "You're part of the family too."

When they reached Miguel and Jacita's *wickiup*, the old blind man was standing in front of it, but Alison could see no sign of Jacita, which puzzled her.

Santo walked through the camp, proudly leading a string of six magnificent horses behind him. He stopped before Miguel, greeted him and Ramon, and then announced that he had come to ask for Jacita in marriage.

"Jacita," Miguel called softly.

Jacita stepped out of the *wickiup,* her head bent shyly.

"Jacita," Miguel said, "do you want me to accept this young man's marriage price?"

"Yes, Father."

Miguel smiled broadly and held out his hands. Santo gravely placed the reins to the horses in the old man's hands. Then Miguel handed the reins to Jacita, who led the horses to the back of the *wickiup* and tied them there, so everyone in the camp could see she had accepted Santo as her future husband.

Miguel asked Santo into his *wickiup* to eat with them, and the young warrior accepted. As they ate, Alison watched the engaged couple from the corner of her eyes. They both seemed so embarrassed, she almost felt sorry for them.

As she and Ramon walked back to their home, Alison asked, "When will they get married?"

"Not for a few days. Santo has to build their marriage *wickiup* first."

"They seem so shy around one another."

"Remember what I told you? They are young and inexperienced."

"But they seem almost afraid of one another."

"I'm sure they're both looking forward to and dreading the wedding night, for fear they'll do something wrong."

"Doesn't anyone talk to them? Explain things?"

"I'm sure Santo isn't a complete innocent. If he hasn't

made a visit to one of the widows who initiate some of the young warriors, he's at least heard the men talking."

"But what about Jacita?"

"I understand women talk too."

From what Alison had heard, they mostly snickered about it. She wanted Jacita to know how wonderful, how beautiful it was. She vowed she would pay the Apache girl a visit and have a little woman-to-woman talk with her.

Three days later, Jacita and Santo rode off to their wedding *wickiup*. Alison was pleased to note that the Apache girl's eyes were glittering with happiness and anticipation. Alison took credit for the last. She hoped she hadn't overdone it when she had told the Apache girl about the joys of lovemaking, or Jacita might be disappointed. After all, Ramon was an exceptionally skillful lover.

"Will they go to the same valley we did?" Alison asked.

"No. No one knows about that valley except you and me."

"Then everyone doesn't go there for their honeymoon?"

"No. It's our secret valley."

Ramon turned to her. "I won't be leaving on another raid for several days. Would you like to go back to the valley for a visit? We can't stay but a day and night though. I need to make preparations for the raid."

Ramon's dark eyes shimmered with sensual promise. "Oh, yes," Alison cried out breathlessly, her heart already racing in anticipation. "When can we go?"

"Tomorrow."

18

Alison and Ramon left early the next morning for the secluded valley where they had spent their honeymoon. As they rode through the mountains, Alison pondered over something that had been teasing at the edges of her mind since the day before. Did Ramon's keeping the valley a secret from the others have some special significance? That, and his suggestion that they return to it, seemed very romantic to her. Had he come to love her, despite what he had said about never loving a woman? A thrill ran through her at the thought. She wanted him to love her, desperately. She'd found out that love, when it was all one-sided, could be miserable.

"You are very quiet today," Ramon remarked.

"I . . ." Alison hesitated, then summoned her courage. "I was just wondering why you kept the valley a secret from the others."

Ramon didn't dare tell her of his sentimentality for the place where they had consummated their union and spent the first weeks of their marriage. To do so would come dangerously close to admitting something that he was having difficulty accepting himself. "A chief feels the need for a place of complete privacy where he can get away from the demands of his responsibilities for a while."

Alison felt a keen disappointment at his words and was glad that she was sitting in front of him on his mount. Otherwise, he might have noticed the sudden tears that came to her eyes. She had been a fool to entertain such fanciful thoughts. Ramon was much too macho, too coldly practical to ever let his heart rule his thinking or his actions.

When they rode into the little valley, however, Alison's disappointment fled as a feeling of utter serenity filled her. There was no doubt about it. The valley did have a hypnotic magic about it. There was no place here for sadness or bitterness or hate, or any of the ugly emotions that man had devised. It was Eden before the fall of Adam and Eve, a place of beauty and happiness and peace.

As Ramon brought his horse to a standstill in the meadow, Alison looked about her. The grass was almost knee high and sprinkled with bluebonnets and salmon-colored paintbrush. And if that were not enough color, the trees were full of birds of every conceivable hue, the most spectacular of which were the little painted buntings whose plumage contained several vibrant colors, making them look as if an artist had gone berserk and splattered every paint on his palette on them. She had never seen so many birds in her life. "Where did all the birds come from?"

"They are on their way back north from wintering in Mexico. At this time of the year, the Chisos are full of them."

"I haven't noticed an increase of birds back at the village."

"They prefer to rest in more isolated areas before continuing their long flight north. The birds have probably been stopping in these mountains for hundreds of years."

Yes, Alison thought, the valley probably had not changed since the beginning of time, except for its seasonal dress. It was one of nature's forgotten jewels just waiting to be discovered and appreciated.

"I see our *wickiup* is still standing," Ramon remarked, "but I'll have to cut fresh pine boughs for it."

"I don't see why you should go to all that trouble," Alison answered, thinking she didn't want him spending their precious time in the valley cutting limbs. "We're only going to be here one day. We can sleep in the open tonight."

"It might be a little cool when the sun goes down."

"We have our blankets, and we can always build a fire to keep us warm." She laughed. "We won't even have to cut wood for it. We can use the old pine boughs."

They spread one of their blankets beside the gurgling stream and ate their lunch. Then they lay on the blanket, basking in the warm spring sun and each other's company. But it was inevitable that their physical awareness of one another would come to the fore and, with it, their passion, for both knew that was their real reason for coming here, to find again a private hideaway to make love.

It was an unhurried loving, one that matched the quiet mood of the valley itself. They undressed each other slowly, savoring the sight of each inch of skin they bared, exchanging kisses and touching, rediscovering the other's secrets as if this were their first time making love.

Ramon rolled Alison to her back and lay half over her, nuzzling her throat and drinking deeply of the sweet scent of her skin and hair. Alison's blood sang at the feel of his warm, bare skin against hers and his hard, muscular body against her soft one. As he placed a trail of butterfly kisses up her neck, she drew him even closer, thrilling as she felt his powerful heart quicken against hers. Oh, how she loved him, she thought, her strong, fierce warrior, her magnificent savage, her exciting lover.

The tip of his tongue teased her lips, then brushed across her teeth, before plunging into her mouth, stroking, swirling, tasting the sweetness within. Alison answered him with her own sensuous strokes, their breaths mingling as the kiss deepened, their tongues dancing wildly and fueling their passion, sending their senses reeling.

Alison moaned in disappointment when Ramon broke the kiss, then sighed in rapture as his lips grazed her shoulders before seeking the softness of her breasts. He buried his face in the valley between those twin mounds, again savoring her intoxicating scent before he covered one breast with soft kisses and little nips, then soothed the tiny stings with his tongue. Her breath caught at the exquisite feel of his tongue rolling and flicking the sensitive, throbbing peak; she moaned as he took it in his mouth.

She clung to him as Ramon turned his attention to its jealous twin, feeling a fire smoldering in her loins as his mouth tugged on her. She drew his dark head closer, never wanting these wonderful sensations to end.

Ramon's head descended, his tongue a fiery dart as he

traced each rib. His hands smoothed over the curve of her hips, then stroked the insides of her thighs, slowly—ever so slowly—inching upward. Alison sobbed, the anticipation almost unbearable, then sighed when his fingers slid over the swollen lips and parted them to explore the damp depths of her femininity. Alison felt the sweet waves of pleasure rushing over her. Her senses spun; her toes curled.

She looked up to see Ramon kneeling between her legs, his silver earrings glittering in the sunlight and rivaling the hot glitter in his dark eyes. As he slipped his hands beneath her hips and lifted her, then dropped his head, Alison's heart pounded in anticipation. As Ramon's lips and tongue worked their magic on her, swirling, flicking, nipping, tantalizing, then dipping lower and probing deeply to taste her honeyed nectar, Alison's breath came in ragged gasps. Before there had been sweet ripples of delight; now there were powerful undulations of ecstasy that shook the very foundations of her soul. He brought her to that shuddering peak of rapture over and over, glorying in his power to bring her pleasure, lavishing it on her until Alison feared she would die if he didn't stop this exquisite agony.

She felt incredibly weak when he lowered her hips and hovered over her, his eyes glowing with satisfaction. Her love for him swept over her like a huge, monstrous wave, and with it she felt a powerful surge of renewed desire. She reached for him, wrapping her hand around his rigid length, once again amazed at the velvety texture of his skin and his scorching heat. She stroked him, his moans of pleasure exciting her even more.

She rolled him to his back, kissing and nipping his bronzed flesh from his neck to his toes, her mouth brushing tantalizingly over his groin as she descended, then licking the insides of his muscular thighs as she ascended until he was writhing beneath her. Again she took him in her hand and lowered her head.

Ramon felt her mouth on him like the heat of a branding iron. His breath left him with a rush, and he trembled all over. As she worked her magic on him, he cupped the back of her head, their positions reversed as she gave him exquisite pleasure. Now he was her willing captive, her tongue dancing, whirling, and tantalizing as she drove him to that peak of unbearable excitement, until he felt his skin could no longer contain him.

Feeling dangerously close to exploding, he uttered a strangled cry and jerked her up to face him, then rolled her to her back. His plunge was swift and true as he buried himself deep in her moist heat, and Alison welcomed him with a cry of gladness. For a moment they lay perfectly still, savoring their joining, their hearts beating in unison. As he began his movements, he bent his head, kissing her long, deeply, lovingly, his thrusts in perfect rhythm. He withdrew completely, teasing and taunting her with the tip of his manhood until Alison thought she would scream for want of him, then slid back into her depths. Again his lips covered hers, and as the kiss grew wilder and more passionate, his strokes became harder, deeper, swifter in a sweet savageness that filled every inch of her body with exquisite sensation and made her blood sing. He held them at the quivering peak, their bodies trembling in intense anticipation, their hearts pounding frantically against each other. Hovering there, prolonging that unbearable tense pitch of excitement, was both heaven and hell.

Alison couldn't stand it any longer. Every nerve in

her body was screaming for release. "Now, please!" she cried.

Ramon gave her what she wanted. With one powerful thrust he lifted her to a wild turbulence of swirling, blinding colors and into a mutual ecstasy so powerful that it seemed to consume their souls and left them both drained and totally sated.

They spent the rest of the day in the enchanted valley just talking and enjoying one another's company, and Alison thought the quiet companionship the best part of their day. She had never felt so close to Ramon, not even when they made love, for passion drugged the senses. The joy, the happiness she felt was pure, a spiritual communion rather than physical.

Ramon didn't make love to her again until that night, and when it was over and they were drifting in that warm, rosy glow of contentment, Alison said, "We should make love in the open more often. It seems more natural, more beautiful than making love in a *wickiup.*"

Ramon was prone to agree. With the blanket of glittering stars above them, the sweet scent of pine in the air, the murmuring creek beside them, their lovemaking had seemed to take on a deeper meaning. With no man-made walls around them, it was as if nature itself had become part of them and shared in their joyous union. "I'm afraid going out into the woods every night to make love would be impractical, to say nothing of the lack of privacy."

Alison was forced to agree. It would be embarrassing if someone were to stumble over them in the dark. "We could pull our pallets into the brush enclosure. We'd be able to see the sky and smell the pines and still have privacy."

When Ramon made no comments, Alison felt silly for making such a romantic suggestion.

She would have been surprised if she had known why Ramon was silent. His mind was occupied with thoughts of what it would be like to make love to Alison in the moonlight, for both times they had come to the little valley there had been no moon. And then an even more tantalizing thought came to him. What would it be like in the rain?

When they left the enchanted valley the next morning, Alison was filled with sadness. She wondered if she would ever feel that special closeness with Ramon again. There she had had him all to herself, but once they returned to the *rancheria* she would have to share him with the others. As chief, he really didn't belong to her but to the tribe, and she knew in her heart that he would always set his people before her. The knowledge that she would never have his heart and soul fueled the deep bitterness she harbored against him for taking away her freedom.

As they rode into the *rancheria*, the first thing Alison saw was the women planting their corn crop in the big field. The bitterness she had been feeling was replaced with a twinge of guilt at taking a day off and not doing her share of the work. Then, as her practical side came to the fore, a sudden thought came to her and she pushed her guilt aside. She wondered briefly if she should approach Ramon with her idea, then decided to risk it. "Will you be going to a marketplace on this next raid?"

"Probably. Why?"

"Would you bring me back something?"

"What?"

"Some vegetable seeds."

Ramon scowled, then said, "I told you we do not have a big enough field for any other vegetables but corn. Besides, we do not need them. Nature provides all we need."

"That's well enough for you to say!" Alison retorted tartly. "You're a man. You're not breaking your back digging in the hard ground for roots and braving the cactus thorns and the yuccas' daggerlike leaves. We women are! If we planted more vegetables, it would make our work much easier, particularly if we planted things that grow aboveground, like squash and melons and beans."

"There is not enough land cleared for all those things."

"We won't need much more, and clearing it won't involve much work. We'll just burn off more grass."

"I told you, Apaches are not farmers . . . except for the Mimbres," he added as an afterthought.

"Who are they?"

"A large Apache band that lives in Mexico."

"If they can farm, why can't we? Or do you think of farmers as being weak and unmanly, since they wield hoes instead of knives and guns?"

Ramon might scorn the Navaho for their agricultural inclinations, but he would never accuse the Mimbres of being weak and unmanly. Despite their farming, they were one of the fiercest and most feared of the Apache tribes. Both Juan José and Mangus Coloradas, two of the greatest and bravest Apache chiefs of all time, had been Mimbres. "They are more settled than we are. They have held the same land for many, many years."

"How long have you been in this valley?"

"Seven years."

"That sounds pretty settled to me. Besides, what can it hurt? All you would lose would be a few seeds and a little labor, and planting more vegetables would be nothing compared to the work the women are already doing."

When Ramon remained silent, Alison asked, "Why are you so resistant to my idea? I'm not trying to tell you how to run the tribe. I don't expect you and your warriors to tend the fields. I'm just suggesting something that would make the women's work easier."

Ramon had never given much thought to how hard the women might have to work—their labor had been the same for hundreds of years—nor had he ever seriously thought about the Mimbres and their success at agriculture. If the Mexican tribe could do it without losing the other Apache tribes' respect, why not try a little farming? More food was always welcome. But . . . "I don't think the women will like your idea. They are used to the old ways."

Alison knew how set in their ways the women were, but she was determined to win them over. "You just get me the seeds. I'll take care of the women."

Ramon said nothing further, leaving Alison to assume that he wouldn't grant her request. He's just being stubborn again, Alison thought angrily. Why, he was just as possessive of his position as leader and decision maker as the stupid medicine men were of their roles, and just as backward in his thinking. But to Alison's surprise and pleasure, Ramon brought her seeds when he returned from his raid.

Alison was so thrilled at the opportunity to try her farming experiment that she hugged Ramon and thanked him profusely, leaving the rugged chief to ponder over the complexity of this white-eyes he had taken for his wife. When he had brought her jewelry, she had thanked him graciously but shown none of the excitement she was now revealing to him. He might not have been as surprised at her reaction if she had been Apache. They had survival down to a fine art. They knew the value of food. But even then, the usual Apache wife would have probably been much more thrilled over a trinket than something as useful as seeds. Women the world over were frivolous creatures, or so he had always thought. Alison had surprised him. He had suspected a strength in her, a determination that equaled his own, but he had never thought a white-eyes, much less one who had been pampered her entire life, to have serious, down-to-earth values. A glow of pride filled him.

As he untied the small sacks of seeds from his saddle, Ramon asked, "How much do you know about farming?"

"Actually nothing," Alison admitted. "I'm a city girl. But it couldn't be any harder than planting corn, and I've learned how to to do that. Just dig a hole in the ground with a stick and put a few seeds in it."

"According to the Mimbres I traded with for these seeds, it's not quite that simple. The old man I talked to said the squash, melons, and pumpkins should be planted on small hills, and the beans should be staked. The vegetables rot if they sit in rainwater."

Alison was grateful for the helpful information Ramon passed on to her. But much to her disgust, she couldn't get the Indian women interested in her farming project. They scorned her idea, no matter how much she argued that farming would be easier than gathering what nature grudgingly provided. Only Jacita agreed to help her burn the field and plant the vegetables, and then only because Alison was her friend. And because the others refused to participate, the two had to settle for cultivating a much smaller plot of land than Alison had planned.

When the vegetables bloomed, the Apache women admired their pretty yellow and white blossoms, but their interest in the garden ended there. They could appreciate it only for its aesthetic value. It wasn't until Alison and Jacita harvested their crop in the summer that the women finally took serious notice. They stood around and watched in awe as Alison and Jacita picked the vegetables right off the ground and filled their burden baskets to the brim in no time at all, without having to contend with one treacherous thorn or sharp-pointed leaf. To Alison's delight, the garden was amazingly productive, enough so that she and Jacita had vegetables to give away. In the end it was the taste of the squash that convinced the Apaches that farming might not be so foolish after all. The vegetables tasted remarkably like the mescal they loved so much and cooked so much quicker than the tough agave hearts. From then on, Alison had to practically fight the women away from the garden, for in their enthusiasm to sample them many picked the melons and pumpkins before they had ripened.

But Alison couldn't get truly angry with them. She was too pleased at how well her project had worked out. And once more, she sensed that Ramon was pleased too.

19

In late August one of men who had been assigned as sentry on a distant mountaintop raced his horse into the *rancheria* and headed straight for where Ramon and his subcaptains were planning another raid beneath the shade of a towering pine. A moment later Ramon and his lieutenants rode from the camp, leaving everyone else in the *rancheria* dying of curiosity to know what was going on. Several hours later Ramon and his men returned, leading a large band of haggard Apaches behind them.

Watching the strange Apaches ride in, their horses hardly more than skin and bone, Alison asked Jacita, "Who are they?"

It was Jacita's husband, Santo, who answered, his black eyes glittering with excitement. "I recognize their leader. That is Chief Victorio!"

Alison stared at the fierce Apache chief she had heard so much about. Victorio was almost as tall and powerfully built as Ramon, with short cropped hair that also had a natural wave, but he was a good twenty years older than the Chisos chief. Then Alison turned her attention to a bent, half-crippled old man standing beside Victorio, noting that his earrings were made from thick gold watch chains. "Who is the old man with the snow-white hair and eccentric earrings?" Alison asked.

"He is probably Nana, Victorio's most trusted subchief and constant companion," Santo answered. "It is said that he is even fiercer and more dangerous and cunning than Victorio."

Ramon led Victorio and Nana to a large *wickiup* that was set aside for official tribal business, and the three men disappeared inside it, while Victorio's warriors, who all wore a circle of red war paint on their cheeks, dismounted and sat on the ground beside their horses. The notorious band was quickly surrounded by the men in the *rancheria* asking about the strangers' purpose for coming to their camp. Much to Alison's disappointment, she didn't hear the renegade Indians' answer. She was rushed away by Jacita to help prepare food for the unexpected guests. By the time the meal had been prepared and served, the men were silent, visitors and Chisos alike, their expressions grim. Even as they ate, the warriors' dark eyes were on the *wickiup* where the two chiefs were having their "smokeout," their council.

The sight of Victorio's men disturbed Alison. To a man they looked bone weary and half starved, their clothing tattered and torn. But it was the desperation she saw in their eyes that distressed her the most. They were clearly men whose dark despair had made them reckless and exceedingly dangerous. She should hate them, she told herself, for the crimes they had committed against her people, but she found she could only pity them.

An hour passed, and another. Everyone in the camp grew increasingly apprehensive. Finally Ramon and

the two Apaches emerged from the *wickiup*, and Alison
knew by the expressions on Victorio's and Nana's faces
that they were not happy with the results of their talk.
The two renegades were clearly angry, while Ramon
betrayed no emotion, his face set like a mask. Alison
knew that expression only too well. Whatever decision
Ramon had made, he was fiercely determined to keep
it.

Two women held out bowls of food to Victorio and
Nana. Victorio waved them aside angrily and quickly
mounted, the rest of his band jumping to their feet and
doing the same. Ramon said something to one of his
lieutenants, and he too mounted. Then, with Ramon's
subcaptain in the lead, Victorio and his warriors raced
from the camp, leaving a cloud of choking dust in their
wake.

Before the renegades had even thundered from the
valley, Ramon summoned his men, and they crowded
around him. From where she stood across the camp,
Alison couldn't hear what Ramon told them, despite his
excellent oratory voice, but she could see mixed emotions on the warriors' faces. A few were obviously disappointed, but most of the warriors seemed relieved by
whatever information Ramon was giving them. As Ramon turned to walk away, the *di-yin* Benito stepped up
to him. Again, Alison couldn't hear what the medicine
man said, but she saw Ramon stiffen and a furious glitter
come to his eyes. Whatever the chief's answer to the
medicine man was, it was brief and adamant. Then
Ramon walked from the circle of Indians, his head held
high and his mouth set in a firm line.

Since Ramon was closer to their *wickiup*, he arrived
there first. He was seated cross-legged on a mat inside
the dimly lit structure, staring at the willow wall across

from him, when Alison entered, holding a bowl of food in her hands.

"I brought you something to eat," Alison said.

"I'm not hungry," Ramon replied tightly.

As he continued to stare at the wall, Alison fought a silent struggle with herself. A part of her was eager to know what Victorio had wanted, and another part cautioned her not to probe into something she knew Ramon considered tribal affairs and none of her business. The minutes of silence that followed seemed like an eternity to her. Finally her curiosity got the better of her and she boldly asked, "What did Victorio want?"

Ramon shot her a hot, warning look, a look that infuriated Alison. "I just asked a question! If you won't tell me, I'll eventually find out from the other women. One of them is bound to have overhead what you said to your warriors, or if not, their husbands will tell them. It may come as a surprise to you, but not all of your warriors are as tight-lipped and secretive as you are."

Ramon was aware that his warriors talked among themselves, and that a few even revealed tribal affairs to their wives, if the women were determined enough to pry the information out of them. But those women were simply curious. Once their husbands had given them the information they wanted, they showed no further interest in the matter, for they knew it was their place to accept and not question decisions, particularly not decisions made by their all-powerful chief. But Alison was an entirely different breed. She wasn't just curious; she was also intelligent and infuriatingly outspoken. If he told her of his decision, she would undoubtedly voice her opinion. It didn't matter that her opinion might be in agreement with his. He was chief! He wouldn't let anyone, not the *di-yins* or his wife, influence his thinking.

But despite his fierce protectiveness over his position, Ramon found he wanted to discuss his decision with someone, that he needed that counsel desperately. In the past, he had told Alison things that he had never revealed to others. So far, she had not interfered with his business, but he secretly feared her influence over him. She was a strong person, as strong as he. If she were a man, Ramon would keep his eye on her, for fear she would challenge him for leadership of the tribe. As incredible as it seemed, even knowing that becoming chief was beyond her capabilities because of her sex, her strength seemed threatening. She was like no woman he had ever known. Woman weren't supposed to be powerful and wise. Those were men's attributes. Unless that woman was the White Painted Woman, that is.

The thought stunned Ramon. Could Alison be the reincarnation of the White Painted Woman come back to help her people in these times of dire need and tribulation? That would explain Alison's strange power to foretell the future. If that was the case, he would be a fool to refuse her counsel. His reason tried to reject the idea. He didn't believe in spirits as the others did. But his Apache upbringing was too strong to completely discredit the idea. He shot his wife a penetrating look.

Alison was acutely aware of Ramon's look, a look that seemed to be peering into her soul and made her very uncomfortable. "Why are you staring at me like that? I just said I'd eventually find out why Victorio came here."

"Who are you?"

A tingle of fear ran over Alison. Why was he acting so peculiar? "What do mean, who am I? I'm Alison!"

Ramon was filled with frustration. Surely, if she were the White Painted Woman she would have admitted it to him. Unless she was testing his faith. But regardless of who Alison was, wife or the reincarnation of the Apache goddess, Ramon found his need to confide in her over-powering. The decision he had made today laid heavily on him. "Sit down. I will tell you what Victorio wanted."

Ramon's sudden announcement bewildered Alison. She sat, wondering what had brought about his complete turnaround.

"Victorio asked me to join him on his warpath against the whites. He is desperate for help, and we are the only band of Apaches in this country that have not been put on a reservation. He has been trying to make it to the Mescalero reservation at Tularosa in New Mexico. They have secretly been supplying him with arms and provisions. But the *pindah* cavalry has him pinned down in Mexico. They patrol entire length of the border and have laid ambushes at every water hole between the Rio Grande and Tularosa. Twice recently, he has been turned back by Colonel Grierson and his buffalo soldiers, at Tinaja de las Palmos in Quitman Canyon and then again at Rattlesnake Springs. Victorio believes if my band joined his, we could fight our way through to Tularosa, but I refused."

That was why Victorio and Nana looked so angry, Alison thought. Thank God Ramon had refused, for she had come to understand and accept the difference be-tween raiding for survival and going on the warpath. If Ramon had committed himself to open warfare against her people, senselessly murdering them out of hate and revenge, it would have killed her love for him. Even if she had come to understand the Apaches' hatred for the whites, bloodshed of innocents would have stood between them like an insurmountable mountain. Or would it have killed her love? Alison wondered. Her deep feelings for the Apache chief seemed to be something beyond reason, something that she had absolutely no control over. No, she was forced to admit, she would have been torn between the man she loved and her loyalty to her people. Thank God Ramon had refused and spared her that torment.

When Alison made no comment, Ramon continued. "It was not an easy decision to make, to turn down another Apache when he is in such desperate need, and I have no love for the white man. But I feared if we joined with him, it would bring the *pindah*'s wrath down on the Chisos. As it is, they make only halfhearted efforts against us for our raiding. But that would not be the case if we went on the warpath against them. They would come down on us with a vengeance, as they have on Victorio. As chief, it is my duty to put the safety of my people first."

Without even thinking, Alison answered, "Yes, it certainly is. You were wise to turn him down. Everyone in the United States is crying out for vengeance against Victorio and his band. The public won't let up until he's crushed. If you had aligned yourself with him, it would have meant certain defeat."

A shiver ran over Ramon. Had she had another premonition? "Why do you say Victorio's defeat is certain?"

"Common sense tells me that. His small band can't hold up against what the American army is pitting against him, and the more the public cries out in outrage, the more soldiers the government will send against him. You said yourself that they have him pinned down at the border, that he can't get supplies and guns. Time is running out for him."

It was the same logic that had brought Ramon to his conclusion and decision. There seemed to be no end to the number of soldiers the *pindah* could send against them. To bring attention to his band by aligning himself to the notorious renegades would have been foolhardy. Victorio's medicine was broken.

Now that her curiosity about Victorio's purpose in coming to their *rancheria* had been satisfied, Alison was curious about something else. "What did Benito say to you that angered you so?"

A long moment of silence followed before Ramon answered, "He called me a coward."

"Because you refused to join up with Victorio?" Alison asked in outrage. "Why that old fool! Doesn't he know it takes more courage to stand up for your beliefs than to do something as stupid and risky as joining Victorio?"

Ramon hoped the people in his tribe would think he acted courageously and wisely too, but in view of what else the old medicine man had accused him of, he wasn't too sure of their confidence in his judgment. "He also called me a traitor to my people, because I refused to give Victorio the guns and ammunition he asked for, nor would I allow him to use these mountains as a place to operate from. All I would give him was food from our emergency supply, but just this once, and only because his warriors were on the verge of starvation. Benito claimed I should have given Victorio more aid in his fight against the hated *pindah,* that a true Apache would have helped his brother Apaches more. I told the medicine man that I was more concerned about the

Apaches in this *rancheria*, that we needed our guns and ammunition to protect ourselves, that I would not bring the white man down on us by offering Victorio refuge or giving him arms to use against them."

Ramon wouldn't divulge to Alison the real reason why Benito had accused him of being a traitor. It wasn't his refusing Victorio that had riled the old *di-yin*. Benito couldn't care less what happened to Victorio and his warriors. The accusation had had a hidden meaning, one that applied to Alison. Twice she had been the instigator of things that were against their Apache way of life, first by insulting the medicine man personally by refusing to call for his aid when Ramon was injured, then by introducing farming to their women. The medicine men feared the white-eyes was gaining influence over their chief, something that the *di-yins* had never been able to do. Benito had hoped his accusation would anger Ramon and bring him to his senses. But instead of his insults turning Ramon's anger on Alison, as the cunning old *di-yin* had hoped, Benito's accusations had only served to make Ramon more determined to follow his own judgment. Alison had had nothing to do with his decision. He had acted as he always had, in behalf of his people. But still, the old medicine man had instilled doubts in the minds of the Chisos, which would serve his purpose just as well, if not better. Benito wouldn't have to worry about Alison's influence if he could remove Ramon as chief. And the medicine man hoped that he could manipulate the next chief.

Alison had no idea of the thoughts that were going through Ramon's mind. She had been busy thinking over everything he had told her. "I'm glad you gave them food," Alison said softly. "Even I felt compassion for them, despite what I knew they were doing to my people. But you were wise to refuse them guns and refuge. Aiding them in that way would have brought the white man down on you just as much as your going on the warpath." Alison paused for a moment, then said, "Yes, I can see where it wasn't an easy decision for you. It must have been very difficult."

It had been. Victorio and Nana had both pleaded eloquently, and Ramon had been deeply touched by their plight. But he hadn't allowed himself to be swayed from his decision, no matter how much he pitied the renegade Apaches or felt for them. There might be others among the tribe besides Benito who would call him coldhearted, a traitor to his own people, but Alison had seen his difficult dilemma and offered her understanding. For some strange reason, that was enough. The twinge of guilt that had been gnawing at his conscience since he had refused Victorio disappeared, to be replaced with a feeling of peace. Regardless of the seeds of mistrust that Benito had sowed in the minds of his people, Ramon knew he had done the right thing.

That fall one of the Mescaleros who had ridden with Victorio appeared at the *rancheria* asking for refuge. It was from him that the Chisos learned of Victorio's tragic ending. It seemed that a joint Mexican-American expedition had traveled into Mexico to Victorio's stronghold in the Candelaria Mountains. Since the Apache chief had been on the warpath against both nations and his favorite way to escape being caught had been to slip over the border and away from the army that was currently chasing him, the two countries had decided to act together to capture the Apache who was dealing them so much misery. But the combined expedition discovered that Victorio and his band had moved

farther south. The Mexican officer in charge, Colonel
Terrazas, sent the American army and Texas Rangers
back, then trapped Victorio and his group in a rugged
canyon in the isolated Tres Castillos Mountains. Completely encircling the islandlike upthrust, Terrazas and
his army of a thousand men attacked. With noplace left
to run or hide, the Apaches were massacred. Victorio
had run out of ammunition. Sixty warriors, including
Victorio, and eighteen women and children were
killed, and seventy were taken prisoner by the Mexicans. A small number, including the man who had come
to them for refuge, managed to escape into the countryside and hide in a ravine, but they survived only by
strangling a baby whose crying almost gave away their
position, and then by crawling through a prairie fire the
Mexicans had set around them.

The shocking tale left everyone speechless. Seeing
the smug smile on Benito's face, Ramon feared the people in his tribe would condemn him for not giving
Victorio guns and ammunition, that they would blame
him for the renegade Apaches' deaths. Then the Mescalero told the Chisos something that shocked them
even more. He related how his chief and their small
band of Mescaleros had wanted to leave Victorio after
their defeat at Rattlesnake Springs, but Victorio would
have none of it. He killed the Mescalero chief and
forced the others to stay. The Chisos couldn't believe
Victorio's disgraceful actions. The Mescaleros had
joined Victorio of their own will. It was their right,
according to the Apaches' strong individualistic code of
warfare, to leave when they so desired. Ramon had
given his warriors the choice to stay or to join Victorio
on that day the renegade chief had ridden out of their
valley. A few had considered it, then decided against it,

and now they were grateful that they hadn't, for they realized that they wouldn't have been allowed to leave either and would have shared the fate Victorio's band had suffered.

When Ramon told the homeless Mescalero that he could stay with their band, the Chisos nodded their heads in approval. Yes, their chief was a compassionate man, and a wise one. Instead of condemning Ramon, they praised him. If not for him, they might have made a fatal mistake. As a result, Ramon's position as their leader was stronger than ever.

It wasn't until Alison and Ramon had returned to the privacy of their *wickiup* that Ramon gave her a quizzical look and asked, "Do you remember when you said Victorio's time was running out?"

"Yes. Why do you ask?"

"Are you sure it was just common sense that made you think that?"

A shiver ran over Alison. "Are you asking if I had a premonition of impending doom? No, it was nothing like that."

Then she couldn't be the reincarnation of the White Painted Woman, Ramon thought, for surely if she was, she would have been able to foretell the disaster that had awaited Victorio. The White Painted Woman was the protector of all Apaches.

Ramon was relieved. He preferred that Alison be just a flesh-and-blood woman. The White Painted Woman belonged to all the Apaches, but this remarkable woman, whom he had come to admire for her strength and wisdom, belonged just to him.

20

The next spring, Ramon's raids were thwarted time and time again. It seemed the entire area that surrounded the Chisos was swarming with calvary, either the *pindah*'s yellowlegs or Díaz's *rurales.* Ramon could hardly ride out from his mountain retreat in any direction before one or the other was chasing him back.

One day, when he had returned from yet another failure, Alison said to him, "I don't understand it. Why are they patrolling this area so closely? Victorio and his band are gone now."

"Victorio is gone, but Nana escaped both the massacre and the holocaust. He took command of what was left of the band and has joined forces with his son-in-law, Geronimo."

Alison frowned. "I've never heard of Geronimo."

"He is a rising war *di-yin* who is rapidly blazing a name for himself. Nana and he are making the warpath Victorio took look tame in comparison. They are everywhere, crossing back and forth across the Rio Grande, one day in New Mexico, the next in Sonora, then in

Texas, then back in Mexico again, killing any Mexicans or *pindahs* they come across and burning everything. They have so terrorized the entire Southwest that even the *pindah* citizens have joined the chase. I don't just have the yellowlegs to contend with, but the Texas Rangers and posses of storekeepers and cowhands, all thirsting for the blood of an Apache—any Apache!"

"Perhaps you should just sit tight for a while," Alison suggested.

"And where will we get our necessities, if not from my raiding?"

"We have food, both from our garden and what nature provides us. And then we have our emergency supply."

"That will not last forever. We will need to replenish it."

"Maybe by that time Nana and his band will have been brought under control."

Ramon didn't see any recourse but to sit tight. It would be suicide to ride out with the area swarming with soldiers and posses bent on vengeance.

But the next week Ramon discovered something that made his blood run cold. The cavalry was probing the Chisos, sending patrols into the mountains that had always acted as his band's sanctuary. It wasn't the presence of the yellowlegs that disturbed him, though. He knew the mountains would destroy them, for they were greenhorns who knew nothing of survival in this harsh, dry land. Rather it was the hard-eyed men who led them, the Texas Rangers, men whose faces were as brown as his and who were as inured to heat and hardships as the Apaches were.

When Alison heard the startling news, she asked, "But why? Why are they so determined to get you?"

"I don't know. Perhaps they think I am supplying Nana and his warriors with arms and supplies. Perhaps it is simply because we are Apaches, and they want to rid this earth of every last one of us."

Ramon monitored the patrols closely. Then one day, when he felt they were getting too close to their camp for comfort, he called for an immediate evacuation.

It was bedlam, trying to pack their belongings while the men rushed them. Finally, when their possessions were packed and loaded on horses, everyone was mounted, many riding double or triple. As Alison rode from the valley with a small frightened child held before her and another clinging to her back, she looked over her shoulder. The only thing that remained of the camp was the *wickiups* and the women's heavy grinding stones. But that wasn't all the Apaches were leaving behind them in the mountain valley. They were leaving their memories too, and the home that had sheltered them from the scorching summer heat and freezing north winds. Then her eyes fell on their garden, which was just beginning to bring forth its harvest, and tears came to her eyes. All that hard work for nothing. Damn the *pindah*! Why couldn't they leave them alone? They weren't hurting anyone here.

Alison realized that she was thinking like an Apache, but she wouldn't take the curse back. At that moment she was Apache. Their pain at being forced from their homes, their anger, their hate for the white man was hers.

Jacita rode up beside her and said glumly, "This is the way it started for Beduiat, the white-eyes chasing him and his tribe from their beloved mountains."

"We aren't leaving the mountains. We're just leaving this valley," Alison pointed out.

"But still, we will never find another home like it."

The two rode in silence for a while, then Alison asked, "Why is it your people don't call one another by your Apache names? Ramon said something about it not being done except in the most dire circumstances, but I still don't understand."

"It is because of the responsibility the Apache name bears. We never address each other by our given names unless we are in mortal danger or it is of the utmost gravity, for if a request is asked for, it cannot be denied, no matter what."

"Are you saying if I asked you for something, no matter what, you'd have to give it to me?"

"Yes. To refuse would be dishonorable."

That explained why Ramon had not wanted her to know his Apache name, for fear she would call him by his name and ask for her freedom. "I'm just curious, but what is Ramon's Apache name?"

Having no idea why Alison was asking, Jacita answered, "It is Chatto."

Alison rattled the name around in her mind. Yes, she thought, it suited him even better than his Mexican name, for it had a strong sound to it.

Ramon settled his band in a small valley on the other side of the mountains, but within days they were forced to move again. With grim determination the soldiers followed their trail. In the next two weeks they moved five times, crossing back and forth across the rugged mountains under the blistering sun, hiding in deep canyons whose walls radiated the heat like an oven, their only water that which they found in little pools, never enough to really assuage their thirst.

Because their horses were worn down from lack of

grass and water, the Apaches were finally forced to walk. Alison trudged along with the others, sweat pouring from her, her head pounding from the sun. Despite her determination to keep up, she lagged behind, and then when everyone else had passed her, she collapsed. She was too exhausted to walk another step. She didn't feel she even had the energy to die.

Ramon appeared at her side, his shadow falling across her and giving her a brief respite from the searing sun. "I can't go any farther," Alison muttered.

"You don't have to. This is where we will camp."

He carried her to one of the caves that were scattered over the side of the mountain. As he sat her down in the cool shade, Alison looked out. The mountain was barren, nothing but solid rock. Suddenly, all the frustrations and hardships she'd had to endure over the past weeks came down on her. She was bone-tired; she ached all over; her throat was dry as parchment, her lips cracked and bleeding. "I can't stand it any longer!" she flung at Ramon. "I can't take any more of the soldiers' constant hounding, any more running and hiding. I'm tired! I'm not as strong as you Apaches are."

She leaned forward and caught Ramon's high moccasins in one of her hands. "Take me back to my people," she pleaded. "Please! Take me back!"

"No. I will not take you back."

"Don't you understand? This is killing me!"

"You are just tired. When you have rested—"

"But that's just it! We're never going to get any rest! They're never going to stop hounding us! If you won't take me back, let me go."

"No! I will never let you go."

"Why? Because of your pride? You can divorce me. And the tribe won't think any less of you for it. You have a perfect excuse. I know how they feel about childless marriages, that they think they're the greatest tragedy an Apache can experience. You can use my barrenness as your reason for dissolving our marriage."

"You are not barren. We have not been married long enough to have a child. Pregnancy is cumulative. We have not made love often enough."

Alison might have laughed outright at Ramon's claim that they had not made love often enough to produce a baby—as often as they made love, they could have produced several—but she was too angry to laugh. It seemed the more he denied her her freedom, the more determined she was to have it. "Damn you! Why are you being so stubborn? Why won't you let me go?"

When Ramon remained silent, a fierce expression came over Alison's face and she said in a hard voice, "Chatto, I am asking you to let me go."

A brief flicker of surprise came over Ramon's face at Alison's using his Apache name before his look hardened. "No."

"You *can't* refuse me! Jacita said you can't refuse any request when your given name is used."

"I am still refusing."

Alison couldn't believe he would refuse, for she knew he took his Apache upbringing very seriously. Was he that determined to keep her, so dead set on it that he would dishonor himself, a man who put honor and pride above everything? "Why?" Alison cried out angrily. "Why are you refusing me?"

It was a long moment before Ramon responded, and then his answer was torn from the depths of his soul. "I can't let you go!" he said in an anguished voice. A noise that sounded oddly like a sob came from him. "I love you."

It seemed to Alison that she had waited a lifetime to hear those words. Her spirits soared as she savored his admission, holding it close to her heart for a long, precious moment. And then her joy was replaced with pain when she realized that his vow of love did nothing to change her fierce desire for her freedom. Above all, she still wanted it, even more than his love. How could he profess to love her, yet deny her what she wanted so badly, what he had stolen from her, what only he could give back? Tears glittered in her eyes, and her voice sounded just as tormented as his had been as she said, "If you loved me, *truly* loved me, you'd give me my freedom."

"I can't! It would be like tearing my soul from my body. I need you. As long as I live, I will never let you go."

Ramon turned and walked down the mountainside. Alison sat back on her heels and cried bitter tears.

It was dark when Ramon returned to the little cave. Alison had recovered from her hysterical outburst, but the bitterness was still there.

He sat beside her on the blanket she had spread and took her hand in his. "Do not let your anger stand between us. I have given you my all. You are my wife, my love, my soul mate. I have laid my heart at your feet."

Alison was helpless against his scorching look. Her love for him was something she couldn't change, no matter what he did. She cupped the side of his face in her hand and said, "I love you too, but—"

"No! Don't place any buts between us."

He took her hand and kissed the palm. Then his dark eyes rose to meet hers. "We have finally proclaimed our love for one another. This night is special. Don't ruin our happiness. Let me love you."

He lowered her to the blanket, placing soft kisses over her face. Despite her bitterness, Alison wanted him as much as he did her. Her passion was an integral part of her love, as impossible to separate as the soul from the body.

There was a poignancy in their lovemaking that night, an underlying sadness that, strangely, made it all the sweeter. There was also a terrible urgency, for they knew not when, or if, they would make love again.

Ramon made love to her over and over. First he loved her with wild abandon, his kisses fierce and demanding, as if he were storming her defenses; then, when they had drifted back down from the rapturous heights he had carried them to, he loved her with gentle tenderness, taking his time and lavishing his attentions on her. But still their strange hunger was not appeased. Alison loved him back, taking him to heights he had never known with her mouth and tongue and hands before they found release in yet another shattering explosion. Even then she wouldn't give him up. She watched his face as he dozed with his head cushioned on her breasts and his manhood still nestled inside her warm depths.

The sun was just coming over the horizon, tinting the eastern sky in soft mauves and pinks, when Alison whispered, "Are you awake?"

"Yes," Ramon answered, his face still pillowed on her soft breasts.

She ran her hands across his shoulders and down his broad back. "I love you with my whole heart and soul, but I can never forgive you for not giving me my freedom. Can you understand that?"

Ramon understood. He too valued his freedom above

all. The only thing that was more precious to him was Alison. "I understand." He slipped his arms around her and embraced her tightly. "But I will never give you up."

21

Two days later the cavalry again came perilously close to the Apache camp, pushed on by their tough Ranger guides, who had been the Indians' mortal enemy since the state of Texas had been a struggling republic. Like bloodhounds on the scent of their prey, the Rangers and the buffalo soldiers —as the Indians called the black cavalrymen because of their tight, curly hair—wouldn't give up the chase. If they couldn't catch the Apaches, it seemed, they were determined to run them to death.

Ramon called for another quick evacuation of his people. But despite his Apache beliefs that there was no dishonor in retreat if it could save lives, the chief had been pushed by the invaders as far as he would go. The exhausted tribe couldn't run any farther. The time had come to turn and fight for their mountain homeland.

Alison had no knowledge of Ramon's plans. Like everyone else in the tribe except his subchiefs, she couldn't understand why he drove them so mercilessly that day, through one twisted, rocky, barren canyon after another, with the hot sun blazing down on them.

He wouldn't even stop long enough to let them ease
their terrible thirst or gnawing hunger. Like many of
the others, Alison stumbled on the treacherous rocky
ground and fell, bruising her knees and scraping the
skin off her hands, and each time one of Ramon's warriors was there to tell her impatiently to get up and
hurry forward.

An anger at the Apache chief rose in Alison, one she
would have furiously vented if she had had the opportunity, but Ramon was nowhere around. Unknown to her,
he was at the rear of the fleeing Apaches, setting his
trap. It was her fury at him for being so unfeeling, so
hard that kept her going that day, that gave her the
strength to struggle on.

When Ramon deemed his tribe at a safe distance, he
attacked the cavalry in a narrow canyon. It was a mas-
terpiece of Apache warfare, for the yellowlegs, mistak-
enly thinking they had finally run the Apaches down
and that surrender of the tribe was at hand, had no idea
they were riding into a deadly ambush. They were
caught completely by surprise when Ramon's warriors,
concealed behind boulders and piles of rocks at the top
of the canyon, opened fire on them. It was the cavalry
who had nowhere to run. They were caught in a furious,
lethal cross fire. The battle was the epitome of the
cavalry's frustration over the years in trying to fight the
Apaches. The sunbaked Indians, stripped down to their
breechcloths for battle, blended in with their surround-
ings. The soldiers couldn't shoot them, because they
couldn't see them. Their enemy would be behind first
one rock, then another. The glaring sun in their eyes
blinded them, while the Apaches had the advantage of
height, picking them off with deadly expertise. In the
few hours left of daylight, Ramon and his warriors gave

them such a terrible beating that what was left of the
patrol retreated under the cover of darkness. By morning the soldiers had left the Chisos, racing their mounts
across the desert to the safety of their fort, not one
daring to look back at the rugged, jagged copperish
peaks where they had been so soundly defeated.

The day after the battle, after posting sentinels on
several high peaks in the Chisos to watch for more patrols, Ramon moved his tribe to another location at the
southernmost edge of the mountains. Below their camp
they could clearly see the Rio Grande and the little
Mexican village that specialized in raising corn. The
tribe settled down and waited.

When a week passed and no further moves were
made against them, the Apaches settled down in earnest. *Wickiups* sprang up everywhere, and for the first
time in weeks the women had time to gather enough
food for the band's hunger to be appeased. The new
location didn't have the beauty that the valley at the top
of the mountains had, nor was it near as cool, but it was a
welcome relief from the soldiers' hounding.

Another week passed, then a month, then another
month, with no sign of the soldiers' return. But Alison
did notice a frequent visitor in the camp, a wiry Mexican who somehow reminded her of a weasel. One day
when she and Jacita were grinding corn on their grind-
stones, she asked, "Who is that Mexican? Over the past
two weeks, I've seen him four times."

"His name Lionecio Castro. He was born in the little
Mexican village below us and rode with Ramon on several raids a few years back. When he left our band, he
said he was going to Chihuahua. Since then we have
seen nothing of him, until just recently."

Alison wondered why the man had come back. Did

he plan on rejoining the tribe? He seemed to be spending an awful lot of time with Ramon.

Several days later Alison found out what the Mexican was doing in their camp. Out of the clear blue, Ramon walked into their *wickiup* and informed her that Castro had come as a representative of the Mexican government with instructions to make a treaty with him.

"A treaty?" Alison asked in surprise, for the Mexican didn't strike her as the kind of man a government would send on such official business. "But he's just an uneducated peon," she objected. "What would a man like that know about making treaties?"

"The Mexican government knew I would never let a strange Mexican anywhere near my camp. They chose Castro because they knew he was a friend of our tribe and knew me personally. He is only acting as their intermediary, carrying out their instructions. You don't have to have an education to do that."

Yes, Alison thought silently, governments usually sent friends of the Indians to bring them in for peace talks, but for some reason she felt strongly suspicious of the Mexican. "Just what are the terms of this treaty?"

"We would be placed on a reservation in Mexico and given provisions and clothing regularly. Castro has promised that we would be well fed and well treated."

"But I thought you said you'd never go to a reservation, that you'd never give up your freedom?"

"That was before the yellowlegs came down on us."

"But we haven't seen anything of the cavalry lately, not since you beat them."

"They are just licking their wounds. They will be back."

"How can you be so sure? They didn't bother to seek you out in the mountains before."

"Has the *pindah* ever let the Apache live in peace?" Ramon asked bitterly. "No! One by one, they have forced the Apache tribes from their homes and put them on reservations. My tribe's turn has come. We are among the last Apaches to still hold our land. The *pindah* will never allow that. They will not rest until they have chased us off, or killed us. And there is noplace left to go as free men, not in even in Mexico."

Alison knew he spoke the truth. Eventually the cavalry would be back. The American public would see to that. They wouldn't be satisfied until they had every Indian in the country on a reservation, or dead. Their unreasonable hatred for the red man came dangerously close to genocide. "But if you're considering settling on a reservation, why Mexico? The Americans would offer you the same terms."

Ramon's black eyes flashed. "I would rather die than go to that hellhole at San Carlos, or any other Apache reservation in this country! They are all the same, stuck off in some scorching desert, swarming with gnats and mosquitoes and flies, infested with disease. There are more ways of killing a man than with a bullet. The Mexicans have promised us a reservation in the mountains, in the Sierra Madres."

Yes, if he and his band settled anywhere, it would have to be the mountains, Alison thought. They were mountain people. They would be miserable anyplace else. "Maybe the Americans would give you a reservation in the mountains."

"Like they did Victorio?" Ramon asked in a scathing voice. "No! I do not trust the *pindah*."

"But you can't trust the Mexicans either! You said they've lured the Apaches with promises time and time again, and then massacred them."

"I would not be trusting the Mexicans. I would be putting my faith in their president. The treaty would come directly from him. I would have his personal promise."

"President Díaz? But he's a Mexican too."

"No, he is a full-blooded Indian. It is from their white Spanish blood that the Mexicans get their treachery."

"Díaz is an Indian?" Alison asked in surprise.

"Yes, a full-blooded Mextec. For that reason, he will treat us honorably. Castro says Díaz does not wish to see our race exterminated, that he feels for all the Indians in his country."

"But he sends his *rurales* and soldiers against you," Alison pointed out.

"Only because he has to, because the Mexican people demand it of him. He would much prefer to put us on reservations, places were we would not be molested by the whites, places were we could live in peace. There are many such places in the Sierras, places so far isolated from civilization that the Mexicans do not want them."

Alison frowned. Díaz's claims sounded familiar. The American government claimed it wanted the Indians on reservations as much for their protection as that of the whites, but the places became prisons where the Indians were half starved and forgotten by the very people who had promised to help them. Ramon himself had enlightened her on the inhumane conditions that existed on the reservations; he had told her how the army failed to protect the Indians. "I still don't understand why you feel you can trust Díaz just because he's an Indian."

"An Indian does not break his word. That is the white man's trick."

"But you don't even have his word, just Castro's."

"I do have Díaz's word, his written word. I have this!"

Alison had not noticed the scroll that Ramon held in one hand. As he unrolled the document and showed it to her, he said, "This is why I have come to you. I cannot read it. Can you?"

"I don't know," Alison answered as she took the paper that was adorned with impressive-looking green and gold seals. "I never learned to read Spanish."

"See if you can decipher it anyway."

Alison struggled over the writing. She could recognize a word here and there, but the document was so eleborately written it seemed a confusing muddle of words, and much of it appeared irrelevant to her. Alison was aware that legal papers were often such, that only a lawyer could sift through the excess of words, and it did look official, but . . .

"Well?" Ramon asked impatiently.

"I don't honestly know what it says," Alison admitted.

"Castro said it is not the treaty. We will still have to settle upon the terms. He said it is proof of Díaz's goodwill toward us, that it had been signed by the president."

Alison flipped through the pages and saw the signature boldly scrawled across the bottom of the last page beside an official-looking impress. She remembered seeing that signature before. "Yes, it's signed with his name, and it looks like the same signature I saw at the bottom corner of Díaz's picture in the courtroom at Presidio, but it could still be a forgery."

"Why do you say that?"

"I just don't trust Castro. He seems sneaky, devious in some way."

"You do not even know the man."

"He has shifty eyes. I've never trusted a man who couldn't look you in the eye."

Ramon laughed. "One eye is crossed. That is why he looks that way."

"I still don't trust him."

"Your suspicions are groundless. The document is signed by Díaz himself." Ramon took the papers from her and rolled them up. "It is settled. I will accept Díaz's offer. We will move to Mexico."

Alison was stunned by his announcement. She had thought Ramon was just considering the offer. She had no idea he was so close to making a decision. Suddenly the doubts and suspicions she had been feeling became something much more profound. A strong premonition of impending disaster came down on her like a heavy, suffocating blanket. "No!" she cried out as Ramon pushed aside the flap at the door and ducked his head.

Ramon froze at the urgency of her voice, holding the flap aside with one hand and staring at her from his half-bent position.

"You mustn't do this!" Alison said, a wild look in her eyes.

"You are only saying that because you have taken a dislike to Castro."

"No! I'm saying it because something disastrous is going to happen if you do. I feel it. I know it!"

An icy shiver ran up Ramon's spine. "You have had another premonition?"

"Yes."

"Then why didn't you tell me in the beginning?" he asked, dropping the flap and coming to his full height.

"I didn't feel it in the beginning. I just felt uneasy. It wasn't until you told me of your decision that this terrible feeling came on me."

"If you can truly foretell the future, why couldn't you predict the disaster that happened to Victorio and his band?"

"I don't know," Alison answered in acute frustration. "The ability seems to come only when it has something to do with you."

When Ramon remained silent, Alison said, "Don't stare at me that way. And don't you dare call me a witch again! I don't know how I know, but I do know something terrible is going to happen if you do this. If you won't stop yourself, then I must. I won't let you!"

Ramon stiffened and a hard expression came over his face. "I am chief! I make the decisions for this tribe. No one tells me what I can and cannot do. I will accept Díaz's offer."

He turned, threw back the flap, and stormed from the *wickiup*. Alison realized she had made a serious mistake. She should have reasoned with him, but she was so upset she hadn't even thought before the words were out. Her fear had made her reckless, and now he wouldn't relent. His stubborn pride wouldn't let him. A feel of hopelessness invaded her, added to the oppressive feeling of impending doom.

Ramon didn't return to the *wickiup* until late that night. His prolonged absence gave Alison time to reflect on all he had said. She couldn't believe he would actually give up his freedom without a fight. It was much too precious to him. The more she thought about it, the more convinced she became that he wasn't doing so willingly. Something had influenced his decision, and she strongly suspected he was doing it for her. She had told him that she couldn't stand being hounded, that she wasn't strong enough to survive, and if they stayed in these mountains, that is what their life would be, perpetually running from the whites who were determined to evict them. Did he think life on a reservation would be easier for her? Was that why he was doing it? Alison had mixed emotions. It pleased her that he loved her enough to put her before his tribe, but it also made her feel very guilty. She realized that wanting him to make her his top priority was selfish. And now, because of her, the entire band might be going to their doom. That was something she couldn't live with. She had to change his mind.

When Ramon entered the *wickiup,* Alison was lying on their pallet in the dark. He stripped off his clothing and reclined beside her. No sooner had his head hit the ground than Alison rolled on her side and placed her hand on his chest. Feeling him stiffen at her touch, she said, "No! Please don't be angry with me. When I said I wouldn't let you do this, I didn't mean it the way it sounded. I wasn't trying to usurp your authority as chief. It was just that I felt compelled to try to stop you. I'm terrified, Ramon, for you, for me, for all of the people in this tribe."

When he remained silent, Alison asked, "Why are you doing this? Is it for me? Is it because of what I said the day the soldiers were chasing us, that I couldn't stand it any longer? I didn't even know what I was saying that day. I felt I had been pushed beyond my endurance, and I was half mad with thirst. But I'm much stronger than that. It was just an outburst, a temporary thing. You don't have to do this for me. I don't want you to."

In truth, Alison had played a big part in Ramon's decision, for two reasons. First, Benito was trying to blame the tribe's recent misfortunes on Alison. By moving the tribe to a safe place, he would be protecting her from the old medicine man's vindictiveness. Second, Ramon thought Alison would be more content to stay with him on a reservation where life would be easier for her. He had been willing to give up his freedom to keep her, to make her happier. "Did you mean what you said about your freedom, that you would never forgive me?"

"Yes, I did mean that," Alison answered in all honesty. "I still feel that way. That's why I can't let you give up your freedom for me. Giving up yours won't give mine back. It won't change anything."

The one and only thing that Ramon couldn't give Alison was her freedom. He didn't think he could bear going through life without her, and he was afraid to give her the choice of choosing between him and his way of life and her people and old way of life. "I will not let you go."

The words hovered in the air over them for a long moment. Tears came to Alison's eyes. Then she said quietly, "I know. But that is something between us, and this treaty involves the entire tribe."

Ramon was silent for a moment, then said, "I will admit that you were a part of the reason for my decision. I thought living on a reservation would be a compromise between our different ways of life. But I did not forget the people I lead. If we do not move peacefully, we will eventually be forced out, and I fear many will be killed if it comes to that. At least this way, we can say it was our own choice, even if it truly wasn't."

"Then fight for your land!" Alison urged fervently.

"I am afraid that too is no longer a matter of choice. We are almost out of ammunition, and with the army keeping such close watch on us and our not being able to raid, there is no way to get more. We are trapped if we stay here." Ramon rolled on his side and ran the palm of his hand down the length of her arm. "Tell me what disaster you see in the future."

"I don't have visions. I told you that before. I just have a feeling something terrible is going to happen."

Ramon was silent for a moment, then said, "I will still accept Díaz's offer, but I will move with caution. We did not survive all these years without carefully watching our backs. I am not a fool."

Alison frowned. Yes, Ramon had proved himself more than capable in the past. Under his guidance, the tribe had done amazingly well to hold back the white tide as long as they had. Surely there must have been times when they were in great danger, but Ramon had brought them through. She should have more confidence in his abilities. But these reassuring thoughts brought no relief from the oppressive feeling of dread that filled her.

She opened her mouth to make one last plea, but Ramon silenced her by placing his fingers against her lips. "No! It is settled. We will discuss it no further."

He rose to his feet, bringing her with him. "We will not be in these mountains much longer. What time we have left here, we will enjoy to the fullest. Come. We will pull our pallet into the brush enclosure."

His voice dropped to a husky timbre that was full of promise. "There is a full moon tonight." Alison could not resist when Ramon took her hand and led her outside.

22

Ramon kept his word about moving cautiously. He sent word to Castro that he wanted further proof of his good faith, and a meeting was arranged between the Mexican representatives and the Apaches to take place at San Carlos. Instead of going himself, however, and risking having the chief of the tribe captured in a trap, he sent one of his subchiefs and two other Indians.

The Apache delegation returned several days later and reported that they were escorted to a town house on the plaza and were met by a number of men in gold uniforms who had every appearance of being military officials. For two days, several details of the proposed treaty were discussed and agreed upon, among them a promise that the Mexican government would provide each Apache with a blanket, a belt, and certain provisions before they set out for their new home in the Sierras. A date had been set for the next month, according to Ramon's instructions, during the full moon.

Three weeks later the Apaches left their beloved Chisos Mountains, men, women, and children, weaving their horses down the narrow, twisting mountain trails that led to the Rio Grande. Alison looked back over her shoulder at the jagged peaks, knowing she would never again see the beautiful valley that had been her home or the little enchanted private valley with its incredible peacefulness. Then, spying a rainbow hovering in the sky over the highest crests, an unbearable sadness filled her, and a tear slid down her cheek. She quickly glanced around her and saw she wasn't the only one who was deeply distressed. Many of the women's and children's dark faces were glistening with tears. Even the fiercest, most hardened warriors looked heartbroken.

They camped that night by the Rio Grande, and then crossed into Mexico, but not until Ramon had put out scouting parties before them. Then, when they were several miles from San Carlos, Ramon called a halt.

"Why are we stopping?" Alison asked from where she sat on her horse beside his.

"I want to be sure they haven't laid a trap for us."

He removed a small mirror from his saddlebags and flashed it in the sunlight. An answering flash of light came from a mountaintop that overlooked the town and the desert all around it.

"Is it safe?" Alison asked.

"Yes. My sentinel has been on that mountaintop since daybreak. There are no soldiers or *rurales* anywhere around. He will stay up there and watch. If any try to sneak up on us, he will alert us."

Alison realized that was why Ramon had chosen a time of the full moon, so his sentinel could keep watch even at night. "But what if they are hiding in the town itself?"

"I have sent scouts up ahead to inspect it. They too

have seen no soldiers or *rurales.* The only strangers in
San Carlos are the officials that Díaz sent to meet us."

His caution soothed the fear Alison had been living
with, but deep down, that feeling of impending disaster
still lingered.

When they rode into San Carlos, the townspeople
came out to greet their old friends warmly, throwing
flowers in their path and cheering. The bells in the
church tower echoed the Mexicans' glad reception, the
joyous pealing ringing out over the tile rooftops and
spilling out over the surrounding desert. Even the government representatives received them cordially,
treating Ramon as if he were a respected dignitary from
some foreign country.

Alison watched from the distance with the others as
Ramon conferred with the officials in front of the town
house on one side of the plaza. The fierce Apache chief
she had come to love towered over the shorter Mexicans, his dark head held proudly, every fiber of his being radiating supreme confidence and power. The same
aura of greatness hung over him that she had noticed
the first time she had seen him that long-ago day in
Presidio. He didn't look at all like a man about to surrender his freedom, but rather like a king who had come to
claim his kingdom. A feeling of immense pride filled
her.

Ramon turned and walked back to the tribe, telling
them that they were to camp in the plaza and stable
their horses behind the old abandoned church until the
next day, when they would be led to their new home.
When the men returned from seeing to the mounts, the
Indians were given provisions in such abundance that
Alison was stunned by the Mexican government's generosity. Wagon after wagon was driven into the plaza,

piled high with blankets, clothing, cooking utensils, sacks of dried beans and corn, barrels of salt and dried beef. Then the Apaches were told to sit down in the plaza, where they would be served a feast.

Alison saw Ramon stiffen from the corner of her eye. "What's wrong?" she whispered.

"The Mexicans have been known to invite us to a feast and then feed us poisoned food."

Alison was horrified. She glanced around her. Seeing that the townspeople were going to partake in the feast also, she said, "But the Mexicans are going to eat too. Surely they wouldn't do that if it was poisoned."

Alison's observation put Ramon's suspicions at rest. He smiled and said, "Now I am the one who is seeing ghosts where there are none. The people of San Carlos would not poison us. They are our friends. They share our happiness at our good fortune."

Alison frowned at Ramon calling her premonition "seeing ghosts where there are none," but she was beginning to wonder if the entire thing hadn't been just a matter of acute anxiety. The Mexicans' happiness for the Apaches seemed sincere, and even the officials seemed genuinely friendly. Perhaps what Castro had told Ramon was true. Because he was an Indian himself, Díaz intended to see that the Indian tribes who agreed to go peacefully to reservations were well treated and cared for.

When one of the officials walked up to Ramon and invited him to sit at a table that had been placed under a huisache tree at one corner of the plaza and dine with them, Ramon answered, "Only if my wife is invited also."

The official had not noticed Alison in the crowd when the Apaches rode in. His full attention had been on the fierce Apache chief he had heard so much about. Even when he had walked up to Ramon he had not noticed her, for she was as lean and brown as the others, and her long hair was just as black. Now when he glanced at her, it was her unusual height that he first perceived. Then, looking at her face and seeing the vibrant blue of her eyes, he was startled. "This is your wife?" he asked in a shocked voice.

"Yes," Ramon answered calmly.

Taking note of Alison's dress, the official asked, "She is Mexican?"

Before Ramon could answer, Alison said, "No, I'm an American."

The Mexican looked very uncomfortable, and Alison knew he was faced with a dilemma he didn't know how to solve gracefully. He didn't dare demand that Ramon release his white captive, for fear the Apache would refuse and break off negotiations immediately. Yet, as a white man, particularly a government official, he was obligated to do just that. Alison feared he might try to use force to make Ramon surrender her, but Ramon had told her in no uncertain terms that he would never give her up as long as he lived. "I am his wife by my own choice."

It was hard to say who looked more shocked by her announcement, Ramon or the Mexican. Because Ramon was staring at her, he didn't see the scornful sneer that came over the official's face before the Mexican quickly hid it. But Alison had seen and knew what he was thinking: that any white woman who would willingly consort with an Indian was the lowest thing on earth. Damn him, she thought angrily. How dare he look down on her! And if he thought to shame her, he was sadly mistaken. She was proud of her love for her

Apache husband. He was more man than all these Mexicans put together. She came to her full, impressive height, raised her chin, and looked the offical defiantly in the eye.

Alison never knew if it was her height or her look that intimidated the man. He stepped back as if he had been slapped in the face and muttered, "Of course your wife may dine with us."

As the official walked away, Alison started to follow, but Ramon pulled her back and whispered, "Why did you tell him that you had married me by choice?"

"Because I knew what would happen if he demanded that you free me, and I was afraid he'd try to force you. I don't want any bloodshed because of me."

Ramon's facial expression didn't betray the keen disappointment he felt. He had been hoping that she had forgiven him. "It was a prudent answer. No one will ever take you away from me."

When they reached the table, Castro was standing there with the officials, a grin stretched from one ear to the other across his swarthy face. "See?" he said to Ramon. "Did I not tell you Díaz would treat you well?"

"Yes, so far he has treated us very well," Ramon admitted. He turned and looked out at the plaza where the women were serving the townspeople and Apache guests. He had never been such huge platters of roasted beef, goat meat, and pork, or such large kettles of *frioles* and steamed vegetables, or so many different kinds of sweetmeats. "Did the government supply all that food too? The people in this town are too poor to put on such a lavish feast."

"Yes, the government supplied it," one of the Mexican officials answered, "and invited the gracious people of San Carlos to the feast as payment for slaughtering the animals and preparing the food."

Ramon briefly wondered at the answer. To his knowledge the government had never paid the peons for anything, much less labor.

The feast continued all day, between horse races and cockfights and gambling games that the Mexicans provided as entertainment for the Indians. The entire town had a festive air about it, and it was hard to say who was enjoying the celebration more, the Apaches or the people of San Carlos.

Because the officials at the table had kept Ramon occupied, he wasn't aware that alcoholic beverages had been brought in to the feast until he, Alison, and Castro walked away from the table much later that day. When he realized that almost every adult male member of his band was well on the way to becoming intoxicated, he was furious. He turned to Castro and asked in an angry voice, "Where did that liquor come from?"

"It was provided by the government. You can't have a fiesta without liquor."

"We were not offered it at our table," Ramon pointed out, his eyes glittering suspiciously.

"Only because it is mescal and tequila. The officials would not insult you, a great chief, by serving you such common, cheap liquor."

"I do not want my people drinking."

"But why not? Fiesta and drinking go together."

"I do not want them to get drunk!"

"They're not drunk. They're just having a good time. Besides, what are you afraid of? You are among old friends here. Come," the Mexican said in a silky voice that made Alison's skin crawl, "we will have a drink ourselves. If anyone deserves to celebrate this day, we do. Together we pulled off this great coup."

"Apaches do not count coup," Ramon replied tightly. "You have ridden with us enough to know that."

"I was just using an expression, my friend," Castro answered nervously, for a dangerous glitter had come into Ramon's eyes. "I simply meant that we deserve to celebrate for all of the work we have both done on this treaty. For weeks we conferred, and I have ridden back and forth between here and Chihuahua City a dozen times to present your case."

If Castro had thought to get Ramon to drink with him out of gratitude, he was mistaken. "I will not drink."

Castro shrugged his narrow shoulders. "If that is the way you feel, I will not insist. But I don't intend to refuse the government's generosity. Today is a great day. I will celebrate with the others."

As Castro walked away, Alison asked Ramon, "Are you going to stop your men from drinking?"

"I will try, but I'm afraid it is too late to stop them. Liquor is the Apaches' biggest weakness, especially that made from mescal. Once they have started, they won't stop until they are in a stupor."

"Can I help?"

"No, you wait over there by the wall of the abandoned church. From there you can see the mountain peak where my lookout is posted. If you see him signaling, come get me."

Just as he had feared, Ramon and the half-dozen sober men he found among the tribe could not keep the others away from the apparently unlimited supply of liquor. Not even the grim reminder of the slaughter of the Apaches at Ramos as a result of their drunkenness could deter them. Ramon finally gave up in disgust several hours after the sun had set, picked up his rifle from his pile of possessions, and returned to Alison.

"Have you seen anything?" he asked as he walked up.

"No, but how can I in the dark?"

"He will light a signal fire."

Ramon sat down beside Alison and leaned against the wall of the church, as she was doing. "Have you seen Jacita or my father?"

"They're inside the church with the women and the children. I imagine they're trying to sleep, but I don't know how they can with all this noise."

"Knife and awl!" Ramon cursed in Apache hitting his thigh with his first. "I ought to ride out of here with them right now and leave those drunken fools here."

"But you won't."

Survival of the tribe was foremost in Ramon's mind. It was the number-one Apache rule, even if it meant sacrificing a few to save the group. But this was not a few. It would mean leaving almost every warrior in his band behind, and a tribe's strength depended upon its warriors. "No, I won't," he admitted, then added ominously, "Not unless I have to."

"Maybe nothing will happen," Alison said, but the words sounded hollow to her ears.

"Perhaps not. I keep reminding myself that the people in this town are our friends. But I do not like the way things are going. It sounds too familiar. The Apaches that were slaughtered at Ramos thought those people were their friends too." He looked across at her. "Do you still feel something terrible is going to happen?"

"The feeling is there. Not as strong as it was at first, but it's still there."

"Perhaps it is a good sign that it is not as strong."

"Maybe." Or maybe it's like pain, Alison thought.

After so long, you don't notice it so much. The body numbs it out.

For a long while they sat in silence, staring at the mountain peak where the sentry was posted and listening to the sounds of the drunken Apaches. One by one the Mexicans who had been celebrating with them staggered to their homes. But the Apaches kept drinking until they were stupefied and lay sprawled all over the moonlit plaza.

Finally Ramon said to Alison, "You are exhausted. Go to sleep. I don't believe we are in any danger from the people in this town. I will keep watch on the mountain. At the first sign of a signal fire, we are leaving. Those who cannot travel will have to be left behind."

"Will we have time to get away?"

"From that mountaintop, in this bright moonlight, you can see for far distances. Yes, we will have time, if we do not tarry."

Alison lay down on the blanket she had spread earlier. "No, go inside the church," Ramon objected. "You will be more comfortable in there on the straw."

Strangely, Alison didn't want to leave his side, but she was too weary to wonder at it. "No, I'll just sleep here. I'm too tired to walk that far."

A few hours later, Alison cried out in her sleep, then sat bolt upright. Instantly Ramon was at her side.

"What's wrong?" he asked in alarm, for her face was as white as a sheet.

"I had a dream," Alison answered in a daze. Then with suddenly clarity of mind, she said, "No, it wasn't just a dream. It was a vision. I saw soldiers surrounding the town."

"But that is impossible. I haven't taken my eyes off the mountain. There's been no signal fire."

"We're surrounded! They're all around us!"

Ramon couldn't understand how such a thing could happen. Surely, in this bright moonlight, the sentry would have seen them, and the warrior he had posted had the sharpest eyes in the tribe.

Alison was seized by a terrible urgency. "Damn you!" she cried out, hitting his chest with her fist. "You've got to believe me! We're in mortal danger!"

At the wild look in her eyes, Ramon believed. He jumped to his feet, saying, "Wake up the women and children. Get them out back to the horses."

Alison scrambled to her feet and ran into the abandoned church, while Ramon tore off to the plaza. At the first sprawled Apache he came across, he bent and shook the man roughly. "Get up! We're about to be attacked!"

When the Apache didn't respond, Ramon yanked him up by his shirtfront. As the drunken Apache's head lolled, Ramon recognized him: he was the sentry that Ramon had posted on the mountaintop. For a moment, Ramon stared at him in shocked disbelief. Then he realized what must have happened. The sentry had grown bored with watching for soldiers, and when he saw none, he deserted his post and came to join in the celebrating, allowing the soldiers to sneak up on them during the night. Furious, Ramon pulled out his knife and slit the stuporous Apache's throat.

The few Apaches who were not intoxicated were coming to their feet. Then, all of a sudden, hundreds of Mexican foot soldiers were rushing at them from all sides. Ramon was stunned. This was not a patrol, but several companies.

Cursing himself, he ran for his Winchester, which he had left beside the church. He heard a rifle shot, followed by a barrage. He looked over his shoulder and saw the Apache who had fired the first shot being riddled by bullets. When he looked back around he came to a dead halt.

Castro stood by the wall where Ramon had been sitting just a few minutes before, holding Ramon's rifle in his hands and pointing it at him. "Don't move, or I will shoot!" the Mexican warned.

Ramon saw a movement from the corner of his eye and glanced at the corner of the church. Three soldiers stood there with their guns aimed at him. Women were screaming from the rear of the abandoned church; they had been caught before they could reach the horses and flee. Behind him there was a brief furious exchange of shots, then silence. He knew that those of his warriors who had been alert enough to resist had been killed. A fury rose in him. He cursed Castro in Apache, "You son of a witch!"

The Mexican paled at what he knew was the Apaches' worst possible curse, a curse they considered so vile that it demanded satisfaction by a fight to the death, for Apaches believed witches to be incestuous. The murderous look in the Apache chief's eyes sent a shiver up Castro's spine, and he was acutely aware of the bloody knife in Ramon's hand. "No, I will not fight you!" he said nervously, afraid that Ramon might attack him despite the guns he and the Mexican soldiers were holding on the Chief. Then, feeling a little braver as three more soldiers ran up behind Ramon, Castro smiled smugly and said, "I will not give you the opportunity to kill me. Then I would not be able to collect my reward from Díaz."

Ramon's eyes narrowed. "Are you telling me Díaz had a part in this treachery?"

"He not only had a part in it, he planned the entire thing. He has been keeping his eye on you for some time now. He was determined to capture and exterminate your band, along with all the others like you that raid Mexico's northern states."

Ramon could accept Castro's betrayal, but not Díaz's, the man whom he had placed his entire faith in. "You lie! Díaz is a full-blooded Indian. He would not stoop to such treachery against one of his own."

"You're a fool if you think that. He cares nothing about the Indians in this country. All he cares about is protecting his position as president."

"He led an all-Indian army during Juarez's war against the French," Ramon countered. "If he did not care about Indians, why did he do that?"

"Juárez was the one who made him a general, because he knew Díaz was the only one who could control the wild savages. Díaz cared nothing for the Indians who fought under him, not if they stood in the way of his ambitions. Did you know that when a regiment refused to fight because they would be facing almost suicidal odds, he had the entire group executed? He forced the Indians to pull his cannons. They were not his soldiers. They were his slaves!"

Castro's revelation was a rude and bitter awakening for Ramon. He cursed himself for a fool. He should have known better than to trust anyone. But there was something he was curious about. "How did he know about you, that we thought you were our friend and trusted you?"

Castro laughed. "He put out word among his *rurales* that he was looking for a man you trusted, a man who could draw your tribe into a trap. Many of his *rurales* are men who were once outlaws themselves. One remembered that he had ridden with me when we were both *bandidos* and recalled that I had spoken of you. He searched me out."

"And found you at the bottom of a dunghill!" Ramon spat scornfully.

"No, in a worse place! In a prison in Chihuahua. Díaz wouldn't have even had to offer me a reward. My freedom from that hellhole would have been enough. But," Castro said with a shrug and a grin, "now I will have both."

Ramon was sick at heart. If only he had listened to Alison. At the thought of her, his heart slammed against his chest. He quickly turned his attention to the crowd of women and children that the soldiers had marched from the church while he and Castro had been talking. He had no trouble finding her, for she towered over the others. A wave of relief rushed over him that she was unharmed. He knew only too well how she valued her freedom and had feared she might have resisted.

And then Ramon was beset by another fear. He was afraid to look her in the eye. But when he forced himself to, he saw none of the condemnation he had expected. Her eyes were filled with understanding and compassion. She lifted her chin and smiled bravely, a smile that crossed the distance between them and infused him with a fierce determination to see his tribe free. He had never loved her as much as he did at that moment.

23

At sunrise the Apaches were marched from San Carlos under a heavily armed guard. Ramon led the pitiful procession, walking alone, his head held high and his hands manacled before him. Behind him staggered the warriors who had been captured and bound while they were in a drunken stupor, looking dazed and confused, while the women and children brought up the rear.

Only one man was allowed to walk with the women—Miguel—and then only after Alison stepped forward and demanded that he be allowed to do so because he was blind and needed someone to guide him. Seeing the Mexicans about to bind him too, she had angrily let go with such a scathing objection that the soldiers had backed down, fearing the woman with the blazing blue eyes would attack them and incite a rebellion among the women.

As they were marched through the streets, the people of San Carlos stood on the sidelines and watched. Ramon knew that the townspeople had known nothing of the planned treachery by the shocked looks on the men's faces and the women's tears, and took small comfort in knowing that they hadn't betrayed him too. Then, in open defiance of the government's cruel and unjust treatment of the Apaches, the village priest came out and blessed the passing Indians, while the church bells tolled mournfully.

The tribe was marched across the burning desert to another small town called Santa Rosa, where they were placed in a stockade. As soon as the soldiers had withdrawn, the warriors rushed to their families. Standing among the tearful reunions, Alison looked around her. She felt a shadow falling across her and knew it could only be Ramon. She turned and embraced him tightly.

It took a moment for her to realize that his hands were between them and not around her. She stepped back and saw that they were still manacled. Seeing that his wrists were rubbed raw, she said, "Sit down. I'll see if I can pry them off with something."

"Forget it. The only way they can be removed is with the key or a file."

"But why did they manacle you? They only tied the others."

"That is one of the disadvantages of being a chief. I am considered much more dangerous."

And justifiably so, Alison thought. She bent and ripped a piece of material from the hem of her skirt, then stuffed it between the abraded skin and the iron bands.

Jacita and Miguel stepped up to them. After the girl had embraced him, Ramon asked Jacita, "Where is Santo?"

Jacita hung her head and answered, "He is over there. He is too shamed to face you."

"That is not necessary," Ramon answered. "I harbor

no hard feelings against any of my warriors. What is done is done. It is best to put it behind us and look to the future."

"What do they have planned for us?" Miguel asked.

"All they have told me is that they have brought us here to Santa Rosa to await departure for the City of Mexico."

"They intend to march us to Mexico City?" Alison asked in shock. "But that must be at least a thousand miles away! We'd never survive."

"Do not underestimate our endurance," Ramon said. "Apaches have been marched to the penal colonies in Lower California and survived. A few even escaped and made the return trip."

"What do you think they plan to do with us once we reach the City of Mexico?" Jacita asked fearfully.

"What they usually do with their Apache prisoners," Ramon answered bitterly. "Take us to Yucatan, separate us, and sell us off as slaves. But I will not allow that. Somehow, I will find a way for us to escape."

Miguel's head suddenly shot up. "Did you say we are in Santa Rosa?"

"Yes," Ramon answered. "Why do you ask?"

"I just remembered something. My brother lives on a *hacienda* a short distance from this town. It is from there that I was stolen when I was a youth. Perhaps he can obtain our release."

"It has been many years since your brother has seen you, even if he is still alive," Ramon pointed out. "Why do you think he would help you?"

"We were very close, unusually close even for brothers. And our family was very influential."

Seeing the doubt on Ramon's face, Alison said, "It's at least worth a try. What harm can it do?"

Ramon relented. "All right. I will ask the soldiers to send word to him that his long-lost brother wishes to see him. What is his name?"

"Don Manuel Rameriz."

The next morning Don Manuel Rameriz came to the stockade where the Apaches were being held prisoner and was escorted to Ramon. He was a tall, distinguished-looking man in an elaborately embroidered charro suit. He looked every inch the aristocrat.

When his escort came to a halt and told him this was the man who had sent the message, a furious expression came over the Mexican's face. "What kind of a trick are you trying to pull?" he asked Ramon. "You are not my brother."

"No, I am your nephew." Ramon stepped to the side to reveal Miguel. "This is your brother and my father."

Don Manuel stared hard at Miguel. He did not look like the youth he remembered. His skin was brown and leathery from the sun, and his hair was snow white. "Who are you?" he asked suspiciously. "If you are my brother, tell me your name."

"I am Don Miguel."

Don Manuel's eyes filled with surprise. It was the name of his brother, and also the name of his mother.

Miguel related the story of how he was stolen by the Apaches, but Don Manuel was a cautious man. "If you are Miguel Rameriz, my brother, you have six toes on your right foot."

The blind man stooped and pulled off his moccasin. "The mountain trails are rocky and hard to travel. Long ago I lost the sixth toe. But you can see the scar where it once was."

The Don looked at the foot and saw the scar. Sudden

tears came to his eyes. Then he stepped forward and embraced Miguel, saying in a choked voice, "My brother! I gave up hope of ever seeing you alive again many years ago."

Ramon and Alison moved away so the two brothers could talk in privacy. They were joined shortly thereafter by Jacita and her husband, the young warrior still looking a little shamefaced. When the minutes slipped into an hour, Jacita asked, "What are they talking about so long?"

"They have many years to cover," Alison reminded her.

Finally the two men joined them, Manuel carefully leading his blind brother. When they were standing before them, Miguel introduced his family to his brother, making Alison wonder how he had known Jacita and her husband had joined them. It could only have been that strange sixth sense of the blind, she thought.

"My brother has told me your plight," Don Manuel said to Ramon. "I will do everything I can to help you."

Despite the fact that the man was his uncle, Ramon did not like the man. He was a *hidalgo* and represented everything he hated in the white man. "I doubt if there is much you can do," he answered brusquely.

"Do not be too sure. General Blanco is an intimate friend of mine. He is a member of the General Council of Mexico and very powerful. The mention of his name and our close relationship may be enough to get your release."

Don Manuel left the stockade. He didn't return until much later, and Ramon knew by the angry expression on his uncle's face that things had not gone as he had hoped.

"They refused to release us," Ramon said when the *hidalgo* stepped up to them.

"Yes! That fool who commands this guard is so stupid he's never even heard of General Blanco! But I did manage to get him to agree to release Miguel as a white captive. He couldn't refuse to honor my demand. But they would not surrender you."

"I would not leave my tribe," Ramon told him.

"I suspected as much," Don Manuel admitted, "but I thought if I could secure your release you could find a way to free the rest of your people."

"And how would I accomplish that, without warriors and weapons?"

"Yes, I see your point," Don Manuel admitted with a deep sigh.

"I will not leave either," Miguel announced.

"But why not?" Manuel asked in alarm. "What purpose would that serve?"

"I chose the life of an Apache. I will not desert them now," Miguel said stubbornly.

"No," Ramon said in a firm voice. "Your brother is right, Father. It would be pointless for you to throw your freedom away. Nothing would be gained by your staying." Seeing that his words were having no effect on the old man, Ramon said gently, "You are old and blind. We have a long, hard march ahead of us. You will slow us down. There will be those in the tribe who will demand that I throw you away. You know this yourself. It is the Apache way. Don't put me in the position of having to choose between my feelings for you and my obligations to the tribe."

Miguel knew that he would be a liability to the tribe, but he still wanted to stay with his family. Seeing how torn he was, Alison's heart went out to him. And then she was struck with a sudden premonition. "You must stay here," she heard herself saying. "You will be of more service to this tribe if you are with your brother."

"In what way?" Miguel asked.

"I don't know," Alison admitted. She shot a look at Ramon and said, "I just sense it."

Seeing his father about to object, Ramon said, "No, you must believe her. She senses things in the future that we cannot. Twice she has warned me of impending danger by virtue of this power, but I did not believe her and came to regret it deeply." Seeing the shocked expressions on Jacita's and Santo's faces, he said, "She is not a witch! Her power is not evil, but good. I believe it comes from the White Painted Woman. But you must tell no one of this."

The young couple nodded their heads gravely and stared at Alison in awe. Miguel believed also, for he had sensed a latent power in the white woman from the very beginning. He turned to his brother and said, "I will go with you."

A look of immense relief passed over the *hidalgo*'s face. "Thank God!" he said. "I was beginning to fear I had found you only to lose you again." He turned to Ramon and said, "I will be back with a letter to General Blanco. But you must guard it well and give it to no one but him when you reach Mexico City. I do not trust any of the others."

"Why are you doing this?" Ramon asked suspiciously.

"For one, you are my family. A Mexican puts his family before everyone. Miguel knew that when he asked for me. For another, I pride myself as a man of honor. Díaz's treachery toward you has infuriated me. I hope my helping you will set things to right."

Ramon thought he would never trust a *hidalgo*,

much less come to admire one, but he did. The beliefs
he had always held about the white and red races had
undergone drastic changes in the past few days. He had
discovered both enemies and champions where he least
expected to find them. He smiled and said, "I am grateful for your help."

Don Manuel returned the next day with the letter
addressed to General Blanco, handing it to Ramon and
again warning him to guard it well.

"I will," Ramon promised. Glancing around to make
sure no one was watching, he slipped it beneath his
shirt.

"There is one more thing I would like to do for you,
but Miguel said I should ask you first," Manuel said.

"What is that?"

Manuel glanced at Alison standing beside Ramon and
said, "I feel sure I can get your wife released too, since
she is white."

Alison saw Ramon stiffen, but before he could answer,
she said, "No, I will stay."

"But why?" Don Manuel asked.

Alison wondered why she was turning down the opportunity to gain her precious freedom. There was only
one reason she could fathom why she wanted to stay. "I
can't desert my husband and his people in their time of
need. That would be cowardly."

Both Ramon and Don Manuel accepted her reason.
Even Alison believed it. She didn't realize that her freedom would be meaningless unless Ramon gave it to her.

The next day the Apaches were marched from Santa
Rosa, the men manacled and tied together. Alison
thought nothing could be as bad as that day Ramon had

pushed his tribe to escape the soldiers, but she found
out that it had been a picnic compared to that of the
long march over the desert to Chihuahua City. During
the daytime the sun blazed down on them, and at night
they had to huddle together to keep warm in the cold
air. They were given very little water and even less
food. Maddening thirst and gnawing hunger were their
constant companions. After a week their moccasins
were in shreds, and the rocky ground cut their feet to
ribbons, so that they all were limping painfully. The
pounds fell off them, leaving them nothing but skin and
bone.

   The babies and young children were the first to suc-
cumb, dying like flies. To Alison their deaths were almost a relief, for their piteous crying and suffering were
more than she could bear. The old were the next to go,
including Benito, Alison's unknown nemesis. Then
some of the adults became ill with fevers and dysentery,
and many of them died too. For a good hundred miles
their trail was marked by a string of graves, and a con-
suming hatred for the merciless Mexican guards filled
Alison. Like her anger at Ramon months before, it was
all that kept her going. By the time the spires of the
churches in Chihuahua City came into sight, two thirds
of the tribe had died under the inhuman hardships that
had been forced on them.

   On the outskirts of Chihuahua City the Apaches were
thrust into the infamous prison know as Acordo, into
the deepest dungeon. Alison looked around her in horror. She had never known places like this existed. It was
damp and cold. The light from the torches on the walls
cast eerie, flickering shadows over all. The smell of
death hung in the air. Feeling something biting her

ankle, she realized the filthy straw on the stone floor
was filled with vermin. A dark despair filled her.

"We will persevere even through this."

Alison jumped at the sound of Ramon's voice, for the
men had been kept separated from the women and
children throughout the entire march. She looked at
him and was shocked by what she saw. His clothes were
in tatters and his moccasins in shreds. There were deep
lines etched in his face and dark circles beneath his
eyes. His cheeks were sunken, giving him an even more
hawkish appearance. On his wrists, where the manacles
had been removed, she saw the deep, festering wounds.
She knew he would carry the scars of those cruel iron
bands for the rest of his life.

Then she was in his arms, feeling his incredible
strength flooding into her. "We'll be free," he whispered against her hair. "I promise you. Somehow I'll
find a way."

For a week the Apaches were kept in the dungeon.
During this time they regained their strength and some
of their weight, forcing themselves to eat the horrid
food that was brought to them, and their lacerated feet
and festering wounds had time to heal. As the second
week crept by, they became increasing restless, for in-
activity was completely against their nature, and Ramon finally demanded to know what the delay was.

For a moment he thought the guard on the other side
of the heavy bars was not going to answer. Then, grudgingly, the man told him they were waiting for the General Council of Mexico to arrive at Chihuahua City to
give Ramon a hearing that would determine his fate.

Ramon couldn't hide his excitement when he told
Alison what he had learned. "Do you realize what this

means? General Blanco is on the council. We won't have to travel all the way to the City of Mexico to present my uncle's letter to him."

For the first time in months, Alison felt hope, and her spirits soared.

24

A few days later Ramon was called to the heavy iron bars across the door by the captain of the guard. He handed the Apache chief a change of clothing through the bars and told him that as soon as he had made himself more presentable, he would be taken before the General Council of Mexico.

"Why do you think they gave you fresh clothing?" Alison asked as Ramon quickly changed in a darkened corner of the dungeon.

"I would imagine the authorities who have been in charge of us would prefer the council not know how badly we have been treated, for fear their decision would be swayed by pity."

"Do you believe they can be swayed?"

"I hope so, and if not, I'm counting on this." He held up the grimy, sweat-stained letter his uncle had given him, then slipped it inside his shirt.

Alison stepped up to him and kissed him on the cheek. "That's for luck."

Ramon folded his arms around her. "I'm going to need more luck than that."

It began as a long, sweet, intoxicating kiss that told her of his love, then deepened to a fierce, plundering, fiery kiss that told her of his passion. Alison had forgotten how wonderful, how wildly exciting his kisses could be, for the prison was too crowded for intimacies of any kind. It seemed it had been a lifetime, instead of only months, since he had held her in his strong arms and made love her. Her passion for him surged to the surface, and she strained her body hungrily against his, thrilling at the feel of his hard muscles, wishing desperately that she could crawl inside him and that this moment could last forever.

Ramon broke the kiss and set her from him. His hands on her shoulders were trembling and his voice was husky with desire. "If I do not stop now, I will not be able to. But that kiss has made me even more determined to see us set free."

He turned, and as he walked through the prison to the door, every Apache's eye was on him. Ramon had never been so acutely aware of his position as their leader and his responsibilities to them. He firmed his resolve and called to the captain of the guard that he was ready to face the council.

The iron bars were swung open, the rusty hinges squeaking in protest. Ramon stepped out of the dungeon, and the bars clanked shut behind him. He found himself surrounded by six guards with their rifles pointed at him. He glanced up the stone stairway and saw, beneath the flickering torches on the damp stone walls, that the entire corridor was lined with armed guards. Knowing that they thought him so cunning and dangerous gave him an immense satisfaction.

Ramon was led up the stairway by the captain of the guard, one flight, then another, then yet another. When they reached ground level, they walked down a long, dimly lit hallway to a set of double doors at the end. The captain of the guard reached for the doorknobs and flung the doors wide open. The sudden bright light after weeks of incarceration in the dark dungeon blinded Ramon. He was roughly shoved from behind into the room.

When his eyes had adjusted to the unaccustomed light, Ramon looked around him. The room was bare except for a long table in the center of the room, and the walls were lined with guards. He glanced at the long, narrow windows where the sunlight was flooding through and saw that they were barred. Beyond them he could see the towering walls of the prison. Suddenly the Mexicans' extreme caution at guarding him so closely seemed ridiculous. Even if he could escape this room, he could never get past those walls. His lips curved in a scornful smile.

A door to one side of the room opened. *"Atencion!"* the captain of the guard called out. The soldiers lining the walls snapped to rigid, upright positions, their guns held before their chests. Five men walked into the room dressed in military uniforms, their coats elaborately gold-braided and their chests covered with medals. Ramon frowned. He had hoped there would be more civilians on the council. He knew only too well the nature of the men who were seating themselves behind the long table. They were hardened soldiers, inured to compassion or any feelings of pity.

When the council was seated, the chairman introduced himself and the others. Ramon paid little attention to their names, except for one. He glanced quickly at one end of the table where General Blanco sat. What

Ramon saw didn't please him. The general looked just as tough and hard-eyed as the others.

"You are El Halcon, chief of the Chisos band of Apaches?" the chairman asked.

It was more a statement than a question, but nonetheless Ramon answered yes.

"You have been accused of crimes against the Mexican people in the states of Coahuila, Chihuahua, and Sonora."

Ramon frowned. He and his band had never ridden as far west as Sonora. Then as the long list of his crimes was read out, he knew he was being judged not only by his own raids but by every raid, every massacre, every bloody foray against the Mexicans that the entire Apache nation had committed. A bitterness filled him, but he was determined to do something he would have never done for just himself. When the reading of the list of crimes against him was finished, he requested that the council listen to him. He pleaded for his people, long and eloquently, pointing out that the band had been reduced to the point that they were no longer any danger to the Mexicans, that they had already paid for their crimes by the deaths of those they had lost. Finally he asked only for the chance to live and breathe the air of their beloved mountains, promising to never set foot in Mexico again.

When his impassioned entreaty was finished, Ramon knew in his heart that the council hadn't been moved. Their faces were set like stone. The entire tribunal had been a farce. He and his tribe had been tried and convicted before the council had even sat down. There was just one last hope to cling to.

He walked to the end of the table where General Blanco sat, removed the letter from inside his shirt, and handed it across the table to him. "This letter is from my uncle, Don Manuel Rameriz. He instructed me to give it to you and you alone."

The general's eyebrows shot up in surprise when Ramon identified himself as his friend's nephew. He took the letter, opened it, and read it. As he read, Ramon watched the general's face closely. There was absolutely no sign of emotion as the officer read Manuel's letter begging him to befriend the Indians, not even a flicker of compassion. Ramon knew even before the man folded it and handed the paper back to him that the general would do nothing in his tribe's behalf.

"You will be notified of our decision," the chairman said.

Ramon knew the hearing was over. He stepped back from the table, then glanced up. Because he had been temporarily blinded when he had first stepped into the room, he hadn't noticed the picture of President Díaz hanging high on the wall behind the table. He knew then why the council had tried him before they even arrived. They were nothing but Díaz's puppets. He stared at the picture with pure loathing, then turned and walked proudly from the room, looking every inch the great, fierce Apache chief he was.

Ramon was returned to the dungeon, where he imparted the disheartening news to his tribe. An hour later the captain of the guard arrived and announced that the council had decided to grant Ramon's request, that the tribe would be moved back to their *rancheria* in the Chisos.

There was a stunned silence in the dungeon after the captain's unexpected announcement. Once she had recovered, Alison whispered to Ramon, "You must have been mistaken. Your pleas must have moved them after all."

"I was not mistaken. It is a trick! They are trying to lure us with false promises again."

"But what would be their purpose in telling you something like that?"

"So we will go with them meekly, like lambs to the slaughter. No, I have no faith in their promises."

"To be honest, neither do I."

Ramon's head jerked up, sending his earrings swinging at the abrupt movement. "You have had another premonition?"

"No, this is one time I wish I could foretell the future, but I can't. Just common sense tells me they're up to something. It was too abrupt a turnaround." She paused, then asked, "What will we do?"

"What I had planned from the very beginning. Escape!"

Ramon gathered his tribe around him in the darkest corner of the dungeon. He told them of his suspicions, then said, "We have only one alternative left. We must escape. Sooner or later they will let down their guard, particularly if we pretend to believe them. I will watch for the right opportunity. When I give the signal, break loose and run. But I warn you, it will have to be everyone for himself."

"But where will we go?" one man asked.

"Back to the Chisos. Whoever arrives there first will light signal fires to guide the others." Seeing the sudden doubt come across the Apaches' faces, he said, "We are strong. We survived the march from Santa Rosa because we were the strongest of our tribe. We will make it."

His brave words filled the Apaches with confidence. There was not one among them who didn't believe. A silence fell over the dungeon, each and every one envisioning his beloved mountain home.

The next morning the Apaches were marched from the prison. As Ramon had instructed, they pretended to believe, allowing themselves to be marched meekly and wearing excited expressions on their faces.

When they were loaded into wagons unbound, Ramon could hardly hide his elation. In their effort to lure the Apaches into believing their promise, the Mexicans were playing into the Apaches' hands and making their bid for escape easier.

As the wagons were driven into the countryside and turned on a major road, Ramon was filled with scorn. Did the Mexicans think they were so stupid that they didn't known north from south? The fools! How did they think the Apaches had been so successful at their raiding if they had no sense of direction? If Ramon hadn't already suspected a trick, he would have known now. The wagons were headed toward the City of Mexico.

As the wagons bounced along the rutted road, Ramon carefully studied the countryside. Despite the fact that the Apaches appeared to be completely relaxed and unconcerned, he could feel their tension and knew they were anxiously awaiting his signal. When the wagons reached an area surrounded by hills that were thickly wooded, he suddenly jumped to his feet and yelled, "Now!"

As the Apaches leaped over the sides of the wagons and ran for the hills, the mounted escort was taken totally by surprise. Between the warm sun and the Apaches' willingness and eagerness to go with them, they had been lured into a false feeling of security and had been dozing in their saddles. One was still looking about him in disbelief when he was yanked from the back of his horse and had his rifle torn from his hand. He was thrown to the ground so hard it knocked the breath from him as Ramon flew into the saddle. By the time he had recovered, it was too late. He was killed with his own gun.

At Ramon's signal, Alison had jumped over the side of the wagon and had run for the hills with the other women, hearing shouts and gunshots behind her. When she reached the edge of the woods, she turned and looked back. Apaches were running in every direction, and a few had gained possession of their guards' horses.

Then she spied Ramon, sitting on a horse at the crest of a hill across the road from her. There was no doubt in her mind that he was looking for her, despite his telling the Apaches that it would be everyone for themselves. He had vowed he would never let her go. The old bitterness she had harbored against him all along came to the rise.

Then he saw her, and their eyes met and held. When he made no move toward her but sat on his horse and stared at her, Alison wondered what was wrong with him. Then suddenly it dawned on her. At the cost of giving up his own happiness, he was giving her back her precious freedom. She had the choice of staying or going with him. If she chose the former, she had only to walk back down the hill, surrender, and then identify herself as a white captive held prisoner by the Apaches. They would not dare rebuff her. Her uncle lived in Chihuahua City, and his name was well known.

Now that Alison had been given both her physical freedom and her freedom of choice, she hesitated, considering her options. If she stayed with Ramon, she would be giving up the way of life she had been born to, her friends and family, her white culture and heritage with all of its comfort and security. Like Ramon's father, once she had chosen the Apache way of life, she would be expected to become Indian to the bone and would share in their fate, a fate that looked very grim at the present, for their escape had yet to be secured. She would be risking more than her newfound freedom; she would be risking her life. And even if the Apaches managed to escape, did she want to go back to a life of running, of being constantly hounded, of having to scratch in the dirt for a meager living? And there would be no turning back. Not ever! Ramon would never give her the opportunity to back out once she had made her choice, of that she was sure. Her choice would be forever.

But if she chose to go back to her white world, she would have to give up Ramon, their remarkable love, their flaming passion, the intense happiness she had found with only him. There was really only one choice Alison could make. Even if their time together would be only an hour, a day, a month, no matter how brief, she would be in his arms, the arms of the man she loved with her whole heart and soul, and therein lay sublime happiness. No woman could turn down paradise. Having made her choice of her own free will, Alison let out a jubilant cry and ran to her man.

As Alison tore back down the hill, her long hair flying out behind her and a radiant smile on her face, Ramon knew he had won his risky gamble and was filled with an incredible joy. The time it had taken Alison to make her choice, even though it had been only a short moment, had seemed like an eternity of hell to him. Briefly he savored his triumph and happiness, then nudged his mount and raced across the clearing toward her, oblivious to the gunshots whizzing all around him. When he reached her, he didn't even slow his horse's speed. He leaned from the saddle, caught her around the waist, and swung her up behind him.

As they raced away, over one hill, then another, Alison clung to Ramon's waist for dear life. Just once she glanced back and saw several other horses and their riders tearing through the woods. Then, recognizing two that were riding double like her and Ramon, she called out to Ramon over the noise of the horses' pounding hooves, "Jacita and Santo made it! They're right behind us!"

Ramon didn't respond to the wonderful news, at least not verbally. He was filled with relief and gladness, but his full attention was on escape. He urged his mount to an even greater speed.

As they flew over the countryside, the wind whipping his dark hair and her tattered skirt about them, Alison laid her head on her husband's broad back. Once she had made her choice, the doubts about their future were firmly pushed aside. She would allow nothing to cloud her happiness. She had every confidence in her magnificent chief, her fierce, savage warrior, her exciting lover. Ramon would take her back to their home, where the mountains floated in the air, where the peaks played with the clouds, and where the rainbows waited for the rain. It didn't matter if the soldiers came. The Chisos was full of hiding places. All that mattered was that she and Ramon were free and together. She had chosen her way of life and her man, one she loved with every fiber of her being, and she wasn't ever going to let him go.

The promise of her waiting rainbow had been fulfilled.

Epilogue

Ramon and Alison were the first to reach their mountain homeland. On the ledge outside of the large cave where they had cached their emergency supplies, they lit signal fires to guide the others back to the Chisos. For months members of the tribe straggled in, sometimes one at a time, sometimes in small groups. Then, when several months passed and no more Apaches arrived, Ramon was forced, with great sadness, to accept the fact that they had been recaptured. His tribe had been reduced to less than seventy people.

Throughout this time Ramon had wondered why the *pindah* army had not sent patrols into the mountains, for the signal fires must have been seen and reported. If they knew his tribe was back, why had they made no move against them? His curiosity finally got the better of him, and he slipped from his mountain retreat and across the desert to Santa Rosa under the cover of darkness, appearing, like a ghost, in his uncle's *sala*.

Then he came to understand why his father and uncle looked so shocked to see him and why the *pindah* had ignored him. The Mexican government had put out word that he and his entire band had been executed. As far as the *pindah* were concerned, the Chisos Apaches had ceased to exist! Before he left his uncle's *hacienda*, Ramon made arrangements with the two men to meet his father and some of his uncle's most trusted *vaqueros* twice a year at an isolated spot a few miles south of the border for a very secret trade. As his uncle had pointed out, the brands on the *pindah* horses and cattle could be easily altered to his own and sold without anyone becoming suspicious.

When Ramon returned to the Chisos, he moved his band back to the big valley, knowing that they would be safe there.

After some time Leonecio Castro returned to the little Mexican village below the mountains. Here he heard the sinister rumor that had crept over the entire Mexican frontier of the Chisos Mountains. It was said that El Halcon's ghost had come back to haunt the mountains, that he had been seen by shepherds guarding their lonely flocks, one time riding along the slopes of the Del Carmen Mountains and another standing on the tip of a rocky point overlooking the Rio Grande, and yet another on the ledge outside a cave. In fact, he had been seen so often near the cave that the Mexicans called it Cueva de El Halcon.

Castro didn't believe the superstitious Mexicans' stories. To prove them wrong, he went into the Chisos. Two days later he returned, ashen-faced, saying he seen the ghost in the cave. That night the signal fire the Mexicans had seen months before burned brightly on the ledge in front of the cave. Terrified, Castro left the country.

The rumor that El Halcon's ghost roamed the mountains became so persistent in the Mexican neighborhood that people were afraid to go anywhere near the mountains. The authorities at San Carlos sent out a patrol to investigate. They searched the mountains, but knowing nothing of the valley in the center, they didn't venture that far. Then they investigated the cave and found withered grass that had been used as a bed, bones of rabbits and other small animals, and the remains of a fire. Since even they knew a ghost had no use for such things, they returned to report that the rumors were unfounded.

Hearing of the report, Castro returned to the little village. No sooner had he made his reappearance than the fires on the ledge outside the cave reappeared. Thinking that the ghost was stalking him to get revenge, Castro fled, never to return.

And so the Apache tribe lived peacefully in the secluded valley. The Mexicans didn't dare to venture too near because of their fear of the ghost, and the rugged, barren, forbidding mountains kept the white man away. If a few horses and cattle disappeared from the Anglo ranches every now and then, the ranchers attributed the thievery to Mexican bandits, since everyone knew there were no Indians in the area and the hoofprints always led to the Rio Grande. Even when a grizzly old Anglo prospector returned from the mountains, claiming the Apaches had returned and were growing vegetables and grazing a small herd of goats in a large valley, no one believed him. Everyone knew Apaches were neither farmers nor herdsmen, and his story was laughed away as the wild fabrication of a senile old man.

As the years passed, children born in the valley eventually left, blending in with the Mexican population in both Texas and Mexico. Even Ramon and Alison's sons left, to lay claim to the *hacienda* their granduncle had left them outside of Santa Rosa. But those who had made their escape stayed in their beloved mountains, for they had sworn they would never leave them.

Alison and Ramon lived to be a ripe old age, their powerful love and passion for one another never wavering or dwindling. She died first. Ramon took her body to the cave and buried it. Then he sat down by the grave of the woman he had loved with his whole heart and soul and waited for his death, never leaving the side of the woman he had vowed never to let go.

A Note to My Readers

I could not end this book without passing on some interesting information. Much of it is based on the life of a great but little-known Apache chief named Alsate, who led the Chisos Apaches and whose story I came across when I was researching another book. Ramon was based on him, and both the part about his trial and his betrayal at the end of the book are true, as is the story of his escape from the Mexican authorities and return to the mountains with his wife and the subsequent ghost stories. Even the last paragraph in the epilogue is true in part. Alsate's mummified body was found in the cave that was named after him.

Ramon and Alison's love story, however, was a figment of my imagination. Alsate's wife was a Mexican woman from San Carlos, and almost nothing was said of her in all the accounts I read about the Apache chief. Since I had become so fascinated with him, I simply created my own love story.

The ghost stories about Alsate have not died with the passage of years. Travelers who became lost in the rugged Chisos Mountains have returned, claiming they were led out of the mountains by an apparition that they thought was a man and woman. Campers along isolated regions of the Rio Grande claim to have found moccasin footprints made by a man and woman within six feet of their beds, yet they had not heard or seen anything. To this day mysterious lights have been seen in the mountains in the vicinity of Alsate's cave. Hundreds of people have seen them. They have even been seen from airplanes. But whenever anyone gets close enough to investigate, they disappear. No one has been able to explain the lights. Old-timers in the vicinity claim they are signal fires that the ghost of Alsate lights for his people who never returned.

I have drawn my conclusions. I will leave you to draw your own.

JOANNE REDD is a native Texan currently living in Missouri City. A longtime obstetrics nurse, Joanne is the author of many critically acclaimed historical romances including *Apache Bride, Desert Bride, Chasing a Dream,* and *To Love an Eagle,* which won the *Romantic Times* Award for Best Western Historical Romance.

In June Dell introduces a new writer, Christina Skye, whose tempestuous love story of two unforgettable characters will stay with you long after you finish her novel, DEFIANT CAPTIVE. We hope you enjoy the following excerpt.

Sussex, England
April 1816

Alexandra jerked open the heavy barn door and darted into the shadowed interior. She turned and put her shoulder to the door, struggling against the wind to close it. When it was at last latched in place, she tossed up her skirt and ripped the pistol free with trembling fingers. The binding around the hammer was the next to go.

Now, she thought wildly. Let him come now. She was ready.

The door creaked behind her, then crashed shut.

He was soaked, Alexandra saw in the brief flare of light from the door, his hair plastered to his head like a dark pelt. He immediately shrugged out of his jacket and strode to the wall behind the door, digging down deep in the hay.

With a grim laugh Hawke exposed the hollow section of wall near the dirt floor. "Just where it used to be, by God." From a hidden chamber behind the wooden plank he lifted a tinderbox and an old lantern without panes. Next came a small wooden keg. "The smugglers use this place to land their silks and brandy," he explained. "When the excisemen aren't nipping at their heels, they rest here by day and move inland with the darkness."

He did not turn around, struggling with flint and steel to light a candle for the lantern. After several failed attempts he succeeded, and rested the flickering light on an upturned barrel.

Once again he dug into the hiding place. This time he brought out two blankets, a length of French lace, and a pair of fine crystal goblets. "Run goods—specially ordered for a bride's trousseau, no doubt. Everything we need to be comfortable until the storm passes, including brandy direct from Paris."

Alexandra's cold fingers cradled the gun concealed in the folds of her skirt. "I should have expected you to know about such things," she said bitterly.

"The smugglers' comings and goings are common knowledge on the coast," Hawke said, shrugging.

"Yes, a murderer would know of such things."

"Murderer?" He frowned then, his attention caught at last. "What are you talking about?"

"You. The Marquess of Derwent. A murderer," Alexandra said shrilly, finally giving voice to those words branded upon her heart so long ago. " 'We hereby order your immediate recall to London, where you will answer charges of bribery, corruption, and gross irresponsibility, which led to a sepoy rising and the subsequent loss of two hundred lives.' Do those words sound familiar, your grace? Do you remember signing your name to that document?"

Hawke frowned. What was the woman about now? "The recall of the governor-general after the suppression of the Vellore mutiny, I believe. I have some notion of the document. Why should it interest you?"

"Did it give you pleasure to grind a man into the gutter," Alexandra cried as if he had not spoken. "To destroy twenty-five years of unstinting service to the Crown in one stroke of the pen? You, who had never done an honest day's work in your whole cursed life?"

"The letter was a joint decision by the whole Board of Control," Hawke said slowly. "A decision reached after two weeks of debate. Someone had erred. Someone had to take the blame. Maitland was in charge and therefore it was his responsibility."

"As simple as that? Neat and clean and settled." Alexandra laughed, a cold, dead sort of sound. "But I'm afraid you're going to find it's not so simple after all, your grace. For that man was my father, and you're going to feel the pain he felt, the burning jolt of the ball that ended his life!"

Slowly Alexandra drew the gun from within the folds of her habit, raising it until the barrel pointed directly at Hawke's temple.

"Well, I'll be goddamned," he said softly.

"Without a doubt."

"Are you mad?"

"Perhaps I am," Alexandra cried, laughing recklessly. "But it's a happy sort of delirium to have you in my sights at last. To see you begin to suffer as he did."

Hawke took a step forward. My God, he thought, she was Lord Percival Maitland's daughter?

"Don't move," Alexandra warned him. "I can shoot the eye of a jack at ten paces."

"Your father again?"

"My father. A man whose name you aren't fit to utter."

"A man who nearly lost his garrison. A man who refused to take responsibility for his flawed decisions at a time of crisis."

"No!" she screamed, and the wind echoed her shrill protest. " 'Twas not his fault, but the fault of men who ordered him to do the impossible. Men who knew not the slightest thing about conditions in India. Men like you, damn your soul!"

Hawke moved slightly closer. "And you planned this whole thing for revenge? You were searching for me that night in the fog?"

"Of course," Alexandra lied. "I came to make you crawl. To make you right this obscene injustice against an upright man." A bolt of lightning crashed overhead and her hand quivered slightly.

"Ah, but I won't crawl." Slowly he began to stalk closer. "But I think you will. Hear that, Alexandra? The storm is nearly upon us. Hear the drum of the thunder." His eyes were silver pinpoints in the gloom. "The devil's fire."

"Stop!" she cried furiously, hating the tremor of her hand, which soon grew to a visible shaking. "Storm or not, I'll put a ball through your skull. At this distance I can't miss, not with such a weapon."

"Did Telford arrange this too?" Hawke asked in a tone of cool dispassion.

"I plan my own revenge!" Alexandra screamed. "I need no one's help. I've been planning this ever since the night I found my father's shattered body."

Hawke's eyes were shadowed and unreadable. "Have you ever shot a man, Alexandra?" he asked softly, taking another step closer. "Have you heard the last rattle of breath, been close enough to see the eyes go flat and vacant when the life is ripped out of them?"

"I'll see it soon," she cried. "I'll laugh when you die."

"I think not. You don't have what it takes, Alexandra."

A ragged bolt of lightning lit the room, and in the sudden flare Alexandra saw his mouth set in a thin line.

In the inky darkness after the lightning passed she saw a different room, bloodred, rank with the suffocating smell of death. Her father's body sprawled across the neatly stacked papers on his desk.

Alexandra's hand began to shake uncontrollably. "No!" she screamed. "You'll die for what you did to him. You and all the others who signed his death warrant!"

"The storm's nearly overhead now. Can you hear the wind?"

"Shut up, you bastard! It won't work!"

"Won't it?" he asked, taking another step until he stood no more than four feet from her. "Listen, Alexandra," he ordered with silken violence. "They call to you.

Like the fiends of hell clawing at the door." As if in answer, the wind screamed, lashing the barn with sheets of rain.

"Stop!"

"They're coming, Alexandra. Can you hear?"

"Murderer!" she cried to drown out the sound of the storm. She shuddered as the Terror began to creep along her spine. "You might as well have shot him in the back. At least I'll face you when you die."

A bolt of lightning crashed directly overhead, exploding like a giant fist across the wooden roof, hammering and rattling the whole building in the storm's unleashed fury. And then there was a new sound against the wind, a wild, ragged keening.

"I must do it!" Alexandra screamed helplessly, but her finger would not move.

"Go on then," Hawke growled. "Do it. Now."

Suddenly there was a flare of light and the lead ball exploded down the barrel, hissing past Hawke's ear and neatly shooting out the candle within the paneless lantern.

"Forgive me, Father," Alexandra cried brokenly, throwing the gun away from her as if it were on fire.

The next moment Hawke's hands were upon her shoulders, shaking her savagely. "So you meant to put a ball through my heart, did you, Alexandra Maitland? You'll wish you did before I'm done with you," he said cruelly, knocking her down upon the hay.

She lay white-faced before him, her hands twisting at her waist. The storm was upon them in all its fury now, and without the lantern they were cast in semi-darkness.

Her breath came in little choking bursts as she fought the tremors that shook her limbs. Her beautiful eyes were wide and staring. "No," she moaned. "No more."

"Much more," Hawke said, dropping beside her to slant his hard body across her in the hay. "But this time it will be me and not a dream."

"Ayah!" she muttered, twisting madly beneath him.

"Wake up," Hawke ordered furiously, trapping her restless body beneath him. "This is no dream. You're here, not back in India! Wake up, damn it! Fight me."

Another violent bolt rent the air. Suddenly Hawke heard a horse's wild neighing and then the muffled drum of hooves. Damn! They'd bolted even though he'd tethered them well.

His captive forgotten, he jumped up and ran to the door, arriving in time to see Aladdin and Bluebell disappear into a gray wall of rain. Hawke cursed long and fluently.

He did not hear the rustling in the hay behind him until it was too late. He turned just in time to see his captive dart blindly past him into the fury of the storm.

Sharp, tiny nails ripped her flesh, a thousand stabbing fingers pulling her down. Hungry teeth snapped at her legs.

Wildly she struggled, only to feel more hands claw her neck and scalp. Still, Alexandra fought, for dimly she knew that to yield would be to die.

"Father?" she screamed, but only the shrieking wind answered, flinging her terror back at her.

The devil's fire slashed through the sky and sent its ghastly light playing over the earth. Long fingers wrapped around her neck and tightened relentlessly. Choking, she struck at the rigid fingers but met only air.

Black waves of fear crashed over her and a queer whine rose in her ears.

They screamed her name in a thousand voices and above the din she heard the sound of her own terror. She choked, desperate for air, and fell to her knees, still flailing crazily.

The iron fingers tightened until blackness licked at the edge of her dreaming mind. Then the wind ripped the last racking sob from her throat.

Cursing, Hawke struggled up the hill against the slashing rain, unable to see more than a few feet in front of him. Stumbling, he ran toward where he had seen Alexandra disappear, praying he would find her before she reached the cliffs.

At the top of the hill he stopped, hunching into the wind and flinging the rain from his face to peer into the unrelenting curtain of gray before him.

That was when he heard her scream.

He plunged forward, half stumbling, and nearly fell over her in the streaming rain. She was caught against a dwarf hawthorn, struggling wildly, her glorious mane of hair caught by a thousand tiny needles. The more she fought, the tighter she was impaled. Still, like a crazed animal, she thrashed until tears soaked her face and her eyes were dazed with pain.

Suddenly she fell to her knees, screaming in blind terror.

"Stop fighting!" Hawke ordered, but the words were flung back at him in the wind, mingled with her wild, hysterical laughter.

He began to tug at her hair, reaching down into his boot for the knife he'd hidden there. It was five minute's work to cut her free and throw her stiff body over his shoulder. Strangely, she did not fight him now.

She was shivering by the time he got her back to the barn. He tossed her down in the hay, and there she lay, her body rigid and unnatural, her eyes glazed and unseeing. Grimly Hawke jerked off her skirt and torn chemise before wrapping her in one of the blankets. He chafed her cold skin roughly, but she gave no sign of noticing.

With a savage curse he reached for the keg of brandy and filled a glass to overflowing, forcing a small amount upon her. She took it without demur, unmoving in his arms. Again he tipped the glass against her mouth, more this time, and suddenly she began to cough as the high-proof smugglers' brandy burned down her throat.

Weakly, she fought with the iron fingers that forced more of the liquid fire between her lips. "C-couldn't do it," she muttered brokenly. "Too much d-death already. Forgive me, Father."

Hawke smiled grimly as he stripped off his own clothes and pulled the blanket around them both. Soon he would give her something to beg forgiveness for, by God.

He slid his hand between their damp bodies, massaging her skin, forcing warmth back into the rigid muscles. Rain hammered on the roof like the hollow sound of his heart and he asked the one question still gnawing at him. "Who sent you, Alexandra? Telford? Was this his idea?"

She mumbled something between short, jagged breaths and Hawke bent closer to listen.

"Who?" he repeated sharply.

"No one. Me. M-my revenge. Against them all."

Hawke knew a harsh, blinding sense of relief. She was not lying this time, for the madness was upon her, and ironically she could not lie in its grip.

"So this thing is between us and us alone," he whispered. His fingers massaged her spine and buttocks, pulling her into his body's heat, never ceasing his powerful strokes. "Wake up, Alexandra. The storm is nearly over. And a new storm is about to begin, by God."

He drew slightly away, bringing his hands around to the cold, taut crests that teased his chest. His thumbs played over her nipples mercilessly, circling and closing again and again. Then his warm, caressing hands slipped lower, tracing her navel and massaging the hollow of her belly.

When he heard her cry of protest, Hawke brought his open palm to the junction of her thighs, forcing her legs apart as he flattened his hand against her softness.

He knew the exact moment her whimper of fear became a moan of desire. Instinct and vast experience told him, even though she had not yet recognized it herself.

He knew and did not stop. He might have had he been capable of rational thought, but by then the madness was upon him as much as upon her.

Searing muscle probed Alexandra's thighs. Suddenly her eyes widened, the ragged edge of dreams giving way to harsher reality. Her breath caught in a sob and she pounded clumsily against his chest. "Let me go, m-murderer!" she cried. "Haven't you done enough?"

With a bitter smile Hawke trapped her fingers in one large hand and rose above her, his manhood rampant between them. "Not nearly." He found what he was seeking, and his smile was thin and cruel as he parted her. "Not for you. Certainly not for me." She twisted wildly but he captured her beneath a muscled thigh while his finger slipped inside, stroking deep and then retreating, over and over, until she arched blindly. "Not yet," he taunted her.

Alexandra felt the lightning play over her, exploding along her raw nerves and bathing her in silver fire. Her body was a thing apart now, molding itself to those expert fingers, her taut muscles desperate for the release he continued to hold just out of reach.

And still she fought him.

Hawke's fingers circled, plunged deep, then quickly retreated. "Now?" he growled.

"N-never!"

"Say it," he ordered roughly.

"Oh, God, stop!" It was a last desperate plea.

"Tell me, Alexandra! No more lies."

It was madness, it was savage, blinding pleasure, and she could fight it no longer. "Please," she cried in a voice not her own but a stranger's.

Abruptly Hawke knelt and cupped her buttocks, watching her face as he lifted her and plunged inside, filling her with living fire and hard, throbbing muscle.

A moan broke from Alexandra's lips. "Damn you!" she cried. "I hate you for this."

But he only laughed and pulled away until she twisted helplessly, desperate for his return. "Yes, Alexandra, like that, with little pleasure sounds upon your lips. Like this." His hands caught her ivory legs and pushed them apart so their bodies met with brutal, stunning force. "Feel it. Feel my fire."

Her mind poised on the edge of darkness, Alexandra moaned hoarsely. Still, Hawke toyed with her, never giving her what he had taught her to need so desperately.

"You're not fighting me now, swan. You're struggling to get closer." He slipped his hand between them and found the tiny ridge of her desire, stroking her with an exquisite touch, careful not to push her over the edge as he relentlessly heightened her pleasure until she panted and tossed wildly beneath him.

"This way," he rasped. "This is how it will be between us. Always. Whenever I love you."

Again and again he brought her to pleasure's threshold, shredding the barriers between them, learning the things that made her moan and twist beneath him. And he remembered it all, turning the knowledge against her a moment later, driving her again and again to the ragged edge of passion only to pull back and prolong the raw torment.

For them both.

No regrets, Hawke told himself in black fury. No aching sense of loss. Only this fierce, gnawing blade of need. Only a man who used a woman as she was meant to be used, teaching her who was master before taking his own pleasure.

As if from a great distance Alexandra heard his ragged groan and felt his thighs tense against her flanks.

"Now, swan!" he cried.

And then the velvet fury was upon her. The ground fell away and she screamed, only to feel his strong fingers surround her. She forgot to breathe, she shattered, she rent the clouds. Through the sky she rode him, feeling the rain that was sweat dampen their skin, seeing the sparks of living lightning leap from his eyes.

Beyond the thunder he took her. Beyond the storm to a greater fury until the lightning played around her and plunged deep within her.

Until she was the storm itself and only he could tame her.

And then Alexandra fell into the maelstrom, scattered into a million charged particles. She died in blackness and in silver, and there he taught her how to be reborn, rising once again from the ashes of their spent desire.

Later, much later, they slept while the rain beat a steady drone overhead. The wind dropped and heavy plumes of mist curled around the corners of the weathered barn. Inside the smell of hay hung heavy upon the cool, damp air.

Hawke was the first to wake. For long moments he did not open his eyes, enjoying a dark, drowsy contentment, warm still from passion kindled and spent not once but many times. He was not yet ready to face the harsh light of day with its crushing burdens of duty and necessity. Instead, he flexed his shoulders, mind and body replete, smiling faintly as he listened to the rain tap upon the roof.

He yawned and lazily stretched out one hand, only to meet warm, silken skin beneath his fingers. The effect was immediate and riveting. He jerked as if struck by lightning, desire scorching a path along his groin as he felt himself swell with a burning hunger to possess her again, his proud, defiant captive asleep beside him.

Lord Percival Maitland's daughter, by God! Wealthy, cosseted, and highborn. A tempestuous beauty who had stunned him with the fury of her passionate response. A woman who'd nearly murdered him, for God's sake. A grim smile played across Hawke's chiseled features as he recalled just how close he'd come to dying in the seconds before she shot the candle's flame right off the wick. A damned good shot—she could have put the ball just as easily through his heart, he knew.

And yet she had not. . . .

Careful, Hawke told himself. Women were God's curse, created to dazzle and betray. Not one of them could be trusted. He had forgotten that once in his reckless obsession with Isobel.

It was not a mistake he intended to make again.

A muscle moved at his jaw as he looked down at the willful creature asleep in the straw, her glorious hair scattered like sunset clouds across her ivory shoulders. She was like no woman Hawke had ever known.

Perhaps it was her rare vibrancy that had taken him by storm. Perhaps it was her bold, flaming spirit after the cold, corrosive years with Isobel.

He did not know. Suddenly he didn't want to know, afraid to explore his feelings too closely. It was enough for now that he wanted her. That he would hold her and have her, again and again, as long as his desire remained.

Whether she liked it or not.

It was the least the wench could do after tracking him to London with the express intention of murdering him.

Hawke scowled as the insistent throbbing in his groin began to build. Smothering a curse, he rose on one elbow, slanting his body so that he could see her face when she came to consciousness.

Something sharp tickled Alexandra's nose and she batted it away.

Warm, soft. So tired.

Again came the tickling at her face, but she twisted to her side, unwilling to leave the snug cocoon of sleep.

Her nose twitched sharply. The smell of straw and damp air and sea salt filled her lungs. Leather and horses. A man's smell.

She smiled slowly, a delicious golden languor heavy upon her limbs. Her fingers met a broad chest covered with dense, springy hair.

Abruptly her eyes flashed open and she jerked upright in the straw, sending the dry strands flying. Two bright circles of color stained her cheeks.

"Titania awakes," the man beside her said coldly. "I see that you slept well. A good tumble in the hay often has that effect. My compliments, Miss *Maitland.* Bedding agrees with you."

"You—you—" Alexandra sputtered. An instant later she was awash in memories, shameful memories, which made her breath check in horror. Memories of exquisite, aching torment followed by fierce, desperate pleasure. She flinched and pulled one trembling hand before her eyes as if to ward off thoughts too painful to face.

Suddenly aware of her nakedness, Alexandra fell back, clutching straw across her trembling body. The streaks of crimson slashed across her cheeks, the only color in her pale, translucent skin. "Savage," she hissed. "Cruel and vicious savage." Vainly she tried to edge away from him, but he rolled smoothly, pinning her beneath one muscular thigh.

"If so, I am a savage who right now holds your father's reputation in his hands. And it was you who came in search of me, may I remind you. You were the one thirsting for my blood, intent on righting what you term a cruel injustice." His eyes were mocking. "I can only wonder what you meant to offer in return for my help."

"Your life, worthless as it is, when I could extinguish it at any moment!"

"But you lost your chance, for you soon discovered you hadn't the stomach for killing. So what was left for you to bargain with?" Hawke jeered, his face only inches from hers.

Alexandra glared back, her fingers balling into fists.

Oh, if only she had a pistol to level between those hard, mocking eyes!

"You do not answer?" Hawke growled, trapping her hands and crushing her beneath him in the warm straw. "This, perhaps?" With cool deliberation he scrutinized the creamy skin of her neck and shoulders which soon flushed crimson beneath his taunting eyes.

"Stop, you contemptible snake!"

"Stop?" A dark eyebrow rose mockingly. "But we're just getting started, Miss Maitland. For such a favor as you ask, I must have something of value in return. If not your body, then what?"

Alexandra twisted helplessly, her breath coming fast and jerky between clenched teeth. *Wretched bloody man!* She was fed up with his mockery and cold manipulation. A few hours earlier he had bent her to his will, taking cruel advantage of her terror during the storm. But it would never happen again, she vowed, fighting the dark memories of his savage lovemaking.

"The desire to correct an injustice to an innocent man," she cried, forcing her thoughts away from those shameful images.

"Unacceptable, I'm afraid. All the evidence pointed to your father's guilt."

"Evidence offered by liars, by men who hated and envied my father! Men he had punished for corruption and who sought to have their revenge by raising spurious charges against him."

"Very stirring, Alexandra," Hawke said softly, his eyes narrowing. "But why, I ask myself? Why would a rich and desirable young woman devote her life to the bitter task of restitution and revenge? Why would she give up the chance for a home and family to pursue such a thankless quest? There is something unhealthy about all this."

"Love!" Alexandra snapped. "Loyalty! Things you would know nothing about, your bloody grace!"

"Love?" Hawke repeated cynically. "Loyalty?"

"For honor too! But then, I forget, a miscreant like you wouldn't know the meaning of that word either."

"And you would?" he scoffed. "No, to others you may lie, to yourself even, but not to me. You are hiding something, Miss Maitland, and I'll have it out of you, mark my words. But until I do we have terms to be set. What have you to offer in return for my help in clearing the charges against your father?"

Alexandra struggled furiously against his iron grip. "D-damn your depraved heart," she sputtered, hating the silver eyes that probed her so relentlessly. With a cry of inchoate anger she twisted sideways and tried to sink her teeth into his hands.

Hawke only laughed and moved his hands out of range. "I see that I must answer for you, then," he growled. "You have only one thing of interest to me and that is an exquisitely responsive body that would tempt a saint to transgress his holy vows. And that, my sweet, *dutiful,* Alexandra, is how you'll repay me."

"Never, you bastard! You can't force me to—"

"Ah, but I don't propose to *force* anything. It's your assent I require, your passion willingly given when you come to my bed. You'll come to me of your own free will or not at all, my dear. I'll have all your passion and all your fire, not one spark less. If you want your father's case reopened, that is my price," he finished roughly.

"Never, you fiend! Never will I do such a thing!"

"So Lord Maitland's daughter is not so loyal after all? Not so eager to endure every obstacle to right her father's injustice? Was all that talk of love just a sham too?" He sneered.

She strained against his cruel grip but could not loosen those rigid fingers. "No, I won't listen! You twist everything. Even white you turn into vilest black." She dragged her hands toward her ears, but Hawke pulled them roughly away.

"A coward, too, I think," he continued ruthlessly.

"Afraid to face your own passion. You know such an arrangement would bring pleasure to you as much as to me, for you have the fiery sensuality of a born courtesan. It shows in a thousand ways—every time you drop your lashes instinctively, every time you moisten your lips with a darting tongue. Every time your eyes burn upon me I see your true nature revealed, my dear Alexandra. And yet not long ago you chided me for lacking honesty. Are you now so afraid to face your own passion? Or is it just that dishonesty has become a habit with you?"

"The only thing I feel for you is passionate hatred," Alexandra hissed furiously, "along with an overwhelming desire to claw that insolent smile from your face!"

"Liar," he growled. "Just like all the rest of your sex. I was a fool to expect you to be any different. But I am a fool no more." His voice hardened. "Today I collected my first installment against the payment you will make me for resurrecting your father's reputation."

Alexandra shivered, his words pounding over her like crashing waves—relentless, cold, and unforgiving.

"Mark me well, I will continue collecting as long as I choose to. Whenever I want. Wherever I want. *Whatever* I want. And you, Miss Maitland, had better pray that my desire lasts until the business is finished."

"P-pray that your desire lasts?" Alexandra choked in fury. "What sort of foul, stinging insect are you? Does your treachery know no bounds?"

"Save your histrionics for a more appreciative audience," he said scathingly. "You were the one with murder on your mind. If we're to talk of treachery, we should begin with that."

"But I—" Abruptly Alexandra bit back her denial, refusing to justify herself to this ignoble creature. Never would she admit that their meeting in London was the work of fate rather than her design.

"Now, which is it to be?" her steely-eyed captor continued relentlessly. "Lord Percival Maitland reviled as a scoundrel down through history or hailed as a hero who walked the precipice and made the best of a dangerous situation? Everything depends on you, Alexandra, you warm and yielding in my bed. So give me your answer. I'll accept your pledge on our bargain, for I believe that you have some twisted notion of honoring your word."

"While you have no honor, and offend every law of man and nature in making such a demand!" Her eyes were storm-tossed against her white face.

"Ah, but you have said I'm the devil himself, so you must not expect anything better of me. Now give me your word or I'll wash my hands of the whole affair."

Alexandra ground her teeth in helpless rage, but she was trapped and they both knew it. She looked up at his shuttered face, hating him, this man who would give her no quarter. Long she studied him, repulsed by his cold arrogance, his insolent assumption of control over her life.

Blaze and be damned! She was helpless before him, and once again revenge was to be denied her. Worse yet, she would be made to yield to her greatest enemy, all so that her father's innocence might be proved at last.

Alexandra shuddered slightly. Her father's reputation restored. That was what he would want, surely. What price was too high to ensure that he would be finally at peace?

"How unspeakably vile you are!" she rasped. "But of course you already know that." She struggled to be as cold and merciless as he was. "Very well, blackguard, you may do what you will with me. But know that I'll be far away from you during those moments. That I come to you only because I love my father more than I hate you. Know always that the only thing I'll ever feel for you is raw hatred," she spat from between drawn white lips.

Hawke's eyes glittered as a small smile twisted his mouth. Although Alexandra did not know it, there was nothing cool about his feelings for her. His lazy indifference went no more than surface deep, a habit learned only after years of practice. "You challenge me exceedingly, Miss Maitland. Yes, I believe it will be an exquisite pleasure to prove you wrong on both those points."

"I don't give a damn for what gives you pleasure!"

His eyes turned smoky and Alexandra looked down to see one rose-tipped breast revealed amid the scattered stalks of hay. With a stifled curse she struggled down into the straw away from his mocking scrutiny.

Hawke's laugh was low and grating. "You ought to, for my pleasure ensures your own. Luckily for you, however, I am not at leisure to pursue the question now. Darkness will soon be upon us, and I must find those damned horses before the light goes. So get dressed, and stop this wanton teasing lest I lose all my fine resolve."

"Teasing be damned!" Alexandra screamed furiously. "The only bloody teasing you're good for is with the end of a whip!"

Hawke smiled cynically and shook his head. "Such language from the lips of a lady." His eyes scoured her face for a moment before he stood up and shrugged into his clothes. He sent her habit and chemise flying toward her face a moment before the heavy planked door crashed shut behind him.

How dare the man? Her mind seething in impotent rage, Alexandra dropped her clothes and grabbed the leather satchel that lay beside her on the straw, hurling it with all her might against the door. If only lightning would strike the cursed man down!

But it appeared that the duke led a charmed life. Alexandra heard no clap of thunder, only his mocking laughter carried on the wind as she shrugged into her chemise and habit, then sat down to tug furiously at her boots.

FREE FROM DELL

with purchase plus postage and handling

Congratulations! You have just purchased one or more
titles featured in Dell's Romance 1990 Promotion. Our goal
is to provide you with quality reading and entertainment, so
we are pleased to extend to you a limited offer to receive a
selected Dell romance title(s) *free* (plus $1.00 postage and
handling per title) for each romance title purchased. Please
read and follow all instructions carefully to avoid delays in
your order.

1) Fill in your name and address on the coupon printed below. No facsimiles or
   copies of the coupon allowed.

2) The Dell Romance books are the only books featured in Dell's Romance
   1990 Promotion. Any other Dell titles are not eligible for this offer.

3) Enclose your original cash register receipt with the price of the book(s)
   circled plus $1.00 **per book** for postage and handling, payable in check or
   money order to: Dell Romance 1990 Offer. Please do not send cash in
   the mail.
   Canadian customers: Enclose your original cash register receipt with the
   price of the book(s) circled plus $1.00 **per book** for postage and handling in
   U.S. funds.

4) This offer is only in effect until March 29, 1991. Free Dell Romance requests
   postmarked after March 22, 1991 will not be honored, but your check for
   postage and handling will be returned.

5) Please allow 6-8 weeks for processing. Void where taxed or prohibited.

Mail to: Dell Romance 1990 Offer
       P.O. Box 2088
       Young America, MN 55399-2088

NAME_____

ADDRESS_____

CITY_____STATE_____ZIP_____

BOOKS PURCHASED AT_____

AGE_____

(Continued)

Book(s) purchased:_____

_____

_____

I understand I may choose one free book for each Dell Romance book purchased (plus applicable postage and handling). Please send me the following:

(Write the number of copies of each title selected next to that title.)

☐ **MY ENEMY, MY LOVE**
Elaine Coffman
From an award-winning author comes this compelling historical novel that pits a spirited beauty against a hard-nosed gunslinger hired to forcibly bring her home to her father. But the gunslinger finds himself unable to resist his captive.

☐ **AVENGING ANGEL**
Lori Copeland
Jilted by her thieving fiancé, a woman rides west seeking revenge, only to wind up in the arms of her enemy's brother.

☐ **A WOMAN'S ESTATE**
Roberta Gellis
An American woman in the early 1800s finds herself ensnared in a web of family intrigue and dangerous passions when her English nobleman husband passes away.

☐ **THE RAVEN AND THE ROSE**
Virginia Henley
A fast-paced, sexy novel of the 15th century that tells a tale of royal intrigue, spirited love, and reckless abandon.

☐ **THE WINDFLOWER**
Laura London
She longed for a pirate's kisses... even though she was kidnapped in error and forced to sail the seas on his pirate ship, forever a prisoner of her own reckless desire.

☐ **TO LOVE AN EAGLE**
Joanne Redd
Winner of the 1987 *Romantic Times* Reviewer's Choice Award for Best Western Romance by a New Author.

☐ **SAVAGE HEAT**
Nan Ryan
The spoiled young daughter of a U.S. Army General is kidnapped by a Sioux chieftain out of revenge and is at first terrified, then infuriated, and finally hopelessly aroused by him.

☐ **BLIND CHANCE**
Meryl Sawyer
Every woman wants to be a star, but what happens when the one nude scene she'd performed in front of the cameras haunts her, turning her into an underground sex symbol?

☐ **DIAMOND FIRE**
Helen Mittermeyer
A gorgeous and stubborn young woman must choose between protecting the dangerous secrets of her past or trusting and loving a mysterious millionaire who has secrets of his own.

☐ **LOVERS AND LIARS**
Brenda Joyce
She loved him for love's sake, he seduced her for the sake of sweet revenge. This is a story set in Hollywood, where there are two types of people—lovers and liars.

☐ **MY WICKED ENCHANTRESS**
Meagan McKinney
Set in 18th-century Louisiana, this is the tempestous and sensuous story of an impoverished Scottish heiress and the handsome American plantation owner who saves her life, then uses her in a dangerous game of revenge.

☐ **EVERY TIME I LOVE YOU**
Heather Graham
A bestselling romance of a rebel Colonist and a beautiful Tory loyalist who reincarnate their fiery affair 200 years later through the lives of two lovers.

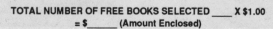

TOTAL NUMBER OF FREE BOOKS SELECTED _____ X $1.00
= $_____ **(Amount Enclosed)**

Dell has other great books in print by these authors. If you enjoy them, check your local book outlets for other titles.